Canadian **Dani Collins** knew in high school
that she wanted to write romance for a living.
Twenty-five years later, after marrying her
high school sweetheart, having two kids with
him, working at several generic office jobs and
submitting countless manuscripts, she got The Call.
Her first Mills & Boon novel won the Reviewers'
Choice Award for Best First in Series from *RT Book
Reviews*. She now works in her own office, writing
romance.

USA TODAY bestselling author **Jennie Lucas**'s
parents owned a bookstore, so she grew up
surrounded by books, dreaming about faraway
lands. A fourth-generation Westerner, she went
east at sixteen to boarding school on a scholarship,
wandered the world, got married, then finally
worked her way through college before happily
returning to her hometown. A 2010 RITA® Award
finalist and 2005 Golden Heart® Award winner,
she lives in Idaho with her husband and children.

ONE-NIGHT HEIRS

DANI COLLINS

JENNIE LUCAS

MILLS & BOON

First published in Great Britain 2024
by Mills & Boon, an imprint of HarperCollins*Publishers* Ltd,
1 London Bridge Street, London, SE1 9GF

www.harpercollins.co.uk

HarperCollins*Publishers*, Macken House, 39/40 Mayor Street Upper,
Dublin 1, D01 C9W8, Ireland

One-Night Heirs © 2024 Harlequin Enterprises ULC

Her Billion-Dollar Bump © 2024 Dani Collins

Nine-Month Notice © 2024 Jennie Lucas

ISBN: 978-0-263-32013-8

06/24

HER
BILLION-DOLLAR
BUMP

DANI COLLINS

MILLS & BOON

This one is for Emmy Grayson and Maya Blake,
my fellow authors in this trilogy.

Thank you for being lovely and generous
and a delight to work with.

PROLOGUE

As Felicity Corning picked up the wastebasket from beside the client's writing desk, a glint of gold script on glossy ebony caught her attention.

You are invited to attend London's premier Benefit for the Arts Gala

The gala was being held at a swanky art gallery in Chelsea two weeks from now.

This is the way, the devilish dreamer on her shoulder whispered. That voice was delusional, always telling her to *keep trying...find a way.*

Given how many obstacles the universe had put in her way, she was ready to throw in the towel on her fashion-design aspirations. She was only twenty-four, but after two years of knocking on fashion house doors that remained firmly closed, she was growing disheartened.

She understood that dropping out of her degree—and having books and books of sketches with only a few physical samples—meant she wasn't seen as a viable candidate for even an unpaid intern position. The designers needed to see more commitment to her craft, but she couldn't help feeling like she had already missed the boat.

If you could show them what you're capable of, the voice persisted, *someone might finally take you seriously.*

"No," she said aloud.

Risking her current job was not the way to go about it. Housekeeping might not be the most glamorous job in the world, but the agency catered to wealthy clients. That was why she had taken it. She often got to put away samples, shopping, and dry cleaning from top designers. Aside from the occasional post-party apocalypse, the work was basic and physical but undemanding. The pay covered her bills. More or less. London was obscenely expensive.

Felicity actually lived a penurious existence. Most artists did. She didn't mind going without lattes or streaming services so she could spend her scant disposable income on bolts of silk and high-end notions, though. Building out her collection was her way forward. It was her passion. It was the only entertainment she needed.

However, her life had fallen into a rut. Every day was a grind that only seemed to entrench her deeper into a place she didn't want to be. She had been thinking of going back to school to finish her degree, which she had waffled her way through the first time round. She had been persuaded by her grandmother into thinking a practical business degree was the way to go, then later switched to visual arts before knocking off to take care of Granny until she had passed away.

Going back to school would create the Catch-22 of having no time outside of her classes and day job to sew. Plus, most fashion houses were looking for a post-graduate degree. It would be years before she was remotely "qualified" in the eyes of top designers.

With a sigh of frustration, Felicity carried the wastebasket into the housekeeping closet, but she didn't imme-

diately empty it into the larger bin. First, she plucked out
the invitation and set it on the shelf of cleaning products.

She wasn't *taking* it, she told her squirming conscience.
She was merely not throwing it away.

Maybe the owner of this three-bedroom townhome—a
well-known supermodel—had tossed it by accident. She
had recently been cast in a blockbuster movie and was out
of town. That was likely why she had discarded the invitation despite the message on the back.

*Delia Chevron and date, courtesy of Brightest Star Stu-
dio*

The studio must have picked up the ticket price for her.
How nice to be so rich and famous you could throw away
a dinner worth a few hundred pounds. Such a waste. A
crime, really, when good people went hungry every day.

People like you, the voice whispered.

"Shut up," she hissed.

But when Felicity left for the day, she told herself she
was only taking the card as inspiration. Someday *she* would
be invited to an event like this—or one of her gowns would,
she thought wryly.

But she knew better. She knew she would take a risk
that could go horribly awry.

On the other hand, it could change her life.

As it turned out, it did both.

CHAPTER ONE

SAINT MONTGOMERY WOULD have been ushered down the red carpet with or without a date, but he was solo tonight, so he chose the less conspicuous side entrance where he was funneled like a steer for branding past a thinner bank of photographers. He couldn't avoid the barrage of questions on his recent breakup, however.

"Saint! Are you and Julie still speaking? What happened?"

He should have brought a date. A new face would have changed the narrative, and God knew he was tired of this one.

Historically, his romantic liaisons were casual and pleasant and ended without conflict. If asked about a particular breakup, he would claim "artistic differences" or some other facetious explanation.

His affair with Julie, however, was the gift that kept on giving. Or taking, as it turned out.

He'd caught her trying to break into his laptop. She'd claimed to be the jealous type who'd suspected him of an affair. He had assured her he was the possessive type, especially when it came to his proprietary software.

Saint wasn't surprised she'd had a mercenary motive in sleeping with him. Most people operated in their own self-interest, including him, but this experience had shaken his already jaded view of his fellow human beings.

When he had begun seeing Julie, he had taken her at face value, believing she hadn't needed anything from him beyond affluent companionship. She was the daughter of a famous sportscaster in the US and stood to inherit millions. She had recently broken up with a star athlete and had told Saint she wasn't ready for anything serious again. She wanted marriage and children "someday" but not today. She had fit seamlessly into his social circle of tycoons and celebrities, flirting and charming wherever she'd gone.

She had seemed an even match for Saint, who always promised monogamy, but little else. He had dropped his guard more than he normally would, never suspecting that Julie had a gambling addiction. Or that she would attempt industrial espionage to pay down her debts.

She could have cost him billions if his bespoke security software hadn't alerted him to her attempt to clone it. He hadn't pressed charges. He'd gone easy on her, expelling her from his life while offering to pay for a treatment program.

She had petulantly refused, then gone on every damned talk show in the English-speaking world, literally selling a tale that *he* had wronged *her*.

This story was well past its shelf life. Saint was beyond ready to change the channel.

"You can wait for your party over there." Ahead of him, the greeter waved a woman into purgatory on the far side of the single door and invited the group ahead of him to come forward.

A kick of desire arrested him as he ate up the vision in blue.

Who was she? She wasn't the most beautiful woman he'd ever seen. More eye-catching in an undiscovered, wallflower way. Most women had arrived dressed to compete with plunging necklines and tiaras and capes made of ostrich feathers. This one's makeup was muted. Her brunette hair fell in subtle waves from a side part. Rather than an ice cap's worth of diamonds, she wore a pair of gold hoops and a thin chain with a locket. Her gown was a simple halter style that tied behind her neck before cradling her ample breasts in soft gathers above a high, wide waistband. The skirt fell in a solid curtain off her wide hips, leaving her legs and shoes hidden.

He let his gaze return to those lovely breasts sitting heavy and relaxed in the gathered cups of silk. No bra. He would swear it on his life. Her nipples were leaving a subtle impression beneath the sheen of fabric. One soft swell lifted and moved without restraint as she brushed her hair back from her cheek.

He swallowed. Saint was a healthy man with a strong sexual appetite, but he rarely felt need. Not like this. Not hunger that was immediate and intense and specific.

Her unease was palpable as she pressed a self-conscious smile onto her lips and eyed the bank of photographers. They were ignoring her in favor of new arrivals at the end of the line.

Wait. Was she looking for a path of escape? She pressed her lips together and took a step.

"Angel," Saint said on impulse, stepping toward her. "I'm so glad you decided to come." He crooked his arm in invitation, aware of the cameras shifting to the pair of them.

"What?" Her amber gaze flashed to Saint, hitting him like a shot of whiskey, sending even more heat pouring into his gut and out to his extremities. The delicious warmth sank to pool low and heavy behind his fly. It was exciting. Dangerous, but exciting.

"Sir." The greeter reacted to Saint trying to bypass him, then stammered, "I beg your pardon, Mr. Montgomery. Of course you may go in."

"We're blocking the entrance," Saint said, steadying his

new date's faltering steps as he guided her into the noisy foyer, then found them a quiet corner in the main gallery.

She blinked, taking in the freestanding sculptures and abstract oils surrounding tables placed like stepping stones into the labyrinth of the gallery's showrooms. The glitterati milled in pockets at the edges. Above them, origami flowers were suspended on threads, drifting and bobbing on gentle, unseen currents, like an upside-down meadow.

The woman's enchantment was cute, her uptilted mouth in that rosy pink nearly irresistible.

"I was stood up, too," Saint said, signaling a server to bring champagne.

"You're joking." Her wide-eyed gaze came down from the ceiling as she took the glass he handed her.

"Prevaricating," he admitted. No one would ever leave him waiting. "I parted ways with my date two weeks ago."

"I'm so sorry." She sounded sincere, which was adorable.

"It's for the best. And you? Who had the poor taste to leave you hanging?"

"Are we prevaricating?" Her chin dropped in a sly, self-deprecating dip. "I actually knew my…um…date wouldn't be here. I came anyway, hoping they'd let me in, which they didn't. So you've aided and abetted a party crasher." She wrinkled her nose.

"I've done worse."

She started to say something, then checked herself, biting her lips with contrition.

"What? You've heard that about me?" That was no surprise. He'd misspent his young adult years on wine, women and song. He was a lot more circumspect these days, but that playboy reputation remained his calling card and had its uses, so he didn't fight it.

"Maybe." Her lashes flickered as her gaze traveled

across the unpadded shoulders of his jacket and down to the buttons that closed it.

He stole the opportunity to take another long drink of her figure-eight figure—which was a solid ten. He came back in time to see the tip of her tongue slide along the seam of her lips.

Her bottom lip was wide and full, the top one thinner with two sharp peaks in the center and an uptilt at the corners that gave an impression she had an amusing secret.

Damn, but he wanted to kiss her. Right. Now.

But when her gaze lifted to his, there was wariness behind the speculation. She quirked a quizzical brow at him.

"Are you really Saint Montgomery?"

"Yes." He liked his name in her accent. It wasn't one of those posh pronunciations that scolded, demanding he behave like his namesake. Her broad inflection held a rueful skepticism that seemed to know he was the furthest thing from a saint.

"So why are you talking to me?"

He liked how direct she was, too. "Is that a real question? I find you attractive."

She choked on the sip of champagne she'd started to take. "No." She tilted her head, eyeing him with suspicion. "At best, you're on a rebound from your recent breakup."

He winced, caught, but, "Both things can be true, can't they? I do find you attractive, but it also suited me to give the paparazzi fresh meat to chew on. Now they're out there wondering who the hell I came in with."

Her eyes widened with alarm.

"Why does that worry you? Who *did* I come in with?"

"I'd rather not say." She glanced around and shook her head with something like incredulity. "I was misrepresenting myself by turning up here and really need to quit while I'm ahead. Thank you for getting me in, but I'm leaving."

"Why?" He put out a hand, needing to touch her again if only to graze her bare elbow. And watch her nipples peak against the thin silk of her gown. "Who was your date? Why did you come if you didn't think they'd let you in?"

"I'm embarrassed to say. Genuinely." Her flush of awareness turned to dark pink stains on her cheeks. Her bright-eyed amusement was very much at her own expense. "I'll do more damage than good if I stick around, so... It was nice to meet you, but I have to go. Even though it *galls* me to walk away from a dinner worth a hundred pounds."

She really was new here. "It's twenty-five thousand."

"What is? This statue?" She halted herself from setting her unfinished glass on the base of a nearby sculpture.

"The plate fee."

"Is twenty-five thousand pounds?" she cried and fumbled her glass, splashing champagne against her knuckles. She added an earthy epithet that he would've loved to hear against his ear while they were between the sheets.

He offered his pocket square, not bothering to mention he'd underwritten a table of ten for his London team of executives and their spouses.

"I'm definitely leaving," she blurted as she handed back his damp square of silk.

"Not before midnight, Cinderella," he cajoled, caressing her arm again, liking how quickly goose bumps rose against his tickling touch. He nodded toward an archway into another room. "I have to make the rounds. Stay and amuse me."

She sobered. "I don't mind laughing at myself, but I don't care to become entertainment for others."

"Why would you be?" He frowned.

"We can both tell I'm out of my league here," she said with reproach. "Why else would you want me on your arm? Social anxiety?"

"I find your sense of humor a welcome balance to people who take themselves far too seriously."

"Gosh, fun as it sounds to meet those people, I'll have to give it a miss." She handed her glass to a passing server.

A lurching sensation pulled in his chest. He wanted to catch at her as though she was falling off a cliff away from him.

"Saint Montgomery. Just the man I need." A woman's hand arrived on his shoulder. She was the forty-something wife of a man Saint had met somewhere for some reason. Her chestnut hair was piled atop her head, her gown a racy haute-couture creation that framed cleavage where a ruby the size of a holiday turkey nested. "I'm planning an eclipse party. I need your clever brain to calculate the perfect time and place. Hello. You're not Julie."

His mystery woman froze like a bunny, then produced a dazzling smile that hit Saint like a ball of sunshine even though it was directed at the other woman.

"I'm not Julie, you're right. I'm Fliss. Sadly, you've missed this year's total eclipse. There will be another in about fourteen months with good views from Iceland, Portugal and Spain. The path is easy enough to find online. I would look it up for you, but I've been called away, so... um...good night." She included Saint in her wave of departure.

"Don't be silly, Fliss. I can't leave you to find your own way home." What a flossy, fluttery name. It suited her perfectly. "Excuse us."

Saint flashed a dismissive smile at the other woman, who was watching them with great curiosity, and steered Fliss against the tide of people still streaming in.

"You don't have to leave. You'll miss a dinner worth a fraction of what you paid for it." Fliss rolled her eyes as they emerged into the press of people still hovering and hurrying through the dusk.

A cool spring breeze slithered through the crowd, ruffling into his collar and dancing against her loose hair.

"You're missing dinner, too. We'll have to find somewhere else to eat." He texted his driver.

"I was being sarcastic. I'll—"

"Saint! Who's your date?" A photographer waiting near the curb began flashing their bulb at them, drawing others to do the same.

Fliss sent an appalled look to Saint.

"Ignore them." He glanced at a muscled security guard wearing an earpiece and a black T-shirt.

The bouncer immediately turned himself into a bulwark against the photographers, opening his arms wide and forcing the photographers back.

"Hey! What's your name? How long have you been dating Saint?"

Fliss was still staring at him with horror.

"There's my car." His driver was coming in on the far side, against the arrival lane, but both directions were clogged with traffic.

He caught her hand and slipped between two limos dispensing passengers, then opened the rear door where his driver had paused in the middle of the street. Saint swept the hem of her gown into the car and slammed the door, then circled to the other side.

"What's going to happen now?" Fliss asked, twisting to look through the rear window as their car crept forward.

"Now I don't have to spend the next three hours talking about astrology. Thank you."

She blinked once at him, then settled into her seat, nose forward. "And here I was about to ask for your sign."

"Scorpio," he drawled. "I only remember because someone told me once that it explains my sting."

"I can see that." She slid him a side-eye. "Bold to the point of fearless. Intense. Likes to be in charge. Did you know that Scorpios secretly believe in astrology?"

"Untrue."

"Well, it wouldn't be a secret if you admitted it, would it?" Amusement twitched the sharp corners of her mouth.

"I'm going to be sorry I ever met you, aren't I?" He wasn't. This was the most fun he'd had in ages.

"Don't worry. Our acquaintance will be very brief." She craned her neck, looking past the driver to the heavy traffic ahead. "After you get me out of here, you'll never see me again."

"I'll have to make the most of my time with you, then. Won't I, Fliss?"

CHAPTER TWO

THE INTIMATE WAY he said her name raised goose bumps all over her body. In fact, he'd been doing that to her from the moment he'd called her Angel and swept her into the gallery.

Fliss knew it was deliberate on his part. She knew who Saint Montgomery was. Or, at least, she knew what the headlines said about him. He was the heir to Grayscale Technologies, one of Silicon Valley's pillars of wealth and innovation. He held a prestigious position within the company, but whether he did actual work was anyone's guess. He was far more well-known for his jet-setting lifestyle and rotating bevy of beautiful women.

He was a player and seemed to want to play with her.

Much to her chagrin, she was allowing it.

Fliss knew better, but every time she looked at him, her brain shorted out. How could it not? He was gorgeous! Rather than the standard tuxedo most men had donned, Saint wore a dark blue jacket with geometric patterns embroidered into it. His black silk lapels framed his black silk tie against a crisp white shirt. His perfectly tailored trousers landed precisely on his glossy black shoes, and none of it distracted from his ruggedly handsome features. In fact, it only accentuated his athletic physique and sheer charisma.

His straight, dark brows gave him a stern look that

reached all the way into the pit of her belly, but the hint of curl in his dirty blond hair, and the stubble that framed his sensually full mouth, were pure hedonism.

Don't stare, she reminded herself, but he really was as good-looking in person as he was in photos. More. He had an aura of lazy confidence that was positively magnetic.

The way his gaze slid over her like a caress was dark magic that ought to have sent her tucking and rolling from the car, not sitting here holding her breath, waiting to see what would happen next.

Just go home.

Coming to the art gallery had been a terrible idea. She had traded away shifts and distressed her credit card to make this gown in time, and it hadn't held up against the ones by the professionals. Not at all. It was fine for a bridesmaid at a country wedding, but her belief that its simplicity was classic had actually been a fear-based decision. She saw that now.

Which, she supposed, meant the night wasn't a total waste of time. *You learn more from failure than success*, Granny used to say. Fliss understood now why she and her work weren't being taken seriously. Insecurity was holding her back from expressing herself.

Her confidence had taken a major hit when she'd arrived and seen how outgunned she was. Rather than try for the red carpet, she'd slinked into the queue for the side entrance only to be shuffled to the side because she wasn't the invitee.

She had been ready to go home, tail between her legs, when this ridiculously famous man had swept her into the party, then into his car, and now—

"My hotel," he told the driver as traffic began to clear.

Such a playboy.

"Presumptuous," she cast at him before leaning forward

to say to the driver, "You can drop me at the nearest tube station."

"For *dinner*. You're the one making presumptions," Saint said indignantly, but laughter twitched his lips.

Amusement tickled inside her chest along with flutters of excitement and intrigue. Was he really this superficial and predictable? Or was there more to him? She wanted to know.

And she *would* rather catch a car-share from a hotel than have him drop her outside the humble row house where she rented a room with four other housemates. Also, she had skipped lunch because she'd been pressed for time and had thought she would be eating well tonight.

Was she rationalizing spending more time with him? Absolutely.

Was she also giving in to that ambitious, calculating part of herself that had gone so far as to put on her own gown and turn up with Delia Chevron's invitation in her handbag, trying to blag her way into a world where she didn't belong?

How had she deluded herself into believing she could be "discovered" on the red carpet? Talk about the ultimate queue jumper!

She was mortified by her own behavior and grateful she'd slipped away without anyone knowing her name. She had only provided her nickname to that woman who'd called her "not Julie." If Granny were alive to hear about this, Felicity would feel the old woman's yardstick, for sure. She'd have opinions about Fliss allowing a serial womanizer like Saint Montgomery to take her to dinner, too.

You'll know the right man when you meet him, Granny's voice had assured her countless times. *Don't waste time with boys who don't appreciate you.*

Fliss had been schooled rather harshly on how disrespectful a boy could be. Saint reminded her a lot of that first and only boyfriend, emanating the same alpha qualities of strength and wealth and handsome popularity.

Fliss knew better than to imagine he was the Mr. Right she was waiting for, but this felt like a chance at something—not fame or gain, but connection. She couldn't pinpoint why it felt so necessary to spend a little more time with him, but when they exited the car outside his hotel, she didn't refuse his dinner invitation and order a car to take her home.

She entered the door the uniformed doorman held for her, aware of Saint's hand in her lower back as he came in right behind her.

The hotel was one that she had only ever heard of as being very posh. She tried not to gawk, but it was like something out of a movie with its checkered tiles and chandeliers, its arches and columns and refined opulence.

The staff treated Saint like a movie star, too. Or, she supposed, like a man who could buy out the place if he wanted to. As they arrived at the dining room, the maître d' escorted them to a table that bore a Reserved sign, leaving a well-dressed party of four grumbling at the reception podium.

"Do you have any allergies?" Saint asked Fliss as he seated her.

"No."

"Have the chef prepare us a tasting menu," he told the maître d'. "Wine to pair, and don't let anyone bother us."

The man nodded with deference and melted away.

"Fliss. Is that short for something?" Saint unbuttoned his jacket as he sat, leaving it hanging open while he leaned back, at ease with who he was and where they were. "Tell me about yourself."

Ugh. "Must I?"

"You don't want to?" His gaze delved deep into her own.

"It's gloomy." She dropped her own gaze, heart clenching. "My parents died when I was eight. They were all I had aside from my granny. She raised me and passed a couple of years ago. I moved to London for a fresh start." Losing her was still a painful knife in her chest.

"I'm sorry for your loss."

"Thanks."

An amuse-bouche arrived to lighten the mood. It was a single bite of ceviche on a foam of fragrant dill served on a silver spoon, topped by a few grains of caviar and a sprinkle of chopped chive. They chased it with a light wine ripe with notes of pear and anise.

Fliss had never noticed such subtleties of flavor before. She thought her senses might've been sharpened by the company she was in. Being in the aura of this man was a thrill somewhere between lion taming and steering a high-performance car through the streets of Monaco.

"What do you do here?" he asked.

"Fashion designer." It might not have been her job, but painters were artists even if they didn't sell their work. "I'm still starting out. You? What brings you to London?"

"Patting the backs of our top performers at the gala this evening."

"Shouldn't you be there, then?"

He shrugged it off. "They'll have more fun without the boss keeping them in check."

"Is that what your work entails? Travel and glad-handing?"

"Much of it, yes." His eyes narrowed with suspicion. "Why are you asking about my work?"

"Why are you interested in mine? We have to talk about something. It's too bad I don't have my tarot cards." She looked to her small handbag. "I could have done a reading for you."

"Do you really believe in the supernatural, or are you stringing me along?"

"Both." She couldn't help grinning. "Granny used to take me to a psychic sometimes, to see if we could talk to my parents. When I was twelve, I won my tarot cards at a fair. It came with a book of interpretations, so I spent the rest of my adolescence learning to read them. I've delved a little into astrology and numerology. Crystals. As far as explaining life's mysteries, they make as much sense as anything else."

"What about ghosts?"

"What about them? Don't say you don't believe in them." She leaned forward to warn, "There's one right behind you."

It was their server, coming to remove their plates. Saint's reaction to the sudden movement in his periphery was a flicker of his gaze, then a shake of his head at her. "You're trouble."

She bit back a chuckle, enjoying herself. This was a unique position. She had no history with him, no future—only now. It allowed her to be completely herself without fear of judgment or consequence. It was thrilling.

"I know how farfetched these things sound," she conceded. "But belief isn't about being rational, is it? It's what we convince ourselves is true when we don't have evidence to tell us otherwise. When I set out my cards, that's all I'm looking for—evidence to support a belief I already have. Should I move to London? Oh, look. I pulled a card that means material success. That must mean I'll achieve my goals if I move to London."

"Sounds more like you're tricking yourself."

"We all trick ourselves." Fliss waved that away. "If you prefer to believe that heaven exists, that's the trick you've chosen because there's no way to prove what really happens after death. Maybe it's my imagination that I hear my grandmother's voice when I set out my cards, but who cares if it is? It brings me comfort to feel like I'm talking to her. And in a way, I *am* keeping her spirit alive by invoking her. Does that make her a ghost whose energy is in the room?"

"You've almost convinced me to believe in something completely illogical." He tilted his head as though trying to understand how she'd accomplished it. "It sounds like you were very close with her."

"I was." She was unable to prevent the pang of loss that thinned her voice. "But her quality of life had deteriorated so much by the time she passed, I really believe she's in a better place. It was still hard to be left behind." She could feel herself descending into melancholy so she added, "She loved to spin a yarn, too. You couldn't trust a word she said. I suppose I keep her alive in that way as well."

Saint's face blanked. "Is everything you've just told me pure BS?"

"Does it matter? You wanted to be entertained, and you are. Thank you." She smiled as the server presented a crystal shot glass filled with layers of gazpacho from dark red beet through a rich green cucumber and avocado to a bright yellow heirloom tomato topped with a morsel of lobster and a sprig of mint.

A Reuilly Sauvignon Blanc was poured into a fresh glass, even though she hadn't finished her first glass of wine and the bottle was still mostly full.

Saint wasn't trying to get her drunk by urging her to finish, though. He caught her concerned glance at the ice bucket and said drily, "The staff won't let the opened bottles go to waste."

The soup was gone in three swallows but left a minty tang on Fliss's tongue that was amplified by a sip of the citrus and vanilla in the wine.

They talked about incidentals over a delicate bouquet of colorful baby lettuce leaves and sprigs of herbs arranged with edible flowers on a pureed dressing, then a main of braised duck with baby turnips and figs.

Saint seemed genuinely interested in her, asking about her taste in music and movies, where she had traveled— London and a school trip to Paris, years ago. He made her feel special, but Fliss knew that was an illusion. She was *here*. That was all.

It was still nice to be on a date. She had a strong sense of self and what she wanted to accomplish with her life, but she suffered certain feelings of inadequacy and lack of experience with romantic relationships.

She veered from thinking about that piece-of-dirt boy-friend she'd had back in sixth form, irritated that she was still letting him affect her, but he'd made sexuality such a complicated thing for her. At first, it had been fun and light, but soon he'd pressured her to have sex. She'd gone along with it out of insecurity with their relationship and nor-mal adolescent curiosity, but it had been very un-special.

First times were often awkward, so she wouldn't have had such hard feelings about it, but he'd begun telling peo-ple she'd given it up to him. Angry, she'd broken up with him only for him to spread nasty rumors that he'd broken things off because she was "the town bike."

She'd lost friendships over it and a lot of trust in boys. For the rest of school and into uni, she had had all the typi-cal curiosity and desires of a healthy, youthful person, but she'd also felt deeply self-conscious when she'd showed so much as a collarbone or an ankle, loath to draw sexual at-tention in case she'd been accused of asking for it.

Eventually, she'd begun to relax and come out of her shell again, but by then, Granny's health had turned. Fliss had moved home, where she had fallen back into old patterns of keeping her head down. In a lot of ways, worry for Granny had tapped her out emotionally, too. There hadn't been room for a romantic relationship, so she hadn't pursued any.

Moving to London had been another fresh start, but between making ends meet and chasing her dreams, she didn't have much time for a social life. Occasionally, she joined her housemates at the pub, but she'd never met a man who interested her enough to choose him over her ambitions.

Until now.

Not that Saint was likely to derail her in any way. He was the most unattainable man in dating history. It was well-documented. He was buying her dinner. That was all this was and all it would be.

She turned the tables on him, though, and learned that his parents lived in New York and that he had a penthouse there but also a home in California because he spent so much time there. He attended plays or movie *premieres*. He was wired for logic and technology where she gravitated to arts and the ethereal. He traveled the globe on a monthly basis.

"We genuinely have nothing in common," Fliss noted wryly. "I have a passport I've used precisely once. I renewed it when I moved to London, hoping I'd need it for work." Surely she would be recognized as a genius and sent to Fashion Week in New York? Or, at the very least, would book herself a trip to attend?

"What about dancing?" He glanced to where couples were stepping and turning in tempo to the pianist's romantic melody.

"Are you asking if I'm any good? Not really. I'm guessing you're an expert?"

"I am." He rose and held out his hand in invitation.

"At least we're both humble," she teased, but he had

every right to his arrogance. Everything about him short-ened her breath in the most delicious way.

Since when did she find a man's hand sexy? The glimpse of his inner wrist above his wide palm and long fingers seemed like the most erotic peek of skin in the world. Fliss wanted to kiss that spot where his skin was a shade less tanned than the rest.

Warming with a blush, she set her hand in his, feeling drawn upward by an unseen force. Pulled and gathered and spun onto a cloud even though her feet weren't yet on the dance floor.

As they arrived, Saint drew her into his arms and her body became a flame, hot and bright and insubstantial.

Then she embarrassed herself by bumping straight into him. As her curves mashed up against his firm, strong body, her stomach swooped and plummeted.

"I'm sorry! See? I'm bad at this."

"Listen to the music. Let me lead." His voice was low and hypnotic. "Trust me."

She didn't trust him. Or shouldn't. But she had quit lis-tening to the voice of caution and now began to feel. The piano notes filled her ears, but she could swear she heard his heartbeat at a deeper level, matching hers. All of her became synchronized to him. The breadth of his shoulders blocked out the rest of the room, making him her world. The faint trace of aftershave against his throat filled her nostrils, and his hand cradling hers sent warmth penetrat-ing into her bloodstream.

The sure way he advanced and retreated, moving her with ease as she gave herself up to his mastery reinforced her sense of belonging to him. Of becoming an extension of him.

This is the one.

The voice that spoke wasn't angel or devil or Granny.

It was her deepest voice of intuitive knowledge. Despite all the evidence to the contrary, a fine vibration within her was harmonizing with his. Fliss gave herself up to it as they moved. Neither of them was leading or following. They were in perfect alignment.

This was how it would feel to make love with him, she understood as sensuality unfurled inside her. Natural and easy. She didn't need her precious tarot cards to tell her he'd be good at sex, either. He'd draw her effortlessly down a path of iniquity, and she would love every second of it.

"What's funny?" Saint murmured, making her realize he was looking at her.

"This situation. It's very surreal to me," she admitted, trying to hide the blush that betrayed where her thoughts had strayed. "It must be very common for you, though? Picking up women?"

There was a flash behind his eyes. Insulted?

He directed his attention over her head, releasing a noise of disparagement. "Women do the picking up. I simply allow it."

"I guess I'm a natural. I didn't realize that's what I was doing." *Was* that what she had been doing?

Their gazes clashed again. This time the flash in his eyes was lightning that struck all the way into the pit of her belly and lower, leaving a scorch in her loins. A certain apprehension washed over her, too. It was the wild combination of exhilaration and fear when tasting nature's raw power. Of being overwhelmed by it.

"It is me this time," he said in that smoky voice that made her skin feel tight.

Picking her up? He was more than a natural at it. He was a world-class wizard.

"I thought this was only dinner?" She dropped her gaze

to the knot in his tie, trying to hide the flare of temptation that came into her eyes.

He probably read her temptation in her tension and the telltale blush that was warming her cheeks.

"It can be, if that's what you prefer." Was there tension in him, too? Her ears were straining to take in every tiny signal between them. "But I like to take my fate into my own hands, rather than rely on the stars to offer me what I want." His mouth curled at the corner. "If there's a chance for more than dinner, I'd like to seize it."

He'd like to seize her, too, apparently, given how his grip tightened slightly on her waist and hand.

Before Fliss realized what he was doing, he guided her away from him in a slow spin that was unexpected enough to make her dizzily catch onto him when she came back into his arms. Then he dipped her slightly over his arm, so she was off-balance, and lowered his head.

He stopped before he kissed her. His whispered "Is there?" wafted across her lips. "A chance?"

Oh, dear.

Her heart was thudding in a mix of anxiety and excitement, and her hands were holding tight to him—because she was literally off-balance. She could have shaken him off and stood on her own two feet rather than let him hold her tipped like this, but her brain had short-circuited again. All she was really aware of was his mouth, right there, filling her with such yearning she could hardly breathe.

She lifted her chin in welcome, offering her mouth to him.

The lightest of touches brushed her lips. A subtle rest of lips to lips. A greeting. Not even a dalliance. He waited for her to make the slight shift and find the angle that fit their mouths together more fully.

Then he rocked his head, a request. *Invite me.*

She did, sighing as his arm grew more firm around her and his tongue probed in a languorous quest. When the tip of his tongue brushed the roof of her mouth, feathery caresses seemed to scroll over her whole body from nape to tailbone, down her arms and legs and high between her thighs, into that pulsing, throbbing place that she'd been trying to ignore but felt heavy and flooded with heat. With longing.

She gasped at the startling way he brought her whole body to life, but he only deepened their kiss, as though seeking whatever she might be holding back from him. Chasing. Demanding.

Fliss had known she wasn't his match financially or socially, but she had been pretending they were equals in a more esoteric way. Wit, perhaps. Or in their lighthearted detachment from this dinner of theirs.

This kiss, however. This kiss demonstrated just how far out of her league she really was. It was a plunge from thirty-thousand feet into thin air. It knocked the breath from her lungs, leaving her ears rushing with nothing but the scream of wind.

His lips raked across hers in an unbridled claim that shook apart all she'd ever known about kissing, which was admittedly a lot less than she'd realized. He cupped the back of her head, and the stubble on his jaw grazed her chin.

When a whimper resounded in her throat, he drew her upright, but desperation had her winding her arms around his neck. *Don't stop.* She stood on tiptoe and pressed herself harder to him. She wanted to be closer. Closer still.

He growled and crushed her to his front and nipped at her bottom lip before soothing and suckling, causing more lightning to strike through her abdomen and into her sex.

More trickles of need and more shivers of ecstatic pleasure traveled down her spine.

Very dimly, she was aware that they were in public, that they should stop, but she couldn't make herself pull away. She tasted wine and traces of clove and inhaled a fading aftershave that would remain imprinted on her senses forever.

Her eyelids had fluttered closed. All that existed was this dark enveloping sense of the world having fallen away. She knew only distant sensations of satin and embroidered wool. Her fingertips found the line where his cool hair cut a precise line against the hot skin at the back of his neck. She was aware of her breasts being crushed against the plane of his chest in a way that was a relief but increased the yearning within her. His hard thighs warmed the fall of her skirt against the front of her legs, and his hand drew a slow, lazy circle in her lower back that was as promising as it was proprietary.

This was what she had been waiting for in her ambivalence toward dating. Not commitment or Mr. Right but this rush of desire that pulsed inside her like a drum beat. Like an imperative.

She had been waiting for a man to kiss her as though she was essential to him. That was how she felt when he started to draw back, then returned as though he couldn't resist one more long, thorough, greedy taste.

He lifted his head and kept her in the shelter of his arms.

She was trembling and grateful for his support. Her knees were gelatin, the rest of her soft as melted wax. His hand was tucked beneath her hair, cupping the back of her neck, thumb moving in a restless, soothing caress against her nape. The other held her body pressed close enough to feel the rapid tattoo of his heart through the layer of his jacket and the thick shape of his erection against her stomach.

They were drawing attention. She covered her burning lips with her crooked finger.

When she stepped out of his arms, he slid his hand down her bare shoulder, leaving a wake of tingles before he buttoned his jacket to disguise the effect she'd had on him.

As they arrived back at their table, he picked up her handbag. "Do you want to stay for dessert or bring it to my room?"

"I—"

Don't, she warned herself.

But that deep, inner, intuitive voice said, *He's the one*.

Her voice was thick as honey. "I'm sure the staff won't let it go to waste if we skip it."

Rather than the smug smile she'd expected, his cheek ticked. He took her hand as they left the restaurant.

CHAPTER THREE

MOST PEOPLE ASSUMED Saint was a risk junkie. Or at the very least, someone who didn't care about risks so long as he got what he wanted.

That wasn't true at all. As a child, he had learned to calculate risk very quickly. If he'd wanted to speak to his father, he'd first weighed whether the subject was worth his father's wrath at having his work interrupted. If he'd tried out for the school play, would it be worth his mother showing up tipsy and making it about her?

Later, when he and his father had found common ground in programming and hardware, his mother had been hurt and jealous. Which would he rather endure? His mother's heartbreak or his father's belittling lecture?

Those early consequences had prepared him for the perils in later relationships: the friend who was only a friend because he wanted access to the newest smart phone, or the girl who liked his money more than she liked him, or the people who invited him to parties to elevate their own social standing.

Saint was always aware when people were trying to use him. He often allowed it. There were silver linings: business advantages, amusing entertainments. Sex.

But he had taught those around him to expect very little from him beyond a sarcastic remark and that he would pick up the bill.

This woman beside him in the elevator, with her quirky sense of humor and understated beauty and fiery depths of passion, felt like a gamble he ought to take more time to calculate. His reaction to her was too sharp. Too intense. That kiss had been so hot, so all encompassing, he'd been seared from hairline to toenails.

This wasn't purely a carnal reaction, though. That was the part making his nerve endings sting with danger. He'd been drawn to her all night—from the first glimpse to his compulsion to leave the gala with her. To learn more about her. To touch her.

She was as puzzling as she was alluring. Both open and closed. That air of mystery, with her refusing to give him her full name, tickled at his well-strung trip wires, but what damage could she possibly do to him if they spent the night together? He didn't have anything in his room that he wasn't prepared to lose. He weathered bad publicity like a seasonal storm.

Hell, he was in a small storm right now, he recalled with annoyance, but that fiasco with Julie reminded him to make clear to Fliss that this evening had its limits.

"I'm due in New York first thing in the morning," he said. "I'll be leaving for the airport in a few hours, but stay the night. Use the room tomorrow if you want. Visit the spa."

The gold in her irises tarnished slightly before she blinked it away. "I have to work tomorrow." Her mouth twitched. "But you've very good at this. Very smooth." She looked down to where she held her purse and gave its clasp a few nervous clicks. "I've always wondered how these things were handled. By that I mean, um, I don't have condoms." She peeked up at him in question.

"I do." Always. There was one in his pocket that he'd pulled from his stash out of habit.

Fliss nodded, but her brows pulled into a frown of consternation.

"Second thoughts? That's fine." He might actually die if she changed her mind, though. He'd never felt horniness like this. So specific. So beastly. Like there was a creature inside him that would run her to ground if he had to, he needed her so badly.

"No, I want to." Her cheeks stained that pretty shade of pink that stoked the fire in his gut. "It's only that I felt swept away a few minutes ago. Now the mood is a little..." She wrinkled her nose. "Logistical. I'm being silly."

The doors opened, and she stepped out, looking to him to show her the way.

Her befuddling honesty and that phrase *always wondered how these things were handled* made him realize she didn't have the experience he did. It provoked a sort of endeared protectiveness in him. As he brought her to the door of his penthouse, he felt almost as though he was initiating a virgin. He wanted to take care with her and meet all her expectations. These sorts of interludes ought to be nothing but pleasure with no reason for regret. He wanted to give her that.

He wanted to give her the best sex she'd ever had so he would remain in her thoughts forever.

And where the hell had *that* come from?

"Do you want a drink?" He let her in and closed the door, sealing them into a lounge lit only by a table lamp. He threw off his jacket, trying to cool his blood. *Patience.*

"No, thanks." She was clicking the clasp on her purse again.

"I don't do this as often you might think, you know."

Not anymore at least. "It suits me to let people think I'm a slut, but I'm actually quite picky."

"Which sounds a little like you're trying to make me feel special. I'll chose to believe you." She set her handbag on a side table and wandered past the sofa to the glass doors that led onto the terrace. Outside, recessed lighting cast pools of gold from beneath the hedges that surrounded the patio table and chairs.

"You are special." He came up behind her and trailed his fingertips down her bare arms, pleased when he heard her breath catch. He was growing addicted to this chemistry that simmered and fizzed between them. It stoked his own arousal, making him twitch and thicken behind his fly. "Do you always react like this?"

"Ha. No." She hugged herself, rubbing the bumps that had risen on her arms. In the faint reflection on the glass, her gaze sought his. "Do you?" Her voice held challenge. Cynicism.

Her question plucked at one of the razor-thin piano wires he used to protect himself. He did not react like this to every woman he met, but he wasn't about to admit it.

"If you want to talk because you're nervous, that's okay." He trailed his fingers down her arms again, making her body twitch in a shudder of sensuality. "But I'd rather you let me sweep you away."

"I am nervous," she admitted breathlessly, voice thinning to a whisper. "But I do want that." She started to turn into his arms.

He stopped her.

"Stay like this," he persuaded, hearing his voice drop into his chest with anticipation.

He drew a line from one side of her neck to the other, scooping her hair onto the front of her shoulder, exposing the bow that secured the haltered front of her gown. He pressed a kiss to her nape.

Such a tiny thing, but it made her shoulders flex. This power he had over her would be heady if there wasn't such an answering ring of need that crashed like a gong inside him. Sexual aggression had its place, but this wasn't it. He kept a tight leash on his inner caveman and nuzzled into the fragrance of almonds and peaches that clung in her hair.

"Can I untie this?" he asked against the strings that dangled against the top of her spine.

"Yes." The word was a rush of breath.

Slowly, slowly, he drew the tail free, watching her shoulder blades pull together as the loops released. He kissed her nape and the tip of her shoulder and scraped his teeth against the tendons at the base of her neck, then bent lower to suck the skin on the fleshy part of her upper arm.

A shiver and a helpless sound was his reward.

As the front of her gown fell forward, exposing her chest in a translucent reflection of pale gold and shadowed nipples, she brought her arms up to shield herself.

He slid his hands around to cup her breasts for her, very aware of the way she drew in a ragged breath at his possessive action. He involuntarily groaned with possessive pleasure as the weight of the warm swells filled his palms.

"Put your hands on the glass." His voice was barely working, coming out graveled by the carnal hunger that was gathering inside him.

The position forced her to lean forward slightly, pushing her ass into his fly and settling her breasts more fully into his hands. He could feel her excitement in the way her breaths trembled, and knowing he was causing it sent electric signals of need straight into his groin.

He stepped even closer, covering her as he continued to kiss her nape and slowly massage the firm globes that filled his hands. He played with her nipples until they were so taut his mouth watered with longing to suck on them. Hard.

She made a noise that sounded like pain.

"Too rough?" He stilled his touch.

"No. It's—I can't..."

"It feels good?" He smiled against her hairline, blowing softly behind her ear as he returned to lightly pinching and toying with her nipples.

"Yes." She hung her head as though tortured beyond her bearing. She shifted restlessly, arching her breasts into his hands while pressing her ass deeper into his crotch, rocking with invitation.

Exquisite.

"Are you feeling needy, angel? Do you want my hands under your skirt? Here?" He released one breast to slide his palm down her stomach, then pressed the fall of silk deep into the hot valley between her thighs. When he flexed his grip against her mound, the noise she made was incredibly erotic, making his skin feel too tight to contain him.

"I like my hand here, too," he assured her in a graveled voice, squeezing in gentle but firm rhythm, enjoying the kinky sensation of trapping her in a vise of pleasure so she shook and wriggled for escape but had nowhere to go.

He nudged her feet open so he could step between them and pressed forward, giving her a firm seat for the grind of her ass against his aching erection while he tongued her earlobe. The sexy noises that emerged from her throat and the rock of her loins against his throbbing sex were an erotic purgatory he could have lived in forever.

"Harder," she moaned, dropping her hand to cover his.

"Keep your hands on the glass, Fliss. Or I'll stop." That was a lie. There was no possible way he wanted to stop. He wanted to fondle her until she broke, but he needed to stay in control. If she started running things, this would be over in a short minute.

He nearly lost it anyway when she dutifully set her hand back on the glass and he glimpsed the way she bit her lips in contrition. Damn, he wanted to kiss that mouth of hers.

But her obedience had granted him permission to continue having his way with her.

With a growled noise of approval, he straightened enough to gather her skirt with both hands until he could burrow beneath the silk to thighs that trembled at his first touch. He stroked all over the warm skin, everywhere that he could reach, from thighs to buttocks to lower back, then forward to her stomach and back down to her thighs.

Her ass wore a V-shaped slash of silver lace held up by three narrow bands of midnight blue strung across her hips. The delicate lace trapped his hand when he slid his touch inside the front. Her plump mound was like holding heaven. She moaned and stepped her feet farther apart, pressing into his touch, all slick and hungry and helpless to her own desires. When she rocked against his fingers, coating them in her essence, he felt omnipotent.

"I want you like this," he said in a guttural voice he barely recognized. "I want to be inside you right here. Like this."

He wanted a thousand other things, too. He wanted his mouth here where his fingers were making her whimper. He wanted her tongue in his mouth and her naked body riding his. He wanted their sweaty bodies contorting into every lewd act he could think of, but right now, he *needed* to be inside her.

Miraculously, she dipped her lower back and lifted her hips with invitation.

"Yes. I want that, too."

* * *

Felicity had thought she was waiting for love. For romance. For commitment and a sense of a future with a man. She didn't look down on women who engaged in casual sex, but she had never imagined it was for her. Until now.

Until this man made her feel that walking away without seeing where this could go would be cheating herself in some way. Even in the elevator, as she'd recognized how effortlessly he made clear this was a one-night stand, she had sensed that if she didn't seize this chance to be with him, even for a few hours, she would regret it.

And here she was, regretting nothing, despite behaving in a way that was so flagrant it bordered on debauchery. She was letting him touch her in very intimate ways. He was commanding her to keep her hands on the glass, and she did it because she needed to have sex with him or she would die. Literally *die*. That was how it felt.

When he removed his hand from her tanga, she moaned in loss. But she could feel the brush of his knuckles against her backside as he released himself from his fly.

The hot weight of his erection sat against the lace that descended into the crease of her buttocks. In the glass, she saw him bite the edge of a small square packet.

"I like your underwear," he told her as he covered himself with the condom. "You'll have to bill me for the replacement."

Before she processed what he meant, the thin cords at her hips snapped and they fell away.

"Oh." The sad sob in her throat turned into a more carnal *"Oh"* as he swept his touch all over the flesh he'd bared, reigniting the fires of need inside her.

Then he was guiding the thick crown of his erection to explore those same slick, eager places, seeking her entrance. Prodding.

She bit her lip, tensing. She'd only done this once before, literally once. Would it hurt the same way?

The pressure increased, hinting at discomfort, but she was so wet and he was so gradual, giving light pulses of his hips as he rolled his fingertip around the swollen knot of her clit. He teased her into relaxing and accepting the unfamiliar intrusion.

At the last moment, she instinctually arched, and that was it. He slid all the way in so his hips were flush against her buttocks. The fabric of his trousers was an abrasion against the backs of her thighs. His steely shape stretched and filled her so she quivered at the thoroughness of his possession.

His hands clasped her hips, holding her steady. His breath hissed, then he leaned over her and his teeth opened against her nape, threatening to bite before he turned it into a hot, wet suckle that had her toes curling in her shoes.

She didn't know how to make sense of all these sensations. The combination of hot arousal and erotic titillation and the wildness of the whole experience was overwhelming, quelling her ability to think. She simply *was*.

He started to move, and the magnitude of the experience exploded.

Waves of pleasure rolled up and down her body with the slide of his hand across her naked torso. The retreat and return of his lovemaking was carnal and raw and so delicious she couldn't help making animalistic noises of pleasure. She was an animal. She'd been caught in the forest by a potential mate, and that was what they were doing. Mating. It was earthy and primal and pure.

"Can you come like this?" he asked against her ear. "Or do you need…" His long fingers swept to the front of her thighs again. He caressed where he was moving with slow, deliberate power, then higher, plucking at her swollen clit.

A storm gathered within her. She couldn't speak because all the energy in the universe had shrunk to a fine point inside her. All that existed was the astounding pleasure coiling in her loins, gathering.

In rough desperation, she pushed herself backward into his thrusts, increasing the impact of his hips.

He grunted in surprise. One hand shifted to bite into her waist, and the speed of his thrusts increased. His hips slapped her buttocks, and the nucleus of need inside her detonated, expanding outward like a supernova.

She cried out with the strength of her climax, but his shout was louder. He pounded into her, engulfing her in a fire that should have incinerated her but only licked and burned and melded her so indelibly with him, she didn't imagine how they could ever be separated.

Saint left later than he should have and had to sleep on the flight rather than using the time to prepare his presentation as he'd originally planned. That was his first misstep.

He hadn't meant to crash on impact, but the dubious thrill of creating slides of market analysis tables was no match for his lack of sleep and abundance of energetic sex.

What the hell had even happened to him? He'd been wrung dry in those first moments in the living room. He'd been emptied of thought and strength and purpose by an orgasm that had bordered on pain it had been so powerful.

He should have soothed them both with a cuddle on the couch and a glass of wine. He'd felt inordinately tender, given how she'd been trembling, but when he'd withdrawn and turned her, their lazy kisses had caught fire again as quickly as their first.

His dumb stick had hardened, and his hunger for her had sharpened to acute. When he'd drawn back, both of them gasping for air, he'd been half barbarian, ordering her gruffly, *Get into my bed. I want to do that again.*

She had said exactly what she'd been saying to him all night. *Yes.*

What a drug. What a night. His orgasms had gotten better and better every time. He couldn't even count how many she'd had. He would've been delivering another several right now if he'd stayed, which he'd been very tempted to do.

That was why he'd made himself leave—while she'd been sound asleep. Otherwise, he suspected he wouldn't have been able to. But this meeting with his father and the rest of the board was too important. The fact that he'd considered risking their ire by rescheduling so he could stay and make love with Fliss had been enough of a caution light that he'd decided it was better to put space between him and the spell she'd cast over him.

Even so, he was still reliving that incredible sex when he arrived in New York and jumped into the shower of the hospitality suite below his office. He was *recovering*, he noted ruefully, and turned the tap of the shower to cold, then downed a hot coffee while he dressed in a clean shirt and suit.

Saint ought to have been mentally preparing for what would be a typically abrasive encounter with his father, but his libido was pacing restlessly inside him, griping, *When can I see her again?*

Never, if he was a jerk about it and failed to express his appreciation for their very exceptional night.

It wasn't like him to be so punch-drunk from any woman, let alone one he'd just met. Hell, he still barely knew her. Most of their conversation later in the night had revolved around, *Does this feel good?*

"Sir?" His assistant, Willow, poked their head in. They

were nonbinary, usually wearing a suit and tie for work while keeping their long red hair in a tidy bun. Occasionally they wore eyeshadow behind the ever-changing frames of their glasses, and they changed their colorful shades of nail polish almost daily. "The board is assembled and ready for you."

"One minute." He handed Willow the notes he'd scribbled as he'd made his way from the jet to the helipad on top of this tower.

He should have been first to the meeting and was already ten minutes late, but he took out his phone and found the number for Smythe's in his contacts.

"Mr. Montgomery." The smooth, feminine voice of Ms. Smythe greeted him in her cool boarding-school accent. "How may I serve you today? I have an opening in an hour."

"I'm in New York," he replied. "But I'd like to purchase some earrings. Something like you showed me last time." He'd intended to give Julie a pair to wear to the gala, but Fliss deserved something he picked out especially for her. "Something with blue in them." The shade of her gown was imprinted in his memory forever.

"Contemporary? Let me text you a few photos. One moment."

Smythe's was a mystery—both shop and owner—but Saint had been warned that prying would result in his no longer receiving invitations to shop there, which would be a pity. He'd dealt with many high-end jewelry merchants throughout his adult life, and Ms. Smythe of Knightsbridge was the best. She was professional and discreet. Her gemstones were ethically sourced and always of the highest quality, the settings one of a kind. Saint occasionally bought investment pieces but more often purchased a parting gift when a liaison was wrapping up.

Today he was looking for more of a welcome gift.

His phone pinged. He flicked through the photos. One showed a chandelier of blue sapphires in yellow gold; another was a platinum cuff with alternate rows of diamonds and sapphires.

"The ones with the marquis diamonds," he told Ms. Smythe. The earrings were the size of a silver dollar. The leaf-shaped white diamonds formed a laurel wreath around an eye-catching twist of round-cut blue sapphires. They radiated elegance and graceful artistry but maintained a playful quality that he thought suited Fliss.

"A lovely choice. Are these for delivery, or shall I hold them for you?"

"Delivery. Her name is Fliss." His inner beast had been too focused on sex to ask for her number before she'd fallen asleep. "She's a fashion designer, but you'll have to do some legwork for me."

Saint had peeked into her purse on his way out the door. He'd found a twenty-pound note, her smartphone, which had been locked, a pair of physical door keys—who even used those anymore?—an invitation to the gala, an Oyster card and a lip gloss. Not even a driver's license or a debit card to give him her full name.

The gala invitation had had Delia Chevron's name on it, which made sense. A model would have friends in fashion. He'd written his number on the card, then slipped away.

"Check the hotel," he said to Ms. Smythe, mentioning the one he always used when visiting London. "If she's still in the room, you can deliver to her there." He had meant to take care of this while he'd been flying to ensure he wouldn't miss her, but so much for that. She'd worn him out, and he'd needed his beauty sleep. "If she's already gone, contact Delia Chevron. They were supposed to attend last night's art gala together, so she'll know how to reach her."

Actually, Fliss had said she had known her date wouldn't be there. Saint spared a moment to ponder that. He'd been so taken with her, he'd glossed over how cagey she'd been about her reason for attending and leaving before it had really started.

"I'd love an excuse to connect with Ms. Chevron." Ms. Smythe's warm voice redirected his thoughts back to the business at hand. "I'll be in touch once your gift has been delivered."

"Thank you." He ended the call and strode down the hall to begin the presentation he would have to make up on the fly.

He wasn't worried. He had spent the last year and a half taking a new approach to military-grade encryption software, personally establishing proof of concept before writing the code for the prototype. This was his baby, and he knew it inside and out.

His father preferred to spearhead product innovation. That would be the stumbling block. Theodore Montgomery had an ego to match the fortune and tech empire he'd built. His control of Grayscale was of the tight, iron-fist variety. In his mind, he was the only genius in the family. His son was far more suited to what Fliss had called "glad-handing."

Saint knew this software would be his contribution to the legacy of his name, though. It would allow him to step out from under his father's shadow and be seen as an innovator in his own right. A leader of the next generation in the technological revolution.

The project was ready for the next stage of development. He needed a team of top-tier programmers to build it out, improve the interface, test it, refine it, then take it to market. That required a huge investment of time, money and other resources. Since it would also become Grayscale's next flagship product, he needed the board on board.

"Good morning," he said as he entered the room filled with middle-aged suits and skirts. On the screen at one end of the room were another half dozen faces, all pinched with expressions of disapproval. His father looked at his watch.

Willow, first-class executive assistant with a minor in miracle making, had translated Saint's chicken scratch into slides that appeared with the click of a button.

Saint dove straight into his business case, emphasizing the value and benefits this software would have for Grayscale, including its appeal to both high-level institutions and small-business users.

"We already offer encryption software," someone said.

"This one is better." It was sacrilege to claim anything his father had designed needed improvement, but it did. "This will become the preferred solution," Saint promised.

The protests kept coming, though, making Saint look to his father, starting to suspect that Ted had poisoned the well before Saint had entered the room.

"You're asking for a lot of money to make a copycat product."

"Are you really prepared to take on a project this complex and carry it across the line? It could take years."

"There's a difference between charm and leadership, Saint."

"Don't hold back," Saint drawled to hide his irritation. "Tell me what you really think of me."

"We think it's half-baked, son," Ted Montgomery said. "Did you not pick up on that?"

"Of course it's half-baked. That's why I'm here. To get an oven," he shot back.

"It feels premature," the CFO said soothingly while looking around to collect nods of agreement.

"No problem." Holding his father's stare, Saint said, "I'll start my own company and develop it myself." It was the contingency plan he had hoped not to need. It would be far more convenient to develop this under the Grayscale umbrella. It would integrate better, and he didn't want it to belong to anyone else when he eventually inherited Grayscale.

"With my money? You're exactly like your mother," his father accused in his scoffing way, right there in front of the assembled board. "You think you can help yourself to what's behind door number three and use it for whatever pissant idea arrives in your head."

"Actually, Dad, I'm exactly like you." Saint took his ire and offense and any other emotion he was currently experiencing and condensed it inside himself. He *became* his father, sharp and hard and clear as a diamond. Able to cut through anything. "This is a business decision. I'm about to revolutionize the sector. If you're so shortsighted that you want to cut me off financially, I'll pick up the phone and ask one of our competitors to develop this with me. Frankly, I'd prefer to focus on this without the distraction of running Grayscale."

Which he did run, whether his father wanted to acknowledge that or not.

Ted wore the title of president and had the final say on top-level decisions, but his social skills were abysmal. Saint spent half his life on a plane. Under the guise of schmoozing, he kept an eye on the executives in their global offices, ironing out wrinkles before they became problems. He resolved sticky issues around politics and international regulations and carried the emotional burden of those who were frustrated by his father's closed-minded leadership so his father wasn't bothered by power struggles and other conflicts.

"I'm well aware you regard this company as a distraction," Ted said with heavy sarcasm, waving toward the screen mounted on the wall. It was back to showing the remote board members, but Saint got the message that his name and face were appearing on screens for all the wrong reasons, thanks to Julie. "You couldn't even stay for dinner last night because you were chasing a new skirt. Clean up your act, son. Show me you're serious about taking the reins, and maybe I could think about retiring. Then you can pour my money into whatever hairbrained scheme you like."

Saint snorted. "You're never going to retire."

The man was seventy and came into the office daily so he could bark orders and continue to feel important. The power he'd amassed here was the only thing that gave him anything close to a sense of satisfaction with his life.

Saint turned his attention to the room at large.

"Just so we're clear, this prototype was built on my own time, on my own equipment, by me. It's mine," he said. "There are people intrigued enough by what I create to want to steal it. They know what I did with the early AI configurations, and they want to know what I'm up to next." That was why Julie had been nudged by her debtors to copy his files. "My work has value. Maybe not to you, but I won't let that slow me down."

He gathered up his laptop and walked out.

"Saint." One of his allies on the board caught him outside the door. "Don't do anything rash. Give me some time to change some minds. There are a lot of people on your side." He nodded toward the boardroom.

"Oh, really," Saint snorted.

"Especially when it comes to your eventual rise to the

throne. But they can't get behind you unless they know you're ready. Maybe take your father's advice? Showing up late today only gave everyone a chance to gossip about you. Maybe if they didn't have anything to gossip about..."

Saint hated to back down or put off his goals, but he also knew his father wasn't stupid. Ted might have flexed his muscles for their audience, but when it came to dollars and sense, he would do what was best for Grayscale.

So would Saint, and honestly, the publicity he'd generated with Julie wasn't great for Grayscale.

"Point taken," he muttered and detoured to the head of their PR department on his way back to his office.

"Xanthe," he greeted as he entered her office.

She was a chic single mother of two who always appeared to be fully in control. Saint suspected she had her days, same as everyone, but the fact that no one ever saw her in a state of stress was a testament to her skill at manipulating optics.

"Saint." She wore her black hair in a neat bun and had her pointed collar turned up around her chin. "You were on my calendar to see today." She left her desk to join him where he was making himself at home on her sofa.

"Because of Julie? I just took a whipping over that, thanks. No one appreciates the free publicity I generate to keep Grayscale a household name."

"Some people are so ungrateful, aren't they?" she mused. "Perhaps if you hadn't poured gasoline on her 'woman scorned' routine by moving on so quickly?"

Fliss? "It was a few photos at the curb. They'll turn anything into a story, won't they?"

"Who is she?" Xanthe asked.

He started to say *No one*, but that didn't feel right. He skipped past answering and said, "I've been informed that my image needs work. What do you suggest?"

"Honestly? Marriage. To someone appropriate," she added quickly. "Conservative. A good family. Well-known, but not famous. Not *in*famous."

"Not interested," Saint said flatly. He'd had a front-row seat on the train wreck that was his parents' marriage. It should have been dissolved decades ago. As far as he was concerned, marriage was nothing less than a cage fight to the death.

"An engagement, then," Xanthe said with her signature ability to pivot. "Temporary. It doesn't have to be real, but it would convey that you're settling down."

Fliss leapt to mind, but he didn't want to bring her into a fake engagement while they had a real affair. Too messy. And if he engaged himself to someone else, he couldn't see her.

"No."

"All right. Final offer." Xanthe used a tone of exaggerated patience and leaned back while crossing her legs. "Celibacy. And I'll circulate rumors that you're *looking* for a wife. That signals you're maturing and developing a sense of responsibility."

"I *have* a sense of responsibility. That's why I'm here. But sure. Run with that." He flicked his hand.

"Did you hear the part about living like a monk? It won't work if you continue having affairs."

"I know."

"Do you?"

He liked Xanthe, he really did, but she was annoying as hell in how well she saw through him.

"Look," he said with the same exaggerated patience she was using. "There is an image that served me well for a long time but no longer does. That's why I'm here. *I* have changed, even if the narrative hasn't."

"I know you don't have nearly as many affairs as you're

reported to have," she acknowledged smoothly. "I also know that when I say 'no women,' you hear 'except that one you really want to have an affair with.' I mean none, Saint."

He looked away, dismayed. He did want an affair with one particular woman. She was all the way across the Atlantic, though. And he hadn't made any promises to her. He could absolutely leave her with the earrings and never contact her again.

"This is important to me," he stated decisively. "I need the board to know I'm all grown up and can be trusted with the keys to the car."

"I'll start the whispers today."

"Thank you." He nodded and rose.

"You're going to call her, aren't you?" Xanthe said, staying seated while watching him knowingly.

"We'll keep it under the radar," he promised. He ignored the *tsk* he heard as he left.

He was far more disturbed by Ms. Smythe's report when he got back to his office.

Delia Chevron didn't know any designers named Fliss.

CHAPTER FOUR

"You can't steal from clients, Felicity." Her supervisor, Luz, was dark red beneath her normally light brown complexion.

"I didn't steal," Fliss argued weakly. "It was in the bin."

But it had been wrong to take the invitation. She had known it was wrong when she'd taken it out of the bin. And when she'd stuck it in her handbag. She had been dead wrong to put it in her clutch and carry that wretched card to the art gallery.

She wanted to sink through the floor with humiliation and guilt that she'd ever even noticed the darned thing.

"You've cost me a good client." Luz's voice rang with anger. "You know I can't keep you on."

"I know," Fliss mumbled, feeling sick.

For three days, she had thought she had gotten away with her futile attempt to advance herself. Photos of her with Saint had turned up online, but none had shown her face very well, so no one had recognized her.

Then, this morning, she'd been told to report here to Luz before starting her shift at a luxury flat in Chelsea. Fliss had known immediately that her dark deed had come to light. Her stomach had begun to churn.

"Did you really have *sex* with Saint Montgomery?" Luz hissed.

"What?" That knocked Fliss back in her chair. "Why do you think that?"

"Because he's *Saint Montgomery*. You went to his hotel with him, then he tried to send you earrings through Delia Chevron. You left them in his room, I presume?" Luz elevated her brows with disdain.

"What? *No*." She touched her earlobe, which was naked, but she had definitely come home with the hoops she'd worn to the gala. She was deeply confused. "I don't know anything about any earrings. That doesn't make sense."

"Which is what Delia said. She pieced together that someone had attended the gala with an invitation addressed to her and had her team investigate how you came by it."

"I didn't pretend to be her," Fliss rushed to assert. She had only implied she was Delia's plus-one, then had been shuffled off to the side to wait for her. She didn't explain that Saint was the one who had actually brought her into the gallery. "He hasn't called *you*, has he? Did you give him my number?"

Luz glared outrage at her.

"I'm not saying you should," Fliss mumbled. Where was astral traveling when you really needed it? She would give anything not to be inhabiting her body in this profoundly mortifying moment.

"I'm really disappointed in you, Felicity. I thought you were someone I could count on. Your final pay will go into your account overnight. I cannot give you a reference, but I wish you well in future." Luz straightened a stack of papers that didn't need straightening, signaling this discussion was over.

"I'm genuinely sorry, Luz." Fliss rose. She was tongue-tied, unable to find anything more to say that wasn't full out groveling.

Her only hope was that this incident wouldn't follow

her around like a bad smell, the way those awful rumors started by her old boyfriend had.

She went home and, since her workday had barely started, pulled up her CV on her ancient laptop. She was immediately disheartened. Scrubbing toilets was her top skill these days, but without a reference she wasn't even fit for that. The fashion design route was even further out of reach.

She couldn't waste time on berating herself, though. There would be ample time for that later. For now, she needed to make rent.

Perhaps she *should* go back to school. It was months until September, though.

Fliss looked around her room with its chipped sill and saggy bed and toilet down the hall. It wasn't much, but it had enough space for her sewing machine and table, her form and a tall, cardboard wardrobe where she stored her finished creations.

She could sell those, she supposed, but that would be counterproductive to her aspirations. Plus, experience had taught her that she would be lucky to earn back the cost of the fabric, especially when she was in a hurry to sell. She rarely got enough to cover her many hours of labor.

As for the gown, she could barely look at it.

She was both appalled and elated when she thought about her night with Saint. Nearly everything about it had been perfect, from the way he'd swept her into the glamor of the gala, then taken her for such a fancy dinner. She'd felt like Cinderella. Maybe she hadn't been fully on his level socially and financially, but she hadn't felt as far away as this life put her.

And the sex. If that was what she'd been missing all this time, she had a newfound contempt for her old boyfriend for making her think sex was something you worked up the courage to offer someone. With Saint, there'd been surprisingly little awkwardness. She had reveled in sharing herself with him. He'd been equally generous with his body and kisses and skill.

When she'd awakened in that wide bed on those luxurious sheets, she'd been pleasantly sore all over, feeling as though she'd hiked to a challenging peak and was brimming with accomplishment. As though she'd won the lottery and could live her life on her own terms from now on.

The first knock of reality had arrived when she had discovered she was alone.

Saint had warned her that he'd had an early flight, so she had tried not to let his disappearance bother her, but it had felt a bit tawdry that he'd slipped away without saying goodbye. She'd splurged on a car share rather than a walk of shame on the tube. She had been home and emptying her clutch before she'd found the number he'd scrawled with *Call me* on the back of the invitation that bore Delia Chevron's name.

Chagrin had wormed into her at that point, boring holes in her midsection. Fliss hadn't lied to him about who she was. She hadn't dropped Delia's name to impress him, but his knowing that she'd possessed that card made her reluctant to text the number he'd given her. If she were a student at this point, she might have felt more confident in connecting with him again, but she was now an unemployed housekeeper and she didn't have a good way to explain that card.

She peered into the nightstand drawer where she had left it, keeping his note like a war bride holding on to a love letter. Should she text and ask What is this about earrings?

Oh, God. He wasn't trying to *pay* her, was he?

That felt tawdry. Sex work was fine for people who chose it, but she was ultrasensitive to how she was perceived sexually, especially when it was a wrong impression. Had he thought that was what her motive had been in going to that gala? Did he think she'd been trolling for a sugar daddy?

Fliss buried her face in her hands, ready to do anything to go back in time and not take that card!

Which would mean she wouldn't have the memory of those few magical hours with him.

No. She dropped her hands from her face. Much as she regretted how things had turned out at work, she didn't regret that night. Saint had helped her discover a passion she hadn't known she could feel. It had been a wonderful experience and now it was over and that left her wistful, but fine. She would suffer the consequence of her impulsive theft of that card, find another job and never see him again. Her boring little life would go on.

She believed that right up until her phone rang the next day. It was a reporter for one of the tabloids.

"Are you the Felicity Corning who was with Saint Montgomery last weekend?"

"People keep asking me for a statement. This is my statement," Delia Chevron said on her social media reel.

Saint took the phone from Willow to watch the slender brunette with a wide mouth and eyelids that sat at a bored half-mast.

"I've never met Saint Montgomery or Felicity Corning. She was working for a housekeeping agency and took an invitation from my home that she used to get into the gala. The next day, Mr. Montgomery tried to send earrings to her, through me. This alerted me to the theft. My security team recommended I end my contract with the agency, so I have. That's all I know. Don't ask me for dirt on any of them. I don't have any."

"I do." Julie had spliced Delia's statement into the front of her own so the video cut to her in the back of a car. She wore a ponytail and yoga clothes to give the impression this was an impromptu reaction, but she wore full make-up and he would bet his encryption software that she was getting paid to wear that brand.

"This is how he operates," Julie told the viewer. "He'll sleep with anyone, even a light-fingered housekeeper. And the earrings? Judging from where they were purchased, they're worth at least two hundred thousand pounds. In fact, they were probably purchased for *me*. I was meant to attend that gala with him. He told me he'd have something pretty for me to wear, then he dumped me. For *her*. Although I wouldn't doubt he was trying to get Delia's attention. Watch out, girlfriend. That man is a playa…"

Saint swore and clicked off the phone, handing it back to Willow.

"I'm going to have to take legal action against her, aren't I?" he muttered.

"Who?"

"What do you mean 'who'? The woman destroying my reputation," Saint snapped.

Willow drew a breath and held it, as though still at a loss.

He swore again. "The woman who is *intentionally* destroying my reputation for the paycheck she's earning off her viral clicks." Although all of these women were contributing to this debacle in their own special way. He couldn't blame Willow for not being sure which one was causing him the most irritation. "Did you send the apology to Delia?"

"With a gift basket and an offer to cover her PR costs."

"Good. And Ms. Smythe?"

"Has the earrings. You're not out of pocket. She has also received a gift basket and some tickets for an opening in the West End as compensation for her trouble. I had the sense that future calls from you might go to voicemail."

No doubt. Saint scratched his eyebrow. How had one night turned into this?

"What about Fliss? Any word from her?" He braced himself as he picked up his phone to look for a text, not sure what kind of reaction he expected from her. Something that monetized her own notoriety? Blame for the attention that had fallen onto her? An apology for not being completely honest with him?

Nothing. Not even a redirection for delivery of the earrings.

"Her socials have been switched to private," Willow said. "She hasn't returned to the house in London. Her housemates are quoted as not knowing where she went."

Fliss had been photographed leaving her home five days ago, when gossip from her coworkers had leaked to the press. She'd since found a good place to hide because she wasn't turning up online. That was both a relief and a frustration for Saint.

He didn't love that she'd hidden so much about who she really was, but she hadn't been outright dishonest, either.

Are we prevaricating?

I'm out of my league.

He was dismayed to hear she'd stolen from a client's home. It was too much like Julie's laptop snooping for his comfort. It made him wonder if Fliss was hiding from paparazzi while she negotiated the best way to capitalize on her night with him—the way Julie had.

"I did find some background on her that was…concerning," Willow continued.

"I've seen what the trolls are saying," Saint grumbled.

"They claim to be childhood friends."

"Friends don't say things like that about friends." And who cared if she'd had an active sex life? So had he.

No, those rumors bothered him for a different reason. They didn't fit with the inexperience she'd expressed.

I've always wondered how these things were handled.

If she was as practiced as those rumors suggested, he would have expected less bashfulness, more assertiveness. She'd been enthusiastic as hell while they'd been making love, which was the part that really mattered, but maybe playing an ingenue was her kink?

Role-play was fine, too, but he hated feeling gullible. He didn't want to believe he'd fallen for an act when he'd been fully involved and as real as he could be for those few hours.

He didn't want to question his own acuity when his father and the board were already doing that for him.

Saint's phone rang. He glanced to see that it was his father and muttered another curse under his breath.

"I'm talking to the lawyers right now," he said in lieu of a greeting, then rolled his wrist at Willow to get on it. He wouldn't out Julie for her gambling addiction, but... "I'll have them threaten a defamation suit if she doesn't cease and desist."

Ted ignored that. "Your mother is asking why you have two hundred thousand pounds for a prostitute's earrings—"

"She is *not*—"

"But I won't bankroll another thoroughbred. Make that go away." His father ended the call.

"Fuuuun..." Saint groaned at the ceiling, crushing his phone in his grip. He was tempted to throw it against the wall.

"Tell Legal to inform Julie that I *will* pursue industrial espionage charges if she doesn't keep my name out of her mouth," he told Willow. He reached for the extra-strength acetaminophen in his desk drawer and swallowed two before he tapped his mother's number. "Interrupt me in ten minutes with a life-or-death emergency."

"Mrs. Bhamra? I'm back," Fliss called over the Bollywood musical playing on the senior's television.

She was later than usual, having picked up a few things on her way home and detoured to view a bedsit. She loved being here. It was almost like being home with Granny, but it had been more than two weeks. She didn't want to overstay her welcome.

Mrs. Bhamra had become Granny's best friend back when the pair had been young widows raising their children on their wages from the lace factory. They had lost their jobs at the same time when the factory had closed but had continued to bolster each other through the rest of life's ups and downs—job changes and weddings and grandchildren, Granny's loss of her son and Mrs. Bhamra's battle with breast cancer.

The pair had had a standing date twice a month where they drank tea and exchanged gossip, romance novels and knitting patterns. Mrs. Bhamra had teased Granny about her belief in psychics, and Granny had complained that Mrs. Bhamra's curry was too spicy. Otherwise, they'd been stamped from the same mold, or so Granny had always said.

As they'd both aged, Fliss had moved back into Granny's modest flat while Mrs. Bhamra had moved to the upscale Mapperley Park, where her son had converted a coach house into a sunny bungalow. It was one floor so she didn't have to climb stairs and had a guest bedroom that her sister used when she visited from Canada. The front window looked onto the landscaped garden where a bridge crossed a pond before its path continued to the steps of the mansion that was the main house.

When Fliss had turned up in the *Daily Mail* next to Saint Montgomery, Mrs. Bhamra had called to ask if the photograph was really her. Since Fliss had been on the verge of hysteria, realizing she was in far worse trouble than simply losing her job, she'd come as clean as she would have to Granny.

Mrs. Bhamra had offered her guest room, much to the chagrin of her son, Ujjal. He wasn't 100 percent thrilled to have Fliss here. He knew as well as she did that the paps would figure out where she was eventually, especially now that she was leaving the house to go to work.

The job was janitorial work for an assisted living facility, thanks to Ujjal making a call, but it was a foot in the door. They were desperate for care aids, too. Fliss could attain her certificate with only a few courses, and that would improve her pay. She was actively looking for her own place, planning to be on her own again very soon.

Provided, of course, that this persistent tummy bug was actually a tummy bug and not what she was starting to suspect it was.

"You worked late today," Mrs. Bhamra said as she muted the television.

"I stopped to buy a few things for dinner." Fliss shrugged out of the baggie hoodie she wore whenever she went out, adding sunglasses like every poorly disguised criminal on the run in every heist movie. "Let me change and wash up, then I'll get started."

"You don't have to cook for me," Mrs. Bhamra protested. She often ate at the house with her family or her daughter-in-law brought a plate if it was a gloomy day and Mrs. Bhamra preferred to stay here.

"I want to." Fliss might've been borderline destitute, but

she drew the line at imposing on the elderly woman's family. She ate groceries she bought, sharing as often as she could but mostly subsisting on peanut butter toast.

If her suspicions were correct, she needed to start eating more vegetables and probably get some special vitamins.

"Do you know I've been thinking of your grandmother all day?" Mrs. Bhamra mused.

"Oh?" Fliss paused in starting toward her room. "I did a reading this morning. I must have conjured her, and she decided to stay and watch your shows with you."

"Pfft." Mrs. Bhamra waved that away with amusement. "I did watch a very nice travel program that she would have enjoyed. The host was some fool traveling around the world. He started at the Eiffel Tower, forgot his sunscreen in Australia, got himself stung by a scorpion in America. Did you know they had those there?"

"Scorpions? No." Fliss pushed a smile onto her lips, but her heart began thudding so hard she grew lightheaded.

The three cards she'd pulled this morning had all been from the Major Arcana—the Sun, the Tower, and the Fool. They were such a powerful combination, she'd barely functioned all day, trying to work out what they meant.

As if the universe was trying to be subtle. The Fool represented blind faith, but it might as well have been a hand mirror. *She* was the fool. The Tower indicated unexpected events. It showed a tower being struck by lightning, throwing two people plummeting to the ground. She was definitely in freefall, but she hadn't meant to cause Saint's downfall along with her own.

Finally, the Sun indicated the beginning of a new life cycle. Given she would have to reinvent herself after losing the life she'd made in London, drawing that particular card made sense. The fact that it showed a naked baby on a horse was just a coincidence. Surely.

"Oh, Granny," she whispered as she slipped into the powder room. "Help me. Please, please, please."

She didn't know what outcome she was praying for as she unpacked the pregnancy test. It seemed ridiculous to even be bothering. She and Saint had used condoms. Yes, they'd had a lot of sex that night, but *they'd used condoms*.

Still, her cycle had always been regular as clockwork. She had nursed denial for five days, desperately trying to believe the stress of hiding from the press was making her late. That lateness was making her feel queasy. She wasn't pregnant.

She knew, though. She knew what she would see.
Positive.

How could such a simple procedure, such a thin pale line, upend her life so completely?

As she sat on the closed lid of the toilet staring at the result, she had to fight the pressure of emotive tears that rose behind her eyes.

She knew she had options. She knew that raising a baby alone was *hard*. Especially when your income was scant and unreliable. At least her grandmother had had a small settlement from the crash that had killed Fliss's parents. That had helped keep the wolves from the door, but that was long gone to Granny's final years of care. Fliss didn't have that sort of cushion. Aside from Mrs. Bhamra, she didn't have anyone who cared about her, and she'd already taken advantage of the elderly woman enough.

There were social services to help, she knew, but even with assistance she was in for a long and difficult struggle. Her dream of becoming a fashion designer was firmly down the loo. Even finding the sort of job that would support her and a baby would be complicated, given this awful black mark of stealing she had on her record. Then there was the notoriety of the baby's father.

In response to all the questions about her, Saint had made a statement that he didn't discuss his private life in the public sphere, but that wasn't stopping the rest of the world from not only pursuing but also capitalizing on her mistake. She'd seen those awful videos from his other lover, disparaging her as a lowly housekeeper and a thief. There were memes all over the internet about her now, too.

My retainer went missing. The housekeeper wore it to the dentist, pretending to be me. Now my celebrity crush is asking for earrings. #RichPeopleProblems

It was excruciating.

I'm being punished, Granny, I really am.

Fliss felt as though she was being punished for ever having dreams in the first place. She shouldn't compound her situation by giving the world more reason to mock her. Bringing a baby into this mess she'd made would be a terrible mistake.

And how would Saint react? Blame her? Maybe he'd accuse her of getting herself pregnant on purpose to come after his money, but she had truly believed she was protected.

He had used condoms.

As the reality of her situation began to take hold, everything in her was folding in on itself. Having this baby would be a huge mistake. A disaster. She could see that clear as day.

But deep inside, she imagined she already felt a physical presence, as though the baby was a living, burning glow. It was the spark of connection to Fliss's parents, whose loss had left her devastated for years. And Granny, who she missed so badly right this minute her eyes began to leak the tears that were brimmed against her lashes.

If she didn't have this baby—for any reason—she would mourn its loss as deeply as she mourned the rest of her family. This baby *was* her family. She wanted a child.

This baby was *hers*. It didn't matter what anyone thought of her or the father—

She caught her breath, blinking to clear the blur from her vision.

That was it! The paparazzi had interviewed some of her old schoolmates who had revived that awful reputation that she was loose. For once, those rumors might actually serve her. She could claim paternity was a gray area.

Could she? White lies had gotten her into this mess, but at least she had a fresh approach to consider as she carefully put the test back into its packaging and crumpled it inside the bag, checking first that there was no receipt with her name on it. She would toss it into a public dumpster at some point, but for the moment her heart was lighter as she looked forward to her new life, one that included the baby she was going to have.

CHAPTER FIVE

SAINT HAD BEEN in London three times since the gala more than three months ago. Each time, he had thought about reaching out to Fliss.

He'd fought the compulsion with difficulty, especially once paparazzi had located her living in Nottingham. She was working in an assisted living facility and picked up casual shifts at a local pub.

Interest in her was finally dying down, though, largely due to the fact that she only ever said "No comment" and shoved her way past anyone trying to pry more out of her.

Saint was grateful for her silence. A strongly worded letter had quieted Julie, and Saint was doing his best to live up to his name for the sake of his project. He arrived early for meetings, bought his mother a filly she wanted and was enjoying celibacy. Not.

The fact was going without sex wasn't that difficult. He'd gone long stretches in his life without anyone warming his sheets. When he was focused on work, as he'd been through much of last year, he became as single-minded and neglectful of others as his father had always been. It was another reason he'd never pursued relationships that lasted longer than a few weeks. He wasn't built for them.

What did make it hard, pun intended, was his memories of Fliss. He regularly woke in the middle of the night, aching and covered in the sweat of arousal, traces of her touch evaporating from his skin.

He'd made great strides in rehabilitating his reputation, though. Xanthe's constructed gossip about his "eye on the future" and readiness "to find his life partner" had gone a long way with the board. He'd been fielding requests for more information from them for weeks. A few had even confided that his success with this project would give them a reason to pressure his father into retirement.

Yesterday, Saint had been invited to attend their regular quarterly meeting in two days. He was certain that meant they were pivoting toward approval.

His father was still holding his cards close to his chest, and Saint had an idea why. This "life partner" narrative had opened a new field of war between his parents. They had begun advancing their preferred candidates for daughter-in-law.

Saint had played this game before. He knew that siding with one would make his life a living hell with the other. It was freaking exhausting.

From the outside, most would assume that aligning with his father was the strategic move. Not only did they share the common interest of the business, but Saint should know which side his bread was buttered on.

Saint refused to be a hostage to his legacy, though. Many, many times he'd stood on the precipice of walking away from his father's dictates and heavy-handed attempts to control him, aware that he would be walking away from his inheritance.

That didn't bother him. He knew his own worth. Yes, his father had paid for his education, but Saint had done the work to achieve top grades and the two degrees he held. He had put in the hours at the office, too, learning the ins and outs of every department and contributing to the company's success from the time he'd begun sweeping floors at eleven.

No matter where he landed, he would never have to start from the bottom.

He hated to draw his mother into his power struggle with his father, though. Unlike Ted, Norma Montgomery had once possessed a heart. It had since been shattered so often by Saint's father that it was a distorted reflection of the woman Saint remembered from childhood, but he felt obliged to protect her from further damage.

Leaving Grayscale would force her to decide whether she wanted to divorce her husband in what would be a very public, destructive battle or lose her son. Ted would have no compunction about demanding she cut ties with Saint if she wanted to maintain the life to which she had grown accustomed—and the horses she loved as much as, probably more than, her son.

Any decision Saint made around walking away from Grayscale would affect Grayscale, too. He didn't want to destroy something that he'd had a hand in building. He didn't want to take his work to a competitor that would attempt to eat what should have been his. He didn't want to see someone else take over his legacy when his father was finally gone, not when it could be his.

No, the most sensible plan was to continue his restraint, earn the trust of his father and the board, and focus on the product he believed in. With recent scrutiny by the government around privacy, his father couldn't deny the value in his new approach. If his father wanted to tie his agreement to an arranged marriage, they would work that out away from the office.

All of which caused the text Saint received to fill him with conflict.

I have to be in London tomorrow. Is there any chance you're here? I need to speak to you, but I don't want anyone to see us together.

She didn't identify herself, but he gave very few people this number.

Seeing Fliss could reignite the publicity and wouldn't be fair to her if she was looking for something longer term. It could undo the progress he'd made where the board was concerned. The smart thing to do was to leave the text on Read. Or simply say no.

But the temptation to see her was mouth-wateringly strong. All he could think about was the feel of her hand tucked into his arm as they had walked into the hotel. Of her secretive smile, as though she knew things he didn't. Of the way she felt when she shuddered with orgasm, triggering his own.

He deserved answers around why she'd misrepresented herself, didn't he?

That was a rationalization. *We all trick ourselves*, she'd said, and he'd come to realize how very insightful she was.

He looked to the calendar. He was due down the hall here at the New York office less than forty-eight hours from now, but he had turned around a flight to London in less before.

He had Willow rearrange his lesser appointments and file a flight plan, then texted her.

A card will be waiting under the name Norma at the concierge. Come to my hotel room at four p.m.

Time crawled, but after a heavy morning of dull meetings, he was in his hotel room, nursing a scotch while he waited. He was half expecting some enterprising reporter would turn up, but when the knock sounded and the mechanism released, Fliss entered.

He wasn't sure what he had expected, but it wasn't her in a pink plaid skirt suit, black knee-high boots and a beret. It was cute as hell and had his gaze dragging itself from the glimpse of her thighs below the fall of pleats to the way her short jacket emphasized the nip of her waist and the generous swells of her breasts.

His inner Neanderthal instantly awoke. *Mine.*

Her features were mostly hidden by oversize sunglasses and a lipstick that had been applied to change the shape of her mouth. She pressed the door firmly closed behind her and stayed against it, hand on the latch.

"Hello." She leaned to set his room card on the nearby table. "Thank you for seeing me. I won't stay long."

She looked and sounded nervous, but he would swear her gaze was traveling all over him. He felt it as viscerally as the way her hands had skimmed across his skin when they'd last been in this room together.

Don't.

"Are you into role-play?" he drawled. "Is that why you're dressed like a hired assassin from a time-travel movie?"

"That's exactly what I am," she said without missing a beat. "I thought it would take more to convince you."

Damn. He didn't want to find her amusing. There was too much at stake.

"Take off your sunglasses. I want to see your face."

She complied, fumbling them slightly as she slipped them into a pocketbook hanging from a long strap over her shoulder. She lifted a frown of consternation to him.

"I actually made this for my interviews at—" She brushed the side of her skirt, making the pleats flutter. "Doesn't matter. I came to London to sell all the clothes I made, but I needed something to wear into this hotel that would blend in. I *am* a designer. I'm just not paid professionally for it."

"You're also a maid. Or you were, until they realized you have sticky fingers."

"It was *in* the *bin*," she said as though she was tired of repeating that. "Delia Chevron threw twenty-five thousand pounds *into the bin*. I thought it was a ticket for dinner and hoped to network or get some publicity for my work. Do you think at any point through all of this nightmare that one single pap has asked me who made my gown? Believe me, I've come to regret the whole escapade." She waved an arm in a wide circle.

"Me, too," he said, stung more deeply than he'd expected by that word *regret*.

She dropped her arm and her mouth pouted with injury, as though that particular word had landed just as hard for her.

Then she set her jaw and lifted her chin.

"Don't pin what happened onto me. I changed my mind about that gala before you'd even spoken to me. You dragged me there, throwing me to them as 'fresh meat to chew on.' Do you know that I thought I was on a date?" She tapped where the pretty yellow lace of her camisole peeked between her lapels. "You might have explained that I was your *paid escort*. Who the hell sends a woman earrings worth a hundred and fifty thousand pounds for *one* night together? I wasn't that good, Saint."

He would beg to differ but only ran his tongue across his teeth.

"Why didn't you text me sooner?" he asked.

"Because you cost me my job and set the hounds of hell upon me. Thanks. Sign me up for more of that. I can't wait."

This was going well. He ran his hand down his face, trying to reset.

"I should have dealt with Julie sooner, instead of giving her an opportunity to feed off your story. That wasn't fair to you."

"You think?"

"Is that why you're here? To tell me you're angry at how this played out?" He would only grovel so far, and she'd just witnessed the extent of it. "Or have you decided you want compensation for your trouble after all?" He moved to the ice bucket. It held a bottle of Prieur Montrachet that he'd had room service deliver. "Have a seat. Do you want something to drink while we discuss terms?"

She didn't move.

He pulled the bottle from the ice and glanced over, catching a look of wounded shock on her face.

"That's really mean," she said.

"What is?"

Saint knew. He was uncomfortable with his guilt and how strongly he was reacting to her. He was doing what he'd learned to do when intense emotions took hold in him—he set them aside and used cold logic while he did whatever was necessary to make the issue go away.

"I can't undo what happened, Fliss. I did cost you your job and threw unwanted attention onto you. People seem to think I don't take responsibility for my actions, but I do." Money might not fix everything, but it bought some very effective bandages. "Tell me what will make you feel better, and I'll see what I can do. A storefront for a boutique perhaps?"

Still she didn't move or speak.

He opened the bottle and poured two glasses, then carried them to the coffee table.

"Come," he invited as he seated himself and leaned back.

After a moment, she came toward him. She seemed very pale as she sat on the sofa across from him, only lowering to perch on the edge of the cushion. She stared at the glass of wine but only clasped her hands in her lap, back very straight. She lifted her gaze to his.

"I didn't come here to ask anything of you," she said with quiet dignity. "Nothing. I mean that. *Nothing.*"

"Except my time," he noted drily.

"Not even much of that," she assured him with a proud lift of her chin. "I'm catching the train back to Nottingham once I've finished the rest of my errands. You'll never hear from me again. But I had to tell you something that didn't feel right to send as a text."

"What's that?" He did his best to sound detached, but his ears were ringing with that word. *Never.* He held his breath, straining to hear over that jarring sound of a train disappearing down a tunnel. His muscles felt both paralyzed and tense with readiness to leap and catch.

"I'm pregnant."

Saint didn't move. She wasn't sure he was breathing.

Then there was a faint, fractured clink before he gave his wine a startled look and swore.

He'd snapped the stem on his glass. He cupped one hand under the other and rose to head to the bar.

"Are you bleeding?" Fliss hurried after him to see him rinse the welling blood from his fingers into the sink. "I'll call the desk." She looked for the hotel phone.

"I can deal with it." He wrapped a clean bar towel around his fingers as he strode into the bedroom.

Fliss covered where her heart had been pounding with anxiety from the time she'd worked up the courage to hit Send on her text. It had increased to alarming levels when she had entered this hotel, picked up the card from a bored-looking bellman, then stepped off the elevator and made her way to this door. Now it was racing so fast she felt dizzy. Her nerve endings were sizzling and her mouth had gone dry.

Entering this suite was like stepping into a dream, but one of those weird ones that repeated every time you closed your eyes, the kind that made you feel stuck and fighting to wake up.

Everywhere she looked, sensual memories accosted her. She'd pressed her hands to that glass door and felt him inside her. He'd carried her through that doorway and stripped her naked, and they'd showered together before taking to the bed where they had touched and kissed each other *everywhere*. He had spoken wicked commands and reverent compliments in a sexy rasp.

Tell me if it's too much. I can't get enough of you.

As she had dressed to come here, she had braced for the impact of that potent sexuality of his. She had known she would react to his rangy, athletic body in his tailored trousers and crisp shirt. She had known she would want to push her fingers into his hair again, to press her mouth to his stern lips and nuzzle the scent in his throat.

She had not been prepared for his aloof, businesslike wall of commerce.

You want compensation after all?

She had suspected he would think that, but she hadn't expected it to stab so deeply to hear it.

"Are you sure it's mine? I used condoms."

She nearly leapt out of her skin, not realizing he'd come back. She grappled at the edge of the bar to steady herself, feeling spun around one too many times by all of this.

"Are you okay?" She looked to his hand. Two fingers wore beige-colored bandages.

"Fine." He folded his arms, feet braced. He'd withdrawn

even further, presenting her with a wall of frost that chilled her to the bone. "This is why you're here, then? You think you've pulled the golden ticket?"

She opened her mouth, but her voice stalled in her throat. In her head, all her words had been carefully planned out, but none of this was going the way she'd expected. Her thoughts were scattered on the wind.

"This is not my first stroll around this particular block, Fliss." Saint's tone grew even more deep and lethal.

"Wh-what…?" She had to press her wobbling lips together to make them work. "What do you do?"

"What do you mean?"

"When it's yours. What do you do?" She dropped her gaze to the elegant buckles on his shoes and the fine detail work across the toes, trying to tell herself that his skepticism worked in her favor. "You don't have any children that you acknowledge, so what do you do when it's yours? Pay for termination or—"

"They've never *been* mine." He spoke through his teeth. "If I had children, I'd acknowledge them, but I don't. That's why I wear condoms, so claims like this don't even arise. And I say this without judgment, Fliss…"

Oh, he was definitely judging her. She flashed a rancorous look up at him.

"I've seen what people have said about you online." His voice and expression were cool and remote. "I can't take your word for it that it's mine."

"Wow." She couldn't hide the slap of that. She looked away, unable to keep from revealing her torment. It wasn't just the memory of those old, cruel rumors. It was demeaning enough that he knew about that time of her life. She couldn't believe he had thrown it in her face like that, though.

"I don't care how many lovers you've had," he said

grimly. "I'm not that much of a hypocrite. I'm only saying I can't take it on faith that your baby is mine."

"You're—" She had to clear the thickness of humiliation from her throat. It came from realizing that she'd nurtured a barely acknowledged hope that this would go differently. Deep in her subconscious, she'd thought he might welcome her back into his life and greet this news with the joy that imbued her.

Fool. Struck by lightning. A new day. A naked child on a horse, proceeding into the future alone.

"You're making assumptions," she said, fighting to inject some semblance of dignity into her voice as she scraped for the words she'd come to say. "I only came to ask you to make a statement that it's *not* yours, so the paparazzi will leave me alone." She fumbled her sunglasses from her pocketbook and put them on before she looked at him again.

He was standing like a pillar, lips parted as though he'd been about to say something. His brows were a thick, foreboding line.

She wished these cheap lenses didn't afford him such a golden glow. He looked like a bronzed statue. A gleaming study in wrath.

"Will you?" she prompted, arteries stinging from the adrenaline running through them.

"It's not mine." Why did he sound so angered? Shouldn't he have been relieved? "That's why you came here today? To tell me it's *not* mine?"

"It seemed fair to warn you." Now the words she'd rehearsed were coming more easily. "It's all over the entertainment sites that you're looking for a wife. It would be awkward if rumors about me started while you were engaged to someone else, wouldn't it? Your intended would be dragged into something she didn't sign up for. I'd rather skip that myself, if you don't mind. So will you? Make a statement?"

"Take off those glasses." He was trying to pierce through their mirrored lenses with the strength of his glower.

"No." She stood straighter, chin up, but she was quivering like jelly inside.

"Is the baby mine or not, Fliss?"

"You wore condoms," she reminded him, refusing to outright lie. "None broke, did they?"

"No, but we had sex. There's a chance it's mine, isn't there? That's why you're here."

"With the legions of men I've entertained? Who's to say?" she said scathingly.

"Don't play games, Fliss."

"This isn't a game," she snapped. "I'm pregnant. The baby is mine. Your only obligation is to tell people to leave me alone. *That's* what I came to tell you today."

She headed for the door, but when she got there, he was there, too, covering the seam to keep it shut. He loomed so close around her she spun to face him, more angry than alarmed.

"Don't make this ugly," she said shakily.

He fell back a step and let his hand fall, but his jaw was clenched, his mouth tight.

"I want a paternity test."

"Why? You want this problem to go away. Let me go away." Fliss reached for the latch.

"So you can, what? Raise my child in some squalid flat on government handouts?"

"I would sell my diamond earrings, but I never received them, did I?" she shot back.

"You're still playing out of your league, Fliss." His hand came up to the door again, leaning on it. "I won't let you use my child against me."

Her heart had become a shriveled thing inside her, leaving a cavern for her voice to reverberate with emotion.

"Don't judge me by your standards, Saint. That's not something I would even think to do. I'm naive that way—which I'm pretty sure you know because I didn't feel played until I heard about those earrings. I thought you were charming and interesting and a generous lover. I thought we were two people who had a really nice time together, but you know which one of us was full of BS that night? You. It was all an act to get me into bed, wasn't it? And you think *I'm* into role-play?" She pointed between her breasts. "You're superficial and callous and kind of a bully. There's no way on *earth* I would raise a baby with you. Now, let me go before I scream the place down."

Fliss made to elbow him in the stomach, forcing him to step back to avoid it. She opened the door and left.

Saint had taken a kick from one of his mother's horses once. This was a similar sensation. He felt knocked clean across a stall.

He was vaguely aware of other sensations. His fingers were still stinging where he'd cut them with the glass. His blood felt thick and congealed in his veins, as though it was pooling in shock. His guts were pure acid.

It wasn't true, was it? There'd been a handful of paternity claims in his past. In the first case, he'd been young enough to buy in very quickly and had nearly bought his partner a ring, only to learn she wasn't even pregnant. Another time, he hadn't been the father.

Those false alarms had not only made him cynical about such claims but made him all the more diligent about wearing condoms. He bought them himself and regularly checked the dates. As Fliss had noted, none had split, so it seemed highly unlikely they had failed.

A compulsion to double-check the dates had him striding into the bathroom where his shaver was in its case. A half strip of condoms was tucked beside it, exactly the way he usually kept it. They were the brand he liked and part of the same strip he'd used with Fliss. The stamp said they were within their use-by date.

She'd been with him every second that night. There'd been no opportunity for her to poke holes in them—

He swore and crushed the strip in his fist, eyes pressing closed. *Fliss* hadn't had an opportunity to sabotage his birth control, but someone else had.

With a grim sense of premonition, he tore one out and sealed its opening to the tap. He filled it with water, then held it at his eye level and watched a droplet of water leak out against the skin. As soon as it fell, another formed. Then another.

With a curse, Saint threw the condom into the shower. It landed with a loud splat. He tried another. Then another. All of them were damaged.

Julie. He couldn't prove she was the one who had done it, but no one else had traveled with him and spent time in his space, and she'd already shown herself short on scruples.

At least he wasn't expecting a baby with *her*.

No. He was expecting one with Fliss.

You're superficial and callous and kind of a bully.

He drew in a breath that burned, hating himself for going full Ted Montgomery on her.

But this circumstance was *exactly* what his own father had faced when Saint's mother had come to him with her unplanned pregnancy. Ted had been on the cusp of what had turned into unprecedented success. Norma had contributed to his ascension in no small way, not that Ted ever gave her that credit. Any warmth or charm that Saint possessed had come from her. She'd compensated for Ted's utter lack of empathy.

But such a one-sided relationship could only be sustained so long. Eventually, their marriage had become a toxic partnership, one that continued to rain nuclear fallout on Saint to this day.

That was why he wore condoms. He didn't want kids. He didn't want to discover thirty years from now that he was as damaging a parent as his own had been.

He was about to become one anyway. He didn't need a paternity test to prove it. He sent another dour look to the discarded condoms in the shower.

Fliss might have walked a very thin line between implying and outright lying about whether her baby was his, but he had no doubt that she was pregnant and that he had put her in that condition. He had even less doubt that she wished it had been nearly any other man.

This isn't a game, she'd said. *The baby is mine.*

Saint found himself thinking, *Mine, too.*

He braced his hands on either side of the sink, reminding himself to breathe while he took that in. Whether he wanted to be a father or feared he'd make a terrible one didn't matter. He was about to be put to the test. This was real. And he *did* take responsibility for his actions—even when his mistake was putting too much trust in the wrong person.

Swearing did nothing to help, but it felt very satisfying to curse out a long, vicious blue streak. Sensation was seeping back into his limbs, and his brain was crawling out of the rubble of emotions that were still piled up around him: shock and fury and guilt. So much guilt toward Fliss. There was something else there, too, deep under the heavy weight of that. Something that was too nascent to excavate. Something almost like relief or… He didn't know what it was and would rather focus on taking action.

He needed a paternity test for his father's sake. Ted would turn this into another black mark against Saint, possibly vetoing the board's approval.

Saint swore again, tiredly this time, and pinched the bridge of his nose.

You want this problem to go away. Let me go away.

As if it were that simple. She was right. As soon as she grew plump enough for people to suspect pregnancy, they would do the math and guess that he was the father. Even if he wanted to take the easy way out that she'd offered and made a statement that the baby wasn't his, she would still be badgered.

And he couldn't turn his back on his child. Not in good conscience. Within a year or two, the baby would look just like him anyway, giving how strongly he resembled his own father.

No, if Fliss was having his baby, *they* were having *their* baby.

Where had she said she was going? Errands. Hell. That could mean anything. If he wanted to catch her, he'd have to be waiting in Nottingham for her.

He went to look for his phone to order the car, ignoring the way Fliss's last words resounded in his ears.

There's no way on earth *I would raise a baby with you.*

CHAPTER SIX

WEEPING IN PUBLIC—on a train, for instance—was a skill Fliss had mastered years ago. As a teen, when she'd been a veritable outcast given the side-eye wherever she went, she had left most of her tears on her pillow. Later, though, when Granny had been struggling and Fliss had felt very helpless, she'd put on a brave face at home and let emotion overwhelm her when she'd been on the bus to work.

It was a matter of having a scarf or a handful of tissues at the ready and taking slow, careful breaths. She liked to wear earbuds so if someone asked with concern whether she was all right, she could claim to be listening to a very sad book. She always kept the sobbing very contained, not making a production of it. She simply let the pain wash over her and leak out her eyes.

Not that Saint deserved her tears. She wasn't crying over him anyway. She was crying over the fact that Granny and her baby would never meet. And because her memory of a magical night had been revealed to be smoke and mirrors. It had been sleight of hand that was akin to a lie. She felt like a sucker.

She was crying because even though she wanted her baby and knew that she would make this work, she was overwhelmed and scared. She didn't have a strong network of support. She had some loose friendships in London, all singletons who were living their single lives, and Mrs. Bhamra, who was healthy for her age but an octogenarian all the same.

Fliss would tell her eventually, but she didn't want to worry the woman. She would wait until she'd paid her back for loaning her the deposit on her bedsit—which was nicer than the one she'd had in London, *Saint*. It had a window onto a well-tended garden and a kitchenette and her own loo. Her landlords were a pleasant older couple who spent their days birdwatching and their evenings talking about it. The house was situated a short bus ride to her day job and a few blocks from the pub where she picked up shifts when she could.

As she approached the station, she mopped the last of her tears, half-thinking she should tell the pub she was available if they needed her to come in tonight, but she was exhausted—emotionally and physically. She had barely slept last night, knowing she would see Saint today, then she'd been up early to get into London.

Her day had been an endurance event of cleaning her room, selling what she could online, then taking the last of her handmade clothing to a nearby consignment shop. She'd had that awful meeting with Saint, then returned to the house to change and catch her housemates as they'd come home from work. She'd said her final goodbye and turned over her key.

The remnants of her time in London were now in a small backpack, a couple of cloth grocery bags and Mrs. Bhamra's rolling suitcase. Fliss might yet sell her sewing machine—a professional-grade Juki—but Mrs. Bhamra had said she would take it as security against the money she'd loaned her, so Fliss was hanging on to it for now.

Wearily, she gathered everything as the train stopped and made her way to the curb.

She was comparing the cost of taking a ride share home against walking to the tram when a swanky black sportscar pulled up before her. The driver's door opened and Saint rose from behind the wheel.

He wore the same clothes as earlier but had added mirrored sunglasses and a leather jacket that made him look *Top Gun* sexy.

Drat. She'd left her sunglasses on the train. She looked back into the station but knew they were gone.

"I've been parked over there for thirty minutes. I was starting to think I'd missed you." He opened the boot.

"I thought I made it clear that your infamy is a liability for me. I don't want to be seen with you." Her heart was in her throat from more than alarm and surprise. What did it mean that he was here?

"So get in. No one will see you." He started to take her suitcase, then checked as he realized how heavy it was. "What the hell is in here? A body?"

"The last man who crossed me, yes." She stared into the two miniature reflections of her own glower.

"A woman in your condition ought to ask for help with heavy tasks like that," he said with false benevolence. "Good thing I'm here now."

"Lucky me." God, she hated him for the effortless way he set the rolling bag into the car. Her bags went in beside it.

She really wanted to tell him to go to hell, but she sank into the passenger seat with a sigh of relief, then slouched low, peering out to see if anyone was pointing a phone their way.

The boot thumped closed, and Saint slid behind the wheel. "Where do you live?"

"Why are you here?" she asked at the same time.

"Why do you think?" he asked.

"You have an unquenchable thirst for sadism? Head north," she said as he pulled away from the curb.

"I checked the condoms. They all leak."

"Oh my God." She sat up, twisting to face him, crying with persecution, "I did *not* sabotage your condoms!"

"I know you didn't." He was maintaining an annoyingly dispassionate tone. "My life is full of vultures and sharks, Fliss. People want to take advantage of me all the time. Sometimes there's collateral damage."

"Who would do something like that?" she asked with astonishment, but she could guess. He seemed to have a talent for alienating the women he'd slept with. "Don't refer to my pregnancy that way," she added in a grumble, falling back into her seat. "It's gross."

"Collateral damage?" He slowed as traffic became congested and turned his head to give her a penetrating look. The turmoil in the dark depths of his eyes belied the remote tone he was using. "Why would you be offended? Unless you're admitting the baby is mine?"

She bit her thumbnail and looked out her side window. "You're going to take the second exit after this one."

Aside from directions, they didn't talk again until he pulled into the cul-de-sac below the cozy brick house situated on a terraced lawn above them. It was accessed by a flight of stone steps cut into the retaining wall.

"You were going to carry this bag up these stairs?" Saint asked with disapproval as he took them from the boot and carried them himself.

"Is it too heavy for you? I can take it." The machine was twelve kilos, and she moved it around all the time, admittedly with an "Oof" of effort every time.

He didn't set the case on its rollers for the uneven path alongside the house to the back porch. He carried it to the door she unlocked, then brought it inside.

"Leave it down here," she said as she started up the narrow, creaking stairs. "I was going to take it to Mrs. Bhamra's on my way home. Now I'll have to do that tomorrow."

"Who's Mrs. Bhamra?" He followed her into the converted attic and looked around.

The single bed was under the lowest side of the slanted ceiling, but Fliss was still able to sit up without smacking her head. There was a bistro table that looked out the dormer window. A four-drawer bureau supported the microwave. There was a mini fridge and two-burner stovetop in the kitchenette, and open shelving displayed her handful of dishes and dry goods.

"Tea?" she offered because she could tell she wouldn't get away with offering him a tip for his chauffeur duties and holding the door for him to leave.

"Coffee?" he countered. "Something stronger?" He was looking at the sketchbook she'd left on the table where she had scrawled out ideas for adding maternity panels to some of her existing clothes.

"You've come to the wrong place for caffeine and alcohol."

"Right." He lifted his head. "How is everything? Have you seen a doctor?"

"Yes." She'd had a scan a week ago, wanting to be sure everything was okay before she'd contacted him. It was.

She filled the kettle and set it to boil.

"I need to hear you say it, Fliss." He stood with his hands hooked into his pockets, his expression mostly hidden behind his sunglasses.

He'd been right—it was annoying to try to read someone when they were wearing such an impervious shield.

"What?" She played dumb.

"Tell me it's mine."

She took off her light jacket and hung it on the hook by

the door, ignoring his request because it felt too much like relinquishing what little agency she had.

"Why are you here?" she asked instead.

"You're having my baby. We have things to talk about."

"Like the fact that you have put me in the impossible position of being either an unfit mother who can only afford a bedsit." She waved at her humble home. "Or a parasite who regards her child as a meal ticket?"

He looked to the window, profile carved from granite except for the way his cheek ticked.

"Are you hungry?" she asked. "Mrs. Bhamra gave me butter chicken when I picked up the case yesterday. There's lots."

"No, thank you. Who is she? Your landlady?"

"A friend of Granny's. I should text her, actually, so she knows I'm back safe." It was nice to have someone worrying about her again. She texted, then started to scoop the cold chicken and rice into a bowl.

"You don't have to eat leftovers. I'll buy you dinner. Where do you want to go?"

"Nowhere. I'm tired." She set the bowl into the microwave and started it, then finished making the tea. In her mind, she heard Granny gasp in horror that she dropped a pair of teabags straight into cups, but she didn't actually own a teapot anymore. The one that had been Granny's had broken—along with her heart—ages ago. She'd never replaced it.

Fliss carried the cups to the table and left them there while she closed her sketchpad and moved it with the pencils to the bed.

"What do you know about me?" Saint asked. "What have you heard or read?"

"Are you asking how much I've stalked you online? I didn't have to. We were mentioned in the same articles.

Although I had to quit reading once I got the gist that I'm a penniless, thieving whore. Better that than a philandering billionaire sociopath, I always say."

He swore under his breath and removed his sunglasses to push a finger and thumb against the inside corners of his eyes.

"Oh, am I supposed to tell you what I've read, not what I know?" she asked without heat. "You're famous for being rich and good-looking. Your father invented a microchip or something. Your mother was a prize model on a game show. That was all before my time, so I don't know much about either of them. Celebrity trivia isn't something I follow. Unless it's fashion related, but even at that I was fifteen when I said to Gran, 'Did you know Stella McCartney's father is a famous musician?' I didn't know who the Beatles were, only that Stella's work was fur-free and leather-free. I knew which of her gowns had been on which red carpets. I know your shoes are Ferragamo and your shirt is Tom Ford. Trousers are a private tailor, I'm guessing. Jacket is Gucci, obviously."

He'd hung it on the chair back, and she could read the tag inside the collar.

"That's kind of impressive." He sounded sincere.

"It's not. All it really tells me is that you're rich and have decent taste." The microwave dinged, so she brought her dinner to the table.

"That smells really good."

"Take this one."

He shook his head, waving at her to eat as he seated himself across from her, but sat sideways in the chair. He braced his back against the wall and hooked his arm over the railed back of the chair. His other arm rested flat on the table.

"My father came from oil money," he said. "His father

was a mean drunk, and Dad's three older brothers were cut from the same cloth. Toxic masculinity is their default." He gave a curl of his lip. "None of them saw any value in my father's passion for computers. My grandfather forced Dad to take business courses and put him in sales, which was the worst possible place for him. As soon as the old man died, he had his brothers buy him out and used the money to develop his microchip. It was a hit."

"Are his brothers nicer to him now?"

"They might be if Dad was nicer to them." Saint played with the handle on his teacup. "Growing up, Dad was the quintessential nerd—before it was cool to be one," he added dourly. "Once Grayscale took off, he was all business. The cutthroat kind. He moved to California and began eating start-ups. He discovered that having money made him very attractive, too. Name a starlet from the eighties and there's probably a photo of him with her."

That actually sounded like a fun game, but Saint kept talking, not giving her a chance to play.

"He met Mom at a party. Like most of his dates at the time, she was quite a bit younger than him, very glamorous looking, but she was straight off the farm in Iowa. Their affair didn't last long. She came with her own baggage, stuff she never talks about. She told me once she was looking for someone who would make her feel safe. Dad was already in his forties, swimming in money, but he'd never been married or had any long-term relationships. At first, she thought he was shy, but it turns out he's withdrawn and incapable of meaningful connection. She broke it off, then she found out she was pregnant."

"Oh?" This story was sounding uncomfortably familiar.

He nodded slowly, not looking at her.

"Dad's friends—advisors, I should call them. They knew he was still on an upward trajectory and had their own reasons for wanting to protect their stake in that. They told him to pay Mom off. She convinced Dad that I deserved to know my father. What if I was a boy? Wouldn't I inherit the company? Shouldn't he raise me to take it over?"

"Sexist. What if you were a girl?"

"Tip of the iceberg," he dismissed with a flick of his fingers. "Mom wanted to keep working. Dad said no. He wanted a trophy wife, one who would smile as she stood next to all the great things he made to improve the world."

"Like you?"

He made a noise of grim amusement. "I stopped trying to be his pride and joy long ago," he admitted drily. "I watched Mom do it for too long and realized it's a lost cause."

"Are they still married?"

"Yes. At first she stayed for me. And because she wanted more children. She didn't want to fail," he added with a wince of understanding. "No one does. But while they were pretending to make it work, Dad had a string of affairs and Mom had three miscarriages. Their prenup was weighted heavily in Dad's favor if she left him. She might not have married him for his money, but she contributed enough to his success that she feels entitled to a bite of it. She could embroil him in a big, ugly divorce if she wanted to, but she doesn't have his level of ruthless disregard and he knows it. It's become a marriage based on spite."

"Family dinners must be fun." Fliss poked at a chunk of chicken, having lost her appetite.

"They're a nightmare," he assured her. "Dad says it doesn't make financial sense to give her half his fortune when I'll only inherit from both of them. It's better to keep it whole. That's his way of claiming he's being stubborn for me. It's not for me." Saint shook his head. "He fears that she'd come after shares in the company. If she got them, he wouldn't have majority control any longer."

"What's your relationship with him like?"

"Terrible," he said conversationally. "But I will inherit Grayscale eventually, and I do want it. I don't overlook what it cost my parents to create this titan of the industry, but I also think, why? Why suffer that long, hating your partner, only to demand I be grateful for their sacrifice? Mom has her horses and Dad has his coven of toadies who scurry around telling him how smart he is, but is that really enough to compensate for all those years of being cruel to each other?"

"When they could have parted and found love elsewhere?"

"When they could have not actively hated each other. I don't understand it. I really don't." He picked up his cup and brought it to his lips but didn't sip. "I only knew that I never wanted to lock myself into a lifetime of the same thing."

Ah. Fliss had wondered why he was telling her all of this.

"I don't expect you to marry me, Saint," she said quietly, ignoring the way her heart felt pinched in a vise.

"I know," he said simply, causing her pulse to lift and dip as she felt understood and believed but also rebuffed. Then his arrow-sharp gaze hit her. "I still have to."

CHAPTER SEVEN

"No, YOU DON'T!" Fliss sat back in shock. "You just gave me a great reason why marriage is a terrible idea. All you have to do is say the baby isn't yours and walk away."

Saint finished lifting his cup to his lips, but his mouth wasn't prepared for whatever this was. It was hot like coffee but weak. It had the color and bitterness of scotch but no bite. He didn't think he'd had a sip of tea in his adult life. Not since he'd tried the stuff as a child and decided he didn't like it.

He still didn't. He set it aside with distaste.

"I don't have the words to express how insulted I am by your thinking I would deliberately reject my child." Especially when he'd just explained how unenthusiastically he'd been welcomed by his own father.

Saint held her wide-eyed stare for a full thirty seconds, until she dropped her gaze to her curry and rice. Then her brows lifted in a silent, cynical *Whatever*.

He was deeply insulted but also uneasy. He *had* put her in an impossible position.

Her bedsit was tiny and definitely inadequate for raising a child. The stairs alone were a guaranteed trip to the hospital, but as humble as this space was, she'd made it homey. It was tidy and organized and more colorful and welcoming than any home he'd ever occupied. Her bedspread was a kaleidoscope of fabric scraps he would bet she had quilted herself. There were doilies in psychedelic spirals under her handful of houseplants. The frame on the photo over the sink was pebbled with a mosaic of what looked like broken china plates.

The photo inside it showed Fliss with her arm around an elderly woman he presumed was her grandmother, judging by the resemblance around their eyes and smiles. Saint had the unnerving feeling that the old woman was watching him from that photo, judging him.

"The baby has become my top priority." He'd had ample time while driving from London to let this situation sink in. He'd already projected through his father's reaction and how this could impact the board's decision. The gossip sites would have a field day, which would affect Fliss and, in turn, their baby. "That makes you my top priority. Your health and safety. I have to look after you, Fliss."

Did her eyes gloss with tears? If they did, she hid it by taking her empty bowl to the sink where she kept her back to him while she rinsed the dish.

"I said some unkind things back at the hotel," he acknowledged. "I was taught to go on the attack when I feel threatened."

"I wasn't threatening you." She turned and crossed her arms, leaning her hips against the front of the sink. "I gave you information."

"I know. I see that now." He was still on the defensive, this time in a different way. It still made him uneasy and caused him to prickle with aggression. "What's important for you to hear is that I don't want my child raised in the sort of atmosphere I grew up in. I won't be so hard on you again," he vowed. "I know you'll hold me to account on that."

"That's not my job. Hold yourself to account."

"I am," he said drily. "That's why I'm here."

She *tsked* and frowned at the foot of her bed. She had changed into jeans and a T-shirt before catching the train. Her faded yellow shirt hung loose over her waistband, so he couldn't tell if her waist was thickening, but he would swear her breasts were fuller than the already deliciously round swells he had worshipped so thoroughly three months ago.

He swallowed, trying not to get distracted with memories.

"We have to try, Fliss. I live a very good life. One that our child is entitled to. I can offer *you* a very good life." He glanced toward the sketchbook, impressed with her flare for a graceful line and a pop of unexpected color or pattern. "Are you really going to put your dreams on hold for the next eighteen years? I can help you achieve them, you know."

"Ew! It's not an achievement if someone hands it to you."

Was that a dig at what he stood to inherit?

"It's not cheating to maximize the opportunities you're given. Try telling me that Ms. McCartney's last name didn't open doors for her. Tell me that growing up in a world where she already had access to designers and celebrities didn't give her a leg up. That's all I'm offering you."

"That's not why I'm having this baby, though," Fliss blurted. "I need you to hear that and believe it."

"Why, then?" he asked, more from curiosity than suspicion.

The tendons in her neck briefly stood out, as though his question put her under great stress. When she spoke, her voice was quiet and held an ache that penetrated far more deeply into him than was comfortable.

"I don't have anyone anymore. Granny is gone and…" She waved toward the photo of her grandmother. "I want a family, even if it's just me and my one child. I don't want whatever it is that you just described." Her splayed hand drew a circle to encompass the conflict that had been baked into his upbringing. "That sounds awful."

"Understood." He didn't blame her for resisting an invitation into his family, but he didn't regret warning her what it was like, either. She needed to know where he'd come from and what she was getting into. "You didn't intend to get pregnant. I know that."

He was heartened by what he perceived as genuinely sentimental feelings toward their baby, too. They didn't keep a jaded part of him from remaining on guard against her, though, speculating whether her show of reluctance to marry was a long con of some kind. He wasn't forgetting about that invitation she'd taken.

All of that aside, however. "We can still make the best of an unexpected situation."

"A rush into marriage is not 'the best.'" She was still hugging herself, shoulders high and tense, brow crinkled with consternation.

"We don't have to marry right away. At least come home with me—"

"To America? I can't leave my life here!"

What life? He bit back the question, rephrasing to a milder, "What would you be leaving behind that you can't live without?"

"Mrs. Bhamra," she mumbled, biting her thumbnail.

"I come to London constantly. I've actually debated buying a property here. We could do that so we have more of a home here."

"So I'd live in London and you'd come and go?"

"New York is a more convenient base for me because I fly to LA as often as anywhere else. Let's start in New York while we figure out how to live together. Ultimately, we'll settle wherever we decide is best for our baby to live."

"I don't have health insurance in America."

"That's not even an argument. I'll fund an obstetrics wing if I have to."

She rolled her eyes. "Must be nice."

"It is. Try it," he said blithely.

Her mouth pursed in dismay.

"What would that even look like? Would we live as roommates or...?" Her tone was overly casual, but he could see how hard she was trying to sound blasé when she glanced at him. Apprehension had stiffened her expression.

He let his head thump back against the wall, watching her through the screen of his lashes. "Is that what you'd prefer?"

Fliss seemed to find something extremely interesting on the side of her elbow. "Well, it's not as if we were planning to continue our affair, is it?"

"I was."

Her gaze clashed with his.

"What do you think the earrings were for?" he chided.

"You tell me. Do you regularly give women such outrageous gifts for a night of sex?"

Saint drew a breath that seared his lungs with fresh liability. She was too good at prying into him, forcing him to self-exam and see where he fell short.

"My relationships have always been superficial," he admitted, rising in a restless attempt to dodge that spiky truth. "You weren't wrong when you called me that. And, as you've discovered, my life can be taxing on those who get involved with me, even briefly. If I can reduce the criticism or soften the impact, I do."

"With jewelry? Just admit you're paying for sex, Saint. This is a safe space. No judgment." She sounded facetious.

"I'm paying for the fact that I don't offer much beyond sex," he prevaricated. "I'm monogamous and materially generous, but I don't fall in love. Emotions are grit in my teeth. That's why I have the reputation I do, so no one expects grand gestures or heartfelt declarations."

"You should be in sales. I can't wait to overturn my life for that."

"You're doing it for our child."

"Right. It's not about me." Her voice sounded tight.

"I'm aware of my limitations, Fliss. Now you are, too. We're going into this with a much clearer vision than my parents had. My mother mistook passion for love and didn't understand why it faded. You won't have those sorts of unrealistic expectations of me."

"And what would you expect of me?" she challenged, expression cantankerous.

"I'd *like* sex, but I don't expect it, if that's what you're asking."

"No—" She made an impatient noise. He didn't think she could hug herself any harder without turning herself inside out. "According to the headlines, you're looking to settle down with 'someone who shares your values.' That's not me. I know that because it's been three months without a word from you. You didn't even ask me to continue that affair you claim to have wanted. Don't—" She held up a stalling finger. "Don't say you didn't have my number. If you can get Delia Chevron's personal number, you can get mine. You're only here—" she pointed at the floor "—because *I* came to *you*. So don't pretend you want *me* when what you really want is sex. If you want honesty between us, be honest about that."

Saint rocked back on his heels, annoyed that she was such a pugnacious fighter but admiring how tough she was at the same time.

"My search for a wife is a smoke screen. I was generating too much unflattering publicity. The board refused to fund an important project until I was able to prove I take

Grayscale and my future seriously. Much as I wanted to call you, I thought it was better to let the attention die down."

"And your silence had nothing to do with finding out I was a lowly housemaid." Her words dripped cynicism.

"The part where you were fired for theft concerned me," he said with gravity. "Not the job you were doing at the time."

Fliss dropped her gaze, not bothering to make more excuses.

"Now you be honest," he commanded gruffly. "Would you have continued our affair if I'd asked?"

"I don't know." She was staring into a corner, profile tortured.

"Really?" The tension of expecting a blow came into his abdomen. "Do you not think of that night as often as I do?"

Her gaze swept to his, wide with exposure, then slid to the bed before snapping away. The flush of pink that came into her cheeks was so ripe with sensual reminiscence he had to fight a smug smile of gratification.

"Okay, then." All he wanted in that moment was to crawl onto that narrow mattress with her and relive every single thing they'd done. Then start making new memories.

"What 'okay'? No. All I'm hearing is that you need a trophy wife," she blurted. "How do you expect an unplanned pregnancy with a scrounging housemaid will go over with your board?"

"Oh, they'll treat it like a national holiday. There might even be a parade."

"Gawd," she cried softly and buried her face in her hands.

"Fliss." He couldn't resist going over to take her hands, forcing her to reveal all the uncertainty gripping her. "I've already thought through how I'll handle it. And once everyone realizes I'm producing Theodore the Third, they'll be very happy for us."

She quirked her brow. "Is your real name Theodore?"

"Now you know my deep dark secret," he said. "Why are you shaking your head? You think our baby is a girl? Gender is a construct."

"Because you're moving too fast, Saint Theodore." She shook her hands free of his.

"Theodore Saint Garvey Montgomery," he clarified. "And what about your experience with me makes you think I move any other way?"

"I thought you wanted a paternity test?" She paced back to the table. "Let's both take a beat while we wait for the results. After that, if we decide to try—" her voice faltered "—living together, I'll give notice at work."

"Do you really doubt that I'm the father?" he asked with a frown.

"I thought you did."

He chewed the corner of his mouth, thinking about the way she'd flinched when he'd said back at the hotel that he couldn't take her word for it.

"My father will want one, but you and I need to be able to trust each other, so tell me the truth—I swear I won't be angry. Is there someone else who could be the father?"

She flinched again, making him want to probe why, but after a moment of hesitation, she pressed her lips together and shook her head, conceding, "You're the only person I've been with."

"Good." A strange sensation washed through him. It was something like relief and something like elation. It sank so deeply into him, it crept toward places he guarded very closely, threatening to get under the door.

"How is that good?" Fliss asked skeptically.

"You're being honest with me. That's very good." He was side-stepping what she had really asked so he didn't have to explain his inexplicable reaction. He was far more comfortable with stepping into action. "Now, you said yourself that you'll be showing soon, so let's get ahead of this. Come to New York with me, and we'll let people see we're in a relationship. We'll announce the baby news when we can no longer hide it." He took out his phone to text Willow. "What's evening traffic like? Is it realistic that we could be at the airport in two hours?"

"*No.* I just finished bringing my things from London. I can't pack up my life again in ten minutes. Where would I even put it?"

"I genuinely don't understand the question." He searched Fliss's distressed expression, trying to see the problem. "I'll pay the rent here until we find a place in London, then I'll hire movers to bring all of this there. Pack what you want with you in New York, which I presume is that photo of Granny and your tarot cards. Text your employer that you quit. We'll say goodbye to Mrs. Bhamra on the way out of town."

Fliss was on Saint's private jet before she had fully absorbed what she had agreed to do, but it was too late for all the qualms that piled on her with the climb in altitude.

This was the real fall from the Tower, she realized. She was literally in the air, the life she'd built, such as it was, falling away. She didn't even have a job to go back to. She had a few hundred pounds in the bank and Mrs. Bhamra's insistence that she should call if she needed anything.

As they reached cruising altitude, the flight attendant offered drinks and asked if they would like her to prepare their meal.

"I've eaten, thanks," Fliss said, stifling a yawn.

"I'll eat later." Saint frowned with concern at her. "Are you tired?"

She'd nodded off in the car on the drive to the airport,

so she ought to have had a little more in her, but, "I was up really early this morning, and it was a long day. I wouldn't mind shutting my eyes for a bit." Plus, she needed time to process all that had happened.

"Use the bed." He unclipped his seat belt and rose. "Come. I'll show you."

It was a throwaway comment. He didn't mean he'd show her how to use the bed, but he sure had the last time they'd been together. As she followed him to the back of the cabin, her cheeks stung with self-conscious heat.

"Are you blushing?" he asked in an amused undertone as he held the door for her.

"Don't tease." She covered her hot cheeks.

"This from the woman who showed up in a schoolgirl skirt today?"

"You said I looked like an assassin," she said over her shoulder.

"The sexy kind from the free-love era. I was looking forward to engaging in hand-to-hand combat, but you got the advantage over me in other ways."

She lost her sense of humor as she moved further into the stateroom. Like the rest of the jet, it was decorated in earthy colors and textures. The head of the bed was a huge, illuminated panel with the silhouette of bamboo plants cast from the backside, giving the impression the forest was just beyond a translucent window. Lamps stood on night tables made of faux granite, and the walls were paneled in mahogany.

"That was a joke," he said in a low voice.

"I know." But it was actually bothering her that she stood to gain anything from this baby, even a free flight to America. She had a dream, but she also had a heavy not-good-enough complex, thanks to years of stumbles and false starts. Shortcuts didn't win. She'd learned that with the invitation debacle.

While she peered into the luxurious bathroom, Saint pressed a louvered panel, opening it to reveal drawers. He pulled blue satin pajamas from one and tossed them onto the bed.

"Oh. Um—"

"For you. I told them not to bother unpacking your suitcase." His eyes were laughing at her again. "You're tired, so I wasn't planning to join you, but I am absolutely open to an invitation if you do want company."

He had told her he wanted sex but didn't expect it. She thought it was pretty obvious that she did expect it. Why else would she have agreed to go to New York with him? Yes, they had things to discuss about the baby, but she could have put her foot down.

She hadn't because she had known from the moment she'd awakened in his bed three months ago that she would like to continue waking beside him. She'd been furious and upset with him when their brief involvement had forced her to flee London, but a barely acknowledged possibility had been dancing in her mind from the time she'd discovered she was pregnant. Their baby had given her a reason to see him and *see*. At her latest checkup, she had asked her doctor if she could have sex. She'd shaved her legs yesterday, knowing she would see him today.

But there was that other tender part of her that had taken a fresh hit when their brief association had turned her into a punchline again.

As Fliss bit her lip and stared at the pajamas with indecision, he said, "No? That's fine." He started to the door.

That hurt, too, that he was able to take it or leave it so casually when she was in such turmoil over whether to have sex and what it might cost her.

Ugh. If she didn't tell him now, she never would.

"Saint."

He paused. His expression was infinitely patient, but her heart started to beat faster. She swallowed, but the tension in her lungs remained.

"I think you should know that…" She looked past him to the door, feeling trapped, but even if she left this bedroom, she'd still be on a plane, thirty thousand feet over the Atlantic. "When I said I hadn't been with anyone else…"

He didn't move, didn't say a word, but she sensed his withdrawal. It was as though his body condensed into ice, dropping the temperature in the room.

"It's not what you're thinking." She scrunched herself into the corner beside the night table. "I mean, you probably thought I meant I hadn't been with anyone lately and that's true, but you're actually only the second person I've ever been with. The first was six—no, seven?—years ago." She winced with apprehension as she said it.

His brows crashed together as he tried to fit that detail into what he thought he knew about her.

"My…um…first boyfriend was mean to me."

"In what way?" The gritty danger that entered his tone sent a chill down her spine.

"Not violent. Just…unkind. He pressured me to have sex with him even though I was on the fence about it. It wasn't assault." Fliss waved her hand, trying to forestall whatever masculine aggression was building behind that glowering, granite expression. "It was my choice but an immature one. I thought he wouldn't like me anymore if I didn't, and I wanted to find out what was so great about it. I didn't get much of an answer," she said in an aside of annoyed disgust.

"It was uncomfortable and unsatisfying. Maybe it would have gotten better with time. With someone else." She folded her arms. "But I didn't want to be intimate again because after we did it, he started bragging around school about it. I got mad and broke up with him, and he retaliated by telling everyone he had dumped me because I was giving it away to anyone who asked. I was only in our social group because I was with him. He was very popular, so when it came to picking sides, everyone chose the stud who'd been wronged over the slut who lied about it."

Saint muttered a curse under his breath, eyes closing. "Then you had sex with me, and..."

"Yeah. That ruined a really nice night." Her throat tightened, thinning her voice. Her chest was burning with self-consciousness. "I hadn't felt like that with him. Like I really wanted sex." *Needed* it. "I knew it would only be one night, but you seemed to know what you were doing and you were nice about it. You said we could stop if I wanted to. I thought it would be cathartic and something that was just for me. And you, obviously, but a nice memory that would replace my old one."

Saint's mouth was tight as he tracked his concerned gaze all over her. "I should have done more to protect you."

"Oh, you think?" She couldn't help her exasperated guffaw over that one.

"From the press," he clarified, mouth sliding sideways with self-deprecation. "But yeah. Physically, too."

"I didn't tell you that to put a guilt trip on you." She looked to the bed and the pajamas, barely resisting the urge to pick them up and press her nose into the cool satin to see if she could smell his aftershave. "I was trying to say that yes, I want to sleep with you, but I'm also scared of what comes after, if things don't work out between us."

"It will work out." He came close enough to cup her elbows and draw her from the corner so she was right in front of him. "I'll make sure of it."

CHAPTER EIGHT

SAINT SPOKE AS though he meant it, so Fliss smiled as though she believed him.

Besides, she was growing overwhelmed by his closeness. Her hand found its way to his chest without her realizing it. Her fingertips tucked themselves behind the placket of his shirt between two buttonholes, and she tugged him closer while she lifted her mouth.

His breath hissed in at her unhesitating invitation. His head dipped, and his firm lips angled across hers.

At first contact, a sensual jolt pulsed through her, so strong it made her groan at the sting of it. Who cared if her life was destroyed by this? Touching him *was* life. He was hot and dynamic and pulsing with energy that shimmered into her, making her feel surrounded and safe and more alive than she ever had.

For three long months, she had been waiting to feel this way again, convinced she never would, but now she was back in this wondrous place where his lips moved over hers with controlled mastery. His palm slid up her arm to the back of her neck, cupping her head while he deepened the kiss at an achingly slow pace.

It was both soothing and inciting. Frustrating. Urgency was rising in her, making her run her hands around to his back so she could pull herself tighter against him.

"I was an animal last time," Saint said, drifting his kiss to her cheek and brow. "You should have told me how long it had been. I would have been more careful."

"I liked it." He'd made her feel irresistible, and she wanted that rush again, maybe to reassure herself it was still there. Or that she held some of the power over him that he had implied, but even though she arched to press her pelvis into the stiffness behind his fly, he only made a sound of gratification and dragged at her hair so he could nuzzle his mouth against her throat.

"I've thought about you a lot. About that night." His free hand skimmed the side of her breast, then climbed beneath the fall of her T-shirt to trace patterns against her waist and lower back, showering her with tingling sensations. "About all the things I would do with you if I ever got the chance again." His hot words stimulated the hollow beneath her ear and stirred the fine hairs at her hairline. "The list is long, Fliss. Very, very long."

She was hearing him on a subliminal level, all her senses drawing tight with anticipation while he only teased her with the brush of his lips on her throat and the unhurried movement of his hand creeping higher and higher toward her breast. By the time his thumb traced the under-band of her bra, she was trembling.

But Fliss had the wherewithal to say, "Don't wreck it. I made it."

He lifted his head. "This?" His clever fingers grew more exploratory, making her wriggle when his tickling touch went into her armpit.

"Yes. And you ripped the knickers I made—"

"I wanted to *keep* them, they were so sexy. Let me see." He took hold of the hem of her T-shirt, forcing her to raise her arms, then skimmed it off and away. His gaze glittered with approval as he took in the jewel-colored scraps of silk, silver lace and black satin straps. "You made this?"

"I had to. I've already gone up a cup size."

"Hell yes, you have."

"Don't look too closely." Fliss touched a tiny wrinkle in the lace edging. "It's full of mistakes. Lingerie is very finicky and unforgiving."

"I'm looking very closely and all I see is perfection," he assured her in a throaty voice. "You should make nothing but lingerie. This is..." Saint slid his finger under the strap where it came over the top of her shoulder. It connected to an eyelet that supported a split strap that framed the upper swells of her breasts in bold triangles before connecting to either side of the balconette cups. He swallowed. "Magnificent."

The feathery trace of his touch was making her breasts tingle and swell. They ached, but even though she drew a breath and shifted, he showed no mercy. His thumb grazed the point of her nipple where it was lifting the amethyst silk.

She didn't realize she'd made a throaty noise until he paused. "Hurt?"

"No. It feels really good." Everything about his hands on her felt really, really good.

A satisfied rumble sounded in his throat. He brushed the strap off her shoulder, then scooped his hand inside the cup to dislodge it. His head ducked and he licked at her nipple, teasing, blowing softly, before he opened his mouth to take the tip deeply into the wet heat of his mouth. He sucked until she was standing on her tiptoes, fist knotted in his hair.

When Saint straightened, his eyes were glazed with lust. He checked in with her very briefly before he freed her other breast and bent her over his arm. He ravished the other one just as thoroughly, sending runnels of heat into her loins and making her cling and arch higher into his mouth and gasp his name.

He didn't let up. No, he pushed his hand into her jeans and knickers and discovered exactly how profound an effect he was having on her. She groaned with aching delight as the restriction of her clothes firmed his touch against her folds. His finger probed, and the plane of his palm sat implacably against the pulsing knot of nerves that had been waiting for this. For him.

"Saint." She was so aroused she was begging, bowed in supplication, lifting her hips to deepen his penetration, trying to increase the friction.

He fluttered his tongue against her nipple, and she lost it. Climax rippled through her, deep and satisfying, tearing a cry from her throat. If he hadn't held her so firmly, she would have fallen down as she fell apart. It was terrifying and exalting and left her so shaken she was still quivering when he removed his hand from her jeans and eased her onto the bed.

"I thought my memory had exaggerated how responsive you are," he said in a rasp. "Are you sure this is okay? I didn't expect you to come so hard and fast." He opened his hand across her abdomen where her muscles were still twitching in the aftermath.

He didn't look *that* worried. He looked kind of smug.

"It's very okay," she said shakily, opening her jeans and lifting her hips to push them down and off with the rest of her remaining clothes.

Saint straightened to yank at his own shirt and pants, his impatience flattering. His erection sprang forth. All of him was like burnished oak, carved and sanded into smooth planes and lovingly accentuated details. He swept his hand across his torso as he looked at her, then slid his hand down, taking hold of himself in a tight fist, expression tense with carnal hunger. He reached for the night table drawer.

"You don't need a condom," she reminded him. "Unless there are other issues? I had a full screen as part of my checkup."

"I was tested..." He frowned in recollection. "It was right before I left for London for the gala. There hasn't been anyone else since. I've never had sex without a condom, though."

"Me, neither. We're both virgins." Fliss sat up to draw the blankets down so she could get under them but paused to ask with false concern, "Do you think we should discuss it first? With a responsible adult we trust?"

"Like who? The pilot?" He threw the covers away and loomed over her, nipping at her lips with his own as he pressed her to the mattress. "Damn, but I've been wanting this."

"I thought about you a lot, too," she confessed in a whisper, stroking her hands down his strong back and over his firm buttocks.

Somehow, he made her feel both delicate and vulnerable but safe. He was proprietary in the way he inserted his legs between hers, effortlessly pushing hers open in a demonstration of how much strength he had—plenty enough to overpower her if he wanted to. But the way he kissed her was a coax.

Let me in. Come with me down this erotic path.

And he went down an erotic path of his own, one that took him over the hills of her breasts and across the field of her abdomen, then into the grove between her thighs.

"You don't have to—" She was already aroused enough, but her voice turned to a moan of indulgence.

"I really do," he said in a low voice, bringing his thumb into play with his tongue.

Fliss couldn't talk after that. All her brain cells were fried by the lazy way he was pulling her toward orgasm again, coiling sensation upon sensation until she was at the tipping point.

"Not yet, lovely," he said, lifting his head and stroking his thumb in the moisture of her folds, avoiding where she most needed to be caressed. "Wait for me."

He set his teeth against her inner thigh just tight enough to threaten pain, then sucked a love bite onto her skin. The discomfort drew her back from the edge but made her sob in denial.

"Soon," he crooned, climbing his wicked mouth over the wobbling muscles of her belly and pausing to worship her breasts once more. The inferno in her loins grew to an ache she couldn't bear.

"You're mean," she accused, so tense with need she thought she'd break in half.

"So mean," he agreed, taking his time with departing from her nipples before he finally, finally rose over her and guided himself to the molten core of her. "I'm going to savor this," he said in sinful warning. "But let me feel it, Fliss. Let me feel you come as many times as you can."

She was still very much out of her league, she realized in those seconds. Not just at his mercy, but willing to do anything for him. For this, the press of his thick shape sinking into her primed, welcoming sheath. Glorious shivers of near climax sent hot-cold sensations across her skin. Her knees bent to hug his sides and her heels dug into his ass, pressing him deeper.

Saint began to move, slow and deep and powerful, and it was all she needed. She twisted beneath him as orgasm detonated within her. Wild noises left her. Breath and thought and any sense of self were all gone in those moments of pure pleasure. Pure being.

"Beautiful," he murmured, sounding barely affected despite destroying her. He continued moving in those precise but leisurely thrusts. "Now another," he commanded, hooking his arm behind her knee to increase the depth of his possession.

She gave him everything he asked for.

"I don't want earrings," Fliss murmured through the dark, hours later, when they were exhausted and damp and drifting off to sleep.

Saint had her spooned into his front. He roused slightly, his ingrained cynicism thinking, *Here we go*.

"What would you prefer?"

"Respect." She sighed and snuggled deeper into his chest. Her hand slid to cover the one he had draped over her waist and grew heavy.

Seconds later, he could tell by the shallowness of her breathing that she was deeply asleep, but he was wide awake, blinking into the darkness, aware of the white noise of the plane's engines and an itch against his conscience.

He had told her he was a generous person, and he was, in a material sense. He could afford to be. But it could actually be argued that it wasn't generosity when the cost to him was very low. On a more emotional level, he was much more miserly. He had built thick, jaded boundaries around himself. Any respect he offered was conditional. Tentative. Everyone would disappoint him eventually. It was not a matter of if but when.

Fliss was authentically generous, though. Considering how she'd been treated in the past and then Saint's neglect of her when she'd been attacked by the press, she would have been within her rights to help him exit the plane without a parachute. It made her openness and lack of inhibition in this bed even more of a gift.

The abuse she'd suffered—and yes, it was abuse—incensed him. On top of that, he was disturbed to realize how little experience she really had with relationships. She needed more than respect. She needed to be handled with tenderness.

He didn't have a capacity for that. Inadequacy chipped at him as he recognized how *he* was likely to disappoint *her*. In his mind, the baby had been the one who needed his protection. Fliss would provide the love their child needed, and Saint would try not to be the same sort of cold bastard his own father had been. Somehow, they would rear a contributing member of society.

Fliss was more vulnerable than he'd realized, though. It was hitting him that she would need more from him than orgasms and an introduction to some top designers. She would need things he might not have within him to give.

Maybe he shouldn't marry her. He might've regarded love as a drug that wore off and left you with a horrific hangover, but she seemed to believe in it. She'd thought his parents should have divorced so they could find it.

That meant that at some point, she might expect him to let her go so she could marry someone else who—

The clench of rejection was so strong inside him, he twitched, causing her to drew a small, startled breath.

"It's okay. Go back to sleep," he whispered, securing her closer while pressing a kiss to the point of her shoulder.

She sighed and relaxed, but he lay awake a little longer, pondering that soar of feral possessiveness in him. Why? It wasn't about the baby. It wasn't even about sex.

Although sex with her was next level. And bareback sex? He would revel in that as much as she was up for. Still, as powerful as his orgasms were, that wasn't the only reason he was obsessed with her. He'd been preoccupied with her from the time he'd left her in London three months ago, thinking about her daily. He had read the gossip stories to know where she had turned up—needing to know she was alive at least. He had wanted to know if she was reading her cards and communing with her grandmother.

He had wanted to know how much of what she'd shown him of herself was real.

That was an uneasy admission. Especially because she was literally in his arms, in his bed, and he was so sexually gratified he ought to be catatonic, but there was a nagging sense of tenuousness keeping him awake.

Every relationship ran its course, whether it was a friendship or someone he hired or a liaison with a woman. He was always aware the association would end, even in the earliest stages of meeting someone new. He could see it as clearly as he saw the person he was meeting.

With Fliss, he hadn't seen the end. He hadn't had time in that initial flurry of lovemaking. Then he'd tried to force the ending, which had sat crooked inside him until he'd seen her again. He still couldn't see the day when they would part for good.

Because of the baby, obviously. Their child would keep her in his life forever, no matter what happened between them.

That was a strange, new concept. The only lifetime relationships he had were with his parents, and those were thorny as hell.

Was that why he always foresaw an end point? Because he liked walking away from people when things got difficult?

It was better than the alternative—sticking it out to stick it to the other person. Wasn't it?

Saint was still thinking about that the following day, when he left Fliss in Willow's capable hands at his New York penthouse and entered the boardroom. He was using a tablet to bring the remote board members into the meeting when his father arrived.

"You're on time at least," Ted Montgomery muttered. "Why are you doing that? Where's your assistant?"

"Good God, Dad. If I'm not capable of connecting a video chat, I have no business working here, do I?" He said into the microphone, "Can everyone hear me? Shall I start the presentation?"

"We've all seen the slides," his father dismissed. "I'm more interested in why you hared off to London. It wasn't in your schedule two days ago."

"I was rearranging some things so we can have dinner with Mother tonight."

"We?"

"It's been added to your calendar."

His father's cheek ticked. "What does she want?"

"I called it. One way or another, we'll need to debrief on what happens today." Saint was being deliberately cryptic as he held his father's challenging gaze.

On their way out of London, Saint had had a private nurse take samples for a lab. The paternity results ought to be available by the time he sat down with his parents tonight. Before he shared that news, he wanted to know where he stood at Grayscale.

"Shall we get to the vote?" he asked.

His father made an impatient noise and sat, then flicked his hand at the CFO to speak.

"Order champagne tonight," the CFO said with her warmest smile. "We wouldn't have asked you to the meeting if we weren't prepared to back you. We're particularly pleased to see how you have shifted the conversation around your personal life. This gives us the confidence that when the time comes, you'll lead Grayscale well into the future." She cut a careful glance toward Ted. "Until that time, we see the value in this new direction you're taking. I move that we support Saint's proposal."

"Second," someone murmured.

The vote was carried and the approval minuted.

"Excellent. *No backsies*, right?" Saint directed that to his father.

"I'll have Xanthe draft a press release," the CFO assured him. "It will go out this afternoon."

"Thank you." Satisfaction and a rush of pure adrenaline for the challenge washed through him. Saint had done so much preliminary work in anticipation of this, he only needed to open the gates and let the horses loose.

His usual single-mindedness was fractured, though. Weirdly, his first instinct was to call Fliss and tell her *I did it*, even though he'd only given her the bare bones of what he'd hoped to accomplish this morning. He had never been one to brag, having learned as a child that there was no point. His father took an attitude that excellence was the bare minimum. He had never been *proud* of anything his son had done.

Ted would be livid tonight, which was why Saint deliberately kept any mention of Fliss and her new place in his life to himself. It was dirty pool, but once the board's support of his project was publicized, it would be a lot harder for them to reverse course.

It would be hard for his father to reverse course once he learned about the baby, but even if it all went to hell in a handbasket...

Saint would hate that. He really would, but Fliss and the baby were his priority now—which was such a lurching departure from his usual way of thinking, he didn't know how to feel about it.

He shook hands with each of the board members, accepting their congratulations as he left them to finish their quarterly meeting.

His father only gave him a curt nod, saying dismissively, "I'll see you at dinner."

* * *

Fliss couldn't decide if she was Rapunzel, Sleeping Beauty or Cinderella.

She'd been half-asleep when they had landed and driven into the city last night. Saint had shown her around his cavernous penthouse before they'd gone back to bed, but she hadn't fully appreciated his home until she'd woken to the sunshine pouring in on her.

Situated eighty floors into the sky, it was two stories wrapped in an arc of glass offering panoramic views of the Hudson River, New York Harbor and the Statue of Liberty. She descended what looked like a glass staircase to the main floor, where a color scheme of slate and midnight blue and quiet cream welcomed her. All of his furniture was modern with rounded corners and long, flowing lines. The floors were marble and hardwood, and the area rugs were so exquisite they had to be handloomed. The contemporary abstracts on the walls were by names she didn't recognize but would look up later.

She and Saint hadn't spoken much. It had still been early, so they'd made love, eaten breakfast, showered, and then he'd dressed in a suit, telling her he had an important meeting with the board this morning. It was a special project that had been derailed by the bad publicity after their initial affair.

Fliss had grown uneasy, deducing that her presence, and pregnancy, could impact his aspirations again.

"There's still time to…not do this," she'd reminded him.

He had turned from the mirror, his tie still dangling loosely from his upturned collar, the top button of his shirt not yet closed. She'd been barefoot in her cotton pajama bottoms and a white T-shirt without a bra.

"Do you want to not do this?" His gaze had flicked to the bed they'd used with enthusiasm.

"I want to do this." She'd pointed at the floor. "Be in this room and never leave. I don't want to do that." She'd waved at the windows. "Be out there as a thing that strangers can judge."

"Good news. Your wish is granted." He'd come across to drop a kiss onto her lips that had been seductive enough that she'd leaned into it, encouraging him to linger. He'd drawn back with reluctance. "For the day, anyway. We'll have dinner with my parents tonight, but it's best if you stay inside until then. Do you mind?" He'd finished buttoning his shirt and expertly tied his tie without looking.

"Dinner? Tonight?" she'd cried. "Where? Here? Am I supposed to cook? What do I wear?"

"Wow. This is not an actual emergency. Take a breath. I've asked Willow— Ah. They're here." He'd pointed toward a muted ping that had sounded from a hidden speaker.

"Who's here? Who's Willow?"

"My executive assistant. Their pronouns are *they/them*. I'll introduce you, then I have to go. Do you mind getting dressed?" His gaze had dropped to her chest. "I like seeing your nipples through your shirt, but I'm getting possessive about who else does."

Her nipples had tightened in a responsive sting that had made her blush. He'd smirked.

She'd hurried to change while Saint had shrugged into his jacket and put on his shoes, then he'd led her down the stairs, saying, "Good morning."

"Good morning," the well-dressed twenty-something had responded. They'd worn a very smart pinstriped suit and boots with a heel. They hadn't batted an eyelash at Fliss, even though they'd known who she was because they'd said, "It's nice to meet you, Ms. Corning. I'm Willow."

"Nice to meet you, too." Fliss had shaken their hand, smiling uncertainly because even in jeans and a fresh T-shirt, *with a bra*, she'd felt very underdressed. "Please call me Fliss."

"I'll go to the office alone," Saint had said to Willow. "I need you to stay and help Fliss get settled. First order of business is to find her an obstetrician."

"Of course." Willow had drawn a phone from the inside pocket of their suit jacket, again seeming completely unfazed. "My sister has a specialist she loves. Let me ask her for the number."

"See if she has a stylist she likes, too."

"For tonight?" Fliss had asked him.

"And the foreseeable future," he'd replied, adding to Willow, "Someone stronger in procurement than opinions. Fliss knows what she wants. Make dinner reservations at that place my mother likes. Warn them that my father will be with us so they can have a steak on hand. I'll text if I think of anything else." He'd checked for his phone, then he'd dropped a kiss onto Fliss's pouted mouth. "Willow is extremely trustworthy. You're in good hands."

Seconds later, he'd been gone and she'd been alone with the stranger.

"My sister," Willow had said with a satisfied smile as their phone had pinged. "The office won't be open yet, but I'll set up a call to interview the doctor as soon as I can get through."

"Thank you. Saint ordered breakfast." Fliss had waved toward the kitchen where they had eaten at the island bar. She hadn't put it away yet. "They must have thought we were a party of thirty. There are pastries and fruit medley for days. Would you like something?"

"I've eaten, thanks, but I'll make myself a coffee." Willow had gone to the industrial grade espresso maker behind the island. "Can I make one for you, too?"

"I prefer tea, but I've had enough for now. You don't seem shocked that I'm here. Or that I...need a specialist."

"I expect the unexpected, working for Saint." Willow had reached unhesitatingly into the various cupboards, clearly familiar with the layout. "It's funny because a lot of my days are very boring. He travels and leaves me with reports to analyze, or I'm picking up dry cleaning. I start to think I'm overpaid and underutilized, then he drops a jigsaw puzzle on the table and tells me to finish it by lunch."

"Am I the jigsaw puzzle?" Fliss had guessed.

"You are. But I love puzzles," Willow had said, lips tilted with amusement.

"Me, too. I used to do them with my granny." Fliss had smiled. Maybe she didn't need to be so intimidated by Willow and their ultra-efficient manner after all.

In truth, they got along like a house on fire. The stylist, Regina, was nice, too. The only hiccup occurred when Fliss balked at ordering more than a handful of items on top of the dress she had picked out for the evening.

She was used to making her own clothing or buying from consignment and altering or embellishing to make a piece her own. There was also the fact that whatever she bought today wouldn't fit her for very long, which Willow picked up on, waiting until Regina had left to say, "Saint wants you to have everything you need for the foreseeable future. That includes maternity wear. If you're not ready to tell Regina, we can work around it, but I'm confident she could source some items without revealing who they're for."

"I'll think about it," Fliss murmured, but she really wanted to keep her pregnancy under wraps for as long as possible, certain it would put her in the spotlight again.

By the time Regina returned with three racks of clothing and a metric crap ton of shoes, it was time for Fliss to get ready. Since her prep for the gala had failed to measure up to Saint's usual crowd, she let Regina's staff do her hair and makeup and even allowed Regina to alter her dress when she would normally do that herself.

She definitely felt like Cinderella when she was pronounced "ready" and made her way out of the spare bedroom and down the stairs.

Regina had leapt on Fliss's appreciation for vintage styles with contemporary touches. She'd brought her a selection from an up-and-coming New York designer including this A-line style skirt in Mediterranean-blue satin with a black fitted bodice. It was off the shoulder while still being meet-the-parents modest. The sweetheart neckline made the most of her ample breasts while creating the illusion that she had a well-defined waist. Her shoes were a closed-toe Mary Jane with a medium heel.

Fliss felt like a screen legend from the black-and-white era but gripped the rail with tension as she came down, half fearing that Saint's parents were here because she could hear him speaking.

He stopped mid-word when he saw her, saying into his phone, "My date is here. Forward that to my parents, and we'll talk more tomorrow."

He ended the call and came to the bottom of the stairs, trapping her on the bottom one so they were eye to eye.

She held her breath as he took in her hair, scooped into a simple twist, her red lips, her bare shoulders and cleavage, then came back up.

"So you do like my taste in earrings."

"These aren't *the* earrings?" She touched the very artistic scroll of blue-and-white stones. Regina had said they would go perfectly with her dress, so Fliss had assumed the other woman had picked them herself from some high-end costume jewelry.

"They are," he confirmed, making her stomach feel funny.

"But you're not giving them to me," she protested. "I said I didn't want any," she reminded, wondering if this meant he'd rather give her sparkly rocks than respect or regard.

"I collected them on my way to Nottingham, so I already had them when you said you didn't want them." His face blanked into the remote expression that was so hard to read. "Would you rather not accept them?"

"They're worth a fortune! It's stressful to wear things this expensive." The dress and shoes were already a lot to worry about. "Why do you want me to wear them?"

"Because you like them and they suit you?" he suggested pithily.

"It's not because…"

"What?"

"Are you trying to prove something or… I don't know," she mumbled as she saw his expression darken.

"I don't care about anyone's opinion but yours. If you like them, then I want you to have them and wear them."

"Thank you." Fliss touched her lobes to ensure each earring was secure. Her stomach was full of snakes. "I feel like you're mad at me now, and that wasn't my intention. I'm just nervous."

"I'm not mad," he said in that acerbic voice. "Not at you. I'm only realizing that the earrings will be noticed and remarked on and that will make you self-conscious. I want you to be able to enjoy wearing a pair of damned earrings if you want to."

"What an apt description. That's what I'll call them from now one. My *damned* earrings."

Saint didn't react, only stared at her.

"Sometimes my sense of humor is misplaced," she admitted with a wrinkle of her nose.

"Now that you've found it, keep it," he drawled, helping her down the final step. "It'll help you get through dinner."

"Because they're going to hate me?" she asked with dread as they waited for the elevator.

"My father hates everyone. Don't take it personally."

"And your mother?" she asked as they stepped into the elevator.

He sighed. "Mother has always believed her looks are her only asset. Dad has never given her credit for bringing more to their marriage than beauty. As such, she despises any sign of aging. The title of grandmother will be a knife to her heart."

"Do we have to do this in public?" she asked as they exited and stepped into the waiting car.

"We do," he said firmly.

The drive wasn't far. The restaurant was smallish, obviously very exclusive given the way they were escorted from the curb up carpeted steps that were protected by a black awning lit by fairy lights. They were handed off to a middle-aged maître d' who had the air of someone who had made a career out of this work.

"Mr. Montgomery. Welcome. I just seated your parents. Please follow me."

Saint had taken hold of Fliss's hand as they'd left the car. He had to feel how clammy her palm was, but he forged the way, allowing her to trail behind him as they wound through the full tables. She tried not to crane her neck, even though she recognized a few celebrities. It was disconcerting to realize they were looking back, noticing Saint and maybe recognizing her from her photos.

She tried to focus on the clothes as a distraction, and it worked a little too well. She nearly crashed into Saint when he stopped walking. He steadied her as he brought her to stand beside him.

"Mom. Dad. I'd like you to meet Felicity."

Fliss's anxiety turned to the sort of morbid terror that

came from facing something she knew wasn't genuinely life-threatening but still turned her blood cold, like a giant spider.

The couple stole a moment to recover from their shock, then rose politely. Ted Montgomery was a peek at what Saint would look like in forty years—distinguished and even more stern, still wearing an aura of power that hadn't diminished at all.

His mother was the source of his star power, though. Norma was easily fifteen years younger than her husband. Her figure was fit, not the least bit matronly. She wore a sequined drop-waist dress that glinted and shimmered in the candlelight. Her beauty would have been a standard blonde-and-blue-eyed variety if not for an intrinsic sparkle that might have dimmed with age, but it was still there, demanding she be noticed.

"How charming. Call me Norma," his mother said, offering her hand in a very brief, weak shake. Her cool gaze skimmed down, taking in every detail of Fliss's appearance, including coming back to the earrings before transferring a silent question toward Saint.

"Ted." His father didn't offer to shake hands. He moved to help Norma with her chair.

"A bottle of Dom," Saint said to the hovering maître d' as he held Fliss's chair.

She sank gratefully into it, knees weak. Her throat had constricted so tightly she felt as though she sipped oxygen through a straw.

"This is why you went to London?" Ted asked with only a flickering glance toward Fliss before shifting his glare back to his son. "You didn't say a word about her in our meeting this morning."

"I was waiting on an email that I've forwarded to both of you," Saint said blithely. "You can read it later, but the important piece is that you're being informed of our happy news at the same time. I'm not playing favorites."

"Hap— Saint." His mother's voice was a gust of betrayal.

"There's no dispute?" His father reached for his phone.

"None," Saint assured him. "I sent it to Elijah so he can begin making adjustments to my will."

Ted sent her a look that was both accusation and disgust. His mother's eyes gleamed with angry tears.

"Wow," Fliss couldn't help saying. "When you said your family dinners were a nightmare, you meant it."

Shock slacked everyone's jaws.

"Oh, did I say that out loud?" She facetiously touched her lips. "I thought that's what we were doing."

Ted's gaze narrowed. Norma's gaze dropped, and her red face turned redder.

Saint sat back, angling to face her.

She'd gone too far, she knew she had, but she had her passport in her clutch and enough room on her credit card to get herself back to London. She could go straight to the airport from here. She didn't have to put up with anyone treating her this way.

"As I said, I'd like you to meet Felicity," Saint drawled. A glimmer of admiration stole into his expression as he continued looking at her. "How you feel about her is irrelevant. How you treat her is not." He sat straight again, making a point of looking at both of his parents in turn. "If you drive her away, you drive me away, so think about the words that are coming out of your mouths."

The bucket of champagne arrived with four crystal flutes.

Saint held up a finger to hit pause on the popping of the cork.

"Are we staying?" he asked them.

CHAPTER NINE

SAINT WOKE AT four in the morning to find the bed beside him empty. The sheets were cool. He lurched up in bed.

"Fliss?"

She wasn't in the bathroom. The door was open, the room dark.

He shrugged on his robe and padded downstairs, finding her in a pool of lamplight, kneeling at the coffee table. A cup of tea was steaming near her elbow. On the table in front of her were three cards face up on a square of black velvet.

"Do you always do this during the witching hour?"

"My body is still on London time. I couldn't sleep." She sipped her tea. "I decided to see what I could see."

"And what do you see?" He started to lower into the chair opposite her.

"That's Granny's spot." She pointed at the cup of milky brown tea on the side table, also releasing a wisp of steam.

"Excuse me, Granny," he said to the empty chair, non-plussed, and moved to sit behind Fliss so he could peer over her shoulder. Three cards were laid in a row. The image in the middle was right side up, but the ones on the outside were upside down.

"The Empress is abundance." Fliss touched the card on the left. "And love. Venus." She pointed to a symbol. "She's reversed because the abundance I'm enjoying is yours, not mine. And because my love is flowing out." She nodded at the empty chair. "Not back to me."

Saint was skeptical of all of this, but he couldn't be dismissive. Her profile was too solemn. She'd been through a lot in the last thirty-six hours or so. If she needed to pretend her grandmother was here so she didn't feel so alone, who was he to judge?

He gave her silky hair a pet and left his hand on her shoulder.

"What about your pregnancy? Venus is the goddess of fertility, isn't she?" He leaned forward to lift the Empress onto its top edge. "Aren't babies usually upside down inside the womb? Maybe that's what it means."

She twisted a glare of mock horror at him and whispered, "Don't touch my cards." She delicately took it to lay it down again. "But thank you. I like that interpretation."

"What's the stick?" He pointed to the one in the middle, labeled *Ace of Wands*.

"That's your fault."

"Oh?"

"It's a new idea that is starting to take root in my mind. You said I should focus on lingerie, and I can't stop thinking about that. It's really hard—"

"The stick?"

"Lingerie." She slid him another admonishing look.

"But you can see from the way that fist is clutching that very sturdy branch, I thought the interpretation was going in a different direction."

"And you can see that the cards never lie. You see what you want to see."

Saint wanted to see her smile. She hadn't since before dinner, but at least her tone had lightened.

"For the record, my lingerie remark was not serious

when I made it." He gathered her hair as he spoke so he was holding the thick rope of it in his stacked fists. He carefully dragged her head back to see her face. "But I wholeheartedly support your shift in focus. In fact, I'll volunteer to be your beta tester."

"You want to wear one of my G-strings to see if it's comfortable?"

"You're a brat sometimes, aren't you?"

"I'm not the one barging in on a reading, pulling hair and making jokes about your penis."

"I never joke about my penis." He released her hair.

"Stick with me, kid," she murmured, straightening the Ace of Wands.

He chuckled and caged her with his knees, massaging her shoulders. "What's with the naked woman and the watering cans?"

"The Star follows the Tower in the Major Arcana. I had the Tower when I realized I was pregnant, so it makes sense that the Star has turned up." She touched the card so it was perfectly aligned with the others. "It's a symbol of hope, like a wishing star or a guiding star. She's watering the seeds that she's planted, but she's naked so she's vulnerable, which we always are when we hope."

"But it's upside down."

"I know," Fliss said pensively. "Reversed means a lack of faith or a likely disappointment. Granny always points out that *star* spelled backwards is *rats*." She tapped the word on the bottom of the card.

"Is she really here? Because there goes my plan to seduce you on the couch." He looked to the empty chair and the untouched cup of tea. "Come back to bed. I promise you won't be disappointed."

She only picked up her tea to sip. "That was a really difficult dinner, Saint."

He knew. That was why he'd been genuinely alarmed to find the bed empty and so relieved to find her here. His parents had stayed and they hadn't said anything that was outright antagonistic or insulting, but they hadn't welcomed her with open arms. Aside from his mother asking about her due date, they'd barely acknowledged the baby.

"And this Belmont Stakes thing? I don't know anything about horses!"

"Is that the reason you couldn't sleep?" he asked.

"It's a house party for a *week*," she said. "Why didn't you warn me?"

"I forgot about it, or I would have. Mom actually has a horse in the race this year. That's not an expression—she really does. So we can't refuse to go." The timing was terrible, though, with his project still in such early stages of getting off the ground. "It's an excellent chance for me to introduce you to everyone, though."

"Who is 'everyone'?"

"Mom's horsey friends." And the Hampton circle along with his father's cronies and the board members who would be sucking lemons over the sleight of hand Saint had pulled by failing to mention Fliss when he had accepted their backing. "Don't worry. It's a week away."

"I looked it up, Saint," she said. "I need outfits. I need *hats*. Your mother was already looking at me like I was an embarrassment."

"I told you, she's vain about her age. She'll come around."

"I always hoped my baby would have a grandmother like I did," she admitted softly.

His gaze flickered to that upside-down Star of disappointment.

"I would give that to you if I could, Fliss." He leaned forward to cup the front of her throat and press a kiss to the top of her hair. "I want to give you everything you need. I really do." When it came to his parents, a sense of failure, of being robbed was so visceral, it was bitter on his tongue.

He did what he always did when emotions reared their head.

"Let's talk to a Realtor tomorrow to find a space for your design work."

"I'd rather use one of the spare bedrooms. I only need a table for my sewing machine, and I'd rather not go out every day and have to worry about being photographed." She began gathering up her cards, then paused. "Do you want me to do a reading for you?"

"God, no." Saint cleared his throat. "I mean, no, thank you."

"Chicken. What are you afraid I'll see?" She was finally smiling as she folded the velvet around the cards and secured the package with a white ribbon.

Too much. The answer slithered through his mind, too slippery to catch and examine, but it was true.

They flew by helicopter, landing in a private airfield where they were collected by a chauffeur who greeted Saint with warm familiarity and a welcoming smile for Fliss.

His mother was less effusive when they arrived at the end of a secluded driveway in a cobbled courtyard surrounding a fountain before a massive stone mansion with wings off either side. It was topped with gingerbread detailing and a tile roof.

Norma greeted them with perfunctory cheek kisses and directed their luggage to "the junior suite."

"I'll leave you to show Felicity around. The florist finally arrived, and they brought the wrong color lilies so I have that disaster on my hands." She stalked away.

"Oh no," Saint said faintly in her wake.

"She just wants her party to go well," Fliss murmured, but if the wrong lilies were a disaster, what did that make her?

During that awful dinner last week, she'd been politely interrogated on her life, from her upbringing to her education right up to her aspiration to pursue fashion design. At no point had she felt that Mr. and Mrs. Montgomery had warmed to her.

As Saint showed her around, Fliss's apprehension grew. His penthouse was gorgeous and worth millions, but this was only *one* of his parents' residences. His father stayed in their Fifth Avenue apartment while Norma spent most of her time at their twenty-two-acre estate in Bedford Corners. They called this mansion their "cottage."

It had been built for entertaining. The main floor was open and welcoming with a great room containing a massive fireplace, a number of smaller conversation areas and a formal dining room with seating for sixteen. Every room had windows and doors onto the back garden where a huge patio was surrounded by flowering shrubs and June blooms.

Saint pointed out the games room and home movie theatre—it easily sat twenty.

"The fitness room and sauna are below our suite in the other wing. I'll show you on the way to our room." He walked her outside past the enormous kidney-shaped pool. "I wanted us to have the pool house, but that's the beauty salon this week. If you chip a nail or want your hair done, just come here. Do you play tennis?" He nodded to the court that was tucked into the trees at the end of a short path.

"Never." She was still craning her neck back at the pool house, which was a genuine cottage with a chimney, a porch, hanging baskets and rickrack detailing.

They stepped onto a boardwalk that wound through

grassy sand dunes, then descended onto the longest, emptiest beach Fliss had ever seen. The ocean stretched out in a gray-blue rippling blanket for about a thousand miles.

"Is that England I see over there?" she joked, pointing randomly.

"That's West Africa." Saint took hold of her shoulders and angled her so she was looking almost straight up the beach. "Northeast is that way, but Canada's elbow is in the way."

"Oh, Canada," she groused. "Can't you see I'm homesick?"

"Are you?" His arms came around her, drawing her back into his strong frame. "I thought you were settling in."

"I am," she fibbed because he could be so sweet sometimes, holding her like this. She draped her arms over his as they watched the waves rolling onto the sand.

At least she had her studio in the penthouse to make her feel at home. It was so much her dream workspace she nearly cried with joy every time she entered it. But the time she spent in there was less about pursuing her dream and more about escaping the reality of this new, foreign life she'd been thrust into.

Her other escape was, of course, this. His arms. The feel of him nuzzling into her neck and thickening against her backside sent tingles showering from her scalp into her breasts. Tendrils of warmth wound into her pelvis whenever he so much as glanced at her. None of her worries could impact her when they spent their nights—and mornings and stolen midday moments—kissing and fondling and pleasuring each other into oblivion.

They cushioned the culture shock of what she was going through, but none of it changed the fact that she felt as though she'd won an all-expenses-paid vacation and was enjoying a holiday fling.

How could she settle into a life that wasn't real?

"Why don't I show you where we'll be sleeping?" Saint suggested throatily.

"You're losing your touch," she teased, reaching back to comb her fingers into his silky hair. "I'm surprised you haven't shown me already."

"The maid needed time to unpack your *six* suitcases." He was also teasing, but all Fliss could think was that they weren't her cases. They might've been rose pink where his were black, but they'd been purchased by him and contained clothing he had bought. She'd approved the outfits after being coached on the robust itinerary of appearances and events and the expected dress code for each. One whole case was dedicated to lotions and cosmetics and hair products.

Hand in hand, they climbed the steps back onto the boardwalk. The house came into view in all its dramatic glory, wings reaching out like arms to cradle the glimmering pool.

"This is really beautiful." She paused, absorbing that this property, along with all those other ones she hadn't yet seen, would be his one day.

"I prefer my beach house in California."

She swallowed a semi-hysterical laugh and let him lead her back to the house, then up some stairs to a massive suite decorated in powder blue and silvery white. Fliss took a moment to wander the sitting room with its small dining nook, then peeked onto the balcony with its view of the ocean. The sumptuous bathroom held a claw-footed tub and a shower that could have doubled as a parking garage. The bed was as big as the pool.

Saint came toward her from checking that both doors to the hall were locked, toeing off his shoes along the way, releasing the buttons at his throat as he did.

Her mouth went dry, always. He was so deliberate yet casual in his sexuality.

"This is the junior suite?" she said with a weak smile.

"The main one has separate bedrooms. Not something we'll ever need, hmm?" He used the back of one crooked finger to caress the edge of her jaw.

Fliss had known he was rich, but this was…impossible. *They* were impossible.

"What's wrong?" He tilted her chin up and frowned as he searched her gaze.

She was drowning. Suffocating.

"Nothing," she lied, offering her lips.

Because, when he covered them, she melted into that different reality where she belonged right here, pressed up against him so tightly she imagined she could feel his chest hairs through the fabric of their shirts.

She was growing bolder, learning what he liked, and slid her hand to the front of his trousers to squeeze him.

Saint grunted and backed her toward the bed, tugging at her clothing as he did.

Moments later, they were naked on the sheets, covers thrown back, kissing passionately. "Be inside me," she urged, finding the bold, aroused length that brushed her inner thigh. She guided him to her center. "I need to feel you."

"Careful," he murmured, caressing her briefly before taking control and sliding the damp tip of his erection against her sensitive inner lips. "You're not ready yet. Why the rush? We have two hours before we're expected to make an appearance."

"I know, but…" Everything would change in a few hours. The gossip sites had cottoned on to their relationship. They'd been photographed going out to dinner and shopping, but now they would be scrutinized up close by his peers—she would.

"Let me make it good for you." He began running his hands over her body as though learning her anew, until every skin cell was awakened to his touch. Then he followed with the lazy graze of his lips. Damp kisses made flames of yearning lick through her so she was aching with need by the time he tipped her thighs back and settled his mouth against her most sensitive flesh.

When she was quivering with tension and on the point of breaking, he rose over her. Now he surged into her the way she needed. She had the taste of herself on her tongue as he sealed his lips to hers in a ravishing kiss. The first ripples of climax had her moaning into his mouth, twisting in the agony of supreme pleasure. He held her in that state with his superior strength and the slow, powerful plunge of his sex into hers.

This was where she needed to be, encased in the electric excitement of raw lovemaking, connected to him in a way that transcended the physical.

Now she only needed to touch his shoulder and he knew what she wanted. He rolled onto his back, and she sat up to ride the rhythm he set. She pinched his nipple and played her fingers over where they joined, knowing he liked it.

Saint's lips peeled back, baring his teeth as he fought to hold on to his control. His cheeks were flushed dark with lust. His fingertips would leave bruises where he gripped her hips, matching the ones fading from last night or the time before that.

When the intensity grew too much for her and she closed her eyes and let her head fall back, succumbing to her thunderous orgasm, he arched beneath her, lifting her off the bed as he shouted with his own release.

Fliss slumped weakly upon him in the aftermath, loving the descent almost as much as the pinnacle. She liked feeling his heart pounding against her breast and hearing the rattle of his breath and knowing she'd done that to him. She liked the twitch of him still inside her, slowly relaxing. She liked the lazy way his hands petted her back in such a tender way.

"See?" he murmured. "We even have time for a nap."

She carefully extricated herself from him and drew the sheet up so it fell between them, forming a small barrier because she had realized what was really bothering her.

People were going to look at her and see not just that she lacked an Ivy League education and wasn't rich and famous and couldn't tell a thoroughbred from a pack mule. She could stand that. She didn't care about them enough to care what they thought of her.

But they would see that this was all she had with Saint. Sex. They hadn't known each other long enough to even form something that could be called a true friendship, let alone the warmer connection of real lovers.

Actually, it wasn't even that other people would guess how little she meant to him. It was her. She was realizing that even though he was considerate and generous and gave her such high-voltage orgasms they could power a small country, he didn't really care about her. Not any more than he would about Willow or a stray kitten they found on the beach. He would look after her and be kind to her, but he wouldn't give her his heart.

And that hurt.

Because there wasn't a damned thing she could do about it.

CHAPTER TEN

"THE BELTON-WEBSTERS ARE some of my parents' oldest friends," Saint told Fliss two days later, when an older man sent a friendly salute of his rolled program from another box at the track. Saint tipped his straw boater hat in reply. "Walter is on the board at Grayscale. They have a home in Water Mill. I was at Harvard with their eldest son, Kyle. If we don't see them at lunch, we'll meet them tonight at their party."

They were in the shade, but it was hot enough that Saint wanted to unbutton the cream-colored vest he wore with matching trousers over a pale blue shirt and a navy bowtie.

The clubhouse lounge, which his mother bought out every year as a giant flex, was air-conditioned and had an open bar along with the buffet she provided to her carefully curated guest list. It wasn't enough to have an owner's box, where a server brought them drinks and snacks on demand and they had a front-row seat to the finish line along with the entertainment between races. He and Fliss also had it to themselves. Norma was currently down at the paddock. Saint's father wouldn't turn up until the big race tomorrow.

"That will be nice," Fliss said with a blank smile, feigning enthusiasm.

He'd been introducing her to people nonstop, first at dinner, then a cocktail party appearance, brunch yesterday, an afternoon garden party and another soiree last night. This was all very rote to him, the faces all slotted into their pigeonholes of usefulness.

Fliss was holding up well. Today she wore yet another perfectly on-point outfit that was sufficiently demure to meet the expected dress code but was also flattering enough to stop traffic. Her pink-and-green floral lace dress hugged her figure and fell to her knees in front, draping longer in the back. The sleeves flared at her elbow, and the neckline plunged enough to make the most of her spectacular chest, which Saint had adorned with a vintage gold necklace he'd chosen for its horseshoe charm. Rather than a hat, she wore her hair in a tight bun wrapped in a pink band. A pair of cats-eye sunglasses and bold fuchsia lipstick completed the look.

Despite the sophistication she projected, she was tense, struggling to smile at each new face. Sometimes he caught her stifling a yawn.

"Dad had an affair with Mrs. Belton-Webster," he said, leaning closer to confide.

Fliss swung her head around and tipped her sunglasses down to look over them, eyes glimmering with shock.

That woke her up. Saint shrugged.

"They don't know I know. I figured out that Mom knew about it when they didn't show up to their daughter's wedding. It's all water under the bridge now. I think one of the reasons Mom stayed with Dad was because she was more afraid of losing that friendship than him. Or her place in all of this." He used his chin to gesture to the racetrack. "You'll keep all of that to yourself."

"Of course." She sipped the straw of her mint-julep mocktail. "Why did you tell me if you thought I would repeat it?"

"You seemed bored." And he'd never had a confidante

to tell. He'd had to let things like that fester inside himself, trying to work out what to do, how to react and when to let it go because his parents had.

"I'm not bored. I've just given up on trying to keep it all straight. I mean, I can't get to know every person *and* every horse. You seem to have friends everywhere, though. You came here often growing up? I don't mean the track. The beach house."

"We came here in the summer if we were living in the city, but we lived in Texas and California at different times. I felt like a military brat, making friends, then leaving for a few years, adjusting to a new situation, then coming back and trying to fit in with the old crowd." Eventually, he'd grown tired of trying. "I do know a lot of people. I don't consider any of them friends."

Her liquid-honey gaze searched his, making his chest itch.

The bell rang.

"Oh!" Fliss swung her attention to the track. "They're off."

At least she was having fun with the betting. She'd been appalled when he had told her he would stake her ten grand. He had threatened to pick her horses himself if she didn't spend it, so she had sat down with the program and her tarot cards, making her selections before they'd even arrived to glimpse the horses.

She'd won the first race, but her bet had been so small, she'd only come away with eight hundred dollars, which she'd tried to give to him.

"Double down," he had insisted, so he knew she had at least that much riding on this race. He'd dropped five grand, and things were not looking good.

"Which one is yours?" he asked.

Fliss's hand came out to grasp his arm. Otherwise, she

wasn't moving, wasn't breathing. She was transfixed by the sprinting horses.

"The one in front?" he guessed, starting to grin as her expression began to glow.

"Shh." Her grip crushed his sleeve.

It was like watching her as she approached climax. Her breath was uneven. Her breasts trembled. Anticipation radiated off her, tightening his own nerves.

It was titillating enough to set hooks into Saint's libido, but he was also amused in a completely non-carnal way. She was mesmerizing, looking so sexy and cutely rapt at the same time. He was twitching into arousal and wanting this win for her in a way he'd never wanted anything, just so he could see her reaction.

If the race had gone one second longer, he would have been fully hard, but there was a collective roar. Fliss screamed in triumph and leapt into his arms, crashing her curves against him, filling his senses with floral and citrus notes that he was learning were innately her. She was warm and soft beneath the thin layer of crepe, light and lovely. Her wild excitement provoked a rusty scrape of laughter in his throat, one that stalled when he noticed his father had turned up after all. He was watching them.

Saint's first, most primal instinct was to draw her protectively closer, but another more harshly learned response recognized that he had revealed a weakness.

He set her back a step. "How much did you win?"

"Enough to pay you back your stake." She was jubilant, smile wide and eyes bright as she straightened the sunglasses that had been knocked askew.

"I don't want it back. It's for you to play all weekend," he reminded.

She did pay him back, though, since she had doubled her money by the end of the day.

"Beginner's luck," she claimed that evening when they were on the terrace at the Belton-Websters'. Word had got around that Fliss had been on a hot streak today. Everyone wanted to know her secret. "Also my lucky horseshoe." She picked up the pendant she wore.

"Have you looked at tomorrow's races?" a middle-aged man asked her.

"I'm saving most of my money for Paprika's Tuft," she said, mentioning Norma's thoroughbred. "But there are a couple others that look promising."

"Show me." The man had his program and a pencil in hand.

Saint excused himself to the bar and was returning with a fresh drink when he ran into Kyle, the son of their host that he'd told Fliss about. Kyle was newly divorced and a little drunker than was wise.

"So that's her, the one who got you in trouble with Dad and the rest of the board?" Kyle snickered, his attention twisted to where Fliss still had her head together with the older man. "I see the attraction. *Nice.*" His hand came up to his chest, cupping imaginary breasts.

"That's your one shot, Kyle. Leave it there, and I'll forget we had this conversation." It was a lie. Saint would never forget. He wanted to blacken both his eyes.

"She's a *housemaid.* You're not serious about her," Kyle scoffed. "Let me know when you're done with her, though."

"We're getting married." Saint squared himself against the man, planting his feet. "She's going to be the mother of my child." He blindly reached to the table beside him to set down his drink.

He missed. The smash of glass on the stones silenced the din of conversation, but Saint didn't look anywhere but at Kyle's disbelieving smirk.

"Swallow what you just said, or I'll shove those words back down your throat for you," Saint warned.

"She's *pregnant*?" Kyle guffawed into the silence. "Man, I gave you a lot more credit than you deserved."

The heel of Saint's palm hit the middle of Kyle's chest before he realized that he was reacting. It was a shove, not a strike, but it was strong enough to send Kyle stumbling backward. His arms flailed as he hit the edge of the pool, then he was plummeting backward into it. The splash washed across nearby shoes, making everyone gasp and step back.

"Saint!" His mother's voice cut through the murmur of shock.

Kyle was slapping at the water, clumsily swimming to the edge, swearing a blue streak.

Saint resisted the urge to stand on the man's head. He looked for Fliss and found her staring at him with the same appalled shock as everyone else.

All heads turned to her now, making her the center of attention as everyone reevaluated her dress, which was three long layers of pleated ruffles from a single shoulder strap, disguising her thickening waistline.

"She *does* bet on the right horse, doesn't she?" an amused voice gurgled.

"Shut up," Saint said in the direction of the voice.

Fliss pivoted on one sandal and walked into the house.

"Fliss!" Saint caught up to her in the music room.

Fliss was so furious she couldn't even look at him. "I need the ladies' room."

"You're not locking yourself in a bathroom," he said through his teeth, looming closer.

"I *will* use the loo when I need one!" She paused long

enough to glare a warning at him. "Take away every other bloody right I have, but not that one."

Heads swiveled in their direction, the level of acute curiosity sizzling on the air like electricity building for a lightning strike.

"It's this way," he said tightly and directed her through an archway and into a short corridor.

Tempted as she was to crawl out the window, she flushed and washed her hands and came out a few minutes later.

Saint was leaning on the wall, arms folded, expression grim. He straightened. "The car is waiting outside."

"Oh, are we leaving?" she asked with facetious surprise.

"You want to stay?" He held her simmering gaze without flinching.

"Does it matter what I want?" She stalked ahead of him to the door.

He waited until they were in the back of the car to say belligerently, "I didn't like what he said."

"I didn't like what *you* said. Can I push you in the pool?"

"Will it get us over this spat as quickly as possible?"

"Is that what this is? Tell me I'm overreacting, Saint. *I dare you.*"

He waited a beat, then spoke in an ultra-calm voice that was so condescending, she wanted to hit him. "The news was going to come out eventually."

"I asked you for one thing." Fliss's voice shook despite her best efforts to keep it level. She removed her necklace and earrings and dropped them into the cup holder that was closest to him in the console between them. For good measure, she toed off her shoes and pushed them toward him with her foot.

"Really? You're going to go barefoot to prove a point? It was his disrespect toward you that got under my skin."

Saint was speaking through his teeth again. "Now they know where you stand in my estimation."

"Do they?" she cried. "You have no idea how hard this is for me, do you? That I have to use *your* money to pretend I belong here when I absolutely do not and everyone knows it? They see straight through me, but I soldier on, pretending for your sake that I can't tell they can barely bring themselves to speak to me. *I'm* trying not to embarrass *you*. And I keep telling myself that it's okay that you don't know how hard this all is because you *can't* know. You've never been in this situation. So I accept your ignorance."

He opened his mouth, and she held up a finger.

"It's the part where you don't *care* how hard this is for me—and just went ahead and made it harder—that I can't forgive. Yes, I know exactly where I stand in your estimation, Saint. Guess where you stand in mine?"

They didn't speak again until they were back in their suite, but all Fliss said was, "I'm going to bed." She removed her makeup and did just that.

She was so tired she fell into a deep sleep immediately, but after a few hours, her turmoil of emotions conjured an old dream that was nightmare and memory combined. Granny was gathering her into her arms, speaking before she'd fully awaked.

I'm sorry, pet. I'm so sorry. At least you were safe here with me and not in the car with them.

"Fliss, wake up." Saint's voice was a hard snap that had her gasping and fighting the blankets and his arms, trying to sit up. "Are you okay?" His hand slid across her back as he gathered her closer, but she pushed away from him, heart pounding, skin clammy.

"Don't." She realized her cheeks were wet and reached to the nightstand for a tissue.

"Was it just a nightmare or...?"

Just? All of this was a nightmare!

She grabbed her pillow and swung it around, managing to catch him by surprise enough that he took a face full of silk and feathers before he cursed and grabbed the pillow, throwing it off the bed.

"You sounded like you were in pain," he said with fresh frustration. "Tell me you're okay. Is the baby okay?"

"The baby is fine. *I* am not okay. I thought I could count on you a *little*. But all you did was tell everyone the only reason you're keeping me around is because your previous lover sabotaged your birth control."

"I did not say that. *No one* knows that part of it."

"*I* know it!" And recalling that particular detail provoked a fresh sense of abandonment that was so acute she could hardly bear it.

Fliss rose and went into the bathroom for a robe, tying it over the pajamas she wore.

"Where are you going?" he asked as she ghosted through the dim room toward the sitting area.

"I want some tea."

"I'll phone for some."

"Oh, my *gawd*. This maid is already up." She slid the belt of the robe higher on her waist so it was more comfortable. "There's no use waking another to boil a kettle." She resisted the urge to slam the door on her way out.

By the time she was filling the kettle in the kitchen—which was such a beautiful space of cornflower blue and daffodil yellow it shouldn't even be cooked in—Saint was arriving.

She pretended to ignore him, but how could she when his white T-shirt hugged his shoulders and chest and his pajama bottoms lovingly draped the firm muscles of his buttocks? How dare he be so mouthwatering and such a complete toad at the same time?

Since she'd already had her daily allotment of black tea, she searched out the peppermint and dropped a bag into a cup while she waited for the kettle.

He clicked the button to warm the griddle, then opened the fridge to take out cheddar cheese. He buttered two slices of sour dough, then set them face down on the griddle, topped them with cheese, then topped each with another slice of bread, butter side up.

"I didn't know you were a chef," she said with only a hint of sarcasm.

"Grilled cheese, eggs and I can stick a banana in a bowl of ice cream and call it a sundae."

"If you plan to cook that sundae, I have notes. Do you want tea?" she asked as the kettle started to whistle.

He shook his head and stayed at the stove while she sat down at the island with her cup. She wasn't hungry—or any less mad at him—but she was fascinated enough by his economical movements to watch him fry a sandwich. He plated them, cut them in half, then added a blob of ketchup to each plate before sliding one toward her.

"I am on your side, Fliss," he said as he took the chair next to her. "You can count on me."

She winced, pained at how much she wanted to believe that but just couldn't.

"You can," he insisted.

"Don't sound so insulted," she mumbled, blowing across the cup she cradled in her cold hands. "Life happens. I should have been able to rely on my parents, but they were struck by a drunk driver on a blind corner."

And were gone. Just *gone*. Then she'd moved in with Granny, which meant the friends she'd had at school were also gone. Making new ones had felt impossible when she'd been so sad. As a teen, she'd finally gotten in with an in-crowd—who had turned her out after her breakup with her puerile knob of a boyfriend. Then Granny had gotten so sick and died on her, and even her loose friendships in London had evaporated after her scandal.

Counting on people had been stamped out of her DNA. She had herself. That was the only person she really believed in and, honestly, she made some pretty stupid decisions sometimes, too.

"I've already started the paperwork to ensure you'll be taken care of, should anything happen to me," Saint said gravely. "Dad has accepted that the baby is mine. Our child will inherit everything that is coming to me. You'll always have access to whatever you need, Fliss."

"This is not about money, Saint." She set down her cup. "Granny was right there, holding me when she told me my parents were dead. I still felt abandoned. That's why I wanted to do this on my own. So I wouldn't count on you, then wind up disappointed."

His cough-curse sounded as though it had been punched out of him.

"*You're* self-sufficient," she pointed you. "Why do you begrudge me wanting that for myself? Instead you want me to rely on you. You made me come live with you and become dependent on you, then you threw away my trust like it doesn't even matter."

"I brought you here because I want you here," he insisted.

"For the baby, I know," she said on a sigh that was more a sob of anguish. "I can see how important it is that our baby grows up like this so they don't feel like I do—as though they're visiting another planet. I'm trying to adapt, Saint, I really am. And I'm trying to keep my expectations low where you're concerned. I don't expect you to love me. I don't expect anything from you except—" She cut herself off.

"What?" he prompted.

"Nothing," she decided, pushing her plate away. "I thought I could expect…kindness? Regard? But I have to find those things in myself. I know that." Why was life so bloody lonely? "I'm going back to bed."

"Did you hear what I just said?" His gritted voice stopped her. "I brought you here because I want *you* here."

"For sex, yes. I know." She turned and put out a pleading hand. "Don't make it sound like more than it is. That's not fair to me."

"It's the truth, Fliss. Yes, I brought you here because of the baby, but the baby isn't even real to me yet. It's a concept. I feel…protective, I guess? I'm anxious for a positive outcome and bothered that I have so little control over that. Mostly it's a gray fog that I don't know how to navigate, so I'm not even thinking about it. I had options, though. I could have arranged protection for you or did as you asked and claimed the baby wasn't mine. I could have worked out a custody arrangement and hired a nanny to cover my side of it. God knows I know what constitutes a good one of those, having been raised by them myself. I didn't want to do any of those things. I wanted *you* here."

"For se—"

"For more than sex," he near-shouted, rising off his stool.

"Keep your voice down," she hissed, hugging herself and looking to the ceiling.

"Yes, I want to have sex with you. You're in the same bed with me. You know it's amazing. That's why you want it, too. But it's more than that, Fliss." He pushed his hair off his forehead and left his hand on his head as though trying to keep the top of his skull from popping off. "You're damned right I want you to rely on me. I don't know what

else to give you. And I don't know how to deal with someone who doesn't want *things*. Who only cares if she's under
a dry roof, not how big it is or which neighborhood it's located in."

Fliss bit her lips because they felt so unsteady and
searched his tortured expression, wary of believing him
because she really, really didn't want to be disappointed
in him again, but she could tell how much this was cost-
ing him to admit.

"You got under my skin from the second I saw you. I
call it lust because if I call it something else, it feels dangerous," he admitted gruffly. "It means that a drunk I see
once every three years can say something about you that
makes me act like a Neanderthal. You think I behave that
way every day?" He waved his hand in a vague direction.
"Never. When I say people know how I feel about you
now, I mean they know they can get to me through you.
It's terrifying."

She didn't want to be moved in any way by that, but she
was. A little. She crushed the sleeve of her robe in her fist,
emotions crashing around in her chest like storm waves.

"Do you see how insulting that is, though?" she asked.
"That you don't want to care about me? That you resent
that you do?"

"You don't want to care about me," Saint shot back, stab-
bing the air between them with his finger. "You don't trust
me. You don't want to rely on me. You're only here for the
baby. You think I don't know you have an exit strategy? If
you search for train tickets to Toronto, where Mrs. Bhamra's sister lives, I'm going to get ads for them in my feed.
How the hell am I supposed to trust *you* when you keep
one foot out the door?"

"She's talking about visiting," Fliss mumbled, looking

down at the elegant arcs of gold painted against her cuticles on her otherwise pink nails.

"I shouldn't have blurted out that you're pregnant. I know that," he said begrudgingly. "You're right that people haven't been taking you seriously. That's on me. I have a history of not taking any of my relationships seriously. But I said it so Kyle would know this is different. Now everyone knows this is different. And yes, maybe it was also a move to lock you in. Not consciously, but... I don't know." He ran his hand over his face. "I want you here, Fliss. You. And I hate myself for hurting you. I'm sorry."

Oh, what was she supposed to do now? Her anger was washing away like footprints in sand, leaving her feeling more vulnerable than ever.

"Can we at least not be angry anymore?" He held out a hand.

"What do *you* have to be angry about?" she grumbled as she stepped close enough to let him draw her into his arms.

"You clocked me with a pillow, for starters." He hugged her securely. "Disparaged my cooking skills. Accused me of human rights violations."

"Pregnant women need the loo. And I was moving the pillow. It's not my fault your face got in the way."

"My mistake. See? I'm getting the hang of relationships."

She hummed a small laugh as she tucked her face against his chest, wanting to stay in this moment of reconciliation forever. But.

"We have to go to the track tomorrow, don't we?" she said with dread.

"No," he said firmly, dropping his arms away from her. "I've already told my pilot we're flying back to the city first thing."

"Saint. Your mom will be devastated if we don't watch the race. If her horse doesn't win, who will console her?

Your dad? It will be awkward for me, I know, but it won't get less awkward if I put it off, so let's get it over with."

"You think Paprika's Tuft won't win?" he asked with a frown. "What did your cards say?"

"I don't ask questions I don't want the answer to."

He narrowed his eyes. "What do your cards say about us?"

"I haven't asked."

CHAPTER ELEVEN

PAPRIKA'S TUFT LOST by a nose. Norma was disappointed but mollified by the quarter of a million dollars that was the second-prize purse.

Fliss had another good day with two wins and a shrewd win-place-show cover of bets in the final race. Her biggest return came when the man who had shadowed her bets gave her his business card.

"Call my assistant the next time you're on your way to Paris. She'll have accounts opened at whichever boutiques you like to visit."

"Oh, that's kind of you, but I couldn't." She looked to Saint, nonplussed.

"I'm up four hundred thousand dollars today. You ought to have a cut of those winnings," the man insisted.

"Take the card," Saint said mildly. "Send him your business plan. See if he'd like to bet on *you*. Fliss designs lingerie," he told the man.

"Ah. Yes. I'd like to see that proposal."

His immediate interest plucked against her sense of not working hard enough to earn such an advantage, but it was a nice outcome to end what had been a tense day. She'd been braced for the worst, but it hasn't been as uncomfortable as Fliss had feared. There'd been too much action and, thankfully, the drunk who'd provoked Saint last night was nursing his hangover and didn't turn up at the track.

They returned to New York later that evening to headlines about her pregnancy, but a political scandal was already overshadowing it.

A small honeymoon period ensued, one that filled Fliss with optimism. She did send her proposal to her potential investor, then flew to California with Saint, where she was accidentally photographed in one of her own bathing suits. Her bump was growing obvious and the rest of her was filling out, too. She wore a seashell-patterned bikini top that tied between her breasts. The matching bottoms were high-waisted and had seashell-shaped cutouts on either hip, each outlined with dark blue piping. She also wore a wide-brimmed hat that she was holding on her head as she tipped her head back and laughed at something Saint had said.

It wasn't a lewd photo. The suit was only partially visible beneath her filmy cover-up, but it was labeled "body positive" and captured an intimate moment between them, so it went viral. All the online influencers wanted to know where her ensemble had been purchased, and when it was identified as her own design, her potential business partner leapt on it, offering her an obscene amount of money to get a line of bathing suits to market as quickly as possible.

From then on, she and Saint both had busy days. While he assembled his team for his security project and oversaw that along with his regular responsibilities she hired her own team, including a buyer in Asia who began sending her amazing fabric samples.

Amid their heavy work schedules, they began hosting dinners. The first was a fun mash-up of his nerdy programmers and her fashion geeks that ended in makeovers and at least one new romance. Then, Fliss began finding her feet with Saint's social circle. They attended cocktail parties and galas. People were more gracious now that they realized she was carrying the next heir to Grayscale and likely to be at these events more often. Fliss didn't kid herself that it was more personal than that, but at least she was growing more comfortable in these settings.

The only hiccup occurred when they were invited to spend an evening in the private box of a celebrity to watch a basketball game. The evening had barely started when there was the sound of a brash female voice calling out drunken greetings, but even as Fliss turned to look, Saint was moving between them, blocking her from seeing the woman. He put a word in someone's ear, and moments later, they were heading to the car.

"Julie," Saint explained with a curl of his lip. "I stopped short of a restraining order when I sent her the cease and desist, but there's no reason either of us need to be in the same room with her. Do you mind?"

"No." They hadn't had a night to themselves in ages. She was more than glad that their evening turned into a cuddle on the couch and some unhurried lovemaking. At times like this, everything about her new life was perfect.

Except…they didn't talk about the baby very often. Fliss was eighteen weeks along and had begun looking through books of names. She also discussed with Saint which room she thought would be best as a nursery. He was agreeable but always seemed a little reticent, which worried her.

He was busy, though. He'd been curtailing travel for her sake, so she wasn't exactly neglected. Also, this pregnancy was happening to her in a very physical way. She had been feeling small internal flutters lately and her baby bump was growing more pronounced, but Saint had yet to feel the baby move.

She had hoped by now he would start to see the baby as more real, but when she pressed his hand to her abdomen in the shower and asked "Can you feel that?" he shook his head.

It was a very subtle sensation inside her, so she wasn't surprised, only disappointed because she wanted him to be as excited as she was. But he wasn't.

"Are you sure there's even a baby in there?" he joked lightly, circling his soapy palm around her navel.

"You think I'm packing on weight for show?"

"Pack it on. I'm not complaining." His lathered hands climbed to cup the weighty swells of her breasts. "I thought you were hot as hell the first time I saw you, but I'm liable to keep you pregnant for years, purely to enjoy this benefit."

"We all need goals," she drawled, amused but also heartened when he spoke as though their future together was a given.

She wanted to believe they would marry and enjoy a long life together, but she also knew the baby would change everything. They would have a whole other human being between them. They wouldn't make love as often or sleep in or go out as much.

There was that other, deeper worry inside her, too. She'd had her world come crumbling down too many times to trust that this new life she was building would last. He might find it threatening that she had contingency plans, and she might have already sat with him and his father as they went over paperwork that explained how the baby's trust would work if something happened to Saint, but all it did was remind her that something *could* happen to him.

She stored copies of the paperwork in a safe-deposit box and opened an account in her own name, one that she used to continue paying rent on her bedsit in Nottingham. She knew Saint took it personally because she told him about it and watched his expression stiffen, but having a fallback position gave her comfort.

Somehow eight weeks of living with him had slipped past and it was time for her twenty-week scan.

"Willow is sending contact details for a real estate agent who will meet with you as soon as we arrive in London," Saint said, pulling her concentration from trying to ignore the fact that her bladder was about to burst. "I'll need two days at the office, then we can spend the rest of the week looking at properties."

He had delayed his trip until after this scan, to be sure she was safe to fly and could come with him, but they were going straight to the jet from here.

"Okay," she said through gritted teeth.

Thankfully, the technician entered with a friendly smile.

Saint took her hand and gave the screen his attention, but Fliss still had the impression he was only being polite and continued to hold himself at a distance where the baby was concerned.

The woman applied jelly to Fliss's belly and began moving the wand, explaining they typically only used the 3D imaging if this traditional two-dimensional black-and-white imaging revealed a concern. She began pointing to silvery lines and blobs, explaining she was measuring the skull and spine. She pointing out the four chambers of the baby's heart.

"Oh, that's a good one." A pair of feet appeared. They were so clear, it was as though the baby had left its footprints in black sand. She snapped a photo.

Fliss became aware of her hand feeling compressed and glanced at Saint.

His eyes were glued to the screen, his expression frozen in a state of fascinated wonder. He didn't seem to realize he was crushing her fingers.

"Saint?"

He dragged his gaze to hers and swallowed.

"Fliss…" He couldn't seem to find words.

She was so touched, she welled up. Her heart grew so big in her chest, it hurt. This was what she had wanted from him. "I know, right?"

His mouth opened, but he only shook his head helplessly and looked back to the screen.

He was still quiet when they were in the car. She waited until they were in the air to ask tentatively, "Are you all right?"

"Not really." He rarely drank these days, mostly in solidarity to her teetotalling, but he sipped a double scotch before saying, "I just found out we're having a baby."

Fliss couldn't help chuckling. "My bad. I should have told you sooner."

"It wasn't a person until today. It was a date on a calendar that I needed to keep clear. It was decisions about furniture and words that Legal needed to write into some documents."

She took his hand in both her own, able to sympathize with his shock because it had taken time for her, too.

He wove his fingers with hers, staring at their joined hands.

"Don't take this the wrong way, but it was easier to think of your pregnancy as a project with an outcome, not the creation of another human," he admitted in a very quiet voice. "Now it's someone I have to worry about. Someone who becomes me. He—" He slid her a look. "Did you think it was a boy?"

They had told the tech they didn't want to know the sex, but Fliss rolled her eyes at how obvious it had been.

"I mean, I'll support whatever gender they feel they are, but yeah. For now, I'll focus on the blue pages in the naming book, not the pink ones. But what do you mean the baby becomes you?"

"Caught in the middle." His thumb rubbed the back of her hand with a little too much abrasiveness to be comfortable.

"I won't use him against you," she vowed. "I know that's hard for you to believe, but I won't."

He nodded absently, gaze fixed on the middle distance.

"You don't have to be like your dad, you know. The company doesn't have to be your sole focus. You can make other choices."

You can love your family. Love us. Love me.

She didn't say it. She was a little put out with herself for thinking it. For yearning for it. They were in a very good place. She didn't want to want more from him.

But she did. Because she was falling in love with him.

"I know," he murmured and brought her hand up to kiss the back of it.

She waited, but he didn't say anything more than that.

They were served a meal soon after, and she moved into the stateroom when she finished, wanting a nap before they landed, but her heart was still panging with yearning.

Fliss didn't know how Saint managed the time change so easily. He rose to shower a few hours after they arrived, whispering that she should continue sleeping. It felt like the middle of the night, so she did exactly that. Granted, Saint wasn't growing a whole other human, but despite her nap on the flight, she was exhausted and thankful for the lazy day where she only had to meet with the estate agent for an hour in the afternoon.

They had dinner with some of his London executives that evening. They were photographed going into the restaurant, but she was used to the attention now. Aside from dressing strategically to promote fellow designers, she ignored the cameras and shouting.

The next day, Saint arranged a car to take her to Nottingham to visit with Mrs. Bhamra. This was for Fliss, since he was busy working all day. They would have a proper dinner with the woman and her family later in the week so Saint could meet everyone.

Fliss picked up a text from Saint as she was leaving the hotel.

I asked the driver to bring you to me on your way out of the city.

At the office? Why?

You'll see.

A few minutes later, the car pulled into a posh square in Knightsbridge. Saint waited outside a beautiful town house.

"Are we looking at a house?" she asked as he helped her from the car.

"No. You look lovely."

"Thank you." She picked up her saucy ballet flat with its colorful pink ribbon, giving the hem of her stretchy knit skirt a lift. The powder blue hugged her bump and hips before falling to her knees. A lacy white crop top with long sleeves and a scalloped hem covered her arms and upper torso.

Saint brought her into the foyer where a guard touched his hat in greeting. At the elevator, Saint tapped in a code.

"This is starting to feel like a secret location for spies or— Oh."

The doors opened into a sparkling wonderland. A jewelry shop. A very, very exclusive one if the thick glass and security precautions and displayed tiaras were anything to go on.

A woman introduced herself as Ms. Smythe. She had long black hair, bright mauve lips and vintage-style sunglasses with yellow lenses that sat low on her nose.

"Ah. My earrings found their owner after all," Ms. Smythe said with warm approval. "They suit you."

"Oh. Thank you. I do love them," Fliss said sincerely, touching one self-consciously.

"Please make yourself comfortable." She waved at a love seat with a low table before it.

Fliss's heart clenched as she saw the array of diamond rings in a specialized black tray waiting on the table.

"I've prepared a selection for you to peruse, but it's only a starting point. I can also create a custom piece once I have a sense of your taste. Shall I fetch some nonalcoholic bubbly?"

"Yes." Saint nodded at Ms. Smythe. "Give us a moment, if you don't mind."

He brought Fliss to the table. She could hardly breathe, realizing what this moment was. Her whole body grew hot, her cheeks stung and her eyes welled.

"I keep thinking," Saint began gravely while circling his hand in her lower back.

She looked up at him, wanting to capture and memorize everything about his proposal. He was as handsome as ever, still looking freshly shaved and crisp from his morning shower. His suit was a lightweight sage green, his collar bone white, as was his tie. His mouth was twitching as though he wasn't as steady on the inside as he looked on the outside, and his dark coffee eyes were so compelling she could have fallen into them.

"For the baby's sake..." he continued in a voice that was growing husky.

For the baby's sake.

She knew that wasn't the best reason to marry, but it was a good one. She wanted more commitment between them. She already knew that she wanted to spend her life with him. She loved him.

Oh, God. She loved him.

Her insides felt as though they tilted and glinted, reflecting rainbows through her as she accepted all the lovely colors of love he provoked—the bright yellows and laughing greens, the passionate reds, the introspective blues and the endless fire of pure, white love.

"We should have more commitment between us. You're shaking." He reached for her hand. "I should have warned you this morning. Asked. I am asking," he said wryly. "Will you marry me, Fliss?"

"Yes," she whispered, blinking to clear her welling eyes, so suffused in the power of her love for him she could hardly speak.

He drew in a breath the way he did sometimes when she touched him intimately, as though the pleasure was more intense than he could bear. He pulled her into his arms and kissed her, mouth hot and hungry but tender and sweet. Thorough and...loving?

As the fires of arousal began to catch in both of them, he drew back, rueful.

"Let's pick a ring."

She swiped under her eyes and drew a breath, trying to catch hold of herself. It wasn't the engagement filling her with so much joy, though. It was this feeling. She was in love. She had found her person.

He is the one.

"They don't have prices," she whispered as she picked up one at random.

"This is not a place for bargain hunters," Saint said drily. "I like this one."

He offered an emerald-cut diamond the size of her thumbnail. A pair of trapezoid-cut diamonds flanked either side. The setting was simple yet different enough to be eye-catching. It was stunning and elegant.

Fliss instantly loved it but made herself scan for something that looked less expensive. All the rings were incredibly beautiful and tastefully extravagant and had to be worth millions of pounds. He wasn't really going to give her a ring like this, was he? What happened to two months' salary?

"Try it on."

Her hand was still trembling. She let him push it onto her finger, but it wouldn't go over her knuckle.

"My fingers are swollen." It was still morning, and all of her was puffy these days.

"I'll resize it." Ms. Smythe appeared with a tray that held two filled flutes of sparkling amber liquid.

"But after the baby comes…"

"I'll do it again." Ms. Smythe handed her a glass, then offered the other to Saint. "It only takes a day or two. It's no trouble."

Fliss didn't know a lot about fine metals, but she knew platinum couldn't be melted down and used again.

"Unless you'd prefer something with color? This yellow diamond would suit your skin tone," Ms. Smythe said.

"I actually like this one." Fliss was still trying to force the ring over her knuckle. It was the one Saint had picked out, and looking into its facets was like staring into an infinity mirror.

That was what she wanted to believe, that he was promising her infinity.

"Excellent. Congratulations. Let me get my gauge."

A few minutes later, they were on the sidewalk again,

standing in the shade of the building while they kissed again.

"Say hello to Mrs. Bhamra for me," Saint said. "Ask her if she'd like to fly back with us. We can drop her in Toronto."

"It's short notice. She might want to wait until next time, but I'll mention it. Thank you. Um…" She was aware of the driver standing at the open the door of the car, waiting for her.

"We'll have dinner tonight, just us. To celebrate." Saint cupped her cheek and dropped a last, lingering kiss onto her lips.

She smiled shyly. Should she say it? She felt it. Meant it. Wanted him to know it.

"I—" Her throat started to close with nerves. "I love you," she confided in a hushed voice.

The relaxed warmth in his expression vanished. The cool, remote man appeared, the one who only thought in binary logic and looked like his dad and said things like, "You don't have to say that."

Her heart was instantly pinched in a vise. "I mean it."

"Well, you shouldn't." His hard brows came together. "We agreed that wasn't something we should expect."

She wasn't asking for his love. That was what she wanted to say. But she was, she realized. She wanted her feelings to be returned.

And they weren't.

"I just thought you should know," she mumbled and turned away to dive into the car.

"Fliss." Saint stopped the driver from closing the door.

"You can't help how you feel, Saint. Or don't feel," she added stiffly. "Mrs. Bhamra will worry if I'm late."

"Damn it." He should have handled that better.

Saint went back to the office, but he couldn't concentrate. He was snappish enough that people gave him a wide berth. A few hours later, he went back to an empty hotel room and texted Fliss.

Are you on your way back?

I'm at my bedsit.

His guts turned to concrete.

Why?

I need some time here.

He swore again, refusing to ask how much time. Was she staying the night? Should he go to her? And say what? He hadn't been built to love anyone, not even himself.

He didn't even know how to *be* loved. The few times his father had shown him something like fatherly affection had been around things that measured up in Ted's estimation of what was important. Did Saint grasp a complex concept? Did he provide a solution that could be monetized? Then yes, Saint was valuable to his father.

As for his mother... Her love had been a needy variety that pulled so hard Saint had never felt like he could possibly be enough to alleviate that emotional chasm inside her.

This was what he had wanted to avoid with Fliss, this sensation of expectations beyond his ability to fulfill. Of not being enough. Of failing.

And he was angry that she'd put this on him. Was she doing it on purpose? Putting herself out of his reach to teach him some sort of lesson? Holding their baby *hostage*...

He pinched the bridge of his nose, not wanting to believe

Fliss would do something like that, but it was the behavior he knew too well from his own upbringing.

Saint and I will be staying at the cottage.

Saint will be coming with me to Texas.

Why don't you spend more time with me at the stables?

Why are you wasting time at the stables when you should be studying?

As recently as a few days ago, his father had asked him scathingly, *Why are you letting that woman distract you? You got what you wanted, so get to work.*

She's pregnant had been his response, but Ted had only snorted with disinterest.

Fliss was more than pregnant. She was carrying their baby.

When Saint had seen those shadows and lines moving on the screen, slowly piecing themselves together into a full picture of the baby Fliss carried, he'd felt it like a punch to the heart. The baby was only the size of a banana, the technician had said, but the magnitude of its effect on him had been world-altering.

He and Fliss had *made* that baby. He was going to be a father. Why was he distracted? Because all he could think about was them. How he needed both of them close so he could ensure they were safe. He wasn't so dependent that he needed to be with Fliss every minute of every day, but he damned well liked knowing he was going back to her every night. Anytime he held her, even if it was only her hand, things inside him settled.

And now all he could think about was seeing their baby. Holding him. Watching him explore the world with Fliss's humor and curiosity.

That was why he'd proposed to her, so they would have that deeper promise to stay together. He wanted her in his life every day. He wanted them to be a unit.

He should have known she would want his heart, though, given how sensitive and emotionally open she was.

Did she not realize his heart was a shriveled raisin of a thing, not worth having?

Frustrated, he paced into the bedroom, noting with relief that she hadn't taken anything more than her purse today.

She must have done a reading while she'd still been in bed because her cards were on the nightstand, not even tied into their velvet cloth. What had she been asking? he wondered. She had told him she didn't ask questions she didn't want the answer to, which was why she hadn't asked about their relationship.

He didn't even believe in these things, but it irritated him that she had said that. He interpreted it as distrust. She lacked faith in their relationship and didn't want her doubts to be confirmed by her cards.

Was his faith in her any better, though? Yes, he had proposed, but when she had told him she loved him, he'd taken it as a personal attack.

From the beginning, he'd known that if he couldn't give her what she needed emotionally, he might have to let her go. Was that what he was supposed to do? What in hell was coming next for them?

He never touched her cards. She had asked him not to, but with the questions ringing in his mind, he impulsively turned over the top card.

Death.

His phone rang, kick-starting his stalled heart.

CHAPTER TWELVE

FLISS'S MORNING READING had encouraged her to say good-bye today.

She had thought she had understood it, especially when Saint had proposed, then things had ended on that sour note at the car and she'd been thrown into confusion.

Slowly, however, as Mrs. Bhamra promised her a knitted blanket for the baby and Fliss visited Granny at the cemetery, she knew which goodbye was necessary and inevitable.

She told her landlords that movers would come in the next few months. She paid them in advance and packed up a handful of personal items, then said her goodbye.

She said goodbye to the person she'd been when she'd lived here in Nottingham, the one who'd held herself back on so many levels and worried she wasn't good enough as a designer or wasn't entitled to live a bigger life.

She said goodbye to thinking that it was impossible for Saint to want *her* when he could have anyone.

He did want her. He'd said it in thousands of ways. She had kept this flat and all her ties here because she hadn't wanted to believe in him. In them. It was scary, especially when he hadn't said *I love you* back to her.

How many other declarations and guarantees did she need, though? He made her life richer in countless ways.

Yes, materially, but he had given her a *baby*. He made her laugh. He coddled her and supported her dreams and built her confidence in herself. He cared about her very deeply. She knew he did.

He wanted to be her person, her safety net, and he couldn't be that person for her if she didn't let him. She had to step off the ledge and have faith that he would catch her. That was how she would learn to trust that he would.

So, even though she was hurt, she was closing out her life here for good so she could make a new one with him.

She had just finished labeling the boxes she wanted shipped to her in New York when he texted.

Dad had a stroke. I'm flying back.

"What?" she cried and hit the button to call him. "I'm coming back now. Don't leave without me," she said as soon as he answered.

"Why?" he asked flatly. "Because you think I'm going to inherit everything now? He's not dead."

It was a slap in the face delivered from three hours away.

"You're upset," she said shakily, as much to remind herself as him. "Have a maid pack my things from the hotel. I'll meet you at the airport."

He ended the call, so she had no idea if he would do as she'd asked.

Saint was stewing in his seat on the tarmac, hating himself for what he'd said to Fliss.

He should have called her back, but he'd been fielding calls from his mother and doctors and the board as word had spread that his father was in hospital.

When he saw the headlights come through the gate toward his jet, he let out a sigh of profound relief that she'd gotten here safely. As much as he'd resented the pilot delaying takeoff—because Fliss had called Willow and told them to hold the plane—he was still shaken by that damned Death card, worried it had been meant for her.

"Willow doesn't work for you," he snapped as she came aboard and took her seat next to him.

"Willow has your best interests at heart, same as I do."

"Do you?" he scoffed. Why the hell was he talking to her this way? Had his father actually died and started inhabiting his body?

"You may go ahead and be an ass to me if you need to let off steam," Fliss said with cool patience. "But I didn't cause your father's stroke." She closed her belt and gave the attendant a tight smile to indicate she was ready for takeoff.

He was being an ass. Why?

Because she hadn't been there when it had happened. He'd thought she was leaving him, and he'd been so hurt, so cast adrift he hadn't known how to deal with it except to go on the attack.

She *was* here, though. Exactly where he wanted her, expression stiff with hurt.

"I am upset," he admitted. "Even if he survives, he'll be too ill to work. The board has already named me interim president. This isn't the way I wanted it to happen. I wanted him to choose me." God, that sounded puerile. "To trust me. To give me *something* that showed—" He couldn't say it.

His father had withheld the same words that Saint had. God, that hurt to acknowledge. He was *exactly* like his father. And if his father didn't survive, that meant Saint wouldn't ever make his peace with the old man.

Fliss's soft hand covered his.

His throat tightened. His eyes grew hot. He used his thumb to pinch her fingers to his palm. He didn't deserve her kindness and wondered what had prompted such generosity.

But he knew. Love. She loved him.

He was a selfish bastard for accepting it, but he drank it up like rare scotch.

The first few days were fraught and filled with *hurry up and wait*.

Saint was pulled in every direction, leaving Fliss helpless to do anything except provide what support she could. She reminded him to eat and curled up to him anytime he sat down, hoping it would pin him down long enough to force a small rest. He always responded by drawing her closer and occasionally nodded off, but he never stayed still long. He was up early and came to bed late.

She invited Norma to eat dinner with them every night so she wasn't spending evenings alone. Norma accepted a few times, but they were somber occasions without much conversation.

Eventually, Ted's condition stabilized enough to determine he had lost the use of his left arm and leg. His facial muscles were affected, and he was having trouble with cognition and speech. His doctors believed he would improve over time, but he would never fully recover.

Saint came home one evening looking very tired after a long meeting with the board.

"How did they take the news?" She knew he'd conveyed Ted's prognosis today.

"Voted me in as president," he said without emotion.

She poured him a scotch and brought it to him, sensing what a bittersweet accomplishment this was for him.

"Thank—" He took the glass with one hand and caught her wrist with the other, looking at the ring on her finger.

"It was delivered this morning." She had fallen in love

with it all over again. "You should have seen the production I went through before they would release it. I thought we were going to have to start our baby-making all over again because they seemed to want our first born."

Saint didn't crack a hint of a smile. He absently set aside his drink and held her hand in his two, studying the stone as if it were a crystal ball.

At his continued silence, her stomach wobbled. They hadn't talked about marriage since she'd driven away from the jewelry shop in London.

"I know this isn't the right time to make announcements. I don't have to wear it if you'd rather I didn't." She started to withdraw her hand, but he held on to it.

"One of the board members asked me today whether we were getting married. I didn't know what to say." His troubled gaze came up to hers. "I was such an ass to you that day. Not just after the news about Dad. Before."

"Saint." She had worked her way through that and wasn't holding any grudges.

"No, let me say this." His mouth pressed flat a moment. His brows did the same. "*Love* is a really loaded word in my world. It always comes with strings. Historically, anyone who said they loved me wanted something, and so everyone said it. Almost everyone. If there was someone who didn't want anything from me, who criticized me and implied I didn't have anything they wanted, then I assumed they didn't love me at all."

He was talking about his father. She wanted to wrap her arms around him, but he was cradling her hand in his two, moving the ring enough that it caught glints of light and threw out flashes of rainbow colors.

"I wanted to put a ring on you. To lock you in. I wanted that from the beginning. That's why I sent the earrings." Saint flicked his gaze to her naked lobes.

She had thought the ring was extravagant enough for an evening at home. She wasn't going to swan around like it was coronation day.

"I wanted to give you everything you wanted. It's the dynamic I understand. Give her a barn full of horses and she'll be happy enough to stay," he said. "I told you to trust that I would take care of you, then all I've done since we got back is lean on you. Thank you for reaching out to Mom, by the way. She doesn't know how to deal with this any better than I do. I think she would come more often, but she feels she's intruding."

"I'll make sure she knows she's not."

"See? We don't know what to do with that, Fliss. Emotional generosity isn't something we have any experience with."

"You're going to break my heart, saying things like that. This is what marriage is, Saint. Leaning on each other when you need to." She slid her arms around his waist and emphasized her statement by letting her weight press into him.

"I thought you were leaving me that day." He folded his arms around her shoulders, voice grave. "When you said you were at your bedsit and needed time. I thought I'd driven you away."

"I was hurt and was being petulant—I'll admit that. But I went there planning to close out my life there. I knew this was where I belong now, with you."

"Yeah?" His features finally relaxed a smidge as he smoothed his hand down her hair, encouraging her to tilt her head back so he could see her face.

"Yes. It's not that I don't believe in you, Saint. I struggle to believe in life. In good things coming to me. I don't trust the future. That's why I'm always trying to read it and prepare for it," she said ruefully.

The glimmer of warmth in his eyes doused. His hand on her back shifted to her arm as though to steady her.

"What's wrong?" she asked, not liking the chill that entered her bloodstream.

"It's foolish. I don't even believe in the damned things, but I was angry about your staying in Nottingham and turned over a card. It was Death. Then I got the call about Dad, but—he's pulling through and now I'm worried..." He searched her eyes.

"Oh, you silly man." She hugged him with all her strength before she tilted her head back to scold. "Don't touch my cards. We've talked about that. Also, the Death card doesn't mean death, it means transformation. And it was *mine*. From my reading that morning. I knew neither of us could feel secure in our relationship until we fully trusted the other to be there. I knew I had to let you see *my* commitment, that I had to cut those old ties, but it was a big step, so I did a reading to help myself process it. If it makes you feel better, the card came up reversed for me, which means I was resisting a change and ought to embrace it."

He only looked marginally satisfied. "What does it mean when it's right side up?"

"It's still a transformation card but indicates a more sudden change, the kind you can't escape or undo. One door opens as another closes. You have to let go of old beliefs and attachments in order to adapt to the new conditions."

"So it is about Dad."

If that was what he needed to believe, she wasn't going to persuade him differently.

He folded his arms around her more tightly and rested his jaw against her hair. "I was scared it meant you or the baby. I don't think I could survive losing either of you, Fliss. I need you."

She smiled against his shirt and roamed her hands under

his jacket, against his back. "I need you, too." And she'd been missing their lovemaking as he'd worked himself to exhaustion every day.

"No, I *need* you, Fliss. Yes, sometimes I'm so aroused I think I'll come out of my skin if I don't get inside you, but I need *you*. To say *I love you* doesn't even cover it because I want to pull everything out of you and hold it inside me like air. Like it's something that will keep me alive."

"Did you just tell me you love me?" she asked in whispered wonder.

"Yes, but it's not enough, Fliss. I don't know how to make my love for you as big as yours is for me. To make you feel it and know it the way I feel your love for me." His arms were so tight around her she could hardly breathe, but she reveled in being crushed by the weight of his love.

She sniffed back tears, clenching her eyes to stem the sting.

"Angel. Don't cry. I'm doing this wrong—"

"No. You're doing it right, Saint. You're absolutely doing it right. Now kiss me and show me—"

He did, pressing his mouth to hers with rough hunger, as though he was starving for her. As though he would consume her.

It was the passion, the need that she had been yearning to feel. She moaned with joy, and he jerked his head back. "I'm being too—"

"Don't stop," she cried. "Love me."

With a growling noise, he backed her toward the sofa. She pushed his jacket off his shoulders, and he dropped it to the floor, picking up the hem of her skirt so he was between her thighs as he pressed her to the cushions. He kept his mouth fused to hers the whole time.

"We should slow down," he rasped against her neck, then opened his mouth to suck a small sting into her skin.

Beneath her skirt, his wide hand roamed her bump before seeking the lace of her knickers. "Can you mend these if I…?"

"Do it."

He snapped them, and she chuckled with joy and excitement and love. She loved when he couldn't seem to get enough of her. And she adored when he murmured "I'll be back" and slid off the sofa to kneel and press his mouth between her thighs, tantalizing her with one slow, wet lick before making her writhe in need.

She didn't want a solo flight this time, though. Fliss needed the connection that felt so indelible it could last a lifetime. She scraped her hand into his hair and tugged. "I need you inside me."

He rose enough to open his trousers and hitch them off his hips, then he dragged her thighs to the edge of the cushion and half sprawled over her as his hard flesh probed hers.

There was a small sting, then he was fully seated inside her. They both sighed and shared a dazzled look. And relaxed.

"I needed to be here," he said, picking up her hand to kiss into her palm, then down the inside of her wrist.

"I needed you here," she murmured, working to loosen his tie. She left it dangling as she opened the buttons of his shirt, then ran her hands across the exposed plane of his chest, the flat disks of his nipples and down to the tense muscles of his abdomen.

His hands were busy, too, shifting her skirt higher, then opening the buttons down the front of her dress to admire the bra she wore.

"This is new."

"I made it for you."

"Then I'll be careful with it." He played his fingertips across the satin cup, teasing her nipple into rising before he tickled his touch across the naked swell that overflowed the top.

"It opens here." She released the catch between her breasts.

"Ah. You do love me." He brushed the cup aside and bent his mouth in fresh worship.

She moaned and lifted her hips, signaling that she wanted him to start thrusting.

"Shh." His hand clasped her hip. "Don't make me come yet. I want it to be together."

She wanted that, too. But it was ever so hard to let him fondle and caress and arouse her with long, lazy kisses while her flesh throbbed around the invasion of his, growing wetter and needier.

"Saint," she gasped, sliding her hand down to where they were joined.

He rumbled another admonishment and caught her hand, pinning it to the armrest above her head. Then he shifted slightly and began to move, slow and tender and deliciously thorough.

"Tell me when," he said against her lips. His whole body was shaking.

She licked into his mouth in a dirty tease, liking that he jolted and thrust harder.

"Like that, is it?"

"Yes…" She groaned. "I'm so close." She pulled her hand free of his so she could cup his head and draw him into a blatant kiss.

He moved with more power, pushing her toward the edge, then falling with her over it, shuddering and muffling her moan of ecstasy with his own.

CHAPTER THIRTEEN

THEY ANNOUNCED THEIR engagement a few days later, and Fliss began nesting in earnest.

She was still working and would have a big launch next year, but for now she was spending her weeks still putting pieces into place and approving production samples.

Saint was even busier now that he was fully responsible for Grayscale as well as overseeing his project. Fliss hardly saw him unless they were checking in with his parents together or making an appearance. Sometimes when he came to bed, if she happened to wake, she would roll toward him and they would kiss and sleepily make love. It was always as deliciously satisfying as ever, but it was quieter. She was well into her third trimester, so he was being extra careful with her, which was sweet, and he always told her he loved her, but she still felt some little distance in him, something she couldn't put her finger on.

One day, about six week before her due date, Willow asked her to come into the office "to review some paperwork."

Fliss was baffled as to why Saint couldn't bring it home, but she didn't want to bother him with yet one more task, so she turned up at the appointed time.

Willow brought her to a boardroom where streamers

and cake and gifts were waiting. They had conspired with a team of parents to throw her a baby shower.

"Willow reminded us that you don't have family here," Xanthe said.

Fliss had met her at different times when they'd made announcements around the baby and their engagement. She didn't mention that she didn't actually have family anywhere.

"Being a new parent is a special club," Xanthe continued. "We're looking forward to welcoming you."

Fliss was incredibly touched, especially when she was given a contact list with each person's professed specialty. "Call me if you have questions about…" They listed everything from colic to preschools to hiring a nanny.

Most of the gifts were unwrapped and wearing only a bow. She admired all of them, thrilled to have so many decisions made for her. She was dishing out slices of cake when Saint came into the boardroom.

"Oh, hello." Her heart leapt when he touched her shoulder and dropped a casual kiss onto her cheek, but her smile faltered as his flinty gaze scanned the strollers and toys and hampers. "Thank you for arranging this," she said. "I really appreciate it."

"I didn't. Willow did." He nodded at his assistant. "I've said many times that Willow is the most valuable member of my staff. This is yet another example why."

Since everyone was looking at them, Fliss joked, "That's why I've asked them to be my birth coach. I already know Willow will do most of the work, and God knows Saint will be tied up with Grayscale business."

That got a laugh from everyone except Saint. His expression stiffened. He set down his untouched cake, said, "Willow," and walked out.

"Excuse me." Willow gave the room a calm smile and followed.

Fliss's heart lurched. "Saint!"

Embarrassed that she'd said something to upset him in front of everyone, she clumsily clambered to her feet and hurried after them, catching up to him and Willow at the elevator.

"Saint—"

"Go enjoy your party. I have something to do." He looked resolute, not angry.

"But…" She searched his expression.

The elevator opened, and she stepped inside with him.

"I'll take the stairs," Willow said, turning away from joining them.

"That was a joke," Fliss said as the doors closed. "I want *you* to be with me at the birth." He'd hired a private coach to come to the penthouse rather than attending classes, but he never missed a session.

"I know. I'm not angry." Seconds later, the doors opened and he held it for her, allowing her to step ahead of him. "Not at you."

"Who, then?"

He led her down the hall and into the glass-walled office that had been his father's. Willow must have sprinted ahead of them because they were dancing their fingers across their tablet, bringing up contacts on the big screen at one end of the room. Some revealed distracted faces, others only showed names. Fliss recognized a few as board members she'd already met.

"Two are unable to attend. Three have not responded. The rest are joining now," Willow said, continuing to assemble the meeting.

"The board," Saint explained with a nod.

"Oh. I didn't mean to interrupt—" She looked to the

door, but Saint took her hand and kept her beside him so they both showed in their own square on the screen.

"You're live," Willow said.

"Good. Thank you everyone for jumping onto this call so quickly," Saint said.

"You said it was an emergency," a gruff male voice said. "Is Ted—"

"I said it was urgent." Saint looked to Willow, who nodded. "Dad's been moved to long-term care and continues to improve each day. No, this is a decision that needed to be conveyed immediately so the board can respond in a timely manner. You've all met Felicity?"

"Hello." Fliss gave a weak smile and wave.

"She is expecting and I plan to be with her at the birth. There. Not here. I am not my father, and I will not become him. I want to be Felicity's husband and the father my child deserves. I'll continue leading the charge on my project, but I am resigning as president."

"Wait! What?" the chorus of voices blustered.

"Saint." She clasped his hand in both of hers, shocked and so moved she could hardly breathe. She stared up at him, blinking eyes that welled with emotive tears. "You don't have to do that for me," she whispered.

"I'm doing it for us. All of us." He nodded at her belly. "I'll continue to head the development of my security project," he said to the board, "but my family is my priority, and you need to know that."

"Oh," Fliss squeaked, ducking her head against his arm because she couldn't believe he was doing this. And she was going to full on start crying in a second, which would be totally embarrassing.

"We'll speak more in the next few days," he told the board. "But I wanted to make you aware so you can start planning for my taking a step back. End the call and leave us, please, Willow."

The on-screen grumbles went silent, and the glass walls tinted to opaque as Willow slipped out, possibly biting back a smug smile, but Fliss only had eyes for Saint.

"Are you sure?" she asked him.

"About not becoming my father? So sure," he said firmly and cupped her cheek. "Do not ask if I'm sure whether I love you. I've been feeling so frustrated, wanting you to know it. When you said that about Willow—"

"It was a *joke*."

"It made me realize that I can say the words, but if I'm not here to show you, then you'll never believe it. Not the way I want you to know it."

"I'll never doubt it again," she swore, because how could she? And she really was starting to cry. "It's a really big feeling to accept."

"Yeah. It's a lot of love I'm carrying for you. Now I've gone and put it on you when you're in such a delicate condition…" He drew her into his arms, hands sliding along the sides of her belly in a sweetly familiar way. His mouth pressed hers.

She went up on tiptoes, letting her arms cling around his neck as they found the right angle for their kiss. The perfect connection. *He's the one.* It wasn't a whisper of intuition anymore. It was a statement of fact.

The baby kicked.

Saint drew back, dropping a startled look to her belly. He gave her a rueful smile that was so carefree it made her pulse leap all over again.

"It will be a busy few weeks while I clear the decks," he warned. "Then I'm all yours. Can you put up with my heavy schedule a little longer?"

She nodded, more confident in the future than she'd ever been.

True to his word, when she started having pains six weeks later, he was in bed beside her.

"Leg cramp?" he murmured when she abruptly rose.

"I think I'm having contractions."

"Really?" He snapped up and reached for his phone.

While he was reviewing the symptoms of labor online, her water broke. She had a quick shower, then they went to the maternity clinic for what amounted to a textbook delivery. By ten thirty that morning, she was coaxing their newborn son to latch and Saint was ordering breakfast for them. Since everything had gone so well, they were sent home with Elliott that evening.

Saint had just spoken to Norma, who seemed eager to meet her grandson, and made a noise as he looked at something on his phone.

"What is it?"

"I was texting Willow to say I won't be answering any calls for a few days. They said the board wants to meet with me about staying on as president. Dad always kept a tight hold on everything, refusing to relinquish control unless he absolutely had to. That's why it's been so demanding on me, but they want to restructure at the executive level to keep me at the top."

"Oh. What do you think of that idea?"

"I think I'll think about it in a few days." He set aside his phone. "Right now..." He lowered carefully beside her to avoid jostling her too much and cuddled her against him so he could watch their son fight to stay awake long enough to nurse.

Fliss looked up at him, catching a look of wonder and tenderness on his face. It filled her with so much love, tears welled in her eyes.

"Angel," he chided, catching her growing misty. He set a lingering kiss on her lips. "You did good today, you know."

"Thanks." She smiled down at her son. "But does it feel weird to you that they just let us bring him home as though we have a clue what we're doing?"

"I honestly don't know what they were thinking."

They both laughed loud enough to disturb Elliott, who frowned and gave a small squawk.

"Oops. Sorry. Shh…" Fliss said.

Still smiling, they quieted to let their son get back to the business at hand.

EPILOGUE

Three years later...

SAINT CAME DOWN the stairs from tucking in Elliott to find Fliss on the floor at the coffee table, shuffling her cards.

"That was fast," she said with surprise.

"He was asleep before I cracked the first book."

"Lapping Nana's farm a few hundred times will do that to a boy."

They always joined his mother for lunch on Saturdays, but today had been an extra exciting visit because she'd rescued a pair of miniature horses. Elliott was convinced they were his, and no one had disabused him of that notion.

"*I'm* thinking of going to bed early," Saint said as he lowered onto the couch behind Fliss. He bracketed her with his feet and gave her shoulders an affectionate massage. "You haven't done this in a while. What's going on?"

"Work. I'm wondering if I'm taking too big a swing with the expansion."

"You're selling out each season. It's time."

"I know, but you've got the launch of your security thingy coming up."

He loved that she called his military-grade privacy software, which was surpassing expectations in its effectiveness and was already being pre-purchased by governments and security forces around the world, his "security thingy."

"That's all under control," he assured her. It was. Willow was leading the charge on its launch. Saint had an amazing top-level team who needed minimal supervision.

"And your mom has a real shot at a triple crown," she reminded him.

Norma could really use a win. They all could. They'd had a rough year after his father had passed suddenly eighteen months ago, shortly after Saint and Fliss had married. Sweeping all three races was a long shot, but Norma wouldn't be crushed if it didn't happen. Her priorities had shifted these days, too. While she still adored her horses, her grandson had stolen her heart the day he'd asked without prompting, *Go see horses, please, Nana?*

"I love that you're worried about the rest of us, but don't hold yourself back," Saint chided Fliss. He nibbled the rim of her ear until his lips brushed the pretty diamond studs he'd given her on her birthday last year, making her shiver in the way that delighted him so much. "Go big. I'm right here behind you to support and help if you need it."

"I know." She made a noise of satisfaction as she wiggled backward, snuggling herself into the cage of his covering chest. She tilted her head so his jaw was against her temple. "I'm just not sure now is the right time to take on more."

"See what the cards say, then."

She set out three cards. They were all right side up. She tapped the first one.

"Ten of Pentacles. Financial reward. That's nice to know."

"And look at those Lovers." He pointed. "They're naked. They need underwear, Fliss." Against her ear, he whispered, "I might have conjured that one."

"I know your thoughts are always in my underwear,"

she teased, reaching back to cup his cheek. "But this card isn't so literal. It represents choice and figuring out what you stand for. Sometimes it means you're facing a moral dilemma."

"Expanding your company is hardly a moral dilemma. It's a business strategy. Your plan is sound. Is that really what that card stands for? I would have thought it meant something more romantic." Saint was genuinely disappointed.

"Like soulmates?" She turned her head so her smile was against the corner of his jaw. "It means that, too."

"I knew it." He dipped his head to burrow a kiss against the side of her neck. "See? Even the cards agree that we should make like lovers and go upstairs."

"I'm almost finished. Look. This is interesting." She tapped the Queen of Cups. "She can be about intuition and compassion and caring. Other times, she's so busy looking into her fancy cup and wondering what's inside that she forgets to look up and appreciate the world around her."

"You've definitely got a lock on compassion and caring, but isn't that warning you to make your dream happen? Not sit here thinking about it?"

"What if I have other dreams, though?"

He sat up taller, then tilted around so he could see her face. "If you have other dreams, you need to tell me what they are so we can make them happen."

"It's something that we talked about at one point, then things got busy. So my dilemma—which isn't a dilemma at all—is to decide which is more important to me. Financial reward or..." She pinched the Queen card and brought it into his line of sight so he could see her thumbnail was drawing his eye to the tiny cherub carved into the throne.

"Angel." His voice shook with the sudden emotion that washed over him. They had talked about another baby very abstractly, only saying that they'd like one eventually but that they ought to wait until things felt more settled.

"It's just a suspicion, but it changes all of this, right?" She set the card beside the others and waved her hand across the line of them.

"Come here." He gathered her into his lap, heart pounding so hard it caused a rushing in his ears. He set his hand against her abdomen. "Really?"

"I think I missed a pill somehow during the trip to Australia. You know how I am with the time changes." She wrinkled her nose ruefully. "And I just feel different. But also a lot like the way I felt with Elliott."

"You know there are perfectly scientific tests that can tell you? You don't have to ask your cards."

"Where's the fun in that?" Her brow quirked indignantly.

God, she was cute. "Fair point. And when have these cards ever let you down? But I don't see a dilemma. I'm here to help with the kids—" He caught his breath as fresh wonder expanded in his chest. "Plural. Can you imagine?"

"You're happy?" she asked with a teary smile.

"So happy."

They couldn't seem to kiss, they were both grinning so wide.

"But I also know that means we're going to lose some of these quiet moments, so let's take advantage of each other while we can," he managed to say, sliding his hand under her shirt in search of her breast.

"Okay, but upstairs. Granny's here." She pointed at the empty chair across the table.

He froze to stare at her, knowing she was full of it. Her mouth was twitching. She had probably staged this entire reading as an elaborate ruse to deliver this news to him in the most playful way possible. To make him believe in cards and ghosts and supernatural forces.

Which he did, because what else was love? Not something that could be measured or tested or proved. It wasn't
even a trick you played on yourself. It was something you
experienced and expressed and *knew*.

"Thank you for the good news, Granny. Make yourself
at home." He rose and helped his snickering wife to her
feet, then kept her hand as he led her up the stairs.

* * * * *

NINE-MONTH NOTICE

JENNIE LUCAS

MILLS & BOON

Gripping his phone, Theo had stood at the lonely railing of his yacht and stared at the red sunset.

Maybe Emmie getting married was for the best, he'd tried to convince himself. Even if her groom was some old man who was just a friend of the family. Maybe the guy could make her happy. Maybe he could share his feelings. Maybe he actually *had* feelings.

Unlike Theo. And at his age, facing down forty, he would never change. At least not for the better.

He opened his mouth to tell Nico he was out of it, that he'd have his new secretary send some bland gift, that he didn't care.

Then—

His baby.

"So you'll call Emmie?" Nico persisted. "Offer her job back?"

"I'll do more than that," he'd replied grimly. "I'll go to her wedding. And talk to her myself."

After finishing the call, Theo told his crew to return to Athens as quickly as possible. Gloating over the ruin on Lyra Island would have to wait. He told his secretary to make sure his private jet was fueled and ready when he arrived.

Flying across the Atlantic last night, he'd barely slept. He took a shower, changed his clothes, paced. The flight took longer than it ever had. He tried to stay calm, but his heart was pounding so hard he could barely catch his breath. From rage.

Emmie had kept her baby a secret.

She'd lied to him with her silence.

She hadn't even given him a chance.

His plane landed outside New York where his motorcycle waited, a mode of travel quicker than any car. He stomped on the gas and sped to Queens, twisting dangerously through traffic, engine roaring in his determination to reach the church in time.

Cold. Cold. He had to be cold. To lose his temper would show weakness; it would show he cared. He would be ice.

He finally reached the old stone church in Queens, crammed between colorful shops and walk-up apartments. He'd been to this neighborhood. Nico's wife had grown up here, alongside Emmie. The neighborhood was blue-collar, working-class, and a happier, livelier place than Midtown Manhattan. As Theo parked his motorcycle, a dog rushed down the sidewalk, barking happily in pursuit of two children on toy scooters.

Grimly, he set down his helmet over his Ducati. Crossing the street, he strode up the church steps and silently pushed open the door.

The minister was already speaking as he entered the crowded church. His motorcycle boots echoed softly against the flagstones, faltering when he got his first look at the elderly bridegroom. What the…? That was the man Emmie had chosen? Over *him*?

The bride turned her face, and he saw his secretary's snub nose and heart-shaped face beneath an appallingly unfashionable knot of tulle sticking out in every direction. She looked uncomfortable, even miserable, and no wonder. Conventional wisdom said that every bride was beautiful, but the white gown seemed lumpy in all the wrong places. It emphasized her huge breasts. *Her huge belly.*

She was giving herself away, along with her baby. Some other man would be the child's stepfather. She'd hidden the baby from Theo in an attempt to cut him out of the equation, to make him powerless—

"Stop," he ground out, stepping into the aisle. "Now."

Everyone in the pews gasped, turning toward him. The minister stared slack-jawed, and beneath her crown of white tulle Emmie turned, eyes wide with horror.

"Theo," she breathed. "What—what are you doing here?"

"Emmie." His eyes dropped to her belly, then lifted dangerously. "Are you pregnant with my baby?"

CHAPTER TWO

EMMIE SWAYED, her heart racing as she gripped her red-rose bouquet. She looked past crowded pews at the Greek billionaire standing in the aisle. The same man she'd dreamed about every night for the last seven months, in hot sensual memories that left her gasping with need.

"Are you pregnant with my baby?"

No! she wanted to shout. *You can't be his father. Because you'll never know how to love him.*

For months, Emmie had kept quiet about her pregnancy, hoping she could dodge this bullet. She'd never lied about paternity—not exactly. She'd just hoped that somehow Theo would never find out. She'd told herself that even if he knew, he wouldn't care. She would just save him the trouble of rejecting her and the baby.

Emmie had to be hard-eyed and sensible. She'd worked herself through community college, taking night classes in accounting. She'd worked for years in a windowless basement for a corporation downtown before becoming secretary for a ruthless, amoral tycoon she despised. In her constantly struggling family, *someone* had to focus on the bottom line.

But even Emmie hadn't been able to be practical in this case. She knew Theo would have given her child support, for legal reasons if nothing else. But though she'd picked up the phone a few times, she just couldn't do it. Even with her father's plumbing business losing money every month. She couldn't call Theo, groveling and begging for cash. Her pride wouldn't let her.

Or maybe she'd just been afraid of giving him that much power over her. Because unlike when she'd quit her job as his secretary, knowing he'd only break her heart further if she stayed—once he knew, she'd never be able to quit being the mother of his child.

But now he was here. Mouth dry, Emmie choked out, "Who told you?"

"Not you. That's the point." Theo Katrakis's voice, slightly accented from his childhood in Greece, was low and angry as he came forward, his hard gaze pinning Emmie by the altar. "You lied to me."

As he stalked past the crowded pews, whispers went through the church like wildfire.

"Her boss!"

"The billionaire!"

And, doubtfully, "*He* slept with *her*?"

His worn black motorcycle boots echoed in the sudden breathless silence. He stopped a few feet away, beneath the steps to the altar.

Suddenly, he was in front of her, close enough to touch.

"I didn't…lie," she choked out.

Theo's black eyes flickered to her baby bump as his low voice cut her to pieces. "You lied."

Shame went through her because she knew he was right, followed by anger because she'd had good reasons.

"So?" she cried, tossing her head in a wave of tulle. "We both know you're not up for it. You don't do commitment or love. What could you possibly offer our child but money?" She lifted her chin. "No, thanks. We're fine without you."

His lips parted with an intake of breath. Almost as if she'd wounded him. No, impossible. He had no heart to wound, though he'd hurt her so badly.

Then his eyes narrowed.

"So you cut me out." His voice was as cold, smooth and dark as the surface of an arctic sea. "You took your judgment of me as license to steal my baby away."

Emmie caught her breath. *Steal?* Was that what she'd done?

"*You're* the father of Emmie's baby?" Harold blurted out beside her. She'd forgotten he was there. Her erstwhile bride-groom seemed to shrink into his tux, goggling at Theo's imposing frame.

And no wonder. Emmie looked up at her former boss.

It seemed a great injustice of the universe that after seven months apart Theo was more handsome than ever. His muscular chest and shoulders were wrapped in a form-fitting black T-shirt, and black denim caressed his powerful thighs down to short black leather boots. His square jaw was unshaven, leaving a dark shadow from hard cheekbones to his sensual lips. Black eyebrows slashed over his harsh, dark gaze.

She felt a sense of despair, of rage and grief that he could still dazzle her and make her want him. She gripped her bouquet, wishing she could smash him over the head with it. She felt a small burst of pain in her thumb as a single thorn pricked her. Putting her thumb to her lips, she sucked the aching spot.

Theo's gaze fell to her mouth. His jaw tightened. He turned to her elderly bridegroom.

"You are no longer required here."

"I can see that," Harold replied with dignity. "You should take over." Patting Emmie's hand, he said quietly, "I wish you all the luck in the world, my dear, in your marriage."

She stared at him, flummoxed. "You've got it all wrong. He's not going to marry me—"

But Harold turned away from the altar to sit in the front pew. His elderly neighbor, Luly Olsen, wearing a flowery dress and pink hat decorated with cloisonné pins of dogs, caressed his shoulder consolingly.

Emmie couldn't blame him for not wanting to face down Theo. Harold was an old-fashioned man and of course assumed Theo would wish to marry the mother of his unborn child.

But her father and brothers were not so trusting.

"Like hell he won't!" From the other side of the pews, her father rose to his feet, his weathered face dumbfounded. "Katrakis. You're the lover in Rio?"

"Her boss!" Beside him, the four big Swenson brothers, well-fed as linebackers, rose of one accord, fists clenched and lower lips stuck out.

Scowling, five Swenson men came forward with the hostility of an opposing football team or army battalion.

"You seduced my daughter. Abandoned her," Karl Swenson accused.

She heard the low mutter across the church. There'd been sympathy for the Swenson family since Margie Swenson died, Margie of the kind word and buttery *fika* pastries. Margie who'd often snuck treats to children and dogs, offering free meals and gentle encouragement to anyone who needed a helping hand.

"There are more important things than money, Emmie," her mother tried to tell her.

But even before she'd gotten sick, Margie had always been dreamy-eyed. At twelve, Emmie had taken charge of balancing her checking account and paying the bills so the power wouldn't get turned off. By fifteen, she managed accounts receivable for her father's plumbing business. Her father was excellent at getting customers to pay what was owed but not so good at keeping track of it.

Everyone in their Queens neighborhood knew not to mess with Karl or his four sons. Broad-shouldered and quick-tempered, her four younger brothers, spanning in age from nineteen to twenty-six, were protective of their only sister.

Theo didn't seem worried. Arrogant in his own physical strength, he only looked at Emmie.

"Tell me," he said quietly. "I want to hear you say it."

She looked up at Theo's darkly beautiful face, his penetrating black eyes and the sharp lines of his cheekbones and shadowed jawline. His aquiline nose was slightly crooked between the eyes, broken in some long-ago fight and never set quite right. Her gaze fell to his cruelly sensual lips that she could still feel against her skin, kissing and caressing every inch of her virgin body.

The light from stained-glass windows left a whirl of red and purple and blue against her white satin skirts. Emmie closed her eyes.

"Yes," she whispered. "He's yours."

"He?" Theo had a sharp intake of breath. "A boy?"

"Yes," Emmie's father growled. "And you're going to give my grandson a name and marry my daughter *right now*."

Emmie's eyes flew open in horror. "No, Dad—"

"Or else."

"Or else," her brothers chorused behind him, clenching their hands.

Emmie flung a terrified glance at Theo, knowing he'd respond with a sarcastic insult that would make her father lose his mind. Any moment, the blows would fly, and someone she loved would be hurt. She spread her arms, trying to create a wall between him and her family. "Please, I promise you, Theo, I don't even *want* to marry—"

Theo gently pushed her aside. Tilting his head, he gave Karl Swenson a hard nod. "Deal."

"You'll marry her?" her father responded suspiciously.

Theo held out his hand. "Agreed."

Her father brightened. "Well, then."

The two men shook hands, as if they'd just agreed to the

sale of a used plumber's torch at cut-rate prices or maybe a truck-mounted sewer jetter with barely a touch of rust.

Looking between the two men, Emmie's forehead creased. "Is this some kind of joke?"

Theo glanced pointedly at the minister, the guests, the church, and lifted his eyebrow as he inquired sardonically, "Do I look like I'm joking?"

Whispers and gasps sizzled through the crowd. By now, many wedding guests were holding up cell phones, because otherwise how would anyone believe it, that a plain, twenty-eight-year-old spinster like their Emmie had managed to entice a handsome Greek billionaire into bed—and into marriage?

Reaching out, Theo took her hand. Slowly, he pulled Harold's engagement ring off her finger. She trembled feeling his fingers slide down her hand. Then he turned back to the elderly man.

"Thank you for standing in," he said gravely, giving him the ring. "I'll take it from here." Holding Emmie's hand, Theo turned to the minister. "Go ahead."

Go ahead?

Emmie tried to pull back her hand. "Are you crazy?" she hissed. "I'm not suddenly going to switch grooms!"

"Why?" he asked coolly, as if *she* were the one being unreasonable.

Emmie didn't know why he seemed as if he wanted to marry her, but after a year and a half as his secretary, she knew Theo Katrakis always got what he wanted, when he wanted it.

But not this time. Oh, no. Not this time.

Yanking her hand away, Emmie said, "We don't have a license. Or a ring! And, oh, yeah—we don't love each other!"

Theo's dark eyes slanted sharply to Harold in the front row with Luly Olsen in her big pink hat. He lifted an eyebrow skeptically. The meaning was clear.

Emmie stiffened. Marrying Harold without love was entirely different—she knew the man could never break her
heart! Desperately, she turned. "Dad."

But her father only patted her shoulder. "You'll thank me
later, sweetheart. It's for the best."

"For the best," her younger brothers repeated, nodding
sagely.

She was being railroaded. Looking around the church, she
saw no allies. Everyone clearly believed she'd been about to
settle for a marriage of convenience with Harold, and so they
expected her to clap her hands with joy at a chance to marry
Theo instead.

How would anyone understand that it was far worse for
her to marry Theo Katrakis, even if he was the father of her
baby, even if he was handsome, even if he was a billionaire?

With a deep breath, she whirled back to him.

"Please don't do this. You'd regret it," she choked out. Black
mascara smeared her fingertips as she wiped her eyes. "You'd
make me regret it."

He looked down at her.

"I'm your baby's father," he said quietly.

Those four words made Emmie catch her breath. Was she
wrong to deny Theo even the chance to try to raise their son
in the same home, just because she was scared?

Scared if she ever let herself get close to Theo again he'd
wrap her heart around his little finger and never let go. And if
he made her love him again, there'd be no escape for her this
time, not if they were married with a child. She'd be chained
to him forever, by the bonds of matrimony and family and by
her own heartsick longing.

She'd spend the rest of her life loving a man who could
never love her in return. The endless rejection would destroy
her, until it finally crushed her into pieces so small she really
would be invisible.

But—what about her baby?

Maybe Theo could never love her. But what if there was hope for him as a father?

Could Emmie really deny their baby the chance to be raised in a secure home with both parents? Could she actually be selfish enough to put her own needs first?

"Just go through the ceremony," Theo told the minister arrogantly. "We'll fix the paperwork later."

"I'm not sure…" the man began, then looked at Theo and shrugged. He turned to Emmie, his eyes grave behind his spectacles as he placed his finger on the correct page. "What do you say, my dear? Should I begin again?"

Lump in her throat, Emmie stared at him uncertainly.

"Do it," Theo said in a low, husky voice. "Say *yes*. Marry me."

She turned, seeing all the staring eyes in the pews, feeling like she was in some awful dream. "I don't know—"

Her voice cut off as he roughly pulled her into his arms. She gasped, breathing in the scent of leather and engines and woodsy aftershave and something even more intoxicating. Something just *him*. Theo's black eyes blazed.

Then, lowering his head, he kissed her.

Theo deployed his kiss like a weapon.

He'd meant to use his sensuality against her, to assert the power of his will and make her agree. He'd done it a few times in the past with other women for much less reason, lazily, almost without thinking. He could always convince a woman to see things his way. And now that he'd decided to marry Emmie, in shocked determination to permanently secure and protect the son he'd just found out about. He had no compunction about his method, just the outcome. The end justified the means.

But as his lips touched hers, something happened that Theo hadn't expected.

The contact of their kiss caused a flash of electricity to curl through him, sizzling up his nerves, burning through his body. It had happened that way before, that night he'd taken her virginity, when they'd conceived their child. But he'd almost convinced himself in the months since then that he'd deceived himself, that he'd been drunk, that he'd been crazy, that he'd imagined that overwhelming ecstasy.

But he hadn't imagined anything.

Kissing Emmie Swenson had made his world spin.

With an intake of breath, Theo pulled her tighter, feeling the firm curve of her pregnant belly and lush fullness of her breasts against his chest, the white satin of her wedding gown sliding against his T-shirt. He gripped her body against his as if she were the answer to the question he'd been asking all his life.

He needed this. Needed *her*. Oh, God. He heard a soft moan and realized it had come from his own throat.

Shocked, Theo wrenched away.

Applause and catcalls rolled through the pews as Emmie looked up at him. Her blue-violet eyes were luminous beneath the ridiculous pile of white fluff on her head. He saw the same agony, the same need and fear, reflected in her beautiful, haunted face. She bit her lower lip, her red lipstick scarlet as roses, emphasizing bow-shaped lips in a heart-shaped face as she searched his gaze. She swallowed, then backed away.

"No," she breathed.

Throwing her bouquet on the floor in an explosion of red petals, Emmie turned and ran from the altar, leaving everything and everyone behind as she disappeared through the side door.

Theo's jaw dropped.

"Guess she needs a little convincing," her father ventured,

in what seemed like the understatement of the year. Theo scowled.

Damn it, why was it always so difficult to convince Emmie of anything? To be his secretary? To tell him about her pregnancy? To marry him?

She'd resisted becoming his wife just as she'd once resisted becoming his secretary. Back then, he'd thought it was proof of her good sense, that she saw through his charm and wasn't easily fooled.

But now…

It seemed Emmie's opinion of him hadn't changed at all. Even after their year and a half of working together, she still thought he was not only a selfish bastard but an utter villain. How else to explain why, after their kiss, she'd looked at him with trepidation almost like fear?

Standing abandoned at the altar beside the minister, as the people in the pews gleefully held up their phones, Theo felt foolish, as he hadn't in decades. His cheeks burned.

He'd never imagined asking any woman to marry him, but he'd always assumed that if for some reason he deigned to select a lucky bride, she'd immediately and gratefully jump into his arms.

Instead, Emmie had *run away.*

"Excuse me," Theo told everyone grimly and turned to pursue his fleeing bride out the side door.

He caught up with her on the other side, in the church hall decorated for a wedding reception.

"Wait," he growled.

Emmie looked back at him, her face troubled. "I'm not going to marry you."

He caught her hand. "Just stop."

"Don't touch me." She wrenched her hand away, her brilliant eyes flashing in the dappled light. Such an intoxicating shade. He thought dazedly of violet flowers, the symbol of ancient Athens. The color of the city's horizon at sunset.

"Fine." Keeping his hands wide of her, Theo took a deep breath. "We need to talk."

"About what?" She lifted her chin. "Maybe we should talk about that little stunt you just pulled, demanding we get married out of nowhere. *Kissing* me? In front of everyone?"

He looked past the reception hall's long folding tables to the homemade wedding cake surrounded by paper plates and stale-looking mints. A hand-painted banner was spread across the back wall, anchored by cheap, drooping balloons. *Congrats, Emmie and Harold.*

His jaw set. "You didn't seem to have any problem marrying that old man."

"Harold's a good person," she protested.

"Why, Emmie? Why him?"

"He offered us a home."

"*I* could give you a home," he said. "Several homes around the world. Why didn't you ask me?"

"Because…" She swallowed, then looked away. Finally she met his eyes. "Why are you pretending you want this, Theo? A wife, a child?"

"I'm not pretending."

She gave a low, bitter laugh. "You forget I know you. Even before I worked for you, I saw how you were. I heard you the morning of Nico's wedding, telling him it wasn't too late to make a run for it! And you were the best man!"

Theo licked his lips. "You heard?"

"I was her maid of honor. I was standing right there. I might have been invisible to you, but…"

"You weren't invisible." He remembered that day, Nico and Honora's wedding on the beach. "You were pretty, in that dress. For once you weren't smothered in the ugliest clothes you could find." His gaze lingered on her lumpy, out-of-date wedding gown, and her cheeks went red.

"You despise the idea of marriage. Why would you ask me?"

Theo looked away, at the arched windows overlooking the courtyard. How to explain something he couldn't even understand himself?

"You're right. I've always avoided commitment," he said haltingly. "In every love affair I've had, I was always planning my exit beforehand. But with you, that night in Rio…"

She waited.

His eyes met hers. "I wasn't careful."

Now Theo heard her sharp intake of breath. She looked down at her hands, clasped in her lap.

"The mistake was mine," he said quietly. She looked up.

"Is that how you see our baby?" Emmie flared. "As a mistake?"

His heart was galloping strangely. "Yes." He looked at her. "A mistake. But it's one I intend to take responsibility for." Looking away, he said softly, "I won't leave you to struggle alone, like my mother had to."

Silence fell. He'd never spoken about his childhood before. Not to anyone.

Emmie's expression changed. "If you want to be a father to our baby, you can." Her tone was suddenly gentle. "I'll let you see him anytime you want. But…that doesn't mean we need to marry."

"The only way I can truly protect him," he said, lifting his chin fiercely, "is by protecting you. The only way I can commit to him…is by committing to you."

Her eyes widened. She took a deep breath, dropping her gaze again. The sweep of her blackened lashes brushed against her cheek like a butterfly's wing.

Makeup made Emmie look…different. More obviously at-

tractive, rather than the secret beauty she'd been, visible to
his eyes alone. Theo wasn't sure he liked it.

The truth was, he didn't like any of this.

Not this cheap reception hall. Not feeling tired and hungry
after his crazed overnight rush here from Europe. Not being
forced into marriage by the conscience he hadn't known he
had.

Not Emmie's badly fitting wedding dress, which showed
off the swell of her baby bump and her full breasts, barely
contained by tight, straining satin. Her pregnant body, laced
into that modestly demure dress, made her look like a sex
goddess of fertility no man could resist.

Except you'd no longer have to resist her, a voice whispered. His body tightened. Not once she was his wife.

He could still feel their kiss pouring through him, liquid
fire in his veins. His gaze kept returning to her face, to her
bruised, reddened lips.

"I'm being rude." She looked back at the closed door to the
church. "All my family and friends are probably still waiting,
wondering what to do. I'm going to tell them it's all off, and
they should go home."

His gaze sharpened. "Emmie—"

"I'm not running away. I'll be back."

After she disappeared through the side door, Theo paced,
tapping his foot. His hand went to his pocket for his phone, by
habit. Then his stomach growled. He hadn't eaten since yesterday. His eyes fell on the wedding cake on the center table.

Crossing past the humble homespun wedding decorations,
he brushed his finger alongside the edge of white frosting on
the plate. Buttercream. Delicious. He heard a noise.

A white-haired woman in a flowery dress and big pink
hat walked through the far door, saying happily to another
woman behind her, "It was the answer to my prayers, I tell
you. When Harold—"

They stopped when they saw Theo, standing beside the wedding cake with one finger on the edge of the frosting.

"We're here to tidy up," one of the women blurted out. He gave them a hard, charming smile.

"Later."

"Of course," they stammered and fled, holding their dainty hats.

Licking the frosting off his finger, Theo reached for the decorative knife, intending to cut himself a slice—the cake obviously wouldn't be needed now—when his phone rang.

It was his lawyer, calling to report that the demolition permits had come through for his new property in Greece. Hearing it over the phone wasn't quite as satisfying as it would have been to see it in person, as he'd intended.

Then the man added, "And we finally found the item you've been looking for."

Theo blinked. "Where?"

"At a pawn shop. In Thessaloniki. We'll dispatch it to your office." Pause. "I heard you returned to New York quite quickly, sir. Was there an emergency?"

"I came back to get married." It surprised Theo how easy it was to speak those words.

His attorney, the biggest attack dog at the white-shoe law firm of Jaber, Greenbury and Moire, heard the word *married* and gasped out, "But you got a prenup first, of course, Mr. Katrakis?"

Hearing Theo's sheepish reply to the negative, his attorney whimpered like a Victorian maiden collapsing on a fainting couch.

Hanging up moments later, Theo marveled at his own stupidity. He'd been standing at the altar, ready to marry Emmie. He hadn't even thought about the risk to his fortune.

What was it about her that caused him to lose his mind?

Well, no more. From now on he'd be cold. Cold and smart.

He'd convince her to marry him—and to sign a prenup. How to convince her? How to get leverage?

The side door opened, and Emmie walked into the reception hall in a swish of white satin, looking pale but determined. He braced himself to argue, to charm, to persuade. "You're going to marry me, Emmie."

She looked at him.

"Fine," she said suddenly. "I will."

CHAPTER THREE

EMMIE'S HANDS WERE still trembling as the two of them went out into the sunlight as if nothing had happened, nothing at all.

After her startling words—startling to her, if not to him—Theo had given her a searching look, then he'd abruptly said, "I'm hungry. Let's talk over lunch."

Outside the church, the colors of her vibrant Queens neighborhood, tiny restaurants with fragrant, unrecognizable spices, and little shops with cheerful clothing fluttering outside swirled around her in a blurry carousel. She blinked, blinded by the blue sky. Blinded by the decision she'd just made.

"It's over there," Theo said, nodding.

"What is?"

"My bike."

Following his gaze, Emmie saw an expensive motorcycle parked arrogantly in the fire lane halfway down the street, a single helmet hanging from the handlebars. "You expect me to ride that?"

"Why not?"

"How would I even hold on to you? With this belly!"

Theo considered her baby bump, then sighed, reaching into his pocket for his phone. "I'll call Bernard."

Bernard Oliver was Theo's chauffeur in New York. But it would take at least thirty minutes for him to drive to Queens. And between them and the motorcycle, she saw clusters of her neighbors and friends in festive hats and their best jackets still filing out of the front steps of the church. Any moment now, they'd turn and see her and Theo at the corner.

She had no intention of spending a half hour answering questions from neighbors. Or letting them see her picked up by Theo's chauffeured Rolls-Royce.

As Theo started to walk ahead, she grabbed his arm. "Let's wait at my apartment. It's not far. We can walk."

His aquiline nose scrunched. "Walk?"

She snorted a laugh. For a man who spent countless hours in boxing gyms and ran marathons, it was hilarious how scandalized he was by the idea of a short walk down the street.

"Yes, walk." She tugged his hand. "Come on."

Emmie dropped his hand as soon as they turned and started walking. It was too hard to touch him. It did strange things to her. Not just her body but her heart.

The kiss he'd given her was still burning through her, from her fingertips to her hair to her toes. That kiss had been so shocking, so overwhelming, it had given her strength to say something the powerful Theo Katrakis almost never heard.

No.

She'd been scared to marry him, scared that he'd end up seducing her body and pillaging her soul, leaving her nothing but an empty husk for the rest of her life.

But when Emmie had gone back alone into the church, something made her change her mind and decide to marry Theo after all.

She'd found her father alone. He'd already told the guests no wedding would happen today so they might as well leave. He'd told his sons they'd already done what they could for Emmie, and they should leave and let the two lovebirds sort themselves out.

But Karl himself had lingered, just in case his daughter needed support. So when Emmie returned, she'd found him alone. They had spoken quietly in a half-shadowed, empty chapel.

"I can't marry him, Dad," she said bleakly. "He'll never love me."

"But you think you could love him?"

She felt a lump in her throat. "Yes."

Her father looked down at the patterns of red and blue and yellow light from the stained glass, pooling against the cool flagstones. Then he lifted his head.

"Your mother was pregnant with you when I married her. You knew that."

She bit her lip. They'd never talked about it. She nodded reluctantly. "I was born six months after your wedding date, so it wasn't hard to figure out."

Karl gave a crooked smile. "Margie didn't love me, either. Not then. She said no the first three times I proposed to her." He ducked his head to surreptitiously wipe his eyes. "When she finally said *yes*, I vowed to make her happy. And I think I did."

"Of course you did." It was startling to think of her romantic, idealistic mother ever not wanting to marry her father. Emmie put a comforting hand on his shoulder. "Mom loved you with all her heart."

"It took a while." He gave her a watery smile, then sobered. "If she hadn't said *yes*, your brothers would never have been born. We would never have been a family."

The thought of that had been so awful, imagining her family disappearing, that Emmie caught her breath.

Her father tilted his head. "If you think you could love Katrakis, well, that's a start, isn't it? And as for him loving you…" His voice trailed off as he gave her a warm smile, his eyes gleaming suspiciously in the dim light. "How could he not? Just give him time."

Time. Emmie didn't think any amount of time could ever

make Theo Katrakis love anyone. But in the time it took for her to say farewell to her father and walk back through the side door into the reception hall, Emmie changed her mind.

She would marry Theo. She couldn't imagine not giving her own baby what she'd had: a happy childhood, in spite of all their money worries and the agony of her mother fighting cancer for ten years. How could she possibly justify saying *no*? Her baby's happiness mattered more to Emmie than her own.

And as for her fear of loving Theo—

Why, it was simple, she thought suddenly as she followed him down the street now. Their marriage just needed a few conditions.

One of those conditions would be that their baby would never have siblings, which was a shame. But it would protect her from inevitable heartbreak—especially because she knew she'd never be enough for Theo and he'd soon grow bored with her anyway. So instead of a romantic, passionate partnership, what if, from the beginning, they strove instead for a deep friendship, based on mutual respect? And trust. Trust most of all.

It was the only way to make their marriage endure.

And yet…

Emmie's memory lingered on that kiss of pure fire he'd given her at the altar. She touched her bruised lips. Her condition would mean there'd be no more kisses, luring her into being reckless, luring her into danger. For the rest of her life.

"Look out."

Theo's strong arm suddenly blocked her path. A beat-up car honked loudly as it whizzed past.

Emmie gasped, realized she'd almost stepped into traffic on the street.

With her center of gravity already so off-kilter, she stumbled back, staggering in her tight mermaid skirt, falling back to the sidewalk—

Theo caught her. As their eyes locked, her white veil was caught by the breeze, whirling around them, lifting upward.

Sunlight frosted his dark hair, framing him with blue sky, making his black eyes luminous. She felt the strength of his body against hers, his powerful chest beneath his snug black T-shirt. The shape and power of his thickly muscled arms beneath her hands.

Her gaze fell to his mouth, and she shivered, breathless with sudden longing…

No!

"Pull me up," she gasped. Struggling, she said hoarsely, "Let me go!"

Wordlessly, he set her on her feet. Cheeks hot, she ducked her head, turning to point at a two-story building on the next corner. "That's it."

Careful not to touch him, she led him past the street-level store emblazoned with old neon from her grandfather's day in loopy cursive lettering: *Swenson and Sons Plumbing.* They reached a nondescript door. Typing in the security code, she led him up the stairs to the three-bedroom apartment where her family had always lived.

"Come in," she said. "It'll only take me a minute to change."

"I'll call Bernard and tell him where…" Theo's voice trailed off as he looked around the living room.

Following his gaze, Emmie saw their cozy, too-small home in a new light. It suddenly looked shabby and cluttered. In the mad scramble before the wedding that morning, the sofa bed where her brother Joe slept had been left a mess of tangled sheets. Dirty clothes from various brothers were strewn over the floor. The kitchen table was covered with piles of empty pizza boxes from last night's dinner, with yesterday's dirty dishes stacked in the sink.

Her cheeks went hot as she followed his gaze.

"I didn't have time to cook last night or tidy up as usual," she stammered. "I was busy with the wedding cake..."

"You made that? Yourself?" Theo's dark eyebrows rose, then he licked his lips. "It was good."

"How do you know?"

Not answering, Theo looked around. "You do the cooking and cleaning for your family," he said slowly, "as well as supporting them financially?"

She stiffened, sensing some criticism of her father. She said defensively, "My family's had a hard time since my mother died—"

"Even before that, you were sending your father most of your paycheck." When she jolted in surprise, Theo tilted his head in amusement. "Do you think I didn't know why you first agreed to work for me?"

Emmie ducked her head, embarrassed. "There were medical bills," she mumbled. "My father's hopeless with anything that doesn't require a hand tool, and my brothers, well—" she smiled weakly "—they wouldn't see a mess if they tripped on it."

"I see." He turned away, looking from the dated, worn furniture to the sparkling-clean windows and old carpet beneath her brothers' discarded clothes, which still had lines from the vacuum cleaner she'd used yesterday morning. Faded photographs, school photos, and black-and-white images of her grandparents lined the walls, covering faded wallpaper.

She flinched a little. She could only imagine what he was thinking. Theo Katrakis could have his pick of gorgeous, glamorous women, heiresses, royalty, movie stars. Was he already regretting the surprise pregnancy that had forced him to propose marriage to a plain, plump nobody from Queens?

She turned away. "Wait here. It'll just take me a moment to pack."

"Don't bother. You won't need anything."

Emmie turned back to him. "What do you mean? Won't we live at your penthouse after we're married?"

He looked over her wedding dress. "Tell me you're not planning to wear *that* again."

"No," she said, insulted by his obvious opinion of her mother's gown. Even if she herself had been thinking it was ugly earlier, that didn't give him the same right.

Theo shook his head. "Then, there's nothing for you to pack. *Especially* not those bargain-bin pantsuits."

They'd been more than a bargain. She'd gotten the suits used from a thrift store for five dollars each. But he didn't need to know that. She lifted her chin. "Maybe I *like* those bargain pantsuits. Did you ever think of that?"

His dark eyes challenged her. "Do you?"

She glared at him, then sighed. "No. Not really. But I have better things to think about and better ways to spend money."

"I thought so. That all changes now. You'll need an entirely new wardrobe as my wife."

"Why?" she said suspiciously. "What do you expect me to do?"

Theo's lips curved. "Be at my side at parties, charity balls, dinners with presidents and royalty." Ticking off the items with his fingers, he tilted his head thoughtfully. "Be the hostess of my homes around the world."

Worse and worse. Emmie had always told herself that her plain appearance didn't matter, not as long as she was clean and tidy and competent. Her boss was the important one, not her. But that was when she'd been his secretary. As his wife…

She shuddered. There was no way she could compete with socialites and debutantes!

Theo stroked his chin, watching her as he continued. "You'll be a leader of society," he mused. "A noted taste-maker."

She stiffened at the wicked gleam in his eye.

"In that case," she responded tartly, "the style next season will be whatever's on final clearance at Goodwill."

He snorted, then came closer. Reaching out, Theo smoothed back a long tendril of her hair.

"Give your new life a chance," he said softly. His dark eyes fell to her mouth. "It might be fun."

Oh, no. She wasn't going to let *that* happen, ever again. The kiss he'd given her at the altar still consumed her. Just his touch on the sidewalk, when he'd caught her in his arms to keep her from falling, had reverberated through her body. Nervously, she turned away.

"I'll be just a minute," she said again and fled down the hall to her bedroom, closing the door behind her.

The tiny bedroom, barely bigger than a closet, still had the travel posters of France and Greece she'd put on the walls as a teenager, long before her mother got sick. Old novels still lined the single shelf on the wall, beside a few beloved stuffed animals from her childhood. Her grandmother's homemade quilt covered her twin bed.

Emmie bit her lip. There was no way she'd let Theo see this—the bedroom of a teenager, a decade old, still frozen in time. Turning away, she grabbed an old duffel from beneath her bed and packed a few precious things, photo books, her stuffed bunny from childhood, tiny onesies she'd already bought for her coming baby. After a moment of thought, she decided to leave the secretarial pantsuits behind. He was right. There was no way Mrs. Theo Katrakis could dress like that. She tossed in some underwear and socks, a few stretchy T-shirts and maternity shorts and some shoes. That was it.

Taking off her wedding dress and kicking off her three-inch white pumps, she exhaled, relieved to leave the hot, constricting clothing behind. She spread her mother's gown carefully on her quilt. She'd have to arrange for it to be dry cleaned and packed away.

She pulled a loose cotton sundress over her ungainly body and stuck her feet into flip-flops. Going to the small shared bathroom, Emmie washed the makeup off her face and pulled all the bobby pins out of the bun, letting her hair fall in soft waves over her shoulders.

She felt like she was free, like she could breathe again.

As long as she didn't think about the man she was about to marry. And what he'd say when he heard about her three conditions of marriage:

First, that they'd live in New York.

Second, that he'd help her family with anything they needed.

And third, that they'd never sleep together again. Ever.

Theo's eyes widened as Emmie returned to the cramped living room of her family's second-floor apartment.

That hideous wedding dress and veil were gone. Emmie now wore a simple sleeveless white cotton sundress and flip-flops. Her face was bare of makeup, her dark blond hair long over her shoulders. His gaze unwillingly lingered on the way it brushed over her collarbones and soft skin.

"Forget it," he said abruptly into his phone. "We'll find our own way. Just pick up the Ducati."

"Who was that?" she asked as he hung up. She was struggling with the handles of a duffel bag that looked fifty years old. Coming around the sofa, he plucked it from her hands.

"Bernard," he answered. "He says there's some politician at the UN choking traffic. He's stuck in congestion by the Midtown Tunnel."

She tilted her head, smiling, and he thought how pretty she was when her violet-blue eyes glowed like that. "So how are you thinking we'll get to Manhattan? Taxi? Rideshare?"

"Sit in the sticky back seat of some stranger?" He shuddered. Setting down the duffel, he typed a search on his phone.

"Subway?" she suggested. "The bus?"

"Bus." He looked up, aghast, then saw her teasing grin. She clearly thought he was being rather silly, which he supposed he was, at least when it came to walking long city blocks or being packed like a sardine into mass transit. But his year living on the streets of Athens at fifteen, trudging sidewalks looking for food or work, trying to slouch in the back rows of buses and train stations long enough to sleep, had been enough for his lifetime. Not that he'd ever tell anyone about that. Turning back to his phone, Theo said, "There's a car dealership two blocks from here."

Emmie's nose wrinkled. "I know. The gentrification is getting ridiculous. Some of my neighbors tried to fight it, but... where are you going?"

"I'm walking there." He paused to let that sink in. He didn't want to be too predictable. His gaze fell to her belly beneath her loose sundress. "Do you want to wait here? I can come back and pick you up."

"I can walk two blocks," she said dryly. "I just didn't know *you* could."

Carelessly lifting the bag with one hand, he flashed her a sharklike grin. "I'm willing to suffer for a good cause."

As they walked side by side down the lively block, Emmie kept glancing at him through her lashes, as if she were trying to work up to something.

So was he. Theo had no idea how to convince her to sign the prenuptial agreement that would be waiting for them at his penthouse beside their lunch spread. But she had to sign it. His attorney had been very definite about that.

"No prenup, no marriage," he'd insisted to Theo on the phone. "Do you understand, Mr. Katrakis? Do I need to remind you what happened to Bill Gates? Jeff Bezos?" He'd paused. "Robert Romero?"

Theo still shivered at the memory. It was true Bezos and

Gates had lost a tidy bundle after prenup-free divorces, but at least those marriages had been long and their wives had helped create those fortunes.

Robert Romero was something else. The self-made frozen-foods tycoon had married a twenty-one-year-old waitress, only to have her file for divorce when they returned from their honeymoon. With her lawyer's help, she'd taken most of the man's fortune. Romero had ended up destitute, shamed, mocked; he died of a heart condition six months later. Whether his heart was broken from losing love or his fortune was an open question.

Mae Baker Romero, the young ex-wife, still lived in a highrise not too far from Theo's, in a swanky penthouse overlooking Central Park. Called Killer by her friends, she often appeared in gossip columns, flashing her big, bright smile and even bigger and brighter diamonds.

Theo shuddered. Every wealthy bachelor in New York knew the story of Robert Romero.

But how could he convince Emmie to sign the prenup, without her feeling insulted and telling him to forget the whole thing? How could he be diplomatic enough to soften the blow, and seduce, and persuade?

He slanted a sideways glance at her.

In bed, he thought. Obviously. When she was close—hell, even when she'd been thousands of miles away—it was difficult for Theo to think of anything but making love to her. He'd made shocking mistakes because his brain ceased working beneath the onslaught of his desire.

Surely, Emmie had the same problem with him.

Surely?

He recalled how she'd trembled beneath his kiss, her hands gripping him tight. When he'd released her, she'd looked up at him like someone newly woken from a dream. That decided it.

Bed.

Bed, his body agreed fervently.

Walking together through the neighborhood, they arrived at the small used-car dealership about fifteen minutes later. It only took five minutes for Theo to select the best on the lot, a pristine cherry-red 1971 Barracuda convertible. It would be a nice addition to his vintage collection, he thought, as well as quick transportation back to Manhattan. He reached for his wallet.

"No," Emmie said.

Theo frowned, turning to her. The salesman stared at the credit card in his hand intently, vibrating like a dog waiting for a particularly choice bit of meat to drop to the floor. "What do you mean *no*?"

"I'm not getting in that thing." She looked at the low convertible doubtfully. "Even if I could lower myself into the seat, I'd never get up again."

"You'll be fine—"

"Forget it."

As they glared at each other, he suddenly missed the old days when he could override her, when he was demonstrably, undoubtedly the boss.

But even then, sometimes they'd battled, usually when she'd decided to stand her ground in order to prevent him from doing something foolish. Like when his private jet had landed for emergency repairs in Florida and he'd nearly bought thousands of acres of swampland out of sheer boredom. Or the time he'd nearly sold an expensive Tokyo property for a single yen because he'd been annoyed his favorite noodle shop was closed.

On second thought, maybe he should let her win this one. Even if it was damned irritating. Setting his jaw, he demanded, "What exactly do you have in mind?"

Her expressive eyes shifted past him on the car lot, and she smiled. "That."

CHAPTER FOUR

THE JUNE AFTERNOON had grown hot and humid by the time
they arrived at his gleaming Manhattan high-rise on the south-
ern edge of Central Park. As Theo pulled the clunky vehicle
to the curb, the doorman hurried forward, scowling.

"Hey, you can't park that here—" The young man drew
back, shocked. "Mr. Katrakis?"

Theo muttered something under his breath, his jaw tight.
Emmie glanced at him with amusement as he put the three-
year-old minivan into Park. He was scowling, but driving a
minivan for the first time was a well-known test and trial for
any red-blooded male. Her smile lifted.

"And—Miss Swenson!" The doorman blinked in surprised
recognition as he slid open her door. His jaw dropped as he
saw the shape of her pregnant belly beneath her sundress. He
stammered, "Er—is it still Miss Swenson?"

"Um...yes." Her cheeks got a little hot, even as she told
herself she had nothing to be ashamed of.

"Not for long," Theo said flatly as he yanked her small
duffel from the minivan's rear with one hand. "We're going
to be married."

The doorman looked speechless, then overjoyed. "Congratulations to you both! Mazel tov! A baby—and married!"
Blinking, he looked back at the minivan. "I guess that explains it."

Theo's scowl deepened.

"Just tell Bernard to find a place for it, Arthur," he said and tossed him the key, which the young man caught midair.

"Will you keep it?" Emmie asked as she followed Theo inside the grand foyer of the high-rise.

He shrugged. "It served its purpose." Glancing back through the window at the street, he gave a sudden impish grin. "Maybe Arthur would like it as his Christmas tip."

As their footsteps echoed over the marble floor, she snorted a laugh. Trust Theo to think of something like that. His good deeds were impulsive, almost always by accident. "He's a little young for a minivan, don't you think?"

"So am I," he said darkly as they entered the private elevator. The door slid closed, and he looked at her. "But it was what you wanted. Were you comfortable on the ride?"

"Yes," she said honestly.

Reaching out, he smoothed back a tendril of her blond hair. "Then, I suppose we can keep it."

Looking up into his black eyes, Emmie shivered, and it wasn't just from the elevator's blast of air-conditioning. She felt something suddenly tremble deep inside her. Was it from the way he'd put her needs over his own in choosing the car? His gentle touch as he smoothed her hair? Or maybe just his casual use of the word *we*?

Whatever it was, Emmie couldn't—wouldn't—let herself be seduced by it. She turned away, stiffening her shoulders. When the elevator door slid open with a ding, she bolted out.

With its high-ceilinged rooms and three spacious terraces, his multi-million-dollar triplex penthouse sprawled across the entire fifty-second and fifty-third floors of the building, equal parts beautiful and cold.

Not just cold in temperature, either, she thought, glancing up at the jagged crystal chandelier of the foyer. Taking a deep breath, she hurried into the cavernous great room, notable for its lack of color and Spartan furniture. The penthouse's design had been done by a famous interior decorator last year. Emmie had organized it herself at her boss's demand, but to her, the result was chilly, a museum of modern art that might be impressive to outsiders and *Architectural Digest* but was utterly unsupportive of the vibrant chaos of actual human lives.

There was no comfort in Theo's home. Nothing but hard sofas that hurt your back to sit in, framed splatters of gray and black on the walls, and cutting-edge technological interfaces running lights, shades, entertainment, security and the rest.

It was impersonal, too. No photographs of family or proof Theo had ever had one. No clutter. No scattered detritus of hobbies, like her brothers' dusty guitars or her father's pile of hardcover thrillers. No pets. No messes. No inconvenient feelings of any kind.

Just as Theo preferred.

And yet she'd just promised to marry him?

Emmie swallowed, trying to calm the sudden rapid beat of her heart. It would be just a partnership, she told herself. Like they'd had before. She'd never let herself love him again. Maybe she'd let herself care just a little, just the amount that was appropriate since he was her baby's father. But no more than that. So what that he'd bought her a minivan? It meant nothing. Buying things was easy for Theo Katrakis. He threw his money around so that no one would ever notice he never put his heart into anything.

At least he hadn't until he'd stormed her wedding that morning and demanded she marry him instead.

Emmie's eyes fell on Theo's muscular back in the snug-fitting black T-shirt as he walked ahead of her, hearing the echo of his motorcycle boots and slap of her own flip-flops on the concrete floor. As his secretary, she'd previously only visited his home in a professional capacity, wearing a skirt suit and three-inch pumps. She'd typed out his orders and instructions on her tablet, or written in shorthand on a yellow legal pad, working long hours to make Theo's life easier, to make it frictionless, in conjunction with Wilson and with Mrs. Havers, the live-out staff.

Now Emmie was slouching through here in a sundress and flip-flops, coming for lunch, like a guest. No. More than that.

Pregnant with his baby. His future wife.

What had she gotten herself into?

Theo's butler stood waiting for them calmly in the two-story great room, in front of a wall of shining glass windows facing the terrace, and beyond that, the wide view of the park and surrounding city.

"Mr. Katrakis. Welcome home."

Wilson seemed imperturbable as ever in his black suit, the penthouse immaculately clean and ready, as if his boss hadn't just appeared with scant warning after seven months' absence.

The butler's eyes warmed when he saw Emmie. "Miss Swenson. I am pleased to see you're back…" Then his gaze fell to her pregnant belly, clearly visible beneath her white sundress. His eyes actually flickered. A first. Clearing his throat, he said only, "Lunch is on the terrace, sir. Along with the paperwork from your lawyer."

"Good."

"What paperwork?" Emmie asked, but Theo only turned away. "Nice to see you, Wilson," she called, then hurried to follow Theo through the sliding glass doors and out onto the terrace.

Outside was as ascetic in decor as inside, with only a few carefully placed tables and chairs. Stark planters with perfectly clipped greenery separated the terraces into separate spaces, for parties. A clear plexiglass railing, sturdy and bulletproof, revealed every inch of the jaw-dropping view of Central Park and New York City.

In the center of the largest terrace was the crown jewel, a grand dining table for twelve, beneath a pergola that seemed entirely constructed of greenery, white flowers and tiny white lights laced through the foliage.

Turning, Theo stood waiting beside the long table beneath the shade, holding out a chair. She quickened her pace.

"Thanks," she said awkwardly, letting him move her chair up after she sat. Theo had certainly never done *that* when she was his secretary.

Emmie looked at the delicious lunch spread across the table and hardly knew where to begin. Roast beef and turkey sandwiches on a platter, made with Mrs. Havers's fresh-baked baguettes; baby greens with walnuts and blueberries and balsamic dressing; juicy watermelon and red strawberries; salty home-fried chips; chocolate chip cookies for dessert, so warm the chocolate was still oozing from the buttery crust.

Sitting beside her, Theo poured a glass of water from the glass carafe and silently handed it to her.

Taking the glass, Emmie drank deeply and immediately felt refreshed by the cold, sparkling water. It occurred to her that she hadn't had anything to eat in hours, since last night really, when she'd forced down half a piece of cold pizza. She'd been too busy to eat, frantically decorating her wedding cake. That morning, she'd been too nervous, scared that her impending marriage to Harold Eklund was a big mistake.

Now, her appetite returned full force. She loaded her plate, and each thing tasted even better than the last, from the sweet-tart fruit to the crispy chips and tangy salad. She washed it all down with juice and more water, then dug in to her third sandwich, with the savory cheddar and roast beef with Dijon on chewy homemade bread.

Then her gaze fell on the clipped stack of papers, perhaps thirty pages of small-font type, sitting on the far end of the long table. Swallowing the last bite of her sandwich, she squinted. "What's that?"

Theo calmly finished his glass of water, washing down his

own plate of food which he'd already refilled several times. "Our prenuptial agreement."

Her mouth fell open. She said, faltering, "Prenup?"

He tilted his head. "Surely you, of all people, knew there'd be one."

After all her time working as his secretary, seeing Theo Katrakis fight for the best deal and always make sure he could never, ever get screwed by an opponent, Emmie should have expected it. But she hadn't.

She stared at the prenup.

Resting on top of the paperwork was an expensive pen, edged with twenty-four-karat gold. It was the pen Theo always used, signing with a flourish, when he felt he'd made a particularly ruthless deal. Her mouth went dry.

He smiled, his white teeth glinting in the sun. "You don't mind, do you?"

Emmie had talked herself into settling for a marriage of partnership if she couldn't have love, but it seemed even that had been too much to hope for.

So much for trust. Theo was already planning their divorce.

"I spoke with my lawyer," he said casually, eating the last chip from his plate, "and I'm afraid I can't marry you without it."

Turning, she stared out past the pergola to the vast greenery of Central Park and distant skyline, sharp against the blue sky.

"Emmie?"

"Fine." Standing up, she grabbed the prenup and returned to her chair. "I'll read it."

She read every word, carefully. She felt him getting restless as the minutes passed. Like many rich, powerful men, Theo disliked unfilled time. He looked down at his phone, reading and typing with his thumbs, fidgeting in his chair.

Emmie took her time, licking a fingertip as she turned the

pages, occasionally marking something in a margin for her own memory.

"It's fine for you to get your own attorney to look it over, if you wish," Theo said finally.

"It's not exactly hard to understand," she said and continued to placidly read in the shade of the pergola as Theo got up and paced the terrace. Finally, she looked up.

"All right. I'll sign it."

He returned quickly to the table, his handsome face relieved. "Good. I'll get Wilson to witness, and we can have a judge here to perform the ceremony in—"

"But I have a few conditions of my own," she said.

Theo sat in his chair, leaning back to cross his ankle over his knee, his body language relaxed, friendly now he'd gotten his way. He smiled. "I would expect nothing less."

"Just three small things."

"I'm all ears."

Emmie took a deep breath. "First. Our primary domicile will be in New York City."

He tilted his head with a frown. "I travel constantly for work. You know that better than anyone."

She looked at him evenly. "And the baby and I may travel with you...sometimes. But I want to raise our child in one place, a real home. Not drag him from place to place living out of a suitcase like some backpacker on a gap year."

Theo set both feet back on the floor, sitting up straight, all his earlier casual friendliness gone now that there was a threat to his future convenience.

"Why here? Why not Aspen, St. Moritz, London?" he asked, listing the settings of his other multi-million-dollar residences. "Or even Greece? I just bought something there today..."

"You might own houses in those places, but they're not home."

"Home can be anywhere we are," he challenged. "We could live happily in five-star hotels in Paris, Tokyo, Sydney. Why not—" his dark eyes lifted to hers "—Rio?"

She shivered. No. She wasn't going to think about that night in Rio.

"New York is my home," she said quietly. She clasped her hands in her lap so he couldn't see them trembling. "My family is thirty minutes away. My friends live here. My *best* friend. And yours," she added, thinking of Honora and Nico.

His jaw tightened. He was clearly irritated at her persistence. As his secretary, she'd always done what he wanted.

"Fine," he bit out. "Your second condition?"

Emmie lifted her chin. "I want your permission to help my family as I see fit. Don't worry, nothing crazy," she rushed to say as he raised his eyebrows. "Just enough to replace what I do in Dad's business and at home. Some money for his retirement. Maybe some of my brothers could go to community college or learn a trade, since I'm not sure they're all interested in plumbing." Another reason the business had been doing so badly the last few years.

"Very well." Theo's handsome face was cold, unreadable. "And the last condition?"

This was the hard one. Emmie took a deep breath.

"I release you from all the adultery clauses in the prenup." She drummed her fingers nervously over the pile of papers. "As far as I'm concerned, you can sleep with whomever you want."

Theo gasped, his eyes wide. She'd never seen him look so shocked.

"What?" he stammered. "Why?"

"Marriage lasts a lifetime. Or it should. And it would be unreasonable for me to expect you to never have sex again. So my final condition of marrying you is—sleep with anyone you want." Emmie lifted her gaze to his. "As long as it's not with me."

* * *

Be married to Emmie and never make love to her?

Had she lost her mind?

Theo set his jaw. Taking a deep breath, he tried to control the pounding of his heart and make his voice sound reasonable. "You're angry I want you to sign a prenup."

"No," Emmie said. Looking up at the pergola's greenery and white blooms, she sighed with a wistful smile. "You are who you are."

Theo had always tried to take pride in that, so why did her words make him feel like he'd somehow let her down? Worse—like he'd let *himself* down?

Stubbornly, he pushed the feeling aside. "So you're trying to punish me for being practical and logical? *You*, of all people? Because that's all a prenup is. A logistical plan."

"Why would I punish you for that?" she agreed sardonically. Dappled sunlight caught gold and strawberry glints in her dark blond hair. "I love that you're already planning our divorce."

He ground his teeth. "I'm not..." Then he realized that a prenuptial agreement was, by definition, laying the groundwork for their divorce. He took a breath. "You must see that any man in my position has no choice but to ask for this. I'd be a fool otherwise."

"And you're not a fool."

"Exactly."

"Because you earned your money the hard way, all on your own."

"Yes."

"And it wouldn't be fair if you were forced to share *your* money with some nobody ex-wife, who'd done absolutely nothing but raise your child."

"Uh..." he said, sensing danger. He changed tactics. "So

you're just trying to delay signing it? By coming up with a crazy idea of celibacy that would only hurt us both?"

"I'm not delaying anything. I'll sign right now." Brushing through the pages, she marked it up with her pen and handed it to him. "Here. Call in Wilson to witness."

Looking down, Theo saw she'd crossed out the clause that would have paid her millions in any divorce caused by his adultery. "You can't be…" As he read further, his eyes widened. He looked up triumphantly. "You made a mistake."

"Did I?"

"You forgot to cross out the same penalty if *you* cheat on me." He snorted. "You can't mean that you'd encourage me to sleep with every woman in the world with no problem, while if you so much as kiss another man, I could divorce you and you wouldn't get a penny, not even if we'd been married thirty years. How would that be fair?"

"It wasn't a mistake," she said serenely.

"What?"

Emmie shrugged. "I'm not going to cheat on you. For me, marriage vows are sacred."

Insinuating that they weren't sacred for him? He ground his teeth. "So let me get this straight. You're telling me to sleep around, while you're planning to remain chaste as a virgin for the rest of your life."

Her cool violet eyes met his. "For the rest of my life."

Theo leaned forward in his chair, furious.

"Why, Emmie?" he ground out. "Tell me why."

She looked down at her clasped hands in the lap of her white sundress, resting close to the swell of her belly. "I don't have to explain."

"You're wrong. I deserve to know." He licked his dry lips. "It can't be…can't…"

It couldn't be that she didn't want him.

Could it?

A hot breeze blew across the rooftop terrace, ruffling the papers on the table, swaying the flowers and vines woven above. Several pages of the prenup broke free from the paper clip and scuttered across the terrace. Rising, he went to pick them up.

All he could think about was their kiss that morning, how he'd felt her respond in his arms, rising like the center of a storm.

And in Rio—

After weeks of work closing a development deal, he and Emmie had both been exhausted. When she'd sighed that they never had time to see anything but the job site and conference rooms in the cities they visited, Theo had decided to prove her wrong. So after they'd closed the deal, he'd called in a favor and taken her to Mount Corcovado above the city after the site was officially closed for the night. The two of them were alone at the base of Rio's most famous symbol, the massive Cristo Redentor statue, lit up in the darkness.

"It's beautiful," she had whispered, shivering. Seeing she was cold, even in the warm night, he'd put his jacket over her, and together they'd looked out at the lights of the city, scattered islands and moonlight over Guanabara Bay.

Then he'd paused, his hands still around her. He felt a tropical breeze blow against his overheated skin. Their eyes caught in the moonlight, and feeling like he was in a dream he'd lowered his mouth to hers.

Kissing Emmie at the top of Mount Corcovado, with Rio sparkling like stars beneath them, he'd felt dazed, drugged with desire. They'd wordlessly returned to the waiting sedan and their hotel on Ipanema Beach. The whole time, his brain was shrieking that he had to stop this, that it was madness, that if he didn't stop it would destroy the best relationship he'd ever had.

Because after nearly a year and a half together, they'd become more than boss and secretary. Working together, day and night, sharing setbacks and triumphs, he'd come to consider Emmie a friend, and those he let even slightly past his guard were few.

But when they'd reached his hotel suite, she'd lifted her violet-blue eyes, hazy with desire, and licked her swollen lower lip.

"Kiss me," she'd whispered.

And he'd been lost. He didn't care that he was her boss. Even if it destroyed him and burned his entire fortune to ash in that moment, he would still have taken her. As the warm wind blew from the open balcony, twisting the curtains, he'd possessed her as his own and, discovering her virginity, known such pure and perfect ecstasy he thought he might die in her arms.

And in some ways, he had.

Emmie had disappeared the next morning, after she'd gotten the awful phone call from her father. He'd expected her to return after the funeral, but instead, she'd called him and said she was never coming back.

And since Rio, Theo had had no interest in other women, no matter how beautiful. What supermodel, what mere *actress*, could possibly compare to the glory he'd known in the arms of his secretary that forbidden night?

The night they'd conceived a child...

Now, Theo's gaze lingered on her bare pink Cupid's-bow lips, falling unwillingly to the swell of her breasts overflowing the modest neckline of her sundress. His body was taut with desire.

And yet Emmie wanted to refuse him her bed? She wanted to push him into the arms of *other women*?

"Whatever your reason, it can't be you don't want me," he said hoarsely. "I know you do. Just as I want you."

Emmie shifted in her chair. The shade from the pergola's

foliage left patterns of light and dark against her skin, the curve of her cheekbone, the sweep of her lashes that seemed to tremble before she turned away, looking out at the Manhattan skyline.

"Wanting you isn't the problem," she said finally.

"Then, what is?"

Rising to her feet, Emmie turned away, walking toward the clear railing of the terrace's edge. She looked out onto the view of Central Park and sun-drenched blue sky. Rising to his feet, he followed her.

"Emmie," he said softly, coming up behind her. "What is it?"

She whirled around. "I'm afraid, all right?"

"Afraid?" He was bewildered. "Of what? Of me?"

"Afraid…" Emmie lifted her gaze, her lovely face anguished. "If I sleep with you again," she whispered, "I'm afraid you'll break my heart."

"Break your…?" Theo staggered back, his brow furrowed in shock. That would have to mean… "You can't be saying that you…love me?"

"I know, right?" She looked away. "What kind of fool would that make me?"

He exhaled in relief. She'd scared him for a second. Relieved, he gave a low laugh. "We both know you're too smart for that. You're practical. Modern. You don't do feelings. You're like me. Plus, you know me too well. Remember what you said when I first asked you to work for me?"

She didn't join his laugh. "I said pigs would fly before I could ever love you."

"So," he tilted his head, "how could I ever break your heart?"

Emmie looked down at her flip-flops.

"No matter what you might think right now, Theo, we both know you can't commit to one woman for long. You can't bear to be tied down. There's no way you could be faithful to one woman for the rest of your life. And no matter how practical I might be," she said softly, "I can't be the lover of a man who won't be true." She looked up. "The only way it won't hurt me is to never sleep with you again. If we can just be partners. Friends."

Theo stared at her, his whole body thrumming with emotion. "You think I can't be faithful?"

Avoiding his eyes, Emmie snorted, shaking her head. It was strange to see bitter cynicism on her young face, usually so earnest. "I've never seen you commit to anyone, Theo. Even before I started working for you, I knew you were a playboy. How could I possibly be the woman to tame you?" She looked down at her old sundress, her flip-flops, the chipped pink polish on her toes. "Look at me. And look," she said as she lifted her chin, "at *you*."

Theo shifted his motorcycle boots against the terrace. His black clothes, which had seemed so reasonable on his private jet that morning, were now far too hot in the sun.

Or maybe it was having Emmie so close.

He exhaled. He knew there was some truth to what she said. He'd never been interested in settling down. No, more than that—he'd actively avoided it, at all costs. He knew he was attractive to women, in a thuggish sort of way, just as he knew that he was good at driving and ruthless in business. He used what he had as a tool to get what he wanted, nothing more and nothing less. His face had been given to him by his parents—by the father he'd never known, and the mother he didn't want to remember. He couldn't take credit for his face, apart from the fight that had broken his nose at fifteen.

He could take some credit for his body, due to frequent exercise at boxing gyms. But that was to alleviate stress. A therapist had once told him exercise could help relax him and calm his mind. He'd never gone back to the therapist—

he didn't like how she'd tried to pry into things best left buried—but he'd taken her suggestion about exercise. It often helped to pound a punching bag or willing opponent until he was exhausted and covered with sweat. Drinking could also work, if he didn't mind the hangover. And sex, though that often had unfortunate consequence of dealing with a woman begging for his love or attention afterward.

Work was the best distraction of all. Until that night in Rio, it had been the only thing he could always rely on, better than any drug, to help smooth the rough edges of the day and the hollow emptiness in his soul.

Then the night with Emmie had changed everything. For the only time in his life, he'd truly been able to forget everything he wanted to forget in an ecstasy so deep it was almost holy.

And now she wanted to refuse him? She wanted to live as his wife, in his home, raising his child—but deny him her body, pushing him into the cold, unappealing arms of other women?

"You're wrong, Emmie," he said in a low voice. He lifted his eyes to hers. "I can be faithful. I *have been*."

She swallowed. "What are you saying?"

Coming closer, Theo pulled her into his arms beside the railing with all of Central Park and New York City at their feet.

"Since our night together, there's been no one else. *No one*. And I swear to you now—" he searched her gaze fiercely "—if you marry me, for the rest of my life you'll be the only one."

CHAPTER FIVE

CANDLES WERE GLOWING across the penthouse terrace as Emmie took a deep breath and stepped out into the warm summer night.

Another wedding, another day as a bride. But this time was so different. The lights of the city sparkled like diamonds, as above, the moon glowed like a pearl in black velvet.

Holding her arm, her father couldn't speak for the tears in his eyes. Her proud, gruff father openly weeping wasn't the only reason he was almost unrecognizable. His gray hair was sleekly trimmed, and he was dressed in a designer suit, with a new gold watch on his wrist, a gift from her bridegroom.

Emmie had received the upgrade treatment, too. She hardly recognized herself, either, in the short, deceptively simple shift dress that could best be described as quiet luxury: hemline at the knee, cowl neckline, long sleeves with a slight bell shape at the wrist. Her hair had been styled in a soft, elegant chignon, and rather than veiled was adorned with a large white rose. Her makeup was discreet, far more discreet than the enormous pearl studs in her ears—those, too, were a gift from the groom, and she was sure they'd cost a fortune. But not as much as the emerald-cut diamond engagement ring on her left hand, which was big enough to be seen from space.

Her cheeks burned as she and Karl walked past the fifty or so standing guests watching them with big eyes. Theo had hired the most expensive wedding planner in the city and demanded a small, elegant ceremony to be produced in four days. The woman had done as he'd asked, for an exorbitant amount that still made Emmie wince to think of it. It was unreasonable how much he'd spent, to achieve something they could have done quietly and easily by going to the courthouse downtown. But what Theo Katrakis wanted Theo Katrakis got.

She shivered.

Walking ahead of them was Honora Ferraro, her best friend who'd returned from the Caribbean especially to be her one and only bridesmaid. She held a single long-stemmed white rose, matching the seven of them in Emmie's elegant bridal bouquet—exactly seven roses, to symbolize harmony and also the four elements and yin and yang and something else. Emmie had been too distracted to follow the planner's explanation, but she figured she'd take all the luck she could get.

The last few days had been a whirlwind of wedding planning and dress fittings and cake tastings. Other than paying for everything, Theo had been absent, busy at the office, as he said, trying to finish up some loose ends so they could leave to honeymoon at some mysterious location. It had been strange to be sleeping in the guest room of this big penthouse, not quite a wife, not his employee, not even really his guest. But in a few minutes, after they spoke their vows, she would have a new place in the world. She'd be Mrs. Theo Katrakis.

Walking across the terrace to harp music, Emmie tottered on four-inch white strappy sandals. Her gaze rested on her four younger brothers, all looking unusually civilized in sleek designer suits that matched her father's.

Her family was far more thrilled about this wedding than they'd been about her prospective alliance to Harold Eklund four days before. Emmie privately wondered if it was possible Theo had bought them all off.

But then, was she any better?

She was marrying him for their baby's sake, she told herself firmly. Their marriage would be a practical one, a partnership to create a stable home for their child. Beyond that, she didn't give two hoots about Theo's wealth. As long as a family could pay their bills, she'd seen no evidence that a big fortune made anyone happier in life. It sure hadn't given Theo much joy that she could see. And yet he kept chasing it.

No, Emmie didn't care about Theo's fortune. She was no gold digger.

But there would be other benefits she did care about...

She shivered as her eyes fell on her bridegroom, waiting in front of the pergola with the judge and Nico, his best man. Behind them, Manhattan sparkled beneath the sweep of the summer moonlight.

Theo's black eyes met hers.

He was wearing a bespoke tuxedo that fit him to perfection, hand-tailored to the hard angles of his powerfully muscled body. She looked up, dazzled by his masculine beauty. Even the slight crookedness of his nose made him more exotic, so strong, so different.

Her heart was pounding.

Theo had insisted on replacing the line in the prenup that she'd tried to cross out. They'd both signed the original version, which listed financial penalties for adultery—by either party. In spite of her weak protests, he'd seemed utterly confident that he'd soon be able to seduce her.

Emmie shivered, fearing he was right. She wasn't sure how long she could keep him from her bed, or even if she should, when she wanted him just as badly as he wanted her. Even now, just looking at him, her body was fire. She didn't realize she'd licked her lips until she tasted lipstick.

She wanted him.

She always had, from the day they'd met at Honora and Nico's wedding years before, Emmie as maid of honor, Theo the best man. Even though he was a handsome billionaire playboy, and she'd been a chubby, working-class nobody, not remotely pretty or interesting. She'd still wanted him. Desperately. She'd hidden her longing with barbed insults for years.

Now Theo was going to be hers.

No. He'd already been hers, though she had not known it. He'd had no other lover since the night they'd conceived their baby.

He'd had no reason to be faithful. They'd never officially been a couple. Why would a playboy be faithful to a one-night stand?

And yet he had. He'd wanted only her.

Knowing that, how could Emmie resist?

"You're practical," he'd told her. "Modern. You don't do feelings. You're like me."

She wished he was right. That she could simply enjoy sex with her husband, without letting her heart get in the way.

But that wasn't her, and she knew it. She had to resist. *Had to.* Because if she succumbed to her desire, there would be nothing to keep her from falling in love with him all over again. Even though she knew her husband would never, ever love her back.

And she'd be lost…

As they reached the pergola, her father transferred her hand to Theo's, and he kept his large hand wrapped reverently around hers. Emmie looked up at the soft flicker of light playing across her bridegroom's rugged face from the columns of tall white candles.

The vows were spoken. A plain gold band for him, a thin platinum band matching the diamond engagement ring for her. There was nothing religious in the judge's words, and yet this moment held a breathless hush to Emmie as they were united, their lives tied together forever.

Then the judge grinned. "You may kiss the bride."

As the guests standing around them applauded and cheered

on the terrace, their noise echoing out into the warm summer night in this sparkling city, Theo lowered his head and kissed her.

And as his lips touched hers, Emmie trembled and was suddenly scared she was already lost.

It was over. He'd done it. They were *married*.

There was no getting out of it now.

As Theo pulled away from the brief kiss, after the judge proclaimed them husband and wife, he looked down at his new bride amid the applause.

Emmie's eyes were luminous, glowing brighter than the candles around them, brighter than the city lights or stars in the darkness above. But he saw something in her expression. Some private grief, some agonized question.

And he felt something tighten painfully in his chest.

"Congratulations, man," Nico said, clapping him on the shoulder. His best man had been a rock through this. That very morning, when Theo had returned to the penthouse at dawn after finding reasons to stay at the office all night, he'd felt cold and clammy and wondered if he was coming down with something.

Fear. He'd been coming down with fear.

Emmie, of course, had no idea of his surfaced doubts. He'd known he couldn't tell her. Their union was already on shaky-enough ground, without him sharing, just hours before their wedding, that he felt sick to the soul at the promise he was about to make.

To love and cherish forever? What was he thinking? No one could promise that. Life was hard and uncertain.

And fidelity? It had been easy to be faithful to her for the last seven months. He hadn't even wanted another woman. But how could he promise that he'd never feel differently? What if he did?

What if Emmie did? What if she—

And it was at that moment he'd realized he was sweating and had picked up his phone blindly, intending to call his pilot and arrange a quick flight to the other side of the world.

But he couldn't do that. He couldn't abandon his unborn son. Not after what Theo himself had gone through when he was young.

So instead, he'd called his best friend—his only close friend, really, aside from Emmie herself. He knew Nico Ferraro had once gone through something similar himself, marrying the granddaughter of an employee in a shotgun wedding—literally—after she surprised him with a pregnancy, knocking on his door in the middle of the night, right before her enraged grandfather showed up with a shotgun, demanding they marry.

But if Theo had secretly hoped that his friend would suggest, as he himself had before Nico's wedding, that it wasn't too late to make a run for it, he'd been disappointed. Instead, Nico had listened, sympathized and then proceeded to tell stories about how glad he was that he'd married Honora, that the marriage had been the making of him, that he couldn't imagine a life without her or their children.

All very well for him. But from a young age, Theo had seen too much in the world to believe in fairy tales. He'd never believed in any of it—that good always triumphed over evil, that love could last forever, that families could love and protect each other to the end.

The only way to survive in this harsh life was to be strong and alone.

But even knowing this, Theo had found somewhat to his surprise that he couldn't desert his son. So he'd gone through with the wedding. It had taken all his strength to make his lips speak the words.

Now, as Theo turned to face his wedding guests, he was a

married man. And looking at his bride's big, nervous eyes, he was wondering if he'd just made the biggest mistake of his life.

"We're so happy for you both." Nico's wife, Honora, was beaming at them. "Our two best friends married? It's a dream come true!"

"I still can't believe you were the father of Emmie's baby all along. Even when I told you she was pregnant by some man in Rio," Nico said, laughing, "you didn't say a word!"

Emmie blushed. "It just happened. We never intended..."

"Yes, we know how that goes," Nico said, exchanging a loving, amused glance with his wife, whose cheeks blushed even redder than Emmie's. Honora turned quickly to her friend.

"Just think, our children will grow up together." She hugged Emmie carefully, so as not to muss her gown. "Our families can take vacations together. The South of France. Italy. Greece."

"Except Theo hates Greece," Nico said, looking at him uncomfortably.

Both women looked at him, startled.

"You do?" Emmie said.

"How could anyone hate Greece?" Honora said.

Theo kept his expression cold. "Actually, I recently bought property on a Greek island."

Nico, who knew only the tiniest bit of Theo's history, looked astonished. "You did?"

Seeing all the other guests waiting to congratulate them, Emmie's family and a few friends from her neighborhood and a whole bunch of his own acquaintances, important society and business people he didn't actually give a damn about, Theo decided he wanted to finish this wedding as quickly as possible. He grabbed Emmie's hand. "We should have our dance."

"Great idea." Nico immediately took his own wife in his

arms. "We must take advantage of being on our own tonight. No babies or grandparents to interrupt us."

"Is that your new definition of romance?" Honora teased, but her eyes flashed with love.

Emmie seemed less keen to dance with Theo. "Already?" She looked around. "But we haven't even said hello to all our guests—"

"We can do what we want," Theo said roughly, by which he meant what *he* wanted.

And so, to the despair of the wedding planner, Theo started the dancing an hour ahead of schedule, before the cocktails or hors d'oeuvres had been served, before cake, before even the champagne toast.

As he led her onto the impromptu dance floor on the terrace beneath the moonlight, he tried to ignore the erratic pounding of his heart. It was only when the music started and he pulled her into his arms that he could breathe again.

Yes. When he held Emmie in his arms, her body pressing against his own, the roar in his ears receded, the panic disappeared.

She looked up at him, her eyes bright, her mouth curving up. "You really don't like weddings, do you? Not even your own."

Especially not my own, he wanted to say, but he didn't because that might have hurt her feelings.

So he said brusquely, "I got a phone call right before the ceremony. I need to go into the office."

"What…now?"

"On the way to the airport."

"Fine," she sighed. She glanced at her father and two of her brothers, now smiling at the married couple from the edge of the dance floor. "What did you do to them? I think they now love you more than me."

He said coolly, "You told me you wanted your family taken care of financially, did you not?"

Her eyes focused on him. "Yes?"

"I told them I'd pay for any upgrades the plumbing business needed, and housing for your brothers, as well as for college or trade school for the ones who preferred to branch out on their own."

"You did what?" Her lips parted. "What did my father say?"

"He demanded that I promise to always take care of you and make you happy," he said shortly. Another promise he wasn't sure he'd be able to keep. All these promises he'd spread around. His heart started to pound again.

"We'll both try to be good partners," Emmie said stiffly, and she looked away, a little wistfully he thought, at Honora and Nico clinging to each other passionately on the dance floor.

Theo looked down at her. In the moonlight, his new wife looked breathtakingly beautiful. The white bloom in her hair gave her the look of a medieval maiden in a pre-Raphaelite painting. The soft white silk dress fit like water running over the swollen curves of her pregnant body.

Turning beneath his gaze, Emmie furrowed her brow, her pretty face turning uncertain. "What is it?" She licked her lips. "Is something wrong?"

The music ended, and he thankfully didn't have to answer. Taking her hand, he led her off the dance floor.

Theo endured the next hour by watching the clock, smiling when required, saying *Thank you for coming* when he was congratulated, speaking directly into his own camera in Greek, sending a video message to Sofia in Paris, telling her he'd see her soon. It was the least he could do, after he'd all but forbidden her to attend his wedding today. She'd cried on the phone when he told her.

But it was better for her to keep her distance. Her life was better without Theo in it. Why couldn't she see that? Hadn't he ruined enough for her?

Pushing thoughts of Sofia away, he focused on listening to Emmie's carefully written, if somewhat stilted, wedding toast. As she teased him about his workaholic ways, causing a ruffle of laughter through the crowd, she also made her deep respect for him clear. By the end of her toast, as she held up her sparkling San Pellegrino, and everyone else held up their Dom Pérignon, Theo felt surprised, touched, but most of all deeply uncomfortable. He knew he didn't deserve praise.

His own toast, spoken off the cuff, certainly made that clear. He'd simply held up his glass and looked at his bride. "To you!"

Even Nico, normally his most loyal friend, looked a little startled at Theo's obvious lack of preparation or his plain ineptitude.

But for the last few days, Theo had been unable to think of writing his wedding toast to his bride without breaking into a sweat. A pity he couldn't ask Emmie to write it for him, but even he could see that wouldn't be appropriate. As it was, he'd been forced to delegate the task to Edna, the elderly secretary sent to him by an agency after Emmie left—Edna with the dyed black hair who distrusted computers, smelled vaguely of mothballs, and repeatedly called Theo *hon*. Sadly, her attempt at a wedding toast, fusty witticisms cobbled together from some long-dead humorist's book of maxims, was unintelligible.

So he'd had to wing it. If brevity was the soul of wit, *To you!* should have been a wedding toast for the ages.

Unfortunately, his bride didn't seem to see it that way. Her lovely face had fallen.

Not the first time Theo had disappointed her. Definitely wouldn't be the last.

"We should go," he said in a low voice while everyone

was still gulping their drinks. "I need to pick something up at the office."

She looked bewildered. "You said we could do it later."

"And now it's later."

Her brow furrowed. "Can't we just send someone for it?"

"I need to do it myself."

"Why?"

"I just do."

"But we haven't even cut the cake. It came from the best baker in the city…" Then she looked at his face more closely. "All right. Let's go."

Theo blinked, feeling a sense of vertigo at her sudden change. He wondered what she'd seen in his face. He didn't like to think of anyone being able to see into his soul. He told himself it didn't matter, as long as he got what he wanted. Which was getting the hell out of here.

Theo gave discreet orders to his butler, and within five minutes, bride and groom were heading for the car, showered with rice, praise and some good-natured teasing by their guests: "I've never seen anyone so keen to start their honeymoon!"

But once the two of them were sitting in the back of the Rolls-Royce, as Bernard drove them through the dark, empty streets of a late weekday evening in Manhattan, it was suddenly far too quiet for Theo's liking. Especially with their suitcases in the trunk for their honeymoon. He'd picked the location as an act of bravado, a way to prove to himself how far he'd come. But had he? Had he really?

For his whole adult life, he'd managed to contain his emotions, to avoid even having them. But now, for some reason, they were suddenly circling.

Emmie's eyes caught his in the back seat, and he looked away sharply, his heart in his throat.

Normally, he would have thrown himself into work for four days or ten, until he was too exhausted and distracted to feel anything. But he could hardly work now, when he'd insisted on dragging his new bride from their wedding. He couldn't exactly jump out of the car and run a quick ten miles, either.

Only one other stress reliever would do.

His gaze slid sideways to the curve of Emmie's breast. They were married now. Leaving on honeymoon. He didn't believe for a second that Emmie actually intended their marriage to be in name only. She'd enjoyed their night together as much as he had. So either she was lying to him, trying to gain the upper hand in their relationship—good luck with that—or else she was lying to herself for some reason. Either way, it was time to clear the air and fall into bed. He couldn't wait until they arrived at their honeymoon destination. And his private jet did have a bed...

In Midtown, he strode into his office building to get this errand done so they could reach that jet as quickly as possible. Emmie followed in her wedding dress. He greeted the security guard, who took in their attire and smiled.

"Congratulations, sir."

"Thanks for coming—" Catching his automatic response too late, Theo corrected himself. "Er, thanks for keeping an eye on things here."

Upstairs, Theo found his empty office floor and all the unfilled cubicles deathly quiet.

"Why are we here?" Emmie asked behind him. He glanced at her, then without responding, kept walking.

His private office was large, with high ceilings, and a very expensive desk. His company had offices in cities around the world, but New York City was technically his headquarters. Unlocking his safe hidden behind a black-and-white Jackson Pollock painting, he pulled out a small, plainly wrapped package, three inches square. His hand trembled a little as he looked down at it in his palm.

"It's funny to be here." Emmie gave a low laugh as she

looked around the office. "So much has changed since I was
here last..."

Moonlight from the high arched window flooded his private office, illuminating dappled patterns on her wedding
dress and the white rose in her hair, her eyes bright. She
looked like an angel. An angel he didn't deserve.

And a sensual one, a divine angel of sin. His gaze fell to
her full breasts and belly, straining against the thin white of
the silk, and he shuddered. There was no way he could wait
until they reached the jet at Teterboro.

Now. He needed her now.

Locking the safe, sliding the painting back over it, he
dropped the small package in his jacket pocket. He crossed
the office, standing inches away from her, towering over her.

Emmie looked up in the moonlight, and her expression
changed. She said brokenly, "Theo—"

But he didn't want to hear arguments or reasons. He didn't
want to think at all. After everything he'd endured to do the
right thing—marry her—he wanted only to claim his prize.

Pulling her roughly into his arms, Theo kissed her. No
soft short kiss, either, like the one he'd given her at their wedding. No.

This kiss was hungry. Dirty. Hard. He plundered her mouth
in an intensity of need. She gasped against his lips, and for a
moment he felt her hesitate. His grip tightened.

Then she returned his kiss with a desperation that matched
his own. A bed, they needed a bed—

The desk. The big desk where they'd spent over a year
working together, where for months he'd tried not to notice
how beautiful his secretary was, when he'd tried and failed
not to desire her. Yes. He'd take her on the desk, right here
and now—

Cupping her breasts through the sensuous silk, he deepened the kiss as she trembled in his arms. Reaching beneath

the fabric of her bra, he felt the warmth of her skin against his palms and stroked her nipples between his fingers.

Ripping away from the kiss, he lowered his head to one nipple, then the other, savoring the taste as each pebbled in the heat of his wet mouth. He heard her moan and was suddenly so hard his whole body shook with need. He had to have her—now. Pushing her against the desk, he fell to his knees in front of her, yanking up her wedding dress, reaching for her white lacy panties, pushing her thighs apart—

"No," she choked out suddenly, and then, "No!"

Roughly, she shoved him away. Startled, Theo stumbled back. Regaining his balance, he straightened. For a moment, they stared at each other in the shadows, blinking in the moonlight.

"I meant what I said," Emmie said hoarsely. "I'm not going to sleep with you."

Then she slid off the desk and, without a single backward glance, left him standing in the shadows of his office.

He stared at the empty doorway, his heart still pounding, dazed with lust.

Seducing her was going to require more effort than he'd thought.

Theo took a deep breath, gripping his hands against the desk. He wanted her. Badly.

And he would have her. They had their whole honeymoon ahead of them. Seducing his wife was now his one and only goal.

Theo intended to be utterly ruthless.

CHAPTER SIX

FLINGING OPEN THE blue shutters, Emmie stuck her head out the window and took an invigorating breath of sea-salt air.

Beyond the whitewashed walls of the tiny Greek hotel, which was really just a few guest rooms above a taverna, she could see the sapphire Aegean sparkling in the morning sun.

Past the fishing boats in the bay, she saw a yacht on the horizon. Was it Theo's, coming to collect them? She hoped not.

This sleepy village was off the beaten path, far from Mykonos or Santorini. Lyra was just a small rocky isle with limited ferry service and no nightclubs or mega resorts, with more grazing sheep than tourists. The island had just one village, also named Lyra, with a few scattered two-story hotels, quiet beach coves, and tavernas overlooking the harbor, where fishermen with stubbly beards and low-slung caps brought in that day's catch with nets on their rusted boats.

And it was all so wonderful, so beautiful and glorious, that it made Emmie's heart hurt with joy.

She turned away from the window, back to their small room. The innkeeper's wife had grandly called it the honeymoon suite, but maybe that was because space was so tight in here, honeymooners were the only ones who'd want it. Seeing her husband sleeping in the small bed, her heart twisted as tightly as the sheets tangled at his feet.

They'd slept together last night.

Just *slept*.

She'd barely managed to push him away in New York. Refusing him, when she wanted him just as badly, was the hardest thing she'd ever done. But she couldn't give in, not without falling for him all over again. And he was not just out of her league: she knew that giving her body to a man who had no capacity for love would only end with her heart bleeding on the floor.

When the driver had taken them to the airport outside New York City and they'd boarded his jet, she'd waited a little breathlessly for his reaction. Would he punish her with the silent treatment? Give up his vow of fidelity and start texting some more accommodating woman? Or, worst fear of all, would he try to seduce her on the spacious white leather sofa of the jet's cabin, when she had nowhere to flee?

If so, she honestly didn't know how long she could hold out, not against him, not against her own treacherous, desperate desire.

Instead, Theo had done something she'd never expected. He'd neither punished her nor pressed his sensual advantage.

He'd acted like a friend.

Theo had been solicitous of Emmie's comfort, asking the flight attendant for food and drinks that he thought might tempt her. When he'd suggested that they change out of their wedding clothes into *something more comfortable*, she'd braced herself—until he'd come out of the back room of the jet's cabin wearing a faded rock-concert T-shirt and slim-fitting sweatpants. He actually wanted her to be *comfortable*.

So a little nervously, she'd changed out of her wedding dress and high heels into comfy leggings and an oversize hoodie emblazoned with the name of her community college. They'd washed down hors d'oeuvres and a charcuterie platter with sparkling water and soda and watched a mutually agreed-upon movie. Nervous of rom-coms, she'd argued in favor of a female-led comedy, and he'd let her talk him into it. It was only later that she realized his negotiation had been only pretense. He'd let her choose.

Midway through the movie, sated and sleepy, she'd fallen asleep. She'd woken over the Atlantic to find Theo sleeping beside her on the white leather sofa, his arm protectively over her shoulders, his cheek resting on the top of her head.

They'd arrived at Lyra yesterday, coming by speedboat from the nearest airstrip at Paros, a few islands over. She'd closed her eyes, feeling the sun on her face and wind through her hair, then heard her husband's apologetic voice beside her.

"The yacht is stuck in Athens till tomorrow, I'm afraid. We'll have to manage at the local hotel tonight."

He'd looked so regretful, as if he really feared he was disappointing her, that Emmie expected to find Lyra an abandoned ghost village and the local hotel a dilapidated shepherd's hovel.

Instead, she'd discovered a charming Greek village clinging to the edge of the sea, full of kind, friendly people. Waking ten minutes ago, she'd felt refreshed, reborn, after a night of deep, delicious sleep as her husband had held her in his arms.

Held her. Just held her.

Maybe this marriage was going to work after all.

As long as their partnership was based only on comfort, support and friendship—

But as she looked back at the tiny double bed in the small room, her eyes forgot they were *friends...only friends...just friends* and unwillingly caressed the length of his powerful tanned body half-hidden beneath the tangle of sheets. The muscles of his chest stood out starkly, the morning sunlight gleaming over his thick biceps and thighs, hardened from his gym habit.

He was wearing only boxer shorts. She dimly recalled hearing him get up at sunrise, quietly change his clothes and go out. When he'd returned, he'd gone to the tiny en suite and turned on the shower. Gauging by the running shoes, T-shirt and shorts left on the floor, he must have gone for a run.

What drove him? she wondered. Why did he throw his body so hard at everything, whether it was working superhuman hours or going for a long run after very few hours of sleep?

Her gaze lingered on his hard-muscled chest, following the dark line of hair down his six-pack abs to the very center of his masculine body, beneath the boxer shorts mostly hidden by the cotton sheets twisted between his sprawled, powerful legs.

"Morning."

At Theo's deep, lazy voice, she looked up sharply, her cheeks hot. With his arm still tossed above his head on the pillow, he gave a wicked, amused smile. He'd clearly caught her perusing his near-naked body.

"Morning." She trembled a little, waiting for him to hold out his hand, to try to tempt her to join him in bed. Could she resist? Could she refuse?

Instead, he sat up in bed, smiling. "I'm starving. Want some breakfast?"

She smiled back, relieved. "Sure…"

Then her throat closed as he rose from the bed, giving her a full view of his powerful, nearly naked body. She saw the scarred flesh of his ankle, burned from an engine fire in a long-ago car race. She caught her breath as he bent over, giving her a view of his muscled back, the boxers straining over the powerful curve of his backside as he dug through his suitcase. Cheeks burning, she turned away, staring out the window at the sea.

"Ready." Dressed casually in a collared linen shirt and khaki shorts, he gave her an innocent smile, even as she thought she saw a glint of wicked amusement in his eyes. And his lips curved upward at the edges—

Oh, heaven. How had her gaze fallen to his lips? She swallowed. "Ready."

But her cheeks still felt hot as they went downstairs to share a late-morning breakfast on the taverna's small patio at the water's edge.

She had dressed modestly in the loose blue cotton sundress and sandals she'd bought in the village yesterday, her hair in a simple ponytail. With only sunscreen applied to her skin, she looked like a tourist and respectable married pregnant lady, she hoped, no different from any other... No one would know their honeymoon was chaste, she told herself. Biting her lip, she stared down at the huge rock on her left hand as the innkeeper spoke to Theo, beaming, clearly delighted to discover that his guest spoke fluent Greek.

Sipping her creamy decaf coffee, Emmie looked around at the other guests who'd straggled down to breakfast late. They all looked like honeymooners for sure, with a post-sex glow. One young couple, holding hands over the table, kept kissing each other when they thought no one was looking. Her heart twisted with unwelcome envy.

"I'm sorry this honeymoon is such a disappointment." She turned to her husband wide-eyed, suddenly terrified he'd read her mind. Sipping his own black coffee, he gave her a mild smile. "With the yacht coming late."

"I don't mind," she answered, relieved. "I like it here." At the rise of his skeptical black eyebrows, she added a little defensively, "Lyra is the most beautiful, charming, friendly place I've ever seen."

He glanced up as the innkeeper brought their breakfasts and departed. "If you say so."

Taking a bite of her flaky pastry—ah, heavenly butter!— Emmie closed her eyes in bliss, mumbling, "If you don't like Lyra, why did you bring us here on honeymoon?"

His eyes flickered. "Our honeymoon starts on the yacht." He stabbed his eggs with his fork. "Our stop in Lyra is just an unpleasant errand I need to finish first."

Lyra unpleasant? She nearly choked on her second pastry. Washing it down with sweet, creamy coffee, she wiped her mouth. "I'm happy here."

"No one is happy here," he muttered.

Did he know this island well? She frowned, trying to remember anything he might have told her about Greece when she was his secretary. But there was nothing. He'd never spoken about his past in Greece, ever. She asked bluntly, "What's your errand?"

Theo looked at her, his jaw tight. "You deserve the honeymoon of your dreams, Emmie. You'll have it. I promise you. You'll be cherished in luxury on my yacht, waited on by a ten-person staff. We'll visit Santorini, where a friend is hosting a party for us. It should be very glamorous. Then Mykonos."

"Glamorous," Emmie sighed.

His lips curved. "Didn't you notice the clothes in your suitcase?"

Emmie had, to her dismay. After they'd arrived in Greece, he'd presented her with a Louis Vuitton trunk graced with her new initials, E. S. K., filled with new designer clothes that fit her pregnant body perfectly, including cocktail dresses and resort wear—obviously arranged by a stylist, at great expense. It was still in lockup at the harbor, awaiting to be loaded onto the yacht.

But she'd seen a flash of prices on the tags. A two-thousand-dollar swimsuit cover-up from Prada? Seriously? Once they were back in New York, she vowed to take it straight back to the stylist for a refund. Even if her husband was crazy rich, that didn't mean their spending should be crazy stupid.

Especially not when, as she and Theo had wandered Lyra's narrow cobblestone village road yesterday afternoon, she'd found swimsuit cover-ups for just ten euros and cotton sundresses for twelve, one of which she was wearing now. She looked down at her hand, twisting her diamond ring nervously. "We could skip Mykonos and Santorini and just stay in Lyra."

"Thank you, but you don't need to pretend. This place is a hellhole." His jaw was tight as he looked up at the charming taverna hotel that she'd taken a million pictures of with her phone since yesterday. "I'm sorry. You deserve better."

Her brow furrowed. Hellhole?

Was he in some alternate reality?

In her time on this island, she'd felt nothing but joy. Emmie wasn't sure why. Was it because, for the first time in her life, she was on vacation? With no responsibilities, no family to cook and clean for, no number-crunching in a basement cubicle or billionaire-wrangling over business schedules?

She didn't have to serve anyone or rush anywhere. She'd just been able to do whatever she pleased. She'd wandered the village on a whim, exclaiming with delight over everything, from the sweet cat curled up on a sunny windowsill, to the children dragging a kite, to the housewife sweeping her doorway and the old man leading a herd of black-faced sheep down the cobblestones. Emmie was in heaven.

And she'd assumed Theo felt the same. But now, looking back, she realized he'd simply followed her, encouraging her happiness without taking part in it. If anything, Theo seemed to go out of his way to be a stranger in Lyra, never introducing himself, avoiding people's eyes, as if deliberately acting the part of the rich, arrogant American tourist.

The truth was, though he'd tried to hide it, he'd been tense since they'd arrived here. She should have realized it earlier, when she saw he'd gone for a long run at dawn. It was how he dealt with stress. Exercise—or sex. Which obviously he wasn't getting.

She swallowed. What was the mysterious errand? "Why don't you like Lyra?"

His jaw tightened again as he looked away. "It's unfortunate the yacht-engine repair took longer than expected. A part had to be flown in from Rotterdam. But we'll be sleeping onboard tonight, I assure you."

Emmie looked past the small fishing boats to the enormous, modern yacht approaching the harbor and felt strangely let down. "Is that it?"

"Yes. Finally." Theo hesitated. "As I told you, I have an errand to run later today. It'll take me a few hours..."

"I'll come."

"No." Then added more gently, "If you're truly enjoying Lyra, I'm sure you'd prefer to spend your last hours shopping and relaxing, rather than dealing with some dreary errand."

"But what is it? Does it have to do with your new property in Greece? The one you mentioned at the wedding?"

Theo carefully ate a bite of dry toast then tossed the rest back on the plate. He gave her a smile that didn't meet his eyes. "You'll be all right for a few hours without me? You won't be lonely on your own?"

Of course she wouldn't be all right. What bride would appreciate being abandoned on the second day of her honeymoon, so the groom could disappear on a mysterious errand he refused to discuss?

But friendship went both ways. She wanted to be supportive, not clingy. So she forced herself to smile. "I'll be fine."

"Good." His handsome face held no expression as he tossed down his linen napkin. Looking at her downcast face, he relented. "But we have a few hours to enjoy ourselves first. What do you say we go to the beach?"

She brightened. "I'd love that."

Smiling, Theo tossed a pile of euros on the table, leaving an enormous tip. As they went upstairs to get changed, Emmie hummed a happy song to herself as they climbed the stairs, thrilled at the thought of spending time on the famous white sand beach of a bona fide Greek island.

"This is going to be so fun—" But as she turned back to her husband on the rickety stairs, his handsome face was twisted with so much grief and rage, she caught her breath.

The darkness in his expression was quickly masked as their eyes met. He smoothed his face into a smile. "I certainly hope so."

And Emmie couldn't help but wonder how it was possible that this quaint Greek island, which to her seemed so sunny and bright, was a hellhole that Theo couldn't wait to leave.

From the moment Theo saw the small rocky island of Lyra, he'd known bringing Emmie here was a mistake.

He'd brought the small, wrapped package from the safe of his Manhattan office to do what he'd been delayed from doing last week: watching from a distance as the charred ruin of his past was finally completely destroyed. Then he'd meant to drop the package into the sea, as Sofia had asked.

But there had been complications. The yacht's faulty engine leaving it docked in Athens. Sofia coming to Lyra after he'd specifically told her to stay in Paris. His wife starting to ask questions.

This wasn't how Theo had imagined his revenge would be.

Just climbing out of the speedboat onto the dock in Lyra's small harbor, returning to this place he'd sworn he'd never set foot on again, had caused a physical reaction. Even now, everywhere he looked made his skin crawl with memory, spiders and centipedes of repressed tragedy, little feet of horror whispering up and down his spine.

Walking through the tiny village which Emmie proclaimed *charming*, all he could see were the ghosts of the past. He'd seen her startled eyes when he'd called it a *hellhole*, and he'd known he'd revealed too much, been too honest about his feelings. But anytime he wasn't in her arms, focused on the long game of his slow seduction, he was on edge.

So far, no one had recognized him. He'd had a different surname then. He'd had so many names as a child. His father's. Then his mother's. He'd had three different stepfathers, none of whom had legally adopted him, but his mother always insisted on calling him by each new surname, as if that could bind her new husband to her son, to make them a family. Hopeless. Stupid.

Then it all ended in flames…

The torture of his own memories caused an overlay of pain over every pretty whitewashed building with blue shutters, an invisible shroud suffocating the rocky shoreline and clear blue water.

He'd been helpless as a boy. Helpless to save his family, even to save himself.

Until he finally had—at unbearable cost…

Theo couldn't relax. Since he'd arrived, he'd barely slept. So he'd gone for a run that morning, pushing himself hard, sprinting the eight-mile trail around the edge of the cliffs, hoping to outrun all his demons.

He ran past an old house and saw the gray-haired, wrinkled version of a woman he vaguely remembered. One who'd once called the police when she'd found him stumbling down the road as a boy, broken and covered in his own blood. Now, the old woman's eyes narrowed as he ran past.

But he didn't stop. He didn't want to be recognized as that boy. Not by anyone. Not even himself.

For decades, he'd seen the charred ruin in his dreams. Theo had bought the ruined property on Lyra because he'd hoped if he took possession of hell, it would loosen its jaws around his soul. But on his run, when he'd seen the burned debris in the distance, he'd stopped cold.

Theo had thought, returning to Lyra as a self-made billionaire with a wife and a child on the way, he'd prove his past was finally behind him, that he'd feel proud and strong, that he'd finally leave the helpless boy behind.

But one look at that scene and he'd realized nothing had changed inside him, not really. Maybe it never would…

"Can you believe it?" Emmie's joyful face looked up at him beneath the wide-brimmed sun hat she'd bought yesterday with *Lyra* stitched across the top in Greek letters. In spite of her stringent application of sunscreen, her legs and arms were already turning tan, with the slightest hint of pink, and he saw freckles on her upturned nose. "A secret beach!"

It took him a moment to brush away old ghosts and come back to the present. By then, Emmie had already dropped her cheap straw beach bag on the white sand. She yanked her white sleeveless cover-up off over her head, revealing a turquoise string bikini as she raced out into the blue water with a joyful whoop.

Standing alone on the beach, Theo stared out at her.

Her bikini caressed her pregnant curves as she kicked at the surf, spreading her arms wide and turning her face to the sun. The little triangle tops of the bra barely contained her overflowing breasts, and the bikini bottom, with strings tied in bows at her hips, was half-hidden by her belly.

Theo was hard just looking at her. But then, he felt like he'd been hard from the moment of their marriage. Repressing his desire, treating her with asexual kindness and concern, cuddling with her while they watched that awful comedy on the jet—and most difficult of all, having her sleep next to him in bed, for the love of heaven, feeling her soft, sensual body move against his groin as she sighed and moaned in sleep—

Remembering, he breathed a strangled curse. A man could only endure so much. He didn't know how much longer he could bear it.

When would his wife finally give in to her own desire and make the first move? When?

It amazed him now that he'd thought her plain before he hired her. How had Emmie contrived to camouflage her incredible beauty for months at the office, in the unflattering suits and tightly prim hairstyles of the efficient, sexless secretary, before he'd finally, truly seen her?

Now, Theo stared at her as she waded into the blue water like Aphrodite, golden beneath the sun. Emmie Swenson Katrakis was the most beautiful woman he'd ever known.

More than beautiful: she was magic. She was the only one who could make him forget. The only one who could chase the ghosts away. Making love to her was all he could think about.

Which meant she was his addiction. Right or wrong, he had to keep her close. So he could keep touching her, looking at her. And when she surrendered to temptation and took him back into her bed, he'd finally feel peace, in the explosion of euphoria as he took her…again and again…

"What are you waiting for?" she called, swimming and kicking in the sea. "Come join me!"

Emmie was chest-deep, the surface of the water clinging to her swollen breasts, sliding slowly over her skin and the tiny clinging fabric. The shock between cool water and warm air caused her nipples to pebble beneath the material. He could see the shape of them, even from here.

He needed no further invitation. He ripped off his shirt and tossed his phone down on top of it. Wearing only his blue swim trunks, he plunged into the water, letting the sea wash him clean before he resurfaced beside her. Pulling her into his arms, he kissed her in the Greek sun, just for a split second, as salty water splashed over them both.

With a laugh, she pulled away and ducked her body back beneath the water. Playfully, she kicked a wave of water over him.

With a low growl, he threw himself in pursuit of her, and with a mock scream she swam away. They played together in the water on the private, deserted beach, and he somehow laughed harder than he had in a long time.

Finally, as the sun started to lower in the sky, he remembered the errand and felt a shadow over his soul. They waded back to the sandy beach. He checked the time and told himself he could take a few more moments, just a few. He spread their blanket beneath the scrawny shade of a single olive tree, clinging to the edge of some rocks.

He dried her off with a towel and froze, looking down at her, his heart pounding. He thought of stretching her out on the sun-warmed blanket and taking her right there on the white sand. But shepherds had sometimes wandered through here following their charges, and even when he was younger there had been an occasional backpacker who heard about the secret beach. But maybe—

"How did you even know about this place?" Emmie asked, yawning as she stretched her limbs out in the sun. "When I asked the innkeeper about a beach, she only told me about one up north. She called it the *tourist beach*."

"This one is kept quiet. For locals."

Her dark eyelashes fluttered open as she peeked at him. "Then, how did you know about it?"

Theo felt the low rumble of tension go through his body, like dark clouds on the edge of his consciousness, crackling the air with threat of a coming storm.

No, he thought. Please. He didn't want to think about it. Let him enjoy this just a little longer. Just an hour. A few more minutes.

"Theo." He felt her small hand reach up to cup his rough, unshaven chin. "What is it? What won't you tell me?"

For a moment, he closed his eyes, holding his breath. Her touch lured him—tempted him unbearably. All he wanted to do was pull her close, to kiss her, to feel her naked body against his own, to plunge into her, to lose his mind in the sweet madness between them.

And yet he forced himself to turn away. "It doesn't matter—"

But Emmie held onto his shoulders. Their eyes locked.

Lifting her head, she hesitated for the space of a breath. Then she kissed him. A brief brush of her lips against his.

Then she drew back, her violet eyes luminous in the Greek sun.

With an intake of breath, he pulled her into his arms, on the soft blanket and kissed her hungrily.

Their lips met like fire, and she clung to him—he clung to her—it was everything he'd waited for and more…

Pulling away with a gasp, he kissed down her neck, his hands roaming over her warm, bare skin—her breasts, her belly, her hips. He reached for the tie of her bikini top at the nape of her neck. His fingers fumbled with the effort, as if he were an untried boy—

Nearby, his phone rang. Squeezing his eyes shut, he tried to ignore the sound. But it kept ringing and ringing until finally, with a curse, he snatched it off the blanket, half-intending to toss it into the sea.

Then he saw the number of the person calling. It was like a splash of cold water in his face. Glancing at Emmie, he stood up unsteadily, putting the phone to his ear, walking away from the blanket beneath the olive tree. He spoke quietly into the phone, in Greek, praying his voice sounded calm, praying his wife wouldn't listen, wouldn't care, wouldn't ask questions.

Speaking quickly, he finished the call as soon as possible. But when he turned back, Emmie was sitting up, staring at him, her face pale beneath her freckles.

"Who's Sofia?" she demanded.

CHAPTER SEVEN

THREE EMOTIONS WENT through Emmie at the phone call, in a chain reaction.

The first was anger. She hated the person calling, whoever it might be. And she was none too pleased at her husband for answering his phone, either.

Then anger was washed away by relief as she realized what she'd nearly let happen: a total collapse of her willpower. Theo had been caressing her hair, both of them still wet from splashing in the surf, his dark eyes smiling down at her, beneath the bluffs and shade of the olive tree. She'd kissed him almost without thinking.

If not for the interruption of the phone call, they might have made love right then and there on the beach, beneath the eyes of any random shepherd passing by on the bluffs above. Really, she should be grateful to the unknown caller for preventing that disaster.

But as her husband paced the beach with his phone, speaking low in Greek, Emmie didn't feel exactly grateful. Her gaze slid over the tanned muscles of his bare back, the hard curve of his backside in the swim trunks, down his powerful thighs and calves, laced with dark hair as she watched him walk back and forth with his bare feet on the white sand.

Her husband's tone was increasingly tense, as if he were trying to convince the caller of something. Then she heard him clearly say a name amid all his impenetrable Greek. A woman's name. Sofia.

And Emmie felt a brand-new emotion. The strongest of all. *Fear.*

Theo hadn't walked away with his phone to be polite, she realized; he didn't want her to know what he was talking about.

Or to whom.

"Who's Sofia?" she'd blurted out as he'd turned to face her. And his expression turned dark.

"You were listening? To my private phone call?"

"I—I didn't mean to," she stammered. Her cheeks went hot. "I couldn't help but overhear."

"Couldn't help but intrude? Even though I walked away from you and spoke in a language I know you don't understand? You still make these accusations!"

"Accusations?" she gasped. What accusations?

"It's late." Scowling, he reached for his shirt, then the bag. "I'll take you back to the hotel."

She felt somehow embarrassed, ashamed, as if she'd been rude and nosy, as if she were the one to blame for the sudden chill between them. She tried to keep up with her husband's long stride, carrying the sagging blanket in her arms as they hurried up the long, winding road back to the village. But how was it her fault? He was clearly keeping secrets from her— and not very well. With so many dark hints, it was almost as if he were goading her to ask questions!

Whatever the reason, Emmie didn't like to be at odds. As they reached the tiny hotel room, she turned to him and said quietly, "Maybe we should talk."

"No time." Yanking off his beach clothes, he didn't even bother to hide his naked body from her as he pulled on a sleek long-sleeved black shirt and tailored black trousers. "I'm already running late. I'll be back in a few hours. Pack your things. I'll escort you to the yacht when I return."

"Okay," she said falteringly. "Have a good—"

But he'd already left, the door slamming closed behind him.

Emmie showered alone in the tiny en suite. When she came out into the bedroom, wrapped in a white towel, the tiny bedroom, which had previously seemed so cozy and tight, seemed cavernous in its emptiness.

Where had Theo gone? What was his errand?

Who was Sofia?

All her earlier happiness had evaporated like mist in sun. Slowly, she pulled on cotton panties and bra and a floral sundress she'd bought at the tourist shop in the village. Brushing her long damp hair, she pulled it back in a ponytail. In the small mirror, she noticed her skin had a healthy glow from the sun.

Or maybe it was from her sudden surge of rage.

How dare Theo treat her like this? Emmie was not his secretary anymore, paid to serve his interests, at his pleasure. She was his wife. She deserved to know these secrets he kept hinting at!

Setting her jaw, she pulled on sandals, grabbed her straw bag and stomped out of the hotel room to look for him.

Ten minutes later, her anger had turned to despair. She would not find him—of course she wouldn't, not if he didn't want her to. It was so unfair. How could Theo make her so miserable, even though she wasn't even sleeping with him? What was the point of denying them both the pleasure, if she was just going to end up miserable anyway?

Walking up the cobblestoned street, she felt a lump in her throat. She put on cheap sunglasses from her bag to hide the tears in her eyes.

Her lips parted when she saw a tall, broad-shouldered man, in a black shirt and trousers which seemed much too formal for the island, walking down a narrow alley with a pretty young black-haired woman. They walked side by side, not touching, but something about the way they spoke quietly insinuated a certain…intimacy.

Emmie ducked back behind a corner, then peeked around it, watching as they continued down the hill toward the marina. Furtively, a little guiltily, she followed the couple down the paths to the docks.

Theo and the unknown girl—Sofia?—walked down the largest wooden dock toward a vintage wooden speedboat waiting with a uniformed crew member at the steering wheel. Farther out in the harbor, Emmie saw her husband's gleaming, modern yacht, named *Future 2*, replacing Theo's starter yacht *Future* of a decade before. She'd never been on either yacht as his secretary.

Emmie watched as he helped the girl climb into the waiting speedboat. On impulse, she bolted toward the marina.

"No!" she cried, running down the wooden dock. "Wait!"

Theo stared back at her with shock. Turning, he spoke in a low voice to the black-haired girl, who shrugged.

As Emmie reached the end, she threw herself into the small speedboat, still panting from her sprint. Theo caught her as she fell. Setting her aright, he glared at her, then let her go, folding his arms.

"I gave you specific instructions. To remain at the hotel."

"I'm not your secretary. You can't give me orders." Emmie's cheeks burned as she turned to the pretty brunette. Sticking out her hand, she said politely, "Hi, I'm Emmie. I assume you're Sofia?"

The girl glanced briefly at Theo, then said, "Yes?"

Was that a question or answer? Emmie couldn't tell if she even understood English. As they shook hands, the brunette raised her eyebrow at Theo, who gave a small, disgusted shake of his head.

"Go," he ordered the boat's driver. The crewman pressed on the gas, whirling the speedboat from the docks toward the yacht in the bay. Other than the loud engine, there was silence. No one tried to explain anything to Emmie.

"So." Emmie licked her lips, feeling awkward and foolish. "What's this all about?"

The girl just looked out at the water.

"Français?" Emmie tried hopefully in her schoolgirl French. Still nothing. And the only Greek word she knew was *efaristo*, which seemed highly inappropriate for her current feelings.

"Since you insisted on coming," Theo told Emmie coldly, "sit down and try not to be a nuisance."

Nuisance? Sitting abruptly in a cushioned seat, Emmie ground her teeth as she looked back at the vanishing shoreline and charming village clinging to the rocks. She'd give *him* nuisance.

The speedboat soon arrived at the enormous yacht, and they were assisted up the steps by uniformed crew, then kicked off their shoes, as apparently everyone went in socks and bare feet on yachts. Not as glamorous as she'd imagined, Emmie thought, surveying her own chipped toenail polish dourly.

They reached the wide deck, with its comfortable chairs and views in every direction. As the yacht started to move, a different member of the crew pushed a flute of champagne into Theo's hand, then the girl's, then even Emmie's.

She looked at the crystal flute, bewildered. Why would anyone give a pregnant woman champagne? In fact, it seemed strange that Theo and the dark-haired girl had champagne, too. Neither seemed to be celebrating.

If anything, her husband looked haunted, his dark eyes shadowed as he kept glancing down at the waiflike brunette. The girl just gripped the yacht's railing and stared out at the sea, her expression pitiable.

Emmie didn't understand any of this.

Holding her untasted flute, Emmie went inside the sliding glass door and handed it to a member of the crew in a white short-sleeved shirt and shorts. "Here, thank you very much, but I don't need this."

"Of course, ma'am." Taking it readily, he touched his cap respectfully and turned away. She stopped him.

"Excuse me, but…um…where are we going?"

The young man looked confused. "To the other side of the island, ma'am. For the best view."

"Ah. Yes. Of course. Thank you," she said, nodding sagely, as she'd sometimes seen her father and brothers do when they had no idea what someone was talking about. Going back out on the open deck, she hugged herself in the warm Greek wind as the yacht sliced through the ocean waves. She looked across the deck toward Theo and the girl.

She couldn't imagine him taking a mistress, not after just two days of marriage, and parading her in front of Emmie! No, surely not. There had to be some other explanation for why he'd come to Lyra, a place he clearly hated, to go on a yachting excursion in secret. With a pretty brunette.

Didn't there?

It didn't take long for them to reach the other side of the island. From this side, the shore was rocky, brown, bare of trees, far from civilization. Her eyes widened when she saw the burned-out ruin of a building clinging alone to the side. A grand old house, long since destroyed.

Going to Theo, she whispered, "What is that?"

His dark eyes brooded as he stared back at the island, gripping the railing. He said flatly, "A house."

"I can see that." Staring at the shell, she thought of Daphne du Maurier's tragic burned Manderley. "But whose?"

Turning to her, he bit out coldly, "Mine."

"Oh," Emmie said, confused. There was nothing left but the

mansion's blackened bones, faded by sun, in ruins for years or even decades. Then she noticed men in hard hats, small from this distance, waiting beside the ruin, a small battalion with heavy machinery, excavators, loaders, bulldozers. She frowned, trying to make sense of it. She said faintly, "You're here to rebuild?"

"No. To destroy." Looking out at the site with grim satisfaction, Theo gestured to the captain, who spoke quietly into a phone. He turned back to Emmie with cold black eyes. "And to answer your question, Sofia is my sister."

Theo watched across the water as men in hard hats, having received the go-ahead, plowed forward with two excavators and a bulldozer, knocking down the last charred walls of the dilapidated house.

Nearby, he heard a choked sniffle. Sofia was gripping the railing, her dark eyes filled with anguish as she looked out at their former home in the twilight.

Without a word, he went to stand beside her. Unsure how to offer comfort, he put his arm around her uncertainly. She leaned against him, silently weeping, never looking away from the island, as the last vestiges of their childhood home were flattened and wiped off the face of the earth.

Looking down, Theo dimly saw a flute in his hand. He'd ordered the very best champagne from his cellar specifically for the occasion. But when he'd pictured this day, destroying the property now that it was his at last, he'd thought he'd feel a sense of joy, triumph—or at least relief.

Instead Theo felt sick, his insides churning. Glancing behind him on the deck, he saw Emmie watching him. He felt her gaze. Her *silence*. She'd been startled when he'd said Sofia was his sister, but she hadn't asked any questions. Now, he was suddenly afraid it was because she didn't need to. More than anyone else, she'd always had a knack for seeing past his defenses, even as his secretary.

And now…

His throat tightened.

Cold. Cold. He had to be cold. To show emotion was weakness. A man had to be strong, or both he and the people he loved would suffer. He had to be ice.

"Cheers," Theo forced himself to say in English, holding up his flute. Sofia stared at him with black tearstained eyes, then finally lifted her own. He clinked his glass against hers, and they each managed a sip of champagne. Reaching into his pocket, he handed her the small brown paper-wrapped package he'd taken from his office safe.

Setting her glass down on a nearby table, she looked at the small package. She said in Greek, "Is it…?"

"Nai." Yes.

Unwrapping it, she pulled out a small gold locket. Clutching it tightly in her hand, she shuddered. "Thank you," she said in a whisper, then took a deep breath. "But…"

"But?"

She looked back at the ruin. "I want to be there."

Theo swallowed. His voice was harsher than he intended as he said, "We're close enough."

"I want the dirt beneath my feet."

"No," he said helplessly, but even as he said it, he knew he would do it. After everything he'd done—and everything he *hadn't* done—he owed her anything she wanted, and more.

Setting his jaw, Theo turned to the captain and spoke a few quiet words. After conferring into his phone, the man replied in the same language.

Theo returned to his sister. "The site's not safe. They still need to fill in the foundation and pull any remaining materials."

She simply lifted her eyes to his, waiting.

Theo sighed. He'd tried to talk Sofia out of coming here today. His original plan had been to film the house's destruction, then send the video to her in Paris. He'd been delayed by his rush back to stop Emmie's wedding in New York. Then Sofia had informed him she'd flown in from Paris to be on the island when the demolition happened.

So he'd revised the plan. He and his bride would sail past Lyra on the yacht, as if by chance, right as the house was demolished. He'd let Emmie believe he was filming the demolition of an interesting ruin, nothing more, then he'd send the video to Sofia at the tiny, unused cottage in the village that she'd inherited from her adoptive family.

But the one-day delay caused by the yacht's needed repair had ended that plan, too. He'd known from the moment he stepped onto Lyra that he didn't want Emmie with him when the house was razed. Having to act casual, to show no emotion, to hide his feelings from her would have been difficult. So he'd decided to leave her at the hotel and go alone on his yacht to film the event from a distance.

Then Sofia had called that afternoon to say she'd changed her mind. She was determined to come with him today and see the teardown in person, and no amount of his arguing had persuaded her otherwise.

First Sofia, now Emmie. Why did the two women he cared about the most insist on fighting his efforts to protect them from pain? Their pain—and his?

Theo looked down at his dark-haired sister. When he'd knocked on her door that afternoon, it had been the first time he'd seen her in person since she was five. He'd had to blink hard to hide the sting in his eyes as he'd hugged her. In some ways, she would always be that child to him. A child who'd deserved a better brother than Theo. And still did.

Now, Sofia set her jaw. "I don't care about *safe*. I need this,

Theo." Her gaze wandered back to the ruin on the hill. "Otherwise, part of me will always be trapped there."

He glanced back at Emmie, still standing alone at the railing a few feet away, pretending she wasn't interested in their discussion, pretending she wasn't offended that they continued to speak Greek in front of her. Theo and Sofia could have easily spoken English; his sister spoke the language well, along with French and German and Spanish. He'd paid for her to attend good schools across Europe.

It was a miracle some enterprising journalist hadn't discovered Theo's whole sordid childhood. The confusion of his five different surnames as a boy had probably helped. It was only after his uncle had brought him to America at sixteen that he'd used his long-dead father's surname of Katrakis.

The name Theo had at fifteen, when his mother and stepfather died, had been Papadopolous. His stepfather's name. It had also been Sofia's surname before she was adopted. The neighbor had adopted only Sofia, not Theo. Who wouldn't want a sweet little orphan girl? Who would ever want a hardened, violent, grief-stricken teenage boy?

His heart was pounding strangely. He felt beads of sweat on his forehead in spite of the cooling breeze. He glanced sideways at Emmie. She was staring down over the slanted sunlight into the dark water below, her shoulders tight beneath the thin straps of her floral sundress.

How he wished she'd just stayed at the hotel. He would have retrieved her after this was all over and done with, and they'd have sailed off into the sunset. She wouldn't have known about Sofia or the house, he'd have had nothing to evade, and they both would have been happier.

"Well, Theo?" Sofia asked in Greek. "Can we?"

"Fine," he said heavily. His belly roiled at the thought of setting foot there. But as he looked at his little sister's pale, haunted face, he knew any pain would be worth it to give her the slightest bit of peace.

As he and Sofia left, he saw the question in Emmie's eyes and answered it with a shake of his head. He didn't want her to accompany them. Because he couldn't tell her the truth about their past, his and Sofia's. And he didn't want to lie to her.

After putting on their shoes, he led Sofia down the steep steps into the small speedboat.

Looking up, Theo had one last glance of Emmie watching from the top deck, the lowering red and orange sun shining through her hair like gold, her expression darkened by shadow. Then the boat took them swiftly—far too swiftly—to shore.

The old dock was long gone, so they had to hop out and wade through knee-deep water. He offered to carry Sofia, but she shook her head. They stumbled onto the beach he'd once paced as a desperate teenager, scared out of his mind.

Theo stopped and looked back at the sun setting over the horizon. Except for the silhouette of the yacht, the view was the same now that it had been then. If he closed his eyes, he could still feel the same panic, the frantic beat of his heart.

Theo was relieved when Sofia called to him, breaking the spell. Together, they trudged the overgrown path up the dry, rocky hill, sea water sluicing off their bare legs and squishing in their shoes.

The big house had been scraped away. When they reached the edge of the site, he stopped to speak to one of the hired demolishers.

His sister staggered forward. Falling to her knees, she touched the dry earth where her bedroom had been, then covered her face with a sob. Theo watched, his shoulders taut, his eyes dry. Digging a hole with her hands, Sofia she took the small gold locket from her pocket and dropped it in. She filled in the hole, smoothing dirt over it. Then she looked down at the cracked stone walls of the old basement on the other side of the structure, half-destroyed and filled with debris, little more than a hole in the ground.

"Tell them to yank it out," she said in a low voice. "Every single stone."

The sun was dying, bleeding red across the sea, by the time they returned to the yacht. Theo's steps were heavy as Sofia fled to the cushioned seats on deck, to sit alone in shadows with her grief. Emmie was nowhere to be seen.

"Where is my wife?" he asked.

"I believe she was fatigued after dinner," the captain replied, "and went to rest in your quarters, sir."

Theo was glad he didn't have to worry about hiding his feelings from her. Being strong in the face of Sofia's grief and pain was difficult enough. He went to sit by his sister, holding her as she cried.

The yacht swiftly returned to the village harbor. Once they were at anchor, he and Sofia took a speedboat to the dock. Sending staffers back to the taverna hotel to pay his bill and collect his and Emmie's things, Theo walked Sofia to her little stone house on the edge of town, a summer cottage now rarely used by her adoptive family. When he left her at her door, she gave him a trembling smile, her eyes luminous.

"Thank you, Theo," she said and hugged him. "I'll be... better now."

Feeling a lump in his throat, he hugged her back. His voice was hoarse as he pulled away. "You deserve every happiness, Sofia." He hesitated. "If I can ever do anything for you, anything at all... Money, help, a quiet word in the right ear..."

Wiping her eyes, she whispered, "Just having you back in my life is all I ever wanted."

With a jerky nod, he turned away. But as Theo returned to the yacht, where his beautiful bride and glamorous honeymoon waited, Theo did not feel better. His muscles ached. His throat hurt. His soul felt sore.

He knew, even if Sofia did not, that his sister was better-off without him in her life. Today surely proved that. He thought of how Sofia had wept, her knees in the dirt, and closed his eyes, sick at heart. However much she might wish otherwise, she'd never forget he was the one to blame.

Reaching the yacht, he stood at the railing, watching as the pearlescent moon rose softly over the Aegean. He thought of drinking whiskey, or maybe guzzling the barely touched Dom Pérignon. He thought of burying himself in work, prepping for his upcoming pitch, the latest iteration of his dream project in Paris he'd pursued for years. None of it appealed.

Only one thing could save him.

Going through the yacht's sliding glass doors, he went down the hall to his private suite. In the darkness, he found his wife sleeping in the large bed.

He woke her with a kiss.

"Theo," she murmured. "What—"

His hand moved to her breast beneath her white sleeveless nightgown, as her lips parted, gasping against his. He deepened the kiss, pressing her back against the bed. He was desperate to touch her, to taste her skin. She wrenched away.

"Stop."

Startled, he stared at her in the slender dagger of moonlight pooling on the bed. She took a deep breath.

"Tell me," she said quietly. "About today."

Theo stiffened. It wasn't enough that Sofia knew his failures. Now Emmie wanted some rope to hang him with as well? "It's in the past. It doesn't matter."

She looked up at him. *Saw right through him.*

"What am I to you? Just the mother of your child? An accessory on your arm that you put in a box when you're done?"

He glared at her. "You know you're more."

"Do I?" She looked down at her hands, interlaced tightly over the blanket. "I want our marriage to work. But how can

I feel like your partner, or even your friend, when you don't tell me anything?"

Theo set his jaw. "I don't want to talk about the past. Ever. It's not a happy story. Forget it. As I have—"

But as he moved toward her again, intending to kiss her into submission, she stopped him with a small hand pressed firmly to his chest. Her eyes pierced his. "Either explain, or get out."

Theo stared at her, his heart pounding. Snatching up a pillow, he rose from the bed. He turned to leave.

Then he stopped, staring blankly at the open door.

Emmie was his wife. If he kept her in the dark, yes, he'd remain safely in control. She couldn't despise him for his past or use it against him.

But what would it mean for their marriage? Now that she knew he was hiding something awful, how long would it be before any chance of intimacy between them—physical or otherwise—was utterly destroyed?

Theo turned back to face her. "Fine," he said hoarsely. "Don't say I didn't warn you."

CHAPTER EIGHT

AFTER A FRUSTRATING night when she'd tossed and turned, trying to understand the incomprehensible events yesterday, Emmie stared at her husband, scared to breathe, scared to break the spell. Was he finally, actually going to reveal his secrets?

Theo's jawline, dark and unshaven, clenched as he looked toward the open porthole, out at the moon-swept sea. Outside, she heard the plaintive call of seagulls.

"The ruin was once my home," he said softly. "Mine and Sofia's."

"In a mansion? On Lyra?" Her lips parted. "I thought you were found by your uncle, roaming the streets of Athens."

"I was—later." His lips curled humorlessly. "It's only because I had so many names as a boy that no one's ever learned the full story. Technically Sofia is my half sister. I was ten when she was born."

"She lives on Lyra?"

He exhaled.

"Paris," he said finally.

Honestly, it was like getting blood out of a turnip.

Clasping her hands in her lap over the king-size comforter, Emmie tried to control her desire to know more. She thought of the emotion she'd seen yesterday as Theo and his sister had watched the destruction on shore. To the untrained eye, he might have seemed stoic, but she'd seen his jaw tighten, his hands clench, his dark eyes blink hard and fast. Someone who didn't know him well might have thought he was angry.

But she'd seen Theo angry. Many times. He'd even been angry at her once or twice, when she'd been distracted by her mother's latest cancer prognosis and accidentally double-booked an appointment, then put a call through from an ex-mistress he was trying to avoid.

But what Emmie had seen in him yesterday went far beyond anger. There'd been an undercurrent of something powerful. Something he hadn't known how to deal with. She'd watched his tender concern for his young sister, who'd seemed devastated. And Emmie had known, whatever this dark cloud was over the siblings, it was so awful it had changed the course of their lives.

Very gently, she asked now, "What happened?"

Sitting abruptly on the bed beside her, Theo searched her gaze, and for a moment she thought he wouldn't answer. Then he said in a low voice, "I'll tell you. Then you'll never ask me about it again. Ever."

"All right."

"You know my father died when I was a baby." Theo looked down, twisting the plain gold band on his left hand. "My mother was an addict. Not just drugs. She was addicted to falling in love. She made…bad choices. My stepfather was the worst. He was handsome, rich. After two divorces, when she met him she thought she finally had the fairy tale. I was ten when we went to live on Lyra. But his money didn't last. He started blaming her. Hurting her. Then he hurt me when I tried to get between them. Then finally…" His throat seemed to close. He said hoarsely, "There was a fire. I was only able to save my sister."

"Oh, Theo," she whispered, reaching out to touch his arm. He didn't seem to notice.

"My mother always thought love would save her," he whispered. "It only brought her grief. And in the end…she died from it."

Emmie saw the tightness in his black eyes, heard the faint wildness of his breath in the shadowy bedroom of the yacht.

"I finally was able to take possession of the house. What was left of it. And Sofia and I needed to see the final demolition. To remember." His lips twisted. "Or maybe to forget."

She could feel the violence of repressed emotion radiating from him in waves. Theo looked up, his handsome face stark.

"Is there anything more you want to know?"

Emmie's heart was pounding. Did she need to know more? Did she even *want* to?

"Theo—"

Then she felt a hard kick beneath her ribs and sucked in her breath. She felt the kick again, and her lips lifted. Every time it happened, she felt the same sense of wonder. "Our baby's kicking."

He frowned. "Now?"

Pushing the covers away, she grabbed his hand and pressed it to her belly over her nightgown. "Feel it?"

His dark eyes widened, and then his jaw fell as he looked down at her. "That's our baby?"

She smiled. "That's him."

"Is that normal? I mean," Theo hesitated, "does it hurt? Do I need to call a doctor? Should I—"

"I'm fine," she said, laughing. "And yes, it's normal. I'm glad you felt it. I want you to be part of everything. Part of our lives."

Their eyes locked, with her hand resting over his larger one, entwined over her baby bump. Emmie's heart twisted. She suddenly realized what courage it must have taken for this intensely private man to tell her so much. She caressed his rough cheek.

"Thank you for telling me. I'm so sorry about what happened." She paused. "But I'll protect you now. For the rest of our lives."

Theo looked down at her in the bedroom filled with shadows. His dark eyes flickered, and the air between them suddenly crackled with electricity.

Cupping her face, he leaned forward and kissed her. No brief, timid peck, but a deep kiss full of yearning. Full of emotion and need.

Beneath her cotton nightgown, her breasts turned heavy, nipples tightening, as desire coiled low and deep inside her. She kissed him back hungrily, clinging to him across the bed.

She felt him shudder. His lips were hard on hers, ravenous, as if he'd been starving and she alone could save him. Then he wrenched back, his eyes gleaming, his voice low.

"Are you sure?"

In answer, she kissed him, pulling him back against her body, her fingertips gripping into his shoulders.

With a repressed gasp, he pushed her back into the pool of moonlight on the bed. As they kissed, they held each other tight, gasping for breath. Suddenly, they were tearing at each other's clothes. His shirt disappeared, then her nightgown, then the rest.

She wanted this. She was no longer afraid. Now she knew that, caring for him as she did, she was going to suffer anyway. Why deny herself what she wanted most? Why deny them both? Avoiding pleasure would not avoid pain.

As he stroked and kissed every inch of her, Emmie held her breath, trembling with need. Her body was taut, aching. She gripped him closer, wanting more, *more*, to feel him inside her, to finally possess him and make him her own. He was the man she'd always wanted. And now he was her husband. Hers forever.

Theo had never needed anyone like this.

He'd never felt so close to her. To anyone.

The shock of emotional intimacy, of being seen and accepted

by the woman he respected most, had cracked through Theo's frozen soul. He'd taken the leap to reveal part of his history to her, and she hadn't let him fall. Holding her naked body against his now was so utterly sweet it was almost unbearable. He'd thought he wanted her before. That had been nothing, a grain of sand in a beach, compared to the way he wanted her now.

As the dark Aegean swayed beneath the yacht, it took every inch of Theo's self-control not to take her hard, now, now, now.

But she was pregnant. He had to be gentle, even if the effort cost him everything he had.

Taking a deep breath, he spread her body across the soft blankets of the bed. Lowering his head, he savored each rosy nipple, cupping her breasts, pale in the moonlight. Until she started to sway beneath him like the waves.

He moved past the mound of her belly, gently stroking her there, placing himself between her legs, parting her thighs with his hands. He felt her shiver and shake as he tasted her, until she gasped for breath, gripping the blankets beneath her to steady herself. She cried out her release into the dark shadows of the bedroom, echoing inside the yacht, beneath the opalescent moonlight, along the ancient Greek sea.

Then, and only then, did he allow himself to slowly push inside her. Before, he'd wanted to take her hard and deep to chase his demons away.

Now he felt...different.

I'll protect you now. For the rest of our lives.

Emmie was his woman. His pregnant wife. It was his job to protect her and take care of her.

He felt a sudden flicker of fear. He'd already failed at protecting those he loved. People had died because of him.

Theo pushed the thought away desperately. This time would be different. He would make sure Emmie was always safe and cherished—

Lying down beside her on the big bed, he reached for her,

lifting her over his body. Her weight was nothing, even though she was pregnant, but his hands shook with the effort it took for him to maintain his self-control as he slowly lowered her over him, her thighs spread to straddle his hips.

She gasped as she felt him push inside her, inch by hard inch, until finally she was pressed to the hilt, stretching her deep. For a moment, he held tight to her hips, not letting her move, as he exhaled, his body tight.

Then, slowly, she began to move, tentatively at first, then riding him harder and faster. His eyes opened, and he looked up at her, seeing her beautiful face with her eyes closed in bliss, her breasts swaying over her belly, her body tight. She tensed again, gripping his shoulders, and he heard her cry out even louder than she had before—

And he lost it. He exploded in ecstasy that he'd never known, in pleasure he'd never imagined even possible. He heard a moan rise to a shout and realized it was his own.

She collapsed over him, sweaty and spent. Exhausted, still dazed by euphoria, he stroked her back. For a few sweet moments he just held her. He felt sated. Safe. Cherished.

For those few sweet moments, he felt like he deserved to still be alive.

The morning sea air was fresh against Emmie's skin as she sat alone at the deck's breakfast table. She touched her lips, still bruised from her husband's hungry kisses.

"Will there be anything else, Mrs. Katrakis?" a young, uniformed crewman asked respectfully, tucking his tray under his arm.

"No, thank you." As he departed, Emmie sipped sweet, creamy decaf coffee and took another bite of *bougatsa*, a buttery, flaky pastry, crunchy and sprinkled with powdered sugar on top, filled with sweet custard. She'd had two big pieces already, along with eggs and fruit.

She smoothed the napkin over her baby bump beneath her simple white shift dress. Brushing her long hair back from her shoulders, she sat back, looking out at the crystal blue sea. She should feel exhausted, with the way she'd spent the last two nights. But she didn't. Sleeping was wonderful, but not half so glorious as being awake with Theo.

They'd been docked here for two days now, just outside Santorini, and she'd never been so happy. Santorini, she thought. Another name for *heaven*.

"Good morning." Her husband fell into the chair across the small table with a wicked smile.

Golden sunlight poured over his high cheekbones and freshly shaven jaw. His open shirt revealed his powerful chest, tanned and caressed by light, shadows etching his muscled pecs and the taut six-pack. Emmie's eyes fell to the line of dark hair tracing down his belly before disappearing beneath the waistband of his swimming trunks.

Theo was handsome as sin. As always. They must have made love a dozen times since they'd left Lyra. How could she still want more? Mouth dry, she managed, "Going swimming this morning?"

"I was thinking about it." He poured steaming hot black coffee from a silver pot into a china cup edged with twenty-four-karat gold. "Care to join me?"

"I'm fine on the deck, thank you," she said, a little primly.

Leaning back in his chair, he smiled at her, his eyes glowing as he placed the edge of the china cup to his mouth. Right against his sensual lower lip.

"Stop that."

"Stop what?" he said innocently and took a sip, as if he hadn't been teasing her, making her imagine other places his mouth had recently been. She flushed, feeling her cheeks burn. He gave a sudden grin. "You're blushing."

"I'm not. You are," she said, a little incoherently. Coughing to cover, she looked out at the blue waves and the island of Santorini in the distance.

Theo stared at her silently, then reached for her hand. "What do you say, Mrs. Katrakis," he said softly. "Would you like to—"

He pulled his hand away as the member of the crew came back out on the deck through the sliding glass doors, holding a covered silver tray. He served Theo his plate of breakfast and departed. Emmie looked at his plate. Just eggs, meat and fruit.

She looked down at her own plate, empty except for the scattering of crumbs. No buttery flaky pastries for him. That was Theo, she thought. No softness, no weakness.

Though he did have a few exceptions. He'd eat a whole loaf of bread, but only from a specific boulangerie in the sixth arrondissement in Paris. He'd devour a bowl of noodles big enough to feed a family of four from his favorite Tokyo shop.

Could she be as uniquely special, as desirable, to him as those hot, crusty baguettes? As that counter-service *yakisoba* from the Ginza district?

If so she'd have his adoration forever.

"What's so funny?" he said suspiciously.

She realized she'd been chuckling to herself—wishing she could be as special as a loaf of bread or stir-fried noodles! Stifling her laugh, she cleared her throat. "Nothing."

Tilting his head, he ate another bite of eggs. "Did I tell you we're invited to a party tonight?"

"That's tonight?"

"Not just a party. A wedding reception in our honor."

She was shocked. She didn't know anyone in Greece. "Who's hosting it?" She thought of the only faint possibility. "Not your sister?"

"No." He chewed and swallowed a bite of bacon, washing it down with more hot black coffee. "I might have another chance at Paris. I'm hoping to discuss it tonight."

At first Emmie thought he hadn't answered her question. Then she realized he had.

"*The* Paris project?" she said. "The one we've chased for years? The property owned by Pierre Harcourt?"

Theo nodded. "There are rumors that he's not happy with the new development team."

"Harcourt is hosting a reception for us?"

Theo pushed his food around his plate with his fork, then said reluctantly, "His daughter."

Emmie blinked, suddenly feeling a slight chill across the yacht's deck, even beneath the warm Greek sun. "Your old girlfriend?"

He shrugged. "Ancient history. Long before your time."

"Celine Harcourt? The one who smashed a plate on your head at Per Se?"

"She smashed it against the wall, at Le Bernardin. Though she was aiming at my head." His lips twisted humorously. "Celine didn't take rejection well."

She hid the tremble of her hands as she set her linen napkin on the table. "No one does."

Theo's handsome face lifted in a sudden grin. "Jealous?"

She muttered under her breath. He leaned forward, taking both her hands in his own.

"You have nothing to worry about," he said. "You're the only woman I want. Forever and ever."

She searched his gaze, her heart pounding. "Am I?"

His head tilted, his expression turning wicked. "Well. Let me think." He kissed the back of her hand, then the other. "Perhaps…" turning the hands over, he kissed her palm "…I should…" he kissed the other palm "…be certain…"

Taking her finger in his mouth, he suckled it, swirling her fingertip with his tongue, as he'd done so expertly to other parts of her that were even more sensitive.

She shivered at the wet heat of his mouth. Her nipples were

hard as desire coiled inside her. Pulling her finger from his mouth with one last kiss, he rose unsteadily to his feet.

"Now I know you'll join me..." He lifted dark eyebrows with a crooked grin. "I'm going for a swim." His powerful legs shifted as he turned on the yacht's deck. "Catch me if you can."

Without warning, he ran straight off the edge of the deck, falling the long distance. She heard a splash far below, against the hard sapphire surface of the water.

Emmie caught her breath. Standing up so fast she felt dizzy, she rushed to the edge to look down.

He was swimming in the water, totally unconcerned about any danger, his slick, wet dark hair shining in the sun. He laughed when he saw her face. "There's nothing for you to be scared of. Come in. The water's fine."

Later that night, Theo sat beside Emmie on the speedboat en route to Santorini, his arm around her. He could not remember the last time he'd felt so relaxed, so sated, so... He didn't know how to describe it.

The summer sun was lowering fast over the Aegean, turning it the color of Homer's wine-colored water. Ahead, he could see the lights of Oia shining in the twilight.

But it was nothing compared to the way his wife glowed.

Theo looked down at her. The red sequins of her short dress shimmered as the boat swayed and leaped over the waves of Amoudi Bay. Her long hair, streaked with honey highlights from their time in the sun, flew behind her, and she'd added a hint of makeup to her flushed, pretty face. His gaze fell to her bare legs beneath the short hemline, her pedicured feet in strappy high heels, her toenails glistening baby pink.

As the vintage wood speedboat flew across the water, her full breasts, pressed into deep cleavage by lingerie, bounced with every hard wave. He tried not to look. Tried and failed and wanted her even now, even though they'd made love three times today, just since they'd gone swimming in the sea.

Would he ever get enough of her?

Emmie's rosy lips suddenly curved, and he knew he'd been caught. He looked up guiltily, but she smiled, her eyes bright.

Something twisted in his heart.

She was just so beautiful, whether in a designer gown, a cheap sundress, or nothing. Naked was his preference.

Two hours earlier, when they were still lazing in bed, Emmie had rolled her eyes when he suggested that for the reception tonight, she wear one of the designer dresses the New York stylist had packed into her trousseau. Reaching for a silk robe to cover her luscious body, Emmie had ducked her head. "Couldn't we just skip the whole thing?"

"I'm afraid we must go," he said, a little remorsefully. Rising from the bed, Theo had stretched his limbs with pleasure after hours of lovemaking. "When Celine heard we were in Greece on our honeymoon, she was nice enough to throw us a party. Plus, I want to find out about Paris."

Emmie's violet-blue eyes were luminous as she pleaded, "You could go without me."

Theo frowned, bemused. "Why wouldn't you want to come? Her father's house is beautiful, the most glamorous on Thira."

Instead of looking pleased, her lips sagged at the edges. She whispered, "I won't fit in."

"That's true." Pulling her close, he'd nestled her body against his own, with only the thin silk of her robe between them. Kissing her neck, he'd gently tugged open the neckline as he whispered, "You're more beautiful than any of them."

Her silk brushed against his skin as he'd pulled her back into bed.

Later, as he followed her out of the shower, he found Emmie wet and naked, digging frantically through her heretofore untouched designer wardrobe now hanging in the yacht bedroom's closet. Surrounded by piles of lovely dresses on the floor, she'd begged him for help.

And he'd given it to her. Oh, how he'd given it to her.

He'd helped her pick out a dress, too.

Now, as their speedboat grew closer to the island, he could make out the magnificent mansion owned by Celine's father. Built a hundred years before, the classical architecture looked slightly out of place, a miniature Versailles dropped willy-nilly onto a Greek island. Other boats already filled the marina. He saw shadows of people arriving, heard the low hum of music and conversation across the water.

Glancing at his wife, he saw she too was staring at the mansion. Her expression was scared. He squeezed her hand.

"The most beautiful one there," he repeated.

She flashed him a grateful look, then looked him over in his tuxedo. "You're not so bad yourself."

It was full twilight, and the moon had just started to rise, as Theo helped her out of the boat onto the enormous dock, lit up by fairy lights. His gaze raked over Emmie in the sparkling red dress, showing off her sensual shape. So pregnant, so sexy, all woman—

A curse went through his brain. How could he want her again already? he thought with wonder.

The three times he'd made love to her today had been explosive, as always, and yet something had been different. Had it been the sunlight? The sea?

Or was it because, three days ago, for the first time in his life, he'd opened up to a woman and revealed something no one else knew?

His body, which had been so relaxed, suddenly tensed.

Had he made a mistake? Had he told her too much about his past? Had he sounded like he was complaining? Like he was weak? Had he said anything that she could somehow use against him?

And he hadn't even shared the worst of his past. He couldn't. Not even with her.

Especially not with her.

If Emmie ever knew the truth—

His heart suddenly felt like it was going to explode out of his chest.

She won't, he told himself. Let the past stay buried. Like their mother's old locket, now smothered beneath the earth on Lyra.

Theo Papadopolous was gone. He'd been born Theo Katrakis at sixteen, when he came to America and became his uncle's heir. He was rich and powerful now. No one could ever hurt him. Cold. He was cold. He had no feelings.

But as his wife clutched his arm, smiling up at him, her eyes shining in the fiery torches lighting up the Santorini hillside, his heart loped in his chest. And he felt the first stirrings of fear. What would happen if Emmie ever really knew?

CHAPTER NINE

EMMIE CLUNG TO her husband's arm as they walked past the torches that led along the path from the dock to the sprawling Baroque mansion, a wedding-cake confection of pink and white, clinging to the hillside above the shore. She felt cold in the warm summer night.

A soft sea breeze blew against her overheated skin, brushing over the red sequins of her sleeveless cocktail dress. The rectangular paillettes shimmered beneath the mansion's lights flooding from the windows, the sequins similar in size and sparkle to the ten-karat emerald-cut diamond on her left hand.

She glanced nervously to the right and left. She saw others arriving who looked elegant and yet casual, in body-conscious beige or black, as if a soiree in a twenty-million-euro mansion in Santorini was just another Thursday night. All Emmie wanted was to fit in. To not embarrass her husband.

To not make him wonder why he'd married her and wish he hadn't.

But it was hard for Emmie, as they walked through grand double doors, and uniformed servers offered champagne from silver trays, not to feel like she was out of step and out of her league.

The other guests had been born into fortune or earned it themselves. Some were special for their athletic prowess, others for their cleverness, others for their beauty.

But Emmie? All she'd done was get herself knocked up.

As they entered the ballroom—a *ballroom*, in someone's private house!—she glanced nervously at Theo. Now *he* fit in all right. He looked gorgeous, his powerfully muscled body civilized by his well-tailored tuxedo. He looked handsome and cold.

Only she knew the depths of emotion and darkness in his soul.

But you don't know, a voice whispered inside her. *You're afraid to know.*

"It's something, isn't it?" Theo flashed her a crooked smile as he looked up at the frescoes on the ceilings above.

"Something," she echoed. Sipping a glass of juice, she glanced around uncertainly. She felt people looking at them, whispering.

"Celine's great-grandfather built this place before the First World War." He added wryly, "Sometimes I feel like that's how long I've been pitching her father about his Paris property."

"How many times have you tried?"

"At least five times. The first was years ago, before I met you. Before I knew Nico, even." His eyes sharpened. "Ah. There she is."

He pulled her forward to a petite, very slender blonde, wearing a simple beige dress with straps and no embellishment.

"Theo." Coming forward, the Frenchwoman lifted on the toes of her stilettos to kiss one of his cheeks, then the other.

"Thank you for throwing us a party," he said, smiling as he looked around the crowded ballroom.

Celine dropped back with a pout, teasingly hitting the lapel of his tuxedo jacket with her hand. "Though, why I should be so good to you, when you never even bothered to invite me to your wedding, I cannot imagine. Hello." She turned the force of her attention to Emmie. "So you are the lucky Mrs. Katrakis."

A moment before, thanks to Theo's compliments, Emmie had been feeling almost pretty. But now, compared to the small, slender French heiress, Emmie suddenly felt as grotesque as a red disco ball—shiny, round and vulgar.

"I am happy to make your acquaintance," she stammered in schoolgirl French. Sadly, it sounded nothing like when she'd practiced in the yacht earlier that afternoon. Her words sounded garbled, like she had marbles in her mouth.

Celine looked startled, then her smile sharpened. She gave Emmie two cheek kisses in response, then said airily, "Enjoy your party."

Cheeks hot, Emmie glanced quickly at Theo, feeling like she'd made a fool of herself. He was watching Celine go.

"Theo."

He turned to her. "Shall I introduce you to everyone?"

But she'd seen the way his eyes had lingered on his ex-girl-friend. She wondered what he was thinking, but then thought that maybe this, too, was something she was afraid to know.

For the next hour Theo introduced her to the wealthy, famous, fabulous people who were his peers and Celine's. Emmie duly shook hands with or was air-kissed by tycoons, government leaders, movie stars and nepo babies.

"Congratulations," they all said to her, as they looked from gorgeous Theo in his well-cut tuxedo to Emmie's flushed face and pregnant belly. And as their lips curved, she knew what they were thinking because she was thinking the same: she didn't deserve to be here.

She met a few more celebrities, followed by harried assistants. Looking at the assistants, Emmie felt sympathy. She almost wished she could be here as Theo's secretary instead of his wife. At least then she'd know how to behave and could

go unnoticed. How she missed it now, the simple sweetness
of being invisible!

After a few minutes of standing idly by, as Theo spoke to
two other men, their conversation switching rapidly between
English, Italian and Spanish, Emmie finally murmured "Excuse me" and wandered to the buffet table.

Quietly, she made herself a plate of hors d'oeuvres and
drank sparkling water. Going to stand in a corner, she
munched her food and watched as the behavior of the guests
steadily deteriorated across the ballroom. As the evening grew
late, they drank to excess and screamed laughter and kissed
one person then another, making Emmie wonder if they'd
taken drugs in the palatial bathrooms or if she'd fallen head-
long into a Roman orgy.

She suddenly wished she was back home, in Queens, attending a potluck with her neighbors and friends who actually
cared about each other, more than shocking or impressing or
competing with rivals and frenemies.

"Madame Katrakis."

Turning, she saw Celine Harcourt. Her throat went tight,
but she gave her best attempt at a smile. "Call me Emmie.
Please."

The slim blonde gave a cool smile. "Thank you." She made
no suggestion that Emmie should similarly call her Celine.
"My dear, you look terribly bored. You must let me entertain you."

"No, I—"

"This way," the Frenchwoman said, and with no good excuse to slight the hostess Emmie set down her plate and followed her, through a secret door that required a code, and up
a slender flight of stairs to a quiet alcove above the ballroom.

Emmie looked down and saw the entire party below: the
band, people dancing, gossiping, couples making out in corners, all the whirl of beautiful people and beautiful clothes.

"Disgusting, isn't it?" Celine sighed, standing beside her. "My father built this balcony so if he fancied some girl, he could bring her up here and make love to her, without having to miss his party. And, of course, so that he could immediately kick her out afterward, with none the wiser."

As Emmie turned to her with shocked eyes, the Frenchwoman lit a cigarette from a pack resting on the small sofa nearby.

"You are far from home, are you not, little secretary?" As she shook out the match, her gaze fell on Emmie's belly beneath the red sequin dress. "You got the golden ticket, and now you are his wife. How did you do it? A hole in the condom? Pretending to be on the pill?"

"Uh…"

"He should have been mine." Celine's eyes looked out toward the spot in the ballroom where Theo was still talking intensely to the two other tycoons. "But I thought it the decent thing to wait six months, at least, before I forced his hand." Her gaze fell back to Emmie's belly. "More fool me."

"It wasn't like that," Emmie protested. "I never tricked him."

She inhaled her cigarette, holding it elegantly, exhaling smoke before she gave a cold smile. "Didn't you?"

The horrible woman tried to make it sound as if Emmie had gotten pregnant on purpose—which she hadn't!

Had she?

After Theo had kissed her on Mount Corcovado at the base of the lit-up statue, she had little memory of the passionate, steamy ride back to Ipanema Beach. She just remembered how she'd trembled as he led her back to his hotel suite.

She'd returned his kiss desperately, with clumsy inexperience, as he'd lowered her to the enormous bed. They ripped off each other's clothes, kissing and tasting and teasing each other until she was gasping with need, until he finally, with agonizing slowness, pushed himself inside her.

She'd felt a sharp pain then, but he'd kissed her, slowly wooing and luring her, until she again felt only pleasure. It was only when she'd finally cried out her fulfillment that he'd finally let himself go.

"There was never any question of…of…" Her cheeks were burning. "We—neither of us—um, we just didn't think about it."

Celine blinked, staring at her blankly, letting her cigarette burn to ash. Then her thin eyebrows lowered. "Do you mean to tell me that Theo just…forgot about birth control? *Theo?*"

This was getting weird. "It's really none of your business," Emmie said, backing away. "Thank you for hosting this party for us, it's so very kind, but I should really get back to my husband now."

Drawing herself up with as much dignity as she could muster, Emmie turned to go.

"You're not good enough for him. Nowhere near good enough." Celine's lovely face was contorted with bewildered rage. She took a puff of her cigarette with a shaking hand. "You? The fat little secretary? You should never be anything but a servant, raising his child, serving his needs, counting out the days till you're paid-off."

Emmie gasped at her rudeness. "That is—"

"You might have convinced him to marry you," Celine interrupted. "But he'll never love you. You know that, don't you?" When she saw Emmie's agonized face, she relaxed and smiled. She took another long drag on her cigarette, then exhaled. "Enjoy the party while it lasts, little secretary."

"So it's true," the Italian said.

"What?" Theo said.

The Spaniard lifted an amused eyebrow, his gaze focused just past Theo's ear. "You have a wife."

"So?" Turning, Theo saw Emmie, following their hostess through the crowded ballroom uncertainly.

Hmm, he thought. Never a good thing to have one's wife comparing notes with one's ex-mistress, even though his relationship with Celine had ended years before. He consoled himself with the thought that there wasn't anything the Frenchwoman could say—that Theo was arrogant, that he was selfish—that Emmie didn't already know. In spades.

His gaze lingered on his wife's sexy shape in the red sparkling dress, at her lovely face as she bit her lower lip in consternation, wobbling a bit in her high heels. A smile traced his lips. Adorable.

"I could hardly believe it," the Italian, Giovanni Orsini, drawled. He took a sip of scotch. "Such a choice."

"I mean, honor is all very *well*, in theory," Carlos Mondragón agreed, "but a little goes a long way."

The three tycoons, acquaintances who saw each other a few times a year, had been discussing sports, mostly cricket and tennis, in spite of Theo's best efforts to work the conversation around to real-estate development in general and Harcourt's property in particular. Now, he blinked at them in bewilderment. "What are you talking about?"

The other men glanced at each other.

"Your marriage," said Giovanni.

"To your secretary," said Carlos.

Theo stiffened. "What about it?"

"You were correct to support the child, and the mother, of course," the Italian said. "But *marriage*? To a secretary?"

"I didn't take you for a snob, Orsini."

He shrugged with an easy smile. "Love affairs are all very well, and accidents *will* happen, if one isn't careful. But marriage is a serious business for men of our station. And taking a mere secretary as your wife... It's hardly the way to start a dynasty, is it?"

Theo was still stinging from Orsini's casual criticism of *if one isn't careful* when he was distracted by that insulting dismissal of Emmie. Hearing his wife, with all her beauty and gorgeously kind heart, described as a *mere secretary* filled Theo with sudden, breathless rage. His hands clenched, and he nearly punched his friend.

But why? Why would Orsini's words make him so angry, when they were obviously true?

What the hell was wrong with him?

Cold, Theo ordered himself. Ice-cold.

He forced himself to turn to the Spaniard, who'd gone quiet. "And you, Mondragón? You agree with this?"

The man shrugged. "As someone who nearly was caught myself recently, all I can say is I was lucky to escape." Gulping down the rest of his scotch, he gave a smile that didn't meet his eyes. "Only a fool marries for love."

Love? Even the word seemed like a judgment to Theo. Love was the worst kind of weakness. "It's not a question of *love*," he defended. "Emmie's pregnant with my son. He must have the protection of my name, and so will she."

"Very noble."

"Very," said Carlos Mondragón, signaling for another drink.

Theo set his jaw, growing more annoyed by the moment. "If it ever happens to you, you'll understand."

"No accidental children for me. I make sure."

"I make *very* sure," Giovanni Orsini added smugly.

"Talk to me if you become a father. Until then, remain silent about what you don't understand," Theo bit out. "If a man does not take care of his own child, he is not a man."

The other two looked at each other.

"True enough," the Italian was forced to concede.

Carlos Mondragón shook his head impatiently. "The subject grows tedious. Let's talk business." Looking both ways in the crowded ballroom, he leaned forward and whispered, "It's true. Pierre Harcourt's looking for a new developer."

Theo sucked in his breath. "For Paris?"

Taking a new scotch off a waiter's tray, Carlos nodded.

He tried to hide the sudden pounding of his heart. The famous Harcourt property in Paris, one of the last undeveloped big parcels in the heart of the city, had been his dream for years. It was how he'd first met Celine Harcourt, years ago, while pitching development plans to her father. Even tonight, he'd stared at her, wondering how to ask if the rumor he'd heard could be true.

Pierre Harcourt was a difficult man to please. For years, the man had dragged his feet on pulling the trigger and developing a property that had belonged to his aristocratic ancestors before they were hauled off on tumbrels.

But Theo had never given up. He'd been dazzled by the potential, from the moment he'd seen the vast car park on the edge of the Seine. Emmie had helped him with that last proposal, when he'd spent millions of euros on architectural and landscape design, investigating government regulations and wooing potential investors. It had all seemed wasted when Harcourt chose a different firm last year.

Until now.

"What about Allmond?"

"Financing fell through. I heard from my mistress whose cousin works there. Harcourt is now looking for stability and deep pockets." Snorting, the Italian saluted him with his lowball glass. "Clearly describes you now, old man."

Theo ignored the teasing. "Is it public knowledge?"

"It will be, tomorrow."

"Is Harcourt here?" Theo demanded, looking sharply around the ballroom.

"You think he'd attend one of his daughter's bacchanals?

He's past that these days. He's in Paris—hey, where are you going?"

Theo had departed without farewell, looking for his wife.

Pushing through the drunken crowds in the ballroom, he finally saw Emmie, bountiful and sexy, a gorgeous red flame amid tiny wispy women in beige slip dresses. Even without red sequins, Emmie would have shone for him like a star.

But her shoulders seemed slumped, and she seemed to stumble in her strappy stilettos. Should he have tried harder to include her in his discussion with the two men? But Theo knew she wasn't a fan of sports, and he'd thought her unlikely to be mesmerized by discussion of the summer cricket season, conducted half in Spanish and Italian. So he hadn't been surprised when she'd wandered away to the buffet table.

But now, he set his jaw grimly. Had Celine said something rude?

There was a loud cheer around them, as the clock struck midnight, and as always at Celine's summer parties, the music changed from classical quintet to pulsing, soaring club music arranged by a famous DJ who charged hundreds of thousands a night. All around them, wealthy, beautiful people poured onto the ballroom floor, as multicolor lights flashed around them.

Their eyes locked across the crowded ballroom. His wife shimmered like a dream, as the beat and haunting melody lifted him to a strange euphoria.

Emmie.

His mouth went dry as something tightened in his chest.

Shaking himself out of his trance, he set his jaw and went grimly through the crowd. When he reached her, he thought she looked pale. He wanted to ask what Celine had said to her, but instead he said merely, "We should go."

"Okay," she said quietly. Maybe she was just tired? He wanted to believe that. He took her arm, in case she needed support, with those damned high heels causing her such trouble. With his other hand, he reached into his tuxedo jacket pocket for his phone.

They left the hillside mansion, overlooking the moon-swept sea. He helped her walk down the path, beneath flickering red lights. The vintage 1950s speedboat pulled up before the two of them even reached the end of the dock. His drivers prided themselves on being quick.

As the boat hurried back toward his anchored yacht, Theo sat in the long back seat beside Emmie, his arm stretched behind her.

"I have some bad news," he told her in a low voice, over the roar of the engine and splash of the wake.

Her big eyes shimmered at him in the moonlight. "What?"

He took her smaller hand in his own. "I'm afraid we'll have to miss Mykonos and cut our honeymoon short."

"Why?" She swallowed, then whispered, "What changed your mind?"

Lifting her hand to his mouth, he kissed it gently. He felt her shiver, just from that, and it made him want... But there was no time for that, he thought with real regret. "I need to go to Paris. Pierre Harcourt's deal with Allmond fell through."

"Paris!" She sucked in her breath, her lovely face filled with shock, then delight. He smiled, touched that she knew what it meant to him. He did not have to explain. She wanted him to have it.

"The yacht will go full speed to Paros, where my jet will be gassed up and waiting to take me to Paris."

"Paros to Paris," she laughed. Then the light in her eyes faded. "Taking you? Just you?"

Still holding her hand, Theo looked up at his approaching yacht, its lit-up windows illuminating Santorini's dark sea. He looked down at their entwined hands barely visible in the moonlight.

"It's going to take all my energy to work up a new pitch," he said in a low voice. "I'll be working sixteen-hour days for the next month."

"*Eighteen*-hour days," she corrected.

She knew him too well. He gave her a crooked smile. "Eighteen."

"Why not bring me with you?" she said slowly. "You know I could help."

He knew. He'd never had a better secretary—ever. She'd been his protector, his partner, his friend. "I can't."

"Why?" she demanded.

Swallowing the temptation, he shook his head. "As you said. You're not my secretary. I promised you'd live in New York, close to family and friends. Plus, you're pregnant."

"So?"

"So?" He stared at her incredulously. "You can't work eighteen-hour days."

"Don't tell me what I can do." Emmie stroked her cheek thoughtfully. "You think developing the pitch will take a month?"

"Or longer," he was forced to admit. "And you'll want to be home, comfortable and safe, with people you love, not bored and alone at the George V, or working at the office till you drop. No." He gave a regretful smile. "I'll leave tonight while you're sleeping on the yacht. As soon as I reach Paris, I'll send the jet back to Paros. When you wake tomorrow, it will take you home."

She stubbornly focused on the point. "Maybe it will be easier than you think. We still have the pitch from last year."

"Harcourt already heard that and rejected it. We have to rethink the pitch entirely. It needs to be visionary. I'll send for additional staff from London and New York." He thought of sending for Edna and shuddered. "I'll get a secretary from the agency. But just being first to pitch isn't enough. This time we'll focus on dazzling not just Old Man Harcourt but also his daughter."

"Daughter." Her gaze darkened. "Celine will be there?"

He shrugged. "She's his only child. He values her opinion." In fact, he valued it too much, in Theo's opinion. Celine didn't give a damn about the property, just the money it would provide her.

Emmie looked out at the moonlit sea and seemed to shiver. No wonder she was cold, with her arms, legs and neckline so bare. He wrapped his arm around her shoulders, forcing his gaze not to linger on the swell of her breasts. No. He wouldn't even look.

"I'll miss your expertise." He quirked a wicked smile. "And a few other things." She wouldn't even meet his glance. He sighed. "Once you're in New York, maybe you could look over the list of secretaries we get from the agency. At least if you approve—"

Emmie turned her head sharply. "I'm coming with you to Paris."

Theo blinked. "What?"

"I'll be your secretary. Just like before."

But you're not my secretary anymore, Theo knew he should say. *You're my wife.*

Something held him back. Having Emmie as his secretary would make it more likely he'd achieve his objective.

Having her as his wife would burn his nights like fire.

"Are you...sure?" he said slowly. "It's really what you want?"

Emmie tilted her head, looking at him beneath the sweep of her dark eyelashes as a little smile played over her red lips. "You're too much to handle for any secretary but me."

"True," he said, amused. He felt a rush of gratitude. "Thank you, Emmie," he said quietly. "You don't know what this means to me."

"I know." Their eyes locked, and his heart skipped a beat.

He pulled her close, wrapping her in both arms, against his chest. Pressed against his white tuxedo shirt, her full breasts seemed barely contained by the sequined neckline, the spaghetti straps about to snap. It was all he could do not to snap them off himself.

All he wanted to do was kiss her, but Yiannis was just now pulling the speedboat close to the yacht. There was no time—

With an intake of breath, he looked at her. "We have two hours before we'll reach my plane in Paros."

"Right." She started to pull away, suddenly all business. "I'll start pulling up research, then call the Paris office—"

"Later," Theo whispered and lowered his head to kiss her.

CHAPTER TEN

"YOU'RE DONE," Theo said suddenly one evening in their Paris office. "I'm taking you out."

"Done?" Emmie looked up blearily from three separate computer screens spread over her desk, showing all the final details of the Harcourt proposal. "What do you mean? We still have—"

Theo gently pulled a stylus from one of her hands and an electronic tablet from the other. "We've done everything we can. We can leave the cleanup and polishing to the team." He looked around the office. "Right, team?"

"We got it, boss," came the cheerful replies in French and English.

Emmie blinked owlishly, disoriented after twelve straight hours of focus. She looked around her. With its cream-colored walls, gilt-framed paintings and old-wood parquet floors, the Katrakis Paris office was very different from the New York office's glass and steel. The nineteenth-century building was in the Étoile district with a view of the Arc de Triomphe. The floor could hold twenty employees comfortably, but was currently bursting at the seams with thirty-two, including the extra staff flown in from London and New York.

For the last month, they'd been working all-out on this proposal—crunching numbers, collating technical and legal data, and creating a beautiful, eye-popping presentation, which they'd show Pierre Harcourt and his daughter tomorrow morning.

Now heavily pregnant, Emmie was finding it a little harder to make it through the sixteen-hour workdays, especially since every night, during time she should have spent sleeping, she made love to her husband once or twice. She didn't regret it. How could she resist Theo's touch, which was like an intoxicating fire?

But still. She'd be glad when the Katrakis team formally presented their proposal tomorrow at Harcourt's office in La Défense. Theo was certain it would immediately succeed. Emmie was less certain. She suspected the Harcourts would request modifications, playing their offer against sales pitches of rivals, in give-and-take of negotiations that could take weeks, if not longer.

She hoped she was wrong and Theo was right. She loved the thought of returning to New York tomorrow night. She yearned for a good night's sleep, for the baby's sake if not for hers, and the chance to nap a little and put up her swollen feet. And to see her family again.

The Swensons were all doing well. Her brothers had all moved out of the family apartment, but Karl was hardly lonely as he and her two older brothers spent their days expanding Swenson and Sons Plumbing. Her second youngest brother, Sam, at twenty-one, had registered for nursing school and was living with his girlfriend in Jersey City. Daniel, the youngest at nineteen, had just departed for Oklahoma to study cybersecurity at the University of Tulsa. Emmie smiled. Call it the Theo Katrakis Scholarship Fund.

Her friends were doing well, too. Honora was pregnant again, and she'd promised to throw Emmie and Theo a baby shower when they were back in New York. Emmie could hardly wait.

But she'd given her word to Theo to help him achieve his

dream. She intended to see it through. All she wanted was for him to be happy, because she—

Because she—

"I'm fine," she told Theo briskly, even as her stomach growled and her knees shook with exhaustion. "I don't need special treatment. I can finish."

"There's no question of special treatment, Emmie. You've fought harder than anyone." Theo's warm black eyes smiled down at her, his gaze like a caress.

This was why she'd worked so hard, she thought. A lump rose in her throat. For *him*. For the last month, she'd thrown herself into being the perfect wife and perfect secretary because she'd yearned to see Theo look at her like this for just one precious moment. With approval. With admiration. With...

Love?

Catching her breath, she shook her head. "I'll stay."

Theo's eyes flickered with respect, then he came closer, drawing her away to a quiet corner, away from the efficient, chattering employees crowding around the screens.

"Remember Rio?" he said softly.

Her lips lifted on the edges. Putting her hands over the full swell of her belly, she said, "Um, yes?"

He snorted, then his eyes grew serious. "You accused me of being a brute of a boss, never allowing you to leave the office even when we traveled around the world. And you were right. So tonight, before we leave France," he took her hand, "I want you to see the City of Lights. To celebrate our coming triumph."

Her eyebrows lifted at the word *triumph*. "Aren't you the one who always says never to count on success?"

"This time is different."

"How do you know?"

He shrugged. "I feel it."

"There are other developers offering proposals, good ones—"

"They'll lose. We'll win." He lowered his head. She felt his lips brush against her ear as he said, huskily, "Let's celebrate."

When he pulled back, his dark eyes caught hers, and she shivered.

"All right," she whispered.

Looking around the office, Theo called, "See you tomorrow at Harcourt's office."

His employees' answering cheer swelled around them, and he responded with a salute. Handing Emmie her sleek new Hermès Birkin bag, he led her to the building's antique birdcage elevator. As they descended, he gave her a sideways glance.

"What is it?" she said, gripping the handle of her bag, beige like her Prada shoes.

"I was just thinking how amazing the last month has been."

"It has."

"And I was thinking, maybe—" He gave a rueful chuckle as they reached the ground floor. "We can talk about it later."

But as they walked through the lobby, Emmie had a feeling he was glad to put off whatever he'd been about to say. Strange. It wasn't like Theo to procrastinate over anything. He was usually like a bull in a china shop, plowing forward with whatever he wanted.

"*Bonsoir, Madame* Katrakis…*monsieur*," the doorman said.

"*Bonsoir*, Jérémie," Emmie replied, holding Theo's arm in his tailored jacket.

She dimly heard the click-click-click of her heels beside his heavier footstep on the marble floor. As he led her out the door to the tree-lined Paris avenue, she looked up at him dreamily. He was darkly handsome, powerful and ruthless in his tailored Italian suit. And she was dressed to match.

Madame Katrakis.

In her cream silk shirt and camel cashmere skirt over her baby bump, wedding pearls in her ears and huge emerald-cut diamond on her left hand, Emmie now looked the part of a billionaire's wife.

When they'd arrived in Paris, Theo had insisted she must have a new, chic wardrobe. "You need the proper armor, Emmie," he'd told her, "to fight at my side in the most glamorous city in the world."

Thinking of Celine Harcourt, Emmie had reluctantly agreed, and a stylist had arrived at their four-story town house that very hour. Her closet was now filled with clothes of quiet, understated luxury: fine fabrics, perfect fit, a total lack of designer logos, and colors that varied between black, white and beige. Every morning at six for the last month, a hairstylist had duly arrived, to blow out Emmie's honey-blond hair and make it sleek and glossy, as makeup was discreetly applied.

Et voilà. Armor.

Theo hadn't been wrong. Emmie saw the respect her costume created in other people. So it was almost worth it, feeling trapped in tight, unforgiving seams, washed out in bland and boring colors, and so hot in the blast of July in Paris.

Once she was back in New York, Emmie promised herself, it would all go straight into the penthouse closet. After this, she intended to finish her pregnancy in loose sundresses, stretchy T-shirts and maternity shorts. She would sleep twelve hours a night or maybe more.

"I'm thinking about tomorrow," Theo said abruptly as they walked a short distance along the avenue.

"About the presentation?" Emmie stopped on the sidewalk. "Should we go back?"

"No. Not that." He licked his lips. "It's about our return to New York."

"What about it?" They'd arranged for a concierge doctor to chaperone their flight, with Emmie so close to her due

date. She gave him a reassuring smile. "It'll be all right if
the negotiations delay us a few days. One of the good things
about owning a private jet. No extra fees for changing one's
schedule."

Theo stared at her for a moment, then looked past her. "Ah.
There he is."

Their gleaming Bentley was waiting for them at the curb
a little way down, a chauffeur standing beside the open back
door. As they walked, Emmie took a deep breath of fresh air.
How lovely to be out of the office.

And in Paris. Just past the leafy green trees and stately
cream-colored buildings with pale blue shutters, she could
see the grandeur of the Arc de Triomphe at the end of the avenue turning pink as the sun was starting to set to the west. As
they climbed into the back of the waiting Bentley, the chauffeur closing the door behind them, the leather felt smooth and
sensual beneath the bare hollows of her knees.

"Where are we going?" she asked her husband.

"Dinner first." Theo kissed the back of her hand, his lips
like fire. His dark eyes burned through her. "I hope you're
hungry."

"Starving," she whispered.

"Good." His expression as he looked down at her made
her throat tight.

Did she see more than desire in his dark eyes? More than
approval for her secretarial skills?

Was it possible that Theo actually—

"He'll never love you. You know that, don't you?"

Celine's spiteful words echoed in her mind, and her brief
hope faded.

Emmie had never had reason to be jealous of the Frenchwoman. She knew that now. Theo's interest in Celine was
the same that he had in Pierre Harcourt. To him, they were
nothing but indecisive property owners who needed to be

convinced to choose Katrakis Enterprises as their real-estate developer.

But that wasn't enough. Celine wasn't the problem.

It was those words. Because Emmie feared—no, she knew—that they were true.

For the last month, Emmie had tried to distract herself from that fact. She'd worked past the point of exhaustion until the pregnancy hormones that amplified her emotions became flattened out and sleepy. She'd allowed herself no time to think, no time to feel.

But now, as their driver took them through Paris, she had no numbers to crunch or images to collate. As her husband held her hand, pointing out the sparkle of the Eiffel Tower at sunset and the silhouette of Notre Dame's famous gargoyles, black against the red twilight, Emmie suddenly felt everything. Including the reason she'd worked so long and hard the last month in Paris to be the perfect wife and secretary. Why she was so desperately trying to win his approval and esteem.

She was in love with him.

In spite of all her efforts, in spite of knowing Theo for the selfish, arrogant cad he could be, Emmie had foolishly given her heart to the complicated man who was her husband.

A man who desired her, and who appreciated her secretarial skills, but had no capacity for love. As he'd told her from the start. She suddenly blinked back tears. Was there any hope?

Following their chauffeured visits to the most unabashedly touristy attractions of the city, Theo surprised her with dinner for two on a private cruise down the Seine.

"I set this up myself." Theo gave a proud smile. He never arranged logistical details himself. When she didn't respond, his smile faded. "But if you don't like it, I could get us a late-night reservation at le Café de la Paix—"

"A dinner cruise, I love it," she forced herself to say.

And she did try to enjoy it. But as they sat on the deck and

enjoyed a private dinner for two by candlelight, floating down
the Seine as they watched the dreamy lights of Paris go by in
the darkness, for some reason she felt like crying.

Theo's handsome face was bewildered as he looked down
at her barely touched plate. "Is something wrong with the
food?"

"No, it's delicious," she said and choked down several bites
of rich chateaubriand in truffle sauce, the buttery cheeses, the
flaky orange blossom tart, washing it down with sparkling,
rose-infused water.

At midnight, their chauffeur drove them back to the eigh-
teenth-century *hôtel particulier* on the Île Saint-Louis overlooking the Seine, which Theo had rented from a penurious
aristocrat at exorbitant cost. He punched in the ten-digit security code at the tall iron gate, drawing her into the small dark
garden as the gate closed behind them with a clang.

"My God, you're beautiful," Theo said huskily. His dark
eyes moved over her in the white silk blouse and camel skirt.
"I've wanted to do this all night—"

He lowered his mouth to hers beneath the streetlights dappled through the trees. Pressing her against the wrought iron
fence, he kissed her hungrily. As his tongue swept hers, elec-
trifying her senses, she clung to him with equal need.

Drawing her to the imposing front door, he punched in
another security code, then led her inside the grand home.

Yanking off his suit jacket, he dropped it to the checkered
marble floor and led her up the wide, sweeping staircase with
its decorative iron curlicues, in a palace built for noblemen
long ago for a life long since vanished.

Leading her to the master bedroom, Theo looked at her in
the semidarkness, illuminated only by faint moonlight and
the passing river traffic below. He pulled off her silk blouse,
revealing full breasts overflowing the white lacy bra. Falling to his knees with an intake of breath, he slowly unzipped

the back of her cashmere skirt, and that, too, dropped to the priceless Turkish rug. He looked up, past her white lace panties and the swell of her pregnant belly, past her full breasts. His dark eyes locked with hers.

She shivered, looking down at him. Shadows played against his high cheekbones, crooked aquiline nose and dark scruff of his jawline. His ruthlessly handsome face was stark with need.

Rising to his feet, he gently lowered her back against the large four-poster bed. He pulled off her high heels, one by one, kissing the insole of each foot before he tossed the designer shoe to the floor. Moving over her, he slowly stroked her, pulling off first her bra, then her panties.

Backing up, he removed his platinum cuff links, placing them carefully on the nightstand with a clink. His dark eyes never left hers as he kicked off his gleaming leather shoes, unbuttoned his tailored shirt, removed his trousers and silk boxers, dropping it all to the floor.

Her husband stood in front of her, naked and unashamed. Emmie's mouth went dry as her eyes roamed down his powerful chest and arms, to his muscled thighs, laced with dark hair, all the way to his scarred ankle. Then the sacred place in the middle, hard and ready for her. Aching with need, she wordlessly held out her arms.

He made love to her passionately in the mansion overlooking the Seine, carefully pulling her up to ride him. He overwhelmed her with pleasure as he'd done every night from the moment they'd wed.

But this time was different.

Afterward, Theo held her in the moonlight, their bodies sweaty in the warm breeze off the river from the open balcony. Her head rested against his bare chest as he caressed her hair.

And she quietly wept.

Now she knew she loved him. And worse.

Emmie wanted him to love her back, for their marriage to

be based on more than just parenthood, more than partnership, more than even sex. She wanted love that lasted forever.

Theo's hand froze as he stroked her wet cheek. "What's this?" He frowned down at her in the dim light. "Tears?"

"No," she lied. Turning, she pressed her face to his skin.

"Emmie?" Sitting up, he sounded worried. "What's wrong?"

"Nothing."

"You're overtired. I've been working you too hard." She didn't answer. He took a deep breath. "You're missing your family," he said quietly. "You're homesick."

Their bodies were still entwined on the shadowy bed, but she'd never felt so far apart.

Emmie lifted her head from his chest. His black eyes pierced her soul, whispering of the pain waiting for her, loving someone for the rest of her life who'd never love her back. She looked toward the open balcony, toward the lowering dark clouds shrouding the Parisian night sky.

"Yes," she whispered. She looked at him. "Don't you want to go home?"

Home.

Theo stared at her in the faint lights of Paris from the open window. They were still naked in bed. Just moments before they'd been lost in ecstasy.

Now, he felt... He didn't even know how he felt. Except that it wasn't good.

All month they'd been in Paris, he'd felt that same relaxed, joyful sensation he'd had in Santorini, only more so. Was that happiness? He didn't know how else to describe it. Working long days with a team he respected on his dream property deal, and feeling the satisfaction of watching it take shape and knowing, *knowing*, he would finally win, was exhilarating. His work this past month had demanded every bit of his attention. It relaxed him, helping him forget everything he didn't want to remember, shutting up the voices inside him that told him he should have been the one to die.

He'd had his Miss Swenson back. Emmie had been in top form, organizing and collating everything from the geologic survey of the plat site to the percentages of different investors in yen versus euros to the visual impact of the marketing materials.

In spite of her advancing pregnancy, Emmie was tireless, running everything with style, grace and flair. Her new wardrobe, with its tasteful luxury, indicated her as a woman of power in her own right. She was the most incredible second-in-command any CEO could hope for, spending every hour of her day in pursuit of one objective: helping Theo achieve his dreams.

Oh, and at night, she suddenly turned into his wife, the sexiest woman in the world, and set his world on fire.

Happiness. Yes. *Happiness* was the word.

Was it any wonder as the day approached when he'd promised to return with her to live in New York, that Theo might wish they could keep living this wonderful life?

Why would he ever want this to end?

The winning property developer would be expected to remain in Paris to oversee construction, perhaps for years. Theo had people who could do that, but what if he preferred to do it himself? Or what if he wanted to jump into a new, exciting project far from New York? The world was full of empty lots, just waiting for him to build cathedrals of industry, palaces of housing, skyscrapers and shops and parks. The future had no limit.

Especially with Emmie by his side.

So he'd had an idea he'd meant to propose to her tonight: that they'd continue to travel the world securing new property deals, moving from place to place. She'd keep working sixteen-hour days at his side. A nanny could travel with them to take care of their child. Perfect.

But first on the elevator, then later as he sat across from her in candlelight on the Seine, Theo Katrakis, feared in board-rooms and amateur boxing rings, had *chickened out*.

No. Not chickened out, he'd told himself. The time just wasn't yet ripe. Timing was everything.

After making love to her, as Theo held her in his arms, he'd stared at the ceiling, trying to think of the right words to make her want the same life he wanted. No ideas were forthcoming.

He wanted to make his wife happy. He did. But he also didn't want to be trapped in New York, waiting for their son to be born, preparing the nursery and dealing with baby showers and endless intrusions from family and friends. He wanted to build his empire. He wanted to work. Work was life.

And he wanted Emmie with him. At his side. In his of-fice. In his bed.

He cared for her. He wanted her respect. She was the only one who understood him, who saw his flaws and limitations but still accepted him, just as he was. He didn't have to hide with her. He didn't have to pretend.

At least he hadn't—until now.

He forced a smile. "Of course I want to go home."

Still naked in his arms, Emmie looked at him, her heart-shaped lips parted in a breathless dawn of a smile. "So you don't mind—"

"But does New York have to be our only home?" He stroked sweaty tendrils of her blond hair from her cheek. "The world is a big place. We could own it all."

Emmie's lovely face clouded in the shadowy bedroom. "I thought you liked New York. It's your headquarters."

"The company's headquarters, not mine."

"You bought a fifty-million-dollar penthouse to live in."

He shrugged. "An investment, no different from my other properties around the world. Emmie—" he clasped her hand "—we could live anywhere."

She stared at him. "But my family is in New York. Our friends." Her eyes filled with shadow. "I agreed to stay and work in Paris till your project was done. But then you promised we could go home."

"Haven't you been happy, Emmie?" His arms tightened around her, their naked bodies intertwined on the bed in a tangle of sheets. "Don't you enjoy our life here?"

Abruptly, Emmie pulled away. She rose to her feet. He had a single moment to appreciate the sensual curve of her backside in the shadowy light, her honey-blond hair tumbling down her back, before she wrapped herself in a white terry-cloth robe from the closet. She turned back, tying the belt.

"I've enjoyed seeing you happy." Meeting his eyes, she added quietly, "Because I'm in love with you, Theo."

Whatever Theo had been about to say was choked off as his throat tightened. Telling himself he'd misheard, he said hoarsely, "What?"

Her violet eyes were huge in the moonlight as she said simply, "I love you."

Turning away, he rose abruptly from the bed, pulling on his robe. He muttered, "You're overtired."

"I'm not, I mean, it's true I am, but that's not why. I'm saying it because it's true. I love you."

It was as if a dam had burst, and once she'd spoken the awful incantation, she couldn't quit repeating it like an evil spell. His mind was whirling. "What does that even mean?"

"I think...*love* means putting the other person ahead of yourself," she said quietly.

His lips twisted downward. "You mean it makes you a slave."

Emmie stared at him from across the luxurious bedroom, with its old oil paintings and marble fireplace full of unlit white candles. Her expression was stricken.

"It's not like that," she protested. Brushing at her eyes,

she gave him a small, wistful smile. "Not if both people love each other."

Love each other.

Memory punched through his heart.

His mother's wild, bloodshot eyes. *"I can't leave him. We love each other."*

"He's going to kill you, Mama. And us."

Breaking out in a sweat, Theo turned unsteadily toward the balcony. Strong, he had to be strong. Gripping his hands into fists, he ordered himself to calm the hell down. Cold. He had to be cold.

But it wasn't working.

"I need some fresh air," he gasped and fled.

Outside on the balcony, the night was warm and clear. Clouds covered the stars and all but a sliver of moon. He could see the inky blackness of the Seine below, the shimmer of lights across the river, and beyond it, the soaring Gothic buttresses of Notre Dame on the Île de la Cité.

Emmie silently followed. Beyond the balcony railing, he could see the dark shape of birds against the lowering clouds, hear their melancholy cries as they flew. He took a deep breath.

"I don't want you to love me," he said in a low voice. "I want an alliance of equals. Where we each can live the life we desire, and no one has to sacrifice. No one gets hurt."

"Sorry."

Her shoulders slumped, her lovely face was downcast. And Theo hated himself for disappointing her. Why was she forcing him to hurt her?

He choked out, "You promised you'd never love me."

Emmie looked down at the black river. A beam of moonlight twisted through the clouds, tracing the smooth curve of her cheek. Lifting her head, she said quietly, "And you promised we'd live in New York. To have a home. With friends. Family."

And Theo suddenly knew the life he'd hoped to have with her was impossible. She would never agree to hire a full-time nanny so that she could spend her days working beside him at the office, helping him conquer the world. Emmie would never be parted from her child for the sake of money or power or fame.

Love was what mattered to her. Love he could not give her.

Pain was like a razor blade in his throat as he turned back to the Seine. Moonlight rested the sharp edges of the water's dark waves.

He felt Emmie's gentle hands on his shoulder. "It's all right, Theo. I know you can't love me. I've known it all along. It's my fault. All my fault." She gave him a crooked half smile. "Well, a little bit yours, for being so irresistible."

Even now, she was making jokes, trying to lighten the mood and offer comfort, though he'd hurt her so badly. He tried to smile back. "If I could love anyone—"

"I know." Balling her fists into the pockets of her robe, Emmie took a deep breath. "I'll get over it. Add it to the list of things we'll never discuss again." She turned away. "Forget I said anything."

But as his wife disappeared back into the bedroom, leaving Theo alone on the balcony in the haunted moonlight of Paris, he knew there was no way he'd ever be able to forget.

CHAPTER ELEVEN

How could Emmie have made such a mistake?

How could she have put their baby at risk?

"All right, Mrs. Katrakis." Dr. Hwang's cool eyes focused on hers, as Emmie lay on a towel over the leather sofa on their private jet now on descent into a New York airport. Standing up, the doctor washed her hands in the small galley sink. "You're only three centimeters dilated. We'll get you to the hospital on time."

"Do you—promise?" Emmie panted, as another contraction contorted her body.

"I don't make promises, but it's very likely." The gray-haired doctor glanced at the flight attendant. "You had the pilot relay the emergency?"

"An ambulance will be waiting when we land," the young woman replied, looking relieved that Emmie wasn't going to give birth on the plane.

Emmie couldn't blame her. She could hardly believe they'd cut it so close.

Her due date was still a week away, and everyone said first babies always arrived late. Emmie had thought she'd have plenty of time to set up the penthouse nursery before she went into labor, upon which she'd serenely grab a prepared overnight bag and Theo would escort her to the Manhattan hospital they'd chosen. She'd get an epidural for the pain, the labor would be hard but endurable, then afterward she'd introduce her baby to family and friends in a comfortable, spacious hospital room filled with flowers.

But Pierre Harcourt had strung them along until that very morning, when after three weeks of asking several developers for modifications and revisions of their bids, he'd finally signed a binding contract with Katrakis Enterprises. Theo had been right. They'd won. But she'd been right, too. It had all taken longer than they'd hoped.

To be fair, Theo had told her more than once that she should return to New York without him. But she hadn't. Even that morning, as they'd been packing for the plane, he'd asked her if it wouldn't be better for them to just stay in Paris until the baby was born. She'd shot down that idea, too.

She'd wanted to prove their marriage could still work. That she could love him and he could totally not love her but they could still succeed together as a couple. As a family.

And this was the result.

"We'll make it to the hospital," Emmie said, forcing her cheeks into a cheerful smile. "That's a relief, isn't it?"

"A relief," Theo agreed, but his handsome face was pale beneath his tan. Going to the galley, he returned with a bottle of cool water and handed it to her as she smoothed her sundress back over her knees, sitting up on the leather sofa.

"Thanks." She drank the water in gulps. "It'll be a funny story to tell our son someday. That we went into labor halfway over the Atlantic."

"Funny," he said, but he didn't meet her eyes.

An ambulance was waiting on the tarmac when they landed at Teterboro thirty minutes later. Emmie was whisked off the plane on a stretcher and placed in the back of the ambulance as the concierge doctor spoke quietly to the paramedics, handing over care.

"Come with me," Emmie called to Theo, who was lingering behind, his shoulders hunched, his handsome face stricken.

"Not enough room. He'll have to follow us, ma'am," one of the paramedics said and closed the ambulance door.

By the time Emmie arrived at the Midtown hospital, the one closest to their house and where she'd planned to give birth, her body was racked with increasing pain. She'd turned in the paperwork weeks before, so was quickly wheeled to a private room in the maternity ward on the tenth floor. By then, the contractions were so bad she couldn't breathe. She nearly threw up from the pain.

"Epidural," she croaked when she saw her obstetrician in the door.

After checking her, the doctor shook her head. "Sorry, Mrs. Katrakis." Nurses came closer, putting monitoring equipment on her belly to check the baby's heart, and on Emmie's finger to check her oxygen levels. "It's far too late for that. You're at nine centimeters. It's almost time to push."

"No—it can't be already—" Emmie couldn't go into labor now, not yet. Not without her husband.

Where was he?

Even without the flashing lights and siren of a speeding ambulance, the drive from Teterboro should have taken forty-five minutes, an hour in bad traffic. Where was he?

"Now, Mrs. Katrakis," her obstetrician said and positioned herself between her knees, "push!"

Emmie gasped for breath and cried and retched, and she pushed. She pushed most of all, bearing down with all her strength, until she thought she might pass out or die and wasn't even sure that would be a bad thing—except her baby...her baby had to live.

When it was finally over, she took a full gasping breath as the doctor turned away with the precious bundle. Emmie craned her head around the doctor, but she couldn't see her baby. Why was it so quiet? What was happening?

"My baby... Why isn't he crying? What's wrong?" She turned, sweaty and crying. "Theo."

But it wasn't her husband she'd heard coming through the door, just a nurse to begin the afterbirth protocols. Emmie turned back to the doctor.

"Give me my baby. Now or I'll..."

A sudden small cry, weak at first, then louder and heartier. The obstetrician turned back toward her, holding a tiny baby wrapped in a clean towel.

"Mrs. Katrakis," she said gently, "I'd like you to meet your son."

The tiny newborn was placed in Emmie's arms, against her bare skin, and she felt a rush of joy she'd never known. The baby blinked in confusion, yawning, looking up at her sleepily with dark eyes. But as their eyes met, Emmie felt a strange recognition. Her son. Hers.

She caressed the baby's cheek, marveling. "And he's all right? He's okay?"

"He took a minute to decide to breathe, but yes. He's fine. Seven pounds, six ounces. A healthy baby boy."

"Thank you, Dr. Sanchez." Her son was born. And he was healthy. He was fine.

But Emmie had given birth alone. Her husband had never arrived. He'd missed the whole thing.

The kindly nurse helped Emmie wash up, helping her into a clean hospital gown. As she was checked by the obstetrician, a different nurse washed her baby, before he was placed back in Emmie's arms.

For long moments, as nurses and doctors buzzed around them in the room, Emmie just sat in the bed holding her baby, wondering at his beauty, touching his skin, holding him close. When he started to whimper, with the nurse's encouragement Emmie tentatively placed her baby to her breast. As he instinctively started to suckle, she watched his tiny face turn blissful and felt relief that was like joy.

But where was Theo?

The sun started to lower behind Manhattan's skyscrapers, and she grew increasingly worried. Had he been in an accident? Was he hurt, dying, his car smashed up on the I-95 freeway?

When the baby slept, she called his phone.

There was no answer. She left a message, then another.

Finally, she phoned Honora, her father, and her brothers, to tell them her baby news. Honora was elated and promised to come at once. Her father and brothers, busy with a big emergency plumbing job, shouted with joy. They promised to come in the morning.

She checked the news anxiously, but there was no mention of a massive pileup on the highway. She left Theo more messages. She received her dinner delivered on a tray and was thinking about calling the police when Honora appeared in the door with her oldest child.

As Emmie's best friend oohed and aahed over Emmie's new baby, Honora's three-year-old, Kara, was less impressed.

"I already have one," the little girl archly informed Emmie, as if to warn her against trying to pawn off the baby on Kara's family. Emmie laughed, but it was strained in her growing anxiety. Where was Theo? Why wasn't he here?

"Adorable." Honora sat on the edge of the bed, glowing but still slender, just recently pregnant herself with her third child. "What are you going to name him? Did you decide?"

"We haven't had a chance..." For all his determination to marry her and secure his heir, Theo never seemed comfortable talking about their baby's future. When Emmie had suggested possible names, he'd always said there was no rush, then changed the subject.

"Really? After two long months of marriage?" Honora said

teasingly, then looked around the hospital room. "Where is Theo, anyway? Did he sneak off for some personal time with his laptop? Off making a super-important phone call?"

Licking her cracked lips, Emmie said slowly, "I... I don't know."

Her friend frowned. "What do you mean?"

"He was supposed to follow my ambulance in his car. But I haven't..." She covered her eyes with her hand, overwhelmed. "That was hours ago. He's not answering his phone. I'm scared he was in an accident."

"Oh, Emmie," Honora said softly. She patted her shoulder. "Don't worry. I'm sure there's a good explanation." She gave a rueful laugh. "If you only knew half of what Nico put me through back in the day..." Whipping out her phone, she placed a call. "Hey, babe," she said cheerfully. "Can you do me a favor?"

Theo was in hell.

From the moment they'd left Paris, he'd felt a rising sense of dread making his body tense and belly churn for reasons he didn't understand.

After all, he'd won the Harcourt prize, just as he'd hoped. Pierre Harcourt had accepted his final bid, and Celine had even congratulated him with kind words, "The best man won," before rushing out of the boardroom to meet up with her new boyfriend.

Assuming the legal paperwork went smoothly, Theo expected to break ground soon. If everything went according to schedule, his new Paris development—a gorgeous mix of retail, office and housing surrounded by dramatic, environmentally friendly gardens—would be finished in two years. It was thrilling.

And yet he'd left it all behind. Abandoned the project at the starting gate. For Emmie.

He'd promised his wife they could live in Manhattan. It was the least he could do. A consolation prize he could give her, he thought bitterly, in lieu of loving her.

Emmie and his son deserved better.

"I'm in love with you, Theo."

Remembering her luminous face as she'd spoken those words still made him feel sick inside.

How long would it be before Emmie realized that Theo, with his cold heart, wasn't good enough for her? Before his son realized it, too?

He'd sent her to the hospital alone. Because he was scared. Because he couldn't bear to see her pain. If that didn't make her love evaporate, nothing would.

He swallowed hard. The truth was, all he could offer anyone was wealth and a job in real-estate development—neither of which Emmie cared about. He'd offered her palaces and gold, when what she wanted, what she *needed*, was his love...

Standing in the grass, Theo leaned his head against the fence, feeling the hard surface against his clammy forehead. Exhaling, he lifted his gaze and looked out at Manhattan's skyline across the Hudson. As sunset fell behind him, the last red rays shimmered over the gleaming steel and glass skyscrapers across the dark river.

When Emmie had gone into labor on the plane halfway over the Atlantic—too late to return to Paris—he'd wanted to flee, to cover his eyes and run. But there was no escaping a plane, not unless one wanted to jump out at twenty thousand feet. Seeing his wife's pain, he'd been overwhelmed with panic and fear. What if he lost Emmie? What if they lost their baby? It would be his fault, for keeping them in Paris so long. Theo had paced in agony, even as he'd tried to look strong and reassuring. But he'd never felt so useless, so helpless, not since—

Not since—

Was Emmie still in labor? Had his son already been born?

Theo had meant to follow her to the hospital, honest to God. But as he'd collapsed into the sports car waiting for him at the airport, he hadn't even driven the short distance to the Lincoln Tunnel before his vision closed in, creating a tunnel all its own.

So he'd veered off into a small park in Weehawken overlooking the river. Parking the car in the half-empty lot, he'd leaned his head against the steering wheel, feeling like he was going to die.

"Theo, what have you done?" The shriek of his mother's voice over the crackle of the fire. *"You've killed him!"*

Pushing the memory away, Theo had stumbled out of the car into the small park, trying to catch his breath.

The August evening was sticky and hot. Leaning against the fence on the edge of the river, he could almost see his breath in the thick humid air, puffs of smoke like the ghosts of those he'd lost. The father he'd never known. The emotionally distant uncle who'd given him a home.

His mother. His stepfather.

Your fault, a dark voice whispered. *You killed them both.*

Now, Theo stared across the water, watching the shimmering glass skyscrapers on the horizon turn orange, then red, then finally violet, as the sun set slowly behind him.

It would be easy, he thought, just to drive back to the airport, and disappear—to Singapore or Dubai or anywhere. People might despise him for abandoning his wife and son.

Only Theo would know the truth: they'd be better-off without him.

Emmie was good and pure, his baby son an innocent soul. What happiness could a man like Theo possibly bring them? What could he do except cause them pain?

"There you are."

Turning, Theo was astonished to see Nico Ferraro crossing the grass. He almost rubbed his eyes, just to be sure Nico, too, wasn't a ghost. His friend smiled.

"My wife called. Said you were having a little trouble finding your way to the hospital." Glancing back, he looked at Theo's parked Maserati with the door still hanging open. "Car trouble?"

"How did you find me—" Then he remembered how last year, after his Lamborghini was stolen, he'd angrily told Nico he was going to put a GPS tracker in every car. His company's head of security would be able to monitor his cars' locations, under strict orders never to share the information with any woman, be she secretary, girlfriend, or wife who might invade Theo's privacy. Emmie had no idea.

"Right," Nico said, nodding with a grin. "I convinced Carter you might be in danger. He's right over there, in fact, with a couple guys just in case." He waved vaguely toward a black van on the far edge of the parking lot. Theo's head of security nodded in return. "So," Nico turned back, "what the hell are you doing here?"

"Nothing much," Theo said tightly.

Snorting, Nico gestured to the van, and his head of security drove away. His friend faced Theo with a sigh. "So you're just hanging out in a park. While your wife just went through labor alone and is now worried your mangled body is going to appear in the morgue. Which made *my* wife send me all over town looking for you, then drive to Jersey in traffic. Thanks for that, by the way." He tilted his head. "What's really going on?"

"I told you. Nothing."

"Uh-huh." Nico looked him over, then shook his head with a low laugh. "Look, I get it. I've been there. But my wife asked me to find you. So you have two choices. Either you phone Emmie and explain the truth about your little park excursion or…"

"Or?"

Nico's dark eyes met his. "Or you come to the hospital with me right now. And I'll explain about your car trouble."

Theo felt trapped in a corner. His hands tightened, and for a moment, he actually considered a third option: punching his way out. Then he looked at his friend's sympathetic but firm expression.

"Fine," he growled.

So Nico drove him to the hospital, arranging for an employee to pick up the Maserati. Walking through the hospital's revolving door, Theo felt numb. He followed Nico onto the tenth floor, past the nurses' desk.

"It's a little late for visiting," a nurse objected as they walked past.

"Not at all. He's the happy father of room 1035," Nico said, pushing him forward.

Theo felt like he was walking through water, or in a nightmare blurry as a Renoir painting, as they rounded the corner into Emmie's room. He saw Honora trying to entertain her toddler with a coloring book. Vases of colorful flowers beneath the hospital's fluorescent light.

Outside, the night was now dark. The window's glass reflected the image of an exhausted woman in the bed smiling down beatifically at the baby in her arms. And Theo saw himself, a dark-haired man standing at a distance like a stranger.

"Look what I found," Nico said, and both women turned to them with a sob of relief.

"Uncle Theo!" little Kara cried, flinging herself around his legs. He looked down at her.

"Hello, sugarplum."

"Theo." Emmie wiped her eyes with a visibly shaking hand. "I was afraid something terrible had happened."

It had, Theo thought. Long, long ago. And it meant he could never be the man she wanted him to be. With a deep breath, he forced himself to smile. "Here I am."

"But where have you been? I left so many messages—"

"Car trouble," Nico said succinctly. "His engine stopped."
It was technically true.

"Uncle Theo, look at my drawing! Look!" Three-year-old
Kara waggled her page covered with squiggles.

"It's...nice," he said, unable to manage his usual charm
that had made him a favorite with the toddler. His eyes met
Emmie's, and suddenly his heart was in his throat.

"We should go," Nico said.

"It's past Kara's bedtime." Meeting her husband's eyes,
Honora quickly gathered up her daughter's crayons. "Grand-
dad will be wondering where we are."

"And so will his wife, since she's been watching him and
the baby." Nico scooped up Kara, ignoring her protests. The
family abruptly disappeared, leaving Theo alone with his wife
and newborn son in the hospital room.

Emmie looked at him.

"You missed everything," she said, her voice strained.

"I'm sorry."

"Well." Her expression relented. "You're here now. Come
meet your son."

His throat was tight as he inched forward to Emmie and the
baby cuddled together. "He's healthy? You're both all right?"

"Fine. Come see him." Looking at the sleeping baby dreamily, she patted the side of her hospital bed.

Awkwardly, he sat down on the very edge. His gaze fell on
some flowers on her nightstand, with a visible card.

You're a brave lady. Best of luck with him.
Carlos Mondragón

Looking around at all the flowers filling the hospital room,
in red, purple, yellow, pink and blue, blue most of all, it struck
Theo how long he'd been missing. Long enough for Emmie to

give birth and his acquaintances to hear about it. Long enough for them to *send flowers*.

Theo really was a selfish bastard. He looked down at his rough, dry hands and repeated helplessly, "I'm sorry."

"No, stop. It's not your fault you had car trouble." But there was something stiff in her voice, as if she didn't believe her own words. As the baby woke and started to fuss, Emmie forced a smile. "Come hold him."

Theo looked nervously at the unhappy baby. "I don't know if…"

"Take off your shirt."

"What?"

"Just do it." Reluctantly, he obeyed, dropping it to the linoleum floor. She lifted her free hand. "Now hold your arms like this."

Jaw tight, he held out his arms. His wife gently lifted the squirming infant, who wore only a diaper, against Theo's bare chest.

Cuddled against his father, skin to skin, the baby gave a little hiccup, then soothed by the rise and fall of Theo's breath, his eyelids grew heavy. His tiny body relaxed back into sleep.

"Good job," she said softly. "Isn't he beautiful?"

Theo looked down at his newborn son. An innocent child who'd depend on him for everything. Not just for his home and education but to show him the meaning of a good life. To teach him how to be a man.

Theo felt something twist his heart, squeezing until it pulled the blood from his veins, choking oxygen from his brain.

Leaning over the bed, Emmie wrapped her arm around Theo's shoulders and looked down at the baby dreamily. "What should we name him?" She gave a light laugh. "Theo Junior?"

He sucked in his breath. Wrap Theo's name, with all its horrifying baggage, around their baby's neck like an anchor?

"Call him what you want," Theo said tightly. "Just don't name him after me."

She turned, clearly mystified. "Why?"

Theo looked into her violet eyes and suddenly knew she needed a better man than he could be. If he stayed, if he was true to his vows, then not just his son but his wife, too, would be sucked dry, giving him love he didn't deserve. They'd give him everything and finally drown beneath the weight of Theo's dark, unredeemable soul.

"I didn't have car trouble." He took a deep breath and told her the truth. "I just didn't want to be here."

CHAPTER TWELVE

DURING THE HOURS her husband had been missing, Emmie had been tortured by thoughts of a car accident, a heart attack, a violent mugging—all the tragedies of life that could happen at any time.

When Theo had appeared in the doorway, her fear had melted away. He was safe. She told herself she'd been foolish to worry.

But looking at his guilty, haunted face, she'd felt a flash of something she didn't want to admit, even to herself. Something dark.

Now she knew what it was. She loved him. She'd somehow thought, if she sacrificed her needs for his, if she was a perfect wife and gave him everything she had, he might someday love her back. Now she knew she'd been lying to herself.

"I want an alliance of equals," he'd told her in Paris. "Where we each can live the life we desire, and no one has to sacrifice. No one gets hurt."

There was no such alliance. Emmie had sacrificed in Paris, working for months on a project she didn't care about, when she'd wanted to be home getting ready for their baby. And Theo had sacrificed, too, leaving his Paris dream project barely started and returning to New York, a place he clearly didn't want to be.

Theo didn't want her life. She didn't want his.

But still, in spite of everything, some part of Emmie had

hoped desperately that they could find a way to be happy to-gether. That somehow, either she would stop loving him—or he'd start loving her...

Now, all those hopes came crashing down.

"You didn't want to be here?" she choked out.

Theo looked down at their sleeping baby in his powerful arms. Holding their newborn against his bare, hard-muscled chest, he was the picture of sexy masculinity.

Except he lacked the joyful face of a new father. For the first time, Emmie noticed the hollows beneath his dark eyes. He had the expression of a man trapped in his worst night-mare. He didn't answer.

"You...don't want our son?" she whispered. Waves of grief and hurt slammed into her.

His black eyes glittered. "He deserves better."

"You're his father. And my husband. Who better to—"

"Someone. Anyone." Standing up, he carefully placed their sleeping baby back in her lap. He took a step back from her bed. "I'm sorry."

Blinking back tears, she tried to breathe, to find her sym-pathy and compassion. But she couldn't. He wasn't just re-jecting her. He was rejecting their son. "No."

"I'm no good, Emmie. I've tried. But the truth is I can never be the man you want. The man he needs."

As he picked his shirt up off the floor and put it back on, she stared at him in the dark quiet of the hospital room.

"You're leaving us," she breathed.

Now that it had finally happened, she realized she'd al-ways known this was how it would end. She would love him; he would leave her. And yet part of her still couldn't believe it. "But you're the one who wanted us to be a family. I was marrying someone else! You interrupted my wedding and wouldn't take no for an answer!"

Head bowed, Theo stood silently next to the bed, hands in

his trouser pockets, black shirt only half-buttoned. His hard face was shadowed by the lamplight. "I know."

"Just because I said I loved you?" she cried. The baby woke and started to whimper. She felt like whimpering, too.

Theo took a breath, started to say something, then just shook his head. "It's more than that."

"Then, why? Tell me why!"

Theo's eyes were bleak. "What do I know about being a father?" He turned toward his distorted reflection in the window. "My father died when I was a few months old. My mother told me he overdosed on pills, trying to sleep over my crying."

Emmie sucked in her breath. "She *told* you that?"

His lips curled. "She was trying to explain why being a parent was so hard. Love was hard for her, too. There was a parade of men through my childhood. She shared drugs with them and fell madly in love." His voice held no emotion. "There was a different man every few months, some of whom she married, none of them very good, often stoned or drunk or stealing her money. And then…"

"Then?"

His dark eyes shadowed. "When I was ten, she met Panos Papadopolous. He was older, and rich. She said she'd met her soulmate who'd take care of her forever. He proposed to her the night they met, and we moved to his ancestral home on Lyra. My mother returned from the honeymoon with two things—a black eye and my sister in her belly."

"What happened?"

He shrugged, twisting the gold band on his left hand. "They fell into a pattern. He'd get mad and smack her around. They'd do drugs together, and he'd graciously forgive her. After Sofia was born, it was worse. Whenever he felt upset about his failing business, or someone disrespected him, or he was worried about his dwindling family fortune, he dealt with it by beating my mother. Just because he could." Looking down, he said in a low voice, "That's what love means to me. Either kicking someone when they're down. Or being the victim on the ground."

Emmie's heart was pounding. Her family life had been chaotic and stressful sometimes, with five children, a sick mother and bills not always paid. But never abusive. Never that. She'd always known her family loved her. "It's horrible. How did you get out?"

"When I tried to protect my mother, he'd beat me, too. Until I became taller than he was. One day, when he punched me, I punched back. We nearly killed each other. I begged my mother to grab my sister and leave, but she wouldn't. She said she couldn't survive on the street with two children and no husband. So she sent me off to a boarding school in England. A school for problem boys. Not to protect me." His lip twisted in a sneer. "To protect *him*."

"Theo..." she breathed, agonized.

He paced across the hospital room's linoleum floor, looking back blindly at the dark window faintly smeared with the lights of Midtown Manhattan.

"I came home from school the summer I was fifteen and found my mother in the hospital with two black eyes and a purple bruise around her neck. He'd gotten notice from the bank that they were foreclosing on the house, so he'd decided to strangle her. And I saw Sofia..." He closed his eyes.

She felt a chill. "What?"

"With me away at school and my mother in the hospital, Sofia was the only one left for him to hurt. I found her hiding in her bedroom closet. He'd wanted money for drugs so he'd demanded her gold locket. Sofia loved that locket. She hugged it whenever our mother was gone because it had her picture inside it. But Panos screamed threats about beating her black and blue and ripped it out of her hand. She was quivering, hiding from him in the dark. She was five years old."

"Oh, no…" Emmie looked down at her sleeping baby and wondered how any parent could hurt their own child.

Theo set his jaw. "Panos had left to find his supplier, so I took Sofia to stay with neighbors in the village. When I returned, I found him high as a kite, smoking and frying honey fritters on the stove. I told him I was taking my mother and sister away for good and if he tried to follow us, I'd kill him."

"What did he do?"

"He screamed insults and threats. When I didn't back down, he picked up the pan of burning oil and threw it at me. I ducked." He glanced down toward his ankle. "Mostly."

"Your scar," she breathed. "It didn't come from an engine fire in a car race."

"No." He gave a grim smile. "I dodged the pan then punched him in the mouth. His cigarette fell into the spilled cooking oil and started to burn. Panos grabbed a kitchen knife and lunged at me. But he slipped and fell. Either the fall knocked him out or the drugs did. I don't know. But when I tried to lift him, to drag him out, I couldn't. He was twice my weight—"

"You tried to save him?" Emmie said, astounded.

He shook his head. "The kitchen filled with smoke, and I could feel the heat burning my skin. I couldn't budge him off the floor. So I turned and ran. I left him to die, Emmie."

"Good. The man got what he deserved," she replied vengefully. He blinked at her vehemence. Looking down at her own baby, who'd fallen back to sleep, she said, "You have nothing to feel guilty about."

His jaw was tight as he looked down at his hands. "Don't I?"

"It's over now, Theo," she tried again. "It's all over."

He looked up at her bleakly.

"It'll never be over," he whispered.

* * *

Theo wanted to flee the hospital and run twenty miles, to punch a bag until he collapsed, to start a fight with someone who'd knock him bloody. Anything rather than face the tenderness and pity and love he saw shining from his wife's face.

His hands clenched at his sides. "The fire was already climbing the walls when I left him. I ran onto the beach and watched the red and orange flames consume the house, crackling and spiraling embers up into the night. As the house burned, I felt *glad*. I thought we were free. Then I heard my mother behind me."

Emmie's lovely face was wan as she listened. He had to tell her the worst. She had to know. His throat was tight.

"Mama was still in her hospital gown and covered with purple bruises, but she'd worried about him, now I was back. She'd come to save him. From me." He still remembered her agonizing shriek.

"Where is he? Theo, what have you done? You've killed him!"

Emmie took a deep breath, her violet eyes luminous with sympathy.

He closed his eyes, not wanting to remember. "She screamed his name and tried to run into the house. When I stopped her, she slapped me in the face, clawing at my eyes, kicking me till I backed away. 'I love him!' she kept screaming. She ran into the house. She was barely inside before it collapsed, exploding into fire."

Theo's knees felt weak, as if he were still that boy again.

Emmie sucked in her breath. Then, still sitting on the bed with their baby, she reached out her hand.

"It wasn't your fault," she whispered. She held out her hand to where he stood alone in the hospital room. "You were fifteen. You did everything you could to protect her. She made her choice."

He didn't move. "Because she loved him."

Dropping her hand, Emmie looked startled. "That's not love."

"Love means putting someone else's needs ahead of your own. Isn't that what you said?"

"Yes, but—"

"The police ruled the fire an accident. But they'd often come to the house after he'd beaten her. She'd always refused to press charges, so I think they felt bad for us. For Sofia, at least."

"And you. You were just a child, too."

"Yeah." His lips curved sardonically. "Well. A neighbor was willing to adopt Sofia. But no one wanted an angry fifteen-year-old. I couldn't go back to boarding school. There was no money. I ran away from a state orphanage and lived on the streets of Athens for a while. I thought I was tough, until a bunch of older boys beat me into a bloody pile on the street because they thought I'd stolen their food. Which I hadn't." Rubbing the back of his mussed hair, he gave her a wry grin. "Though, I'd wanted to."

Theo looked across the hospital room at his sweetly sleeping baby boy. "The funny thing was, they did me a favor. A social worker found me at the hospital and told me my uncle from America had been looking for me."

"See?" Emmie said warmly. "That's another example of love—"

"My uncle was lonely. His wife had just left him. He wanted a companion who wouldn't leave. I started learning his business, property development. My uncle was kind, in his way. But weak."

"Weak, how?"

Theo thought of his Uncle Andrew's face as he'd taken him to his small, shabby office in Upstate New York.

I'll teach you how to pitch. Work is the thing that can

save us. That will never leave you. It's cold and logical. Live
to work, and no one can ever hurt you."

And Theo had learned that well. He'd thrown himself into
business like an anchor into a bottomless ocean. Over the
last twenty years, he'd turned his uncle's small business into
a global empire.

He sighed. "Even after his ex-wife married another man,
Uncle Andrew never got over it. When he was sad, he'd drive
by her house. When he was drunk, he'd look her up online.
Other than that, he'd work, but he didn't even do that very
well, since he was distracted by his yearning for her, like a
missing piece of his body." His jaw tightened as he looked at
Emmie. "That's what love does to you."

She looked away. "You're right. Love is awful. But also,"
she said and lifted her gaze, her lovely face filled with emotion, "it's the only thing that makes life worth living."

Theo staggered back a step, looking at the light and love
shining in her eyes.

"I wish I could love you," he whispered. He shook his head
hollowly. "My life has burned my heart out of me."

"But you told me everything—didn't you?" At his trembling nod, she gave him a slow-rising smile. "There are no
more secrets between us. Now you've trusted me that much,
maybe things can be different. We can be different."

"I don't want you to be different, Emmie. You're sweet and
good. I won't have you throwing your love away on someone
without a heart. I'm not going to drag you down." His gaze
fell to their son. He said softly, "Or him." He turned away.
"Good-bye."

"Theo!"

At the agony in her voice, he froze. He closed his eyes. He
couldn't look back and see her imploring face. If he did, he
knew he'd never have the strength to leave. But he had to. For
Emmie. For his son. He pressed his fingertips against his eyes.

"Forget the prenup," he whispered. "You can have anything you want. Money, cars, houses. Just take it. Everything I have is yours—"

His voice caught, and he fled the room. He didn't look back. Stumbling down the hall, he couldn't wait for the elevator so ran down ten flights of stairs. At the ground floor, he knocked the exit door against the wall in his desperation to escape. Staggering into the street, he hailed a yellow cab, feeling like he was going to die.

Knowing that the best part of him just had.

CHAPTER THIRTEEN

THEO STARED DOWN at the divorce papers that had just been delivered overnight to his Paris office. Along with Emmie's diamond engagement ring.

Emmie hadn't gotten a high-powered attorney to fight for her rights, as she should have done. These papers looked like something she'd printed off the internet. She didn't ask for the penthouse or any other residence. She wanted no alimony, not even the million dollars the prenup had entitled her to. She asked only for two things: child support, which he was already legally required to pay. And the used minivan he'd bought on impulse in Queens.

Closing his eyes, he exhaled. It was so Emmie. She wouldn't protect herself, so he'd do it for her. He'd tell his own shark of a lawyer to give her more than she'd asked for. Far, far more.

It had been two months since he'd left her in the hospital, and though he'd immediately returned to Paris and tried to bury himself in work, he still felt her absence, every second, every moment. For the first few days after he'd abandoned her, she'd tried to call and left messages. Then she'd abruptly stopped. Emmie finally must have accepted what they both knew to be true.

But he hoped she was happy. God, how he prayed she was, her and his son. He'd almost reached out to Wilson, the penthouse's butler, just to confirm Emmie and the baby were all right. But he hadn't. He was barely holding on as it was. He had to make a clean break.

Theo was looking at that clean break right now. Holding it in his hands. All he had to do was forward the divorce papers to his lawyer in New York to get the ball rolling.

Divorce. It was what Theo had wanted. Wasn't it? So why didn't he feel at peace? Why did he feel like punching the wall?

"Stop—wait—you can't go in there," his elderly secretary protested in French.

"Try and stop me," came the pert response in the same language, and suddenly the door to his private office was flung open, and his sister strode in. Sofia's eyes lit up when she saw him. "Thank heaven I caught you. I need you to take my present with you."

What was she talking about? He stared at her as his secretary came in, clearly discomfited.

"I'm sorry, *monsieur*, she—"

"It's all right, Gertrude." Theo gestured for his secretary to close the door. After she left, he lifted an eyebrow at Sofia. "You couldn't call first?"

"I tried that. You always ignore my calls when you're at work."

Through the window, he could see the gray rain over Paris, the eternal traffic around the Arc de Triomphe. "I call you back eventually."

"You take too long." With a tsk, Sofia sat down in the hard chair across his desk. "And even then, you're too busy to talk. Sensible people go out to dinner with friends and enjoy life. You just work, exercise and sleep!"

"That is how I enjoy *my* life." But even as Theo spoke those words, he knew he was lying. He couldn't remember the last time he'd enjoyed anything. Even Paris's famous cuisine tasted like ash in his mouth.

"Nobody could enjoy the life you live. Spending two months away from your wife and child! It's lucky for you I'm here to make sure you're not utterly miserable." His little sister smiled at him, and for a moment he almost smiled back.

He'd never intended to have a regular relationship with Sofia. But since she'd returned to Paris last month, after a summer traveling the world, she'd absolutely refused to take his hints that he'd prefer to be left alone. No. She showed up at his hotel room and suggested a stroll through the Jardin du Luxembourg. She'd twice phoned him in a panic, once claiming her date had abandoned her and later that her purse had been stolen, and when he arrived in a rush, he'd found her smiling like a cat with a canary feather hanging from its mouth, standing in front of a chic restaurant, where she'd gotten them reservations. "It's the only way you'd come," she explained. As if that excused it!

For the last two months, no matter how hard Theo tried to push her away, Sofia had persisted.

"That's love."

He heard the words as if Emmie had spoken them in his ear.

Theo sucked in his breath. No. He couldn't let himself think that way. Not now. Not after everything he'd done—

"So, what do you want?" he demanded now.

"Not much, big brother." Sofia sat back in her chair serenely. "Just a small favor. Very small."

She'd really changed since they'd left Lyra, he thought. The young woman looking at him now, in her red lipstick and chic little suit, had deep self-confidence and a determined glint in her eye. She'd come into her own. But no wonder, when… He did mental arithmetic. He was almost forty. That meant Sofia was almost thirty.

How the hell did that happen?

"What favor?" he growled.

"It's nothing." She placed a small blue box on his desk. "Just this."

Theo stared down at the wrapped present with its big blue bow. "What the hell is that?"

Sofia sighed. "I got your wife's invitation. I meant to RSVP weeks ago but then got caught up with my new job at the museum. Also, I've been seeing someone, and..." She snorted. "Why am I explaining? You understand. You always wait till the last minute. I was counting on it when I came here."

"Emmie invited you to a party?" Theo was bewildered.

She rolled her eyes. "I felt bad about ignoring her when we were in Lyra, so I decided to blow her away at the shower." Smiling down proudly at her wrapped gift, she confided, "They're little blue baby booties I knitted myself." Lifting a manicured hand high in the air, she pretended to do a mic drop. "Now, *that's* how you make amends. But I didn't finish making them till last night, and by then, even the fastest shipping wouldn't make it in time. Then I remembered you were still in Paris. I must say, sometimes it's nice to have a workaholic brother with his own plane." She grinned, rising to her feet. "Thanks, big brother. I really appreciate this."

"She's having a baby shower." He'd gotten that much.

"Yes." Frowning at him, she spoke with exaggerated slowness, as if explaining something simple to someone not so bright. "And I need you to bring it with you when you fly to New York today. For the party tonight."

His throat suddenly hurt. "Sorry. I'm not going."

"Of course you're going. The invitation said coed. I assumed you were the reason. Emmie wanted you to be there." Her brow furrowed. "Are you really not going?"

Theo felt a hard twist in his chest. He cleared his throat.

"I'm too busy to leave Paris at the moment." To prove it, he moved the cursor vaguely around his computer screen. "We're about to break ground on our project. The biggest in central Paris in decades. That doesn't leave much time to loll around eating cake with friends."

Sofia looked at him pityingly. "I see."

And that was just it. He was afraid she did see.

Theo rose to his feet. "I'm sorry I can't take your gift personally, but my secretary will arrange it to be sent in time by express courier. Where's the party?"

"A friend of hers is hosting. Some beach house in the Hamptons."

Beach house. That meant Honora and Nico. His closest friends, other than Emmie. He felt a razor blade in his throat.

Pushing papers around his desk, he said hoarsely, "Thanks for coming by, but I have a lot of work to do…"

Sofia didn't move. She was staring at those papers. *"Theo."*

He followed her gaze to Emmie's diamond ring resting on the divorce papers.

"Emmie's leaving you?" Sofia breathed. She looked up. "What happened?"

He set his jaw, looking away. "I don't want to talk about it."

"You can't have broken up. Why?"

Turning from his desk, Theo went to the large arched window and looked out at the gray drizzle of Paris. Leaning his arm against the glass, he looked down at the busy lanes of traffic swarming around the Arc de Triomphe. Swallowing hard, he forced himself to say, "Emmie and I realized we weren't suited for marriage. It was a mutual decision."

"No way." His sister's voice was incredulous. "The woman I met in Lyra was totally in love with you."

Theo set his jaw. For a moment, he thought of ordering her out.

But this was his little sister. Was he really going to shut her out of his life? Now, after everything?

He'd lost Emmie, who'd been his best friend, first as his secretary, then as his wife. He figured he'd lost Nico and Honora, too. He didn't want to hear their criticism, so he hadn't returned their messages. He'd left them as gifts to Emmie, along with his penthouse, his cars, his fortune.

And his son. He suddenly realized he didn't even know the boy's name. The only way he'd survived the last two months was by avoiding knowing.

Cold. He had to stay cold.

But as he folded his arms, he was suddenly sweating in his tailored suit. "She's better-off without me. You know what I am."

"What are you?"

Theo stared at her bleakly.

"A murderer," he whispered.

Sofia came forward, her eyes wide. "No."

"She died because of me."

"Mama made her choice. You tried to save her, you *tried*. But she chose him over us. Over and over."

"I should have found a way." His voice caught. As he sank into his desk chair, his eyes were stinging.

His sister put her hand on his shoulder. "You were only fifteen, and you saved us—both of us. Because of you, I had a good life. You sacrificed everything for me," she said quietly. "Don't you remember?"

"No." The emotions he'd repressed for decades seemed to be whirling around him, making him dizzy. He felt like he couldn't breathe. He yanked off his silk tie.

"After Mama died, Mrs. Samaras wanted to take me in. But I wouldn't go there without you. I clung to you. The social worker was going to send both of us to the orphanage instead. Then you took me aside and said I had to go with nice Mrs. Samaras. You said I'd be warm and loved with plenty to eat. You told me you had somewhere wonderful to live, too. It was only later I realized you were lying. You were alone."

Theo stared at her. In the brutal aftermath of the fire, he'd wanted to cling to his baby sister, too. She'd been his only family left. But he'd known Sofia would have a better life if she was adopted by Eleni Samaras, a childless widow who baked fresh bread in her tidy kitchen and had a garden full of flowers and chickens.

He closed his eyes. "You were young, innocent. The fire wasn't your fault."

"It wasn't yours, either. You still ended up starving on the street." Her hand covered his. "You've watched out for me your whole life. Protecting me from my father. Finding me a home. Sending me to college. Even letting me butt in, when you returned to Lyra and wanted to demolish the house alone. You've always put me first." She took a deep breath. "Mama taught us all the wrong things about love. But Theo...you showed me what the best of love could be."

Theo stared at her, shocked into silence.

His sister smiled. "It's why I'm taking you to dinner next week. To tell you about the man I've met." She blushed. "It's getting serious. He's going to ask me to marry him. And I'm going to say *yes*."

"Sofia..."

She grinned. "So expect a phone call from me soon, with me in a fluster about my Fiat getting a flat tire. Right in front of a very nice two-star tavern in the *Septième*." Her smile faded, even as her eyes shone in the gray light of the Paris office. "Because I finally found a man who can live up to my brother. The kindest, strongest, most loving man in the world. A man who protects those he loves. At any cost."

Theo's heart was pounding. The way his sister described him was so different than how he saw himself. Not a monster? A hero?

He was the one who'd taught Sofia how to love?

"Love means putting the other person ahead of yourself," he said slowly, repeating the words of his wife.

Sofia smiled through her tears. "Exactly."

Against his will, Theo pictured Emmie, imagining her holding their child tenderly, singing a low lullaby. He could see her beautiful, luminous face.

What did their baby look like now, at two months?

Would he suddenly be thirty, and a man—turning into an adult, as Sofia had suddenly, when Theo wasn't paying attention?

Had Emmie moved on, too, since he'd left? Had she given up on Theo and found a better man? Had she found a replacement father for their son?

Theo suddenly felt like he was on fire. He yanked off his tailored jacket, dropping it to the floor. Dripping with sweat, he unbuttoned the collar of his shirt.

"Emmie doesn't want me," he whispered. "I'm not good enough for her. Or our baby."

"If she thought that, why would she name the baby after you?"

He froze. "What?"

Digging into her purse, Sofia produced an invitation. "See?"

He snatched it up. Decorated with baby animals, the invitation listed the party details, along with the baby's weight, length, and name. *Theodore Karl Katrakis.* Emmie had named their child after him.

He knew his wife loved their baby more than her own life. Why would she name her adored son after the man who'd deserted them?

Was it possible she still loved him? Believed in him? In spite of everything he'd done to drive her away?

Love means putting the other person ahead of yourself.

Theo looked up with an intake of breath. His heart was racing like a motor as he turned to the divorce papers sitting beneath the cold sparkle of Emmie's diamond ring.

Was it too late?

Looking around his elegant cream-colored office with the

oil paintings, he realized he'd been lying to himself about what he was doing in Paris.

All this time, he'd told himself he was pursuing his big dream, building a real-estate development blending mixed-use retail, housing and green space that would be his legacy.

The truth was the real thing he'd been building in Paris was a wall around his heart. Around *himself.*

The only way to be free was to let himself feel.

Forget being cold. Forget being strong.

The only way to live was to let himself love her.

Theo looked up with a gasp.

"I have to go," he told his sister, and grabbing the gift, he ran for the door.

The autumn evening was fresh and clear and cool. The sprawling terrace of the Ferraros' beachside mansion, with a view of the Atlantic, had been elaborately decorated for a baby shower, with colorful lights hanging across the trees with yellow and orange leaves, heaters between the tables to keep them warm.

Emmie had dressed up a bit for the occasion, beyond her usual T-shirt and jeans, wearing a soft pink dress that was comfortable and flattering to her still-curvaceous figure. Her hair was in a casual ponytail, but at least it was freshly washed. Her only makeup was tinted lip balm. She'd never win any beauty contests but she didn't need to. She didn't need to prove anything to anybody. She was Bear's mother, and Karl's daughter, and good with numbers, and a hard worker. She baked really good *fika* pastries, too, from her mother's recipes. Being on her own for the last two months, she'd had two choices: either collapse in despair or decide she was okay, just as she was. She had a baby to look after. So she'd decided to be okay.

"Thank you all for coming," Honora said as Nico left to put their yawning toddler Kara and baby Ivy to bed, and their household staff cleared the dinner plates from the tables. "Now—who's ready for some shower games?"

Honora was in her element as hostess. Now visibly pregnant, she'd welcomed them with her husband and young children, Honora's grandfather and his wife. Emmie's father was there, of course, and all four of her brothers, even Daniel, who'd flown all the way from Tulsa. Sam had also brought his girlfriend, Imani. Things were getting serious there.

Surrounded by her friends and family, Emmie had forced herself to smile all night till her cheeks hurt, pretending she was enjoying herself. She wanted to.

She'd told Honora she wanted men allowed at her baby shower, which was traditionally a female affair, because she wanted her father and brothers there. Secretly, Emmie had hoped for a miracle. But by the time they'd mailed out the invitations last month, she'd realized how ridiculous her hope was, and she'd thrown Theo's invitation in the trash.

She needed to stop *hoping*. Longing for him, waiting for him, crying for him. Hope was poisoning her. She'd always love Theo. But he didn't love her. He didn't want to be married to her. He'd made that clear.

She had to let him go.

So two days ago, she'd filled out the divorce papers. She wondered how he'd reacted when he'd gotten them yesterday in Paris. She assumed he'd been relieved. She'd given him exactly what he wanted.

As October twilight fell across the ocean, Emmie surreptitiously wiped her eyes. She had to believe there was a better life waiting for her. She couldn't settle for unhappiness. She'd take inspiration from Harold Eklund, the elderly plumber she'd nearly married last June. She'd seen him in Queens last week, and he'd told her he was engaged to Luly Olsen, of the outrageous hats.

"I thought with my wife gone, I could never be happy again," he told Emmie. "I was going to settle for second best. But now, Luly and I...we're so in love. I guess it's never too late."

Emmie was glad for him. She didn't even mind being referred to as *second best* because for Harold, that's exactly what she'd been. Without love, what was the point?

Bear gurgled happily nearby from his bouncy seat, and she focused back on her baby with a smile. But her throat still ached. Had she done the right thing?

"Are you happy, sweetheart?" her father asked quietly beside her. "Truly?"

She watched as her brothers bobbed for pacifiers—instead of apples—with the intense rivalry of a party game. Daniel rose from the bucket of water triumphantly with a pacifier in his teeth, his whole head wet.

Emmie smiled, though her heart was hurting. She took a deep breath. "Actually, Dad, I'm thinking of moving back to Queens."

"Really?" He looked astonished, then delighted. "What about the penthouse in Manhattan?"

"It's a little too fancy." She'd been lonely there since Theo left. High up in the sky, far from human contact, the huge triplex had felt isolating, imprisoning, not luxurious. "I'd rather get an apartment near you. Maybe I can set up to do bookkeeping, taxes and payroll for the neighborhood. I could work and still keep Bear with me."

"That sounds wonderful, honey. But…"

"But?"

Karl hesitated. "If you're moving to Queens, that must mean Theo, he…" He licked his lips. "The two of you, you're not…"

"No," she whispered, staring at her cup of punch. "We're not."

Her father took a deep breath, then reached for her hand. "I'm sorry, honey."

"Me, too." But Emmie did her best to smile, for the sake of

the people she loved, who'd gone to so much trouble to celebrate her and Bear.

He was the best baby in the world, especially since he'd learned how to sleep five hours at a time at night. Always smiley—though, some uncharitable souls might declare it mere gas—he was growing plumper and more adorable by the day. She tried not to notice Theo's features in his face. Bear was his own person. And already the light of her life.

As they ate delicate little cakes and drank coffee, the wind grew cold off the Atlantic. In spite of the heat lamps, Emmie shivered in her dress and light cardigan in the autumn evening. If only things had been different. If only Theo could have been here, his handsome face smiling, his powerful arm over her shoulders.

Sitting on the cushioned furniture on the decorated terrace of the beach house, Emmie opened gifts for her baby, thanked her family and friends and didn't let herself cry.

"What's going on with Theo, Emmie?" Vince asked suddenly. Her eldest brother was sitting beneath a nearby heat lamp, holding her sleeping baby in his arms. He winced at their father's sharp glare, but persisted. "Why isn't he here?"

"Is your marriage over?" her brother Joe asked.

A lump rose in Emmie's throat. There was no point in hiding it from everyone. Even if it cast a pall over the evening, getting the truth out in the open would help her finally make a fresh start. Taking a deep breath, Emmie said slowly, "You might as well know... Theo and I—"

"Am I too late?"

Emmie's breath caught as she turned her head.

Theo stood in the doorway of the house, coming out onto the terrace. His tailored dark suit was wrinkled and rumpled, but somehow he'd never looked more handsome. The night breeze off the Atlantic ruffled his dark hair, as his black eyes met hers.

"Theo!" Honora hugged him, and Nico shook his hand.

But he had eyes only for Emmie. He came toward her where she sat on the sofa beneath the round, colorful lights swaying in the dark trees.

Heart pounding, she looked up at him. "What are you doing here?"

"I brought you something." Pulling a small, beautifully wrapped present from his jacket pocket, he placed it in her hands. Trying to ignore the way she'd shivered at his touch—the night was cold—she unwrapped the package.

Inside, she found lumpy blue baby booties, clearly homemade. She looked up with an intake of breath.

"From Sofia," he explained.

Emmie told herself she'd treasure the gift from Bear's aunt, of course she would, but even so, she felt a swell of bitter disappointment. Licking her lips, she set the booties aside. "Thank you. It was kind of her." Then she frowned at him. "You flew here just to deliver it for her? All the way from Paris?" It seemed strange that Theo had agreed to such an errand.

"That wasn't the only reason," Theo said softly.

"Why…?" Suddenly she knew. "Oh. Of course. You came to New York to see your lawyer. About the divorce."

There was an intake of breath from friends and family at the word *divorce*. Theo didn't seem to notice or care. His dark eyes burned through her.

"Is there someone else, Emmie? Is that why you want it to end?"

Her jaw tightened as she said coldly, "I'm not the one who wanted it to end, Theo." Her gaze fell on Bear, snuggled in her brother's arms on a nearby chair. "But yes. There's someone else."

Another gasp. Theo staggered back a step on the shadowy terrace. As he rubbed his eyes, the plain gold band on his left hand gleamed in the lights.

"I… I really didn't think…" For a moment, he seemed unable to speak. Then he shook his head. "Good for you," he said hollowly. He forced a smile. "You deserve to be happy, Emmie. You deserve all the love in the world."

His handsome face was miserable. And suddenly, even after everything, it was hard for her to see him in pain.

Taking a deep breath, she straightened her spine. She didn't know what he was doing here, but she wasn't going to be his puppet, falling at his feet whenever he deigned to appear.

He'd made his choice. Now he could live with it.

"I know I do," she said coldly. "So does Bear."

"Bear?" he said guardedly.

Rising to her feet, Emmie collected their baby from her brother and brought him to her husband beneath the swaying lights. "It's our nickname for him."

"Bear." Theo exhaled, looking down at their baby in her arms, who was more adorable than ever in fuzzy footie pajamas. He cleared his throat, his expression oddly vulnerable as he said, "My sister's invitation said you named him after me."

Was that why Theo had come? To give her a hard time for their baby's name?

"Yes, well," Emmie glanced wryly at her father, who snorted and rolled his eyes, *"Theodore* is a lot of name for a baby. I started calling him Teddy. Then Dad called him Teddy Bear…"

"Then just Bear," Karl replied, smiling between his daughter and grandson, before glaring at his son-in-law.

"Bear. I like it." Theo looked at the baby. The infant now regarded his father with equal interest, and with the same black eyes. He said in wonder, "He's gotten so much bigger already."

"I know."

Theo licked his lips. She was staring at his mouth when she heard him say shyly, "Can I hold him?"

"Of course." Theo wanted to hold their baby? Trying to

calm the pounding of her heart, telling herself this didn't mean anything, she helped him take the baby, showing him how to support his head.

As Theo held him, Emmie saw a swirl of emotion on her husband's handsome face she'd never seen before. Adoration. Fear. And something else. Something more...

"Thank you, Emmie." Theo looked up, and to her astonishment she saw a suspicious sheen in his eyes. "Even though our marriage is over, I'll always be grateful that you're his mother. The best woman in the world," he said softly. He swallowed. "I'll sign your divorce papers. But even if you love someone else now, I intend to be Bear's father. I'll always be there for him from now on." Looking at her with haunted yearning, he whispered, "And I'll always be here for you. For anything."

The look he gave her went far beyond desire. The floor suddenly trembled beneath Emmie's shoes. What was happening?

"It's Bear," she blurted out. "He's my someone else."

Theo blinked. His brow furrowed. "What?"

"The other man in my life now. It's Bear. Just Bear."

Her husband sucked in his breath, his wide black eyes searching hers. "Is it really true?"

Emmie lifted her chin. "But I still don't understand what you're doing here. Why you came all the way from Paris."

All her friends and family were staring between them in a breathless hush beneath the colorful lights leaving latticed shadows of the half-bare trees in the autumn night. In the distance, she could hear the roar of the surf. Or was it the pounding of her heart?

Theo stepped forward, his dark eyes piercing her soul. "Is there a chance, Emmie?" he whispered. "Do I still have a chance?"

She trembled, caught by his gaze. Afraid to say a word. Afraid this was all a dream.

"Because if I thought I had a chance, I'd..."

"You'd what?" she said softly.

He took a shuddering breath. "I'd throw myself at your feet."

"Get the baby," her father muttered, and Nico discreetly plucked Bear out of Theo's arms.

Her husband turned to face her. And as he came forward, taking both her hands in his own, everyone and everything else around them vanished. She saw only him.

"Leaving you was the biggest mistake of my life," he said in a low voice. "For all my life, I've been scared to love anyone. The day we wed, I was terrified out of my mind."

Her jaw dropped. Theo Katrakis admitting fear? Aloud? In front of all her family and friends?

"Because I already knew what would happen," he continued. "I knew I'd fall in love with you. That I already had."

"What?" breathed Emmie. What had he said?

His hands tightened over hers. "What if I gave you my heart and you left? What if you died? What if I couldn't be the man you wanted? I didn't think I could survive it. So I tried my hardest to be like ice. To never let you in."

She was afraid to breathe. "And?"

His dark eyes flickered. Raising his hand, he stroked her cheek. "Your love melted my defenses," he whispered. "You left me bare. When you went into labor, I felt helpless. Powerless. I felt panicked and ashamed. So I left you." His gaze fell on Bear, cuddled in Nico's arms. "Both of you."

Remembering that awful day, Emmie closed her eyes, feeling a painful twist in her heart. "You hurt me."

"I know. I'll never forgive myself. And I've been punished every day since. I ran away to be a big shot in Paris. To follow my so-called dream. And I learned something important."

"What?"

He took a deep breath. "The whole world is a wasteland without you. No matter how many palaces or gardens I build.

Without the woman I love…this earth is as empty as my heart."

His voice cracked. He looked down at their intertwined hands. Then, as he'd threatened, he fell to his knees before her.

"Give me a chance to win you back, Emmie," he whispered, pressing her hand against his rough, unshaven cheek. "Tell me I have a chance to regain your trust. Whether it takes weeks or months. *Years.* All I ask is that you let me try." He looked up at her, and his eyes were luminous with tears. "Because I'm utterly, completely in love with you."

Emmie gasped. She heard her friends and family do the same.

"I love you, Emmie. And it's true what I said. You deserve a better man that me." He pressed his forehead to her clasped hands in a medieval, almost holy, gesture of fealty. "But if you give me the chance, I'll spend the rest of my life trying to be the man you deserve."

Beyond the terrace, beyond the shadows of autumn trees with their hanging lights, Emmie saw the sweep of moonlight over the black Atlantic waves. Could she forgive him? Could she let him back into her life—back into her heart?

A dozen people waited breathlessly for her answer. She closed her eyes, hearing the soft whir of the heat lamps, the call of seagulls in the cold October night.

Then she exhaled, opening her eyes. Reaching down, she pulled him to his feet. "I've always known you were a pain, Theo." Tears overflowed her lashes as she gave him a slow-rising smile. "And I've always known you're worth it."

He searched her gaze with an intake of breath. "Yes?"

"I never stopped hoping for a miracle. I never stopped loving you, Theo—"

"Oh, my darling," he whispered and pulled her into his arms. For a long moment, he just held her tight. Emmie closed her eyes, her cheek against his chest. She breathed in the scent of him, woodsy and masculine, and she felt like she'd finally come home.

"Kiss her!" someone yelled.

Lifting his head, Theo looked back with a grin at their friends and family. "I was thinking the same thing."

And he lowered his head to hers in a kiss of pure fire. Emmie dimly heard the wild roar of the surf, echoing the rush of blood in her veins, as his hot, sensual embrace told her everything she needed to know, pledging love forever... or maybe longer.

Their baby son, held too tightly by Nico, gave an indignant squawk. Theo and Emmie pulled apart with a laugh and reached to bring their son into their arms.

"I love you," Theo told his son, then he cupped Emmie's cheek. "And I love you, Emmie."

Around them, friends and family cheered, as if they had just turned from the altar, newly wed.

And that was how it felt to Emmie. Except instead of a bridal bouquet, Emmie held their baby. Instead of a glitzy diamond ring, she held her husband's powerful hand in her own. Instead of words vowing to love and cherish, she saw the promise in Theo's dark eyes.

And in that moment Emmie knew she'd be loved, seen and adored for the rest of her life. All her dreams, especially the ones she'd believed could never come true, were all around her.

EPILOGUE

IT WAS STRANGE, Theo reflected eight months later. For a man who'd once claimed to not want family, he now had quite a lot of it. Strange—and wonderful.

"Who gives this woman to be married to this man?"

Eyes stinging, Theo looked down at his sister in her white gown. "I do."

Placing Sofia's hand into her bridegroom's, Theo returned to sit with his wife in the front row of the whitewashed Greek church.

Looking up with a tender smile, Emmie put her hand over his. Her emerald-cut diamond, now back in its rightful place on her left hand, glinted in the dim light. His heart swelled as he thought how much he loved her. He was the luckiest man on earth.

When the ceremony ended, Theo watched as the newly married couple kissed, then left the tiny church hand in hand. Fifty-odd guests followed them, walking the half mile to the new house that had been built in Lyra, over the ashes of Theo and Sofia's childhood home.

Well, not exactly. The new house had been built in a slightly different location, closer to the beach, their favorite place to play as children. On the spot where the old house had burned, where their mother had died, they'd built a garden, to remember and find peace, and they planted the roses their mother had once loved.

It was a lovely June morning. Walking with Emmie along the cliffside path, Theo breathed in the sea air. Emmie was wearing a soft, lovely dress, and he was dressed in a suit to match, pushing a top-of-the-line baby stroller.

At ten months, Bear was making happy *la-la-la* sounds, grabbing his own feet, his adorably chunky thighs sticking out of dapper blue shorts. The baby hadn't quite figured out how to walk yet, but the kid was so energetic, Theo fully expected once he learned he'd be running within the hour. There'd be no stopping him.

Just as there was no stopping his wife. Theo glanced at her as they walked. Even the beauty of Greece couldn't compare to Emmie's soulful, gorgeous voluptuousness. Her honey-blond hair tumbled over her shoulders, lit by the golden sun. Her violet eyes outshone both the vivid blue sky and sapphire-hued Aegean.

At four months pregnant, her belly was barely starting to show beneath her dress, but her breasts were already in full bloom. His gaze lingered on her breasts, then her exquisite pink lips. After a year of marriage, he still couldn't get enough of her body, her beauty and, most of all, her soul. Emmie was the heart of their family, which meant for Theo she was the heart of the world.

Emmie's extended family, her brothers, her brand-new sister-in-law, her father and even her father's new girlfriend were straggling behind them on the cliffside path, laughing and teasing each other. Theo had had to get a bigger private jet to bring them all here. He smiled. His jet was now their minivan.

But he found he liked the happy chaos of Emmie with her four brothers. Five children sounded about right. He hoped this second baby would be just the start.

Ahead of them, Honora and Nico were walking with four-year-old Kara in her flower-girl dress, pushing their toddler Ivy and baby Jack in a double stroller. The Ferraros were now their neighbors. Theo and Emmie had sold the penthouse and bought a brick town house in Greenwich Village on their friends' small street. Their new house had seven bedrooms, a rooftop terrace and even—most luxurious of all in Manhattan—an actual backyard. Emmie was already hinting about getting a dog. As if there wasn't enough mayhem already, he thought ruefully. But now he knew there was always room for more. There was always more to love.

Though Theo occasionally still traveled for work, unless there was serious reason, he was always home every night at six. He often visited Paris to check progress but allowed his extremely competent employees to oversee the day-to-day project. That way, Theo was able to have dinner with his wife and son, read Bear bedtime stories, and give Emmie a break, a little shoulder rub and ask about her day before they fell passionately into bed.

He enjoyed his business. He *loved* his family.

Theo's life had changed so much. He no longer tried to be cold to avoid hurt or the possibility of loss. Those were just part of the package with feeling love and joy. They all went together.

So he embraced it. All of it. It was the bravest thing he'd ever done. And the hardest. And the best.

Control was an illusion. Love was real.

Dancing with his wife at his little sister's wedding reception, held in a big white tent beside the Aegean, Theo laughed with delight as they swayed ineptly to the loud, raucous music of the French rock band his sister and her new husband adored. Surrounded by the newlyweds' young, cheering friends and the even noisier cheering of Theo's big new family, he felt his heart was a million miles wide.

"Are you crying?" Emmie whispered.

He rubbed his eye. "Got some dirt in my eyes."

By her knowing smile, she wasn't fooled, which was fine,

because he didn't intend her to be. Theo wanted his wife to know him, both the good and bad, and for him to have the gift of knowing the good and bad of her. Though, as he teased her, he had yet to find any bad. But when it came, he would accept it with open arms, as she'd accepted him.

Emmie had given him a second chance, when he hadn't really deserved a first one. He would love her till the end of his days.

Nuzzling her neck on the dance floor, he whispered, "You're the most beautiful woman here. Anywhere."

"Oh, stop."

Theo looked down at her tenderly. "I mean it."

She blushed, looking down, hiding a smile. "You have to say that because I'm your wife."

"I have to say it," he said and stroked wonderingly through her long blond hair, "because it's true."

And as he lowered his head to kiss her, right there on the dance floor, surrounded by people they loved in the big reception tent, Theo knew Emmie had given him more than family. She'd given him his life.

* * * * *

MILLS & BOON MODERN IS
HAVING A MAKEOVER!

The same great stories you love,
a stylish new look!

Look out for our brand new look
COMING JUNE 2024

MILLS & BOON

COMING SOON!

We really hope you enjoyed reading this book.
If you're looking for more romance
be sure to head to the shops when
new books are available on

Thursday 18th July

To see which titles are coming soon, please visit
millsandboon.co.uk/nextmonth

MILLS & BOON

MILLS & BOON®

Coming next month

ITALIAN'S STOLEN WIFE
Lorraine Hall

'I am very well aware of who you are, *cara*.'

His smile felt like some kind of lethal blow. Francesca could not understand why it should make her feel breathless and devastated.

But she had spent her life in such a state. So she kept her smile in place and waited patiently for Aristide to explain his appearance. Even if her heart seemed to clatter around in her chest like it was no longer tethered. A strange sensation indeed.

'I am afraid there has been a change of plans today,' he said at last, his low voice a sleek menace.

Francesca kept her sweet smile in place, her hand relaxed in his grip, her posture perfect. She was an expert at playing her role. Even as panic began to drum its familiar beat through her bloodstream.

'Oh?' she said, as if she was interested in everything he had to say.

No one would change her plans. *No one*. She narrowly resisted curling her free fingers into a fist.

'You will be marrying me instead.'

Continue reading
ITALIAN'S STOLEN WIFE
Lorraine Hall

Available next month
millsandboon.co.uk

LET'S TALK

Romance

Follow us:

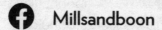 Millsandboon

@MillsandBoon

 @MillsandBoonUK

@MillsandBoonUK

For all the latest titles and special
offers, sign up to our newsletter:
Millsandboon.co.uk

afterglow BOOKS

Afterglow Books is a trend-led, trope-filled list of books with diverse, authentic and relatable characters, a wide array of voices and representations, plus real world trials and tribulations. Featuring all the tropes you could possibly want (think small-town settings, fake relationships, grumpy vs sunshine, enemies to lovers) and all with a generous dose of spice in every story.

♪ @millsandboonuk
◎ @millsandboonuk
afterglowbooks.co.uk
#AfterglowBooks

For all the latest book news, exclusive content and giveaways scan the QR code below to sign up to the Afterglow newsletter:

Never Date A Roommate
PBO 9780263322897 £8.99
Ebook 9780008938420 | Audio 9780263324860
For publicity enquiries please contact
millsandboonpressoffice@harpercollins.co.uk

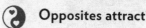

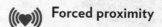

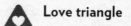